Legacy of Mercy

Books by Lynn Austin

www.lynnaustin.org

Legacy of Mercy

LYNN AUSTIN

BETHANYHOUSE
a division of Baker Publishing Group
Minneapolis, Minnesota

Published by Bethany House Publishers
11400 Hampshire Avenue South
Bloomington, Minnesota 55438
www.bethanyhouse.com

Bethany House Publishers is a division of
Baker Publishing Group, Grand Rapids, Michigan

Printed in the United States of America

Library of Congress Cataloging-in-Publication Data

Names: Austin, Lynn N., author.
Title: Legacy of mercy / Lynn Austin.
Description: Minneapolis, Minnesota: Bethany House, a division of Baker Publishing Group, [2018]
Identifiers: LCCN 2018019419 | ISBN 9780764217630 (paper) | ISBN 9780764231728 (cloth) | ISBN 9781493416141 (e-book) | ISBN 9780764233050 (large print)
Subjects: | GSAFD: Christian fiction.
Classification: LCC PS3551.U839 L44 2018 | DDC 813/.54—dc23
LC record available at https://lccn.loc.gov/2018019419

This is a work of historical fiction; the appearances of certain historical figures are therefore inevitable. All other characters, however, are products of the author's imagination, and any resemblance to actual persons, living or dead, is coincidental.

Scripture quotations are from the King James Version of the Bible.

Scripture quotations in chapters 21 and 32 are from the Holy Bible, New International Version®. NIV®. Copyright ©1973,1978,1984,2011 by Biblica, Inc.™ Used by permission of Zondervan. All rights reserved worldwide. www.zondervan.com

Cover design by Dan Thornberg, Design Source Creative Services

18 19 20 21 22 23 24   7 6 5 4 3 2 1

To my family:
Ken, Joshua, Vanessa, Benjamin,
Maya, Snir, and Lyla Rose

With love and gratitude

Prologue

CHICAGO, ILLINOIS
AUGUST 1897

My dearest Oma Geesje,

It was hard to say good-bye to you so soon after meeting you and discovering that you are my grandmother. I wanted so much to stay in Michigan and get to know you and all of my other relatives in Holland a little better. But as you wisely pointed out, I needed to return to my life in Chicago and the adoptive parents whom I dearly love.

My brief stay this summer at the Hotel Ottawa was life-changing. I have always known that Mother and Father adopted me at an early age, but now, after living the first twenty-three years of my life with no information about my past, I was excited to finally discover who I really am. Reading the story of your life and how you immigrated to America from the Netherlands fifty years ago helped me see that I am part of a much larger story and a much larger family. And for you, dear Oma, I know that I'm the living continuation of my mama Christina's story—a story that ended much too soon.

7

But where do I go from here? I have returned home hoping that my faith in God will keep growing. Yet from the moment I returned to Chicago, I have been swept up in the many social events and expectations that I ran away from when I fled across Lake Michigan to the Hotel Ottawa this summer. I have very little time to read my Bible, let alone pray. But whenever I start to feel overwhelmed, I remember your wise words—that God has put me in this place, with the life I have, for a reason. There are lessons here in Chicago that He wants me to learn, and I know He has a plan and a purpose for me.

I'm still trying to accept the loss of my real mama, but at least I understand now that the empty place I have always felt in my heart had once been filled by her. My grief after losing her when I was three years old was always there, even though my adoptive parents filled my life with love and stability. I have also been facing the memories of the shipwreck and my near drowning—an event that has silently shaped my life, making me fearful and anxious. Now that I know the source of my fears, perhaps I can begin to change.

Father has allowed me to hire the Pinkerton Detective Agency to try to learn more about Mama and those missing years between the time she left home with Jack Newell in October of 1871 and when she died in the shipwreck in September of 1877. I am curious to learn if Jack is my real father and to discover what happened to him and Mama after they left Michigan. I will be sure to let you know what I discover, since my story is also your story. We are taking this exciting journey together, Oma.

Meanwhile, my plans to marry William are moving forward with the hope that the changes I saw in him on the night of the Jenison Park Hotel fire will prove to be lasting. He told me that night that he would be willing to listen more closely when I talk about spiritual things, and he said he didn't want my newfound faith to come between us. After learning how Father risked his life to save me when the Ironsides *sank, I'm more eager than ever to marry William so I can help Father with his financial problems. Although I must confess that as William lays out his plans for the rest of our life together, I sometimes feel a sense of panic, not excitement. Mother calls it the bridal jitters.*

Please give my greetings to Derk when you see him. He played a significant role in everything that happened this summer, and I will always consider him a dear friend. I miss you, Oma!

With love,
Anneke

HOLLAND, MICHIGAN
SEPTEMBER 1897

My dearest Anneke,

It was so wonderful to hear from you. I was happy to learn that you are well and that you are settling back into your life in Chicago.

All of the excitement in our little town of Holland has finally ended now that our town's fiftieth anniversary celebration is over. I let myself be talked into riding on a parade float down Eighth Street along with some of the other original Dutch settlers, but I felt very foolish to be on display that way. The story I wrote about how I immigrated to Michigan with Dominie Van Raalte and the

*very first group from the Netherlands has been put into
a book along with the other settlers' stories. But you are
the only person who has the original version, where I
confessed all of my doubts and fears and loves and losses.
The published version tells only the facts.*

*My dear, I advise you not to let William or your parents
or anyone else pressure you to make a decision you are
not ready for. As you know from reading my life story, the
results are never good when we make decisions in haste,
especially with a decision as important as marriage. And
as much as you may wish to help your father, I don't think
he would want you to marry William purely for financial
reasons.*

*Derk stopped by the other day to say hello and to let me
know that his studies at the seminary are resuming. This
is his last year there, and then he will become a minister.
He said to tell you he thinks of you often and wishes you
all the best.*

*With love,
Oma Geesje*

CHAPTER 1

Anna

CHICAGO, ILLINOIS
1897

I am still in bed, languishing in that lovely state between dreaming and wakefulness, when the note arrives. Our housemaid has brought it to my bedroom on a tray along with tea and toast and a soft-boiled egg. The moment I see whom the letter is from, I am fully awake. My life is about to change. I tear open the envelope and pull out the card.

> *From: The Pinkerton Detective Agency*
> *Agents R. J. Albertson and M. Mitchell*
>
> *To: Miss Anna Nicholson*
> *Please be advised that we have found information concerning your mother, Christina de Jonge, that may be of*

11

*interest to you. We await word of a convenient time to
call on you to relay our findings.*

I toss the covers aside and leap out of bed, causing the maid
to step back in surprise. "Is the courier who delivered this note
still waiting for my reply?" I ask her. I can't recall the maid's
name. She is new and young and very skittish. Mother demands
a lot of our servants, and few of them last very long. I have
already seen this poor girl in tears.

"I-I'm not sure, Miss Anna. Shall I go and see?" She glances
around as if looking for a place to set the tray. The cup rattles
against the saucer.

"No, wait a moment, please." I rummage through my desk
for stationery and a pen to scribble a reply. I'm certain my social calendar is filled with scheduled events today, but I'm too
excited to recall a single one. The Pinkerton detectives have a
fine reputation for unearthing secrets from the past, and I have
been growing impatient as I've waited for them to report back
to me. I scribble a note to Agents Albertson and Mitchell, inviting them to come today at three o'clock, then I fold the note,
place it in an envelope, and seal the flap. "Take this down to
the courier right away," I tell the maid. I grab the tray from her
and shove the envelope into her hand. "Hurry!"

"Yes, Miss Anna."

As soon as she's gone, I remember that I have a luncheon
engagement with my fiancé's mother and sister that is certain
to drag on until three o'clock. I will simply have to excuse
myself early. Mother will be annoyed, but it can't be helped. I
have been waiting for weeks for news of my real mama, ever
since returning from Michigan in July.

The detectives' report is all I can think about as I sip tea and
eat tiny sandwiches at the garden party later that afternoon.
William's mother has planned this luncheon to introduce me

as her son's fiancée to some of her longtime friends and their daughters. The fall afternoon is so lovely that the luncheon is held outside in the beautifully kept gardens behind the Wilkinsons' mansion. Tables and chairs dot the grass between the flower beds, and the tables are set with white linen cloths, fine china, and silverware. Maids serve the tea from sterling silver pots, the sandwiches from silver platters. It's a serene setting, with birds twittering and the air perfumed by the last of the summer roses climbing the trellises.

Mother looks as regal as a queen as she chats with William's mother. She is beaming as if she is the bride-to-be instead of me. This marriage will raise her status in Chicago society by several notches. I'm seated at a table a few feet away with William's sister, Jane, his Aunt Augusta, and two cousins. I should be filled with genteel enthusiasm as I listen to them talk about William and share some of their wedding day experiences, but I'm restless. My only role is to look pretty, make polite conversation, and enjoy the luncheon, yet I feel a lingering uneasiness, as if I'm supposed to be doing something else. I have no idea what. But something useful.

By the time dessert is served, I'm tired of smiling. I'm timid by nature and unused to being the center of attention. I can't stop glancing down at the little watch brooch pinned to the bodice of my gown—a present from Mother and Father. Time seems to crawl at a snail's pace. Mother catches me watching the time and discreetly shakes her head, a signal to mind my manners. I never had a problem following all the rules that my social position requires until I spent a week in Michigan with my grandmother Geesje in the summer and saw how liberating a simpler life can be.

Jane, who is five years younger than me, leans close to whisper something. She is slender and dark-haired like William, and her brown eyes sparkle with mischief as she discreetly gestures to a fashionably dressed young woman sitting near the fountain. "Have you met Clarice Beacham yet?" she asks.

"Only briefly. Why?"

"William courted her for some time before he met you. Clarice was furious at being tossed aside for you."

"I'm surprised she came today."

"My mother and her mother are very old friends. It was their idea to pair her with William in the first place, not his."

"I see." Clarice is easily the most beautiful woman at the luncheon, with shining auburn hair pinned up in the latest Gibson girl style. She exudes a self-confidence that I've never had, visible in the way she sits and walks and converses effortlessly with the other women. Yet the word I feel that best describes her is not a kind one: *haughty*—as if wealth and luxury and privilege are her birthrights. I dare not judge her, though, because I have held the same attitudes for most of my life, even though my position in society comes through adoption, not birth.

"Clarice has been keeping a close eye on you for months," Jane tells me, "waiting to pounce if things between you and William don't work out."

I'm wondering why Jane would confide in me this way. As if reading my thoughts, she adds, "I'm only telling you this so you'll be careful what you say around her. Clarice would do anything to get William back."

I'm unnerved to know that I have a rival, let alone a beautiful, ruthless one. "I see. Thanks for the warning, Jane."

"You're welcome. I like you a lot better than Clarice. I hope we'll become friends."

"I do, too." I reach to give her hand a squeeze. How I have longed for a close friend!

The maids glide around the garden in ruffled aprons, refilling teacups, holding out trays of delicate tea cakes. I glance down to check the time again, and when I look up, Clarice is walking toward me.

"Congratulations on your engagement," she says with a smile. She sits down in an empty chair beside mine as the other guests begin to rise from their places to mingle.

"Thank you, Clarice."

"William's mother tells me you have recently returned to the city after being away for a few weeks this summer."

"Um . . . yes." I wonder if Mrs. Wilkinson also told Clarice that it was because William and I briefly ended our engagement before reconciling again. "Mother and I spent some time at a resort in Michigan," I tell her. "It was lovely and relaxing."

"What made you decide to leave Chicago?" It is very brash of her to keep probing for information, and I'm grateful for Jane's warning.

"Chicago can be so hot during the summer months," I say with a little wave of my hand. "Were you able to escape the city at all?"

"I wouldn't want to. There are so many exciting things to do that I would be afraid I would miss something. Besides, if I had a fiancé as handsome as William, I wouldn't leave his side for a single day." I have no reply to that. "Listen, Anna," she says, resting her hand over mine. "We don't know each other very well yet, but I hope we can become friends. My family and William's have been friends for ages, so you and I will be almost like sisters now that you're marrying him. When might you have a free afternoon so you can join me for lunch? We can get to know each other a little better, just the two of us. Please say you'll come."

"That's very kind of you. We'll have to arrange a time very soon." I wonder what she is plotting. I'm relieved when Mother joins us before Clarice pressures me to choose a date. Mother has more experience with scheming women than I do. As she and

Clarice talk, my thoughts drift to my meeting with the Pinkerton detectives in another hour, wondering what they might have discovered. Any news about my real mama will be welcome, but I'm also hoping to learn who my biological father is. According to my grandmother, Mama had been madly in love with a man named Jack Newell, and they ran away together the day after a fire destroyed most of Holland, Michigan, including the factory where Jack worked. The two were headed for Chicago and didn't know that a huge fire had also destroyed much of the Windy City on the very same night. I have read firsthand accounts of the Great Chicago Fire and wonder where Mama and Jack would have found work and a place to live after such devastation.

It's half past two when Clarice finally wanders away. I rise and tell Mother I would like to leave. Her serene façade vanishes. "We can't leave now," she whispers. "It would be rude."

"Some of the other ladies are leaving," I say, nodding toward two departing guests.

"But you are the guest of honor!"

"You may stay longer if you'd like, Mother. I'll send the carriage back for you."

The color rises in Mother's cheeks. It's hard to tell if she is furious with me for wanting to leave early or for daring to defy her. Perhaps both. I start to walk away, but she stands and grips my arm, holding it in her firm grasp to keep me from leaving. "What is this all about, Anna? Are you unwell?"

I could lie and pretend to be sick, but it would be wrong. "The detectives Father hired are coming today at three o'clock. They have news about Mama. I need to leave."

I can see she is torn between staying so she won't miss anything and going with me to keep an eye on me. She decides to accompany me, and as we thank our hostess and politely take our leave, I brace myself for the lecture that is certain to come. We climb into our carriage to start for home and she doesn't disappoint me. "When your father and I agreed to help you hire the Pinkerton detectives, we never imagined it would interfere with your life this way."

"I'm sorry. But I forgot all about the luncheon when I told the detectives to come at three o'clock today. Besides, the luncheon was nearly finished anyway."

"That's no excuse. As the guest of honor, you should be among the last to leave, not the first."

"I'm hoping that the detectives have information about who my real father is."

Mother purses her lips as if it will help hold her anger inside. When she finally speaks she sounds calm, but I know she's not. "Isn't it enough to know your mother's story and how she died? You need to leave the rest of it alone, Anna, and get on with your life."

"But I'm curious about my father, too. If he really is Jack Newell, I would like to know what happened to him and why I don't remember him at all."

"You may learn something very unsavory. It's a stone best left unturned."

"I can't leave it. I want to know."

"Listen to me." She grips my arm again and hushes her voice as if she doesn't want anyone to overhear, even though the only person near enough is our driver—and he would never tell family secrets, would he? "It's entirely possible that your parents never married, Anna. If that turns out to be true, we would be obligated to make William and his family aware of it."

"Of course I'll tell William. He's going to be my husband. He'll want to know who I really am as much as I do."

"That isn't true. You are the only one who is obsessed with this. William and his family would prefer not to know."

I stare at her in surprise. "Did they tell you that? William never mentioned it to me."

"His mother let me know in a very delicate way that they would be happier not to have the past exhumed. Most of Chicago society has no idea you're even adopted, let alone what your background is, because frankly, it's none of their business. William's mother and I both feel that the past should remain buried. As William's wife, you must be above reproach. We cannot allow any unsavory details about your parents to taint your reputation."

"I promise that no one outside our family will ever know what I discover. But I have to keep searching until I learn the truth."

"Once it's out of the box, the truth can rarely be concealed. The harder one tries to hide it, the juicier the gossip becomes. And you also must think of your children. Anything you learn about your past becomes part of their past, too."

"I'm not ashamed of my mother. She died saving me."

"And your adoptive father put himself in danger to rescue you. Don't forget that. You owe him a measure of discretion, too."

I know she's right, but I still can't contain my curiosity. I remain silent for the rest of the drive home, promising myself that I will listen to the detectives' report and let that be the end of it. When we arrive home, a small carriage is parked out front, and our butler tells me that the two Pinkerton agents are waiting in the front parlor. I pluck off my hat as I hurry inside to greet them. After the preliminary niceties, Agent Albertson hands me a typewritten report, and we take our seats on the sofas to settle down to business.

"We found a record of marriage in your mother's name. Christina de Jonge married Jack Newell in October of 1871."

My heart leaps in my chest. "They did get married!" I look up at Mother and can see that she is relieved to learn that my birth was legitimate. I'm relieved, as well. I silently rehearse my real name—Anneke Newell. "Were you able to find any more information about Jack?" I ask.

"We're following up on some possible leads. You told us he was a laborer, so we're searching through membership lists of various trade unions for his name. I'll let you know as soon as we find something."

I look down at the report again. "According to this, they were married two weeks after the Chicago fire," I say. "That's two weeks after running away from home in Michigan."

"Yes. The ceremony was performed by a justice of the peace in the village of Cicero. Since the fire destroyed central Chicago and all of the city records, most legal transactions in the city were disrupted. That's why we decided to comb through the marriage records in neighboring towns, which is where we found it. You told us that Christina and Jack came to Chicago to find work, and there were plenty of construction jobs after the fire, but housing was scarce. You'll see that Christina listed an address in Cicero as their place of residence."

"Did you go to that address? Is the house still there?"

"We did. It's a boardinghouse that has been in operation for some thirty years. We spoke with the landlady, Mrs. Marusak, and from our description, she thinks she may remember your mother."

I leap up from the divan, too excited to remain seated. "I want to talk to her. Can you take me there?"

"Certainly, if you'd like." Agent Albertson rises, as well.

"Anna, dear. Are you forgetting that you have plans this evening?" Mother asks, pretending to be calm. "I'm afraid there won't be enough time for my daughter to travel all the way to Cicero and back with you this afternoon," she explains to the agents.

"How about tomorrow?" I ask.

"That won't be possible, either," Mother says. "Your calendar is quite full, dear, for the remainder of this week."

"But there must be an afternoon when I can get away. Can't

we cancel something?" After consulting the calendar that she meticulously keeps, Mother informs me that with our multiple social engagements and two important dress fittings, the earliest opportunity to travel to Cicero will be a week from tomorrow. I don't know how I'll be able to wait that long. I remember my silent vow to abandon this search, but my curiosity outweighs any fear I have about what I might discover about my parents in Cicero.

I show William the typewritten report when we meet for dinner later that evening. "It was such a relief to know that my birth wasn't disgraceful," I tell him. He nods but shows little enthusiasm, briefly scanning the page before folding it in half and laying it aside. We are in the elegant dining room of the private men's club that he and Father belong to, in the only area where women are allowed. The plush surroundings and hushed atmosphere make me feel as though I must whisper.

"Shall I order for both of us?" William asks when the waiter appears.

"Yes, but nothing too heavy. Your mother hosted a luncheon for me today." William orders, and the waiter leaves. "Some days it seems that all I do is climb in and out of my carriage, change from one dress to another, sip tea, and politely nibble my way through a series of extravagant meals. When I stayed with Oma Geesje in Michigan, we once ate a dinner of fresh tomatoes from her garden with cheese and bread. It was a wonderful meal."

William offers me a patient smile and reaches for my hand. "I wanted to dine alone with you tonight because we have so much to talk about. It seems there is very little time to converse about important things when we're together at social functions." I glance at the detectives' report that he has set aside. That is what is most important to me at the moment, but I can see that William isn't interested.

"You're right," I say. "We hardly ever dine alone. Tell me what you're thinking."

"We still haven't chosen a date for our wedding. Mother tells me that you ladies need plenty of time to make all the preparations, but how much time, exactly?"

"I don't know. I've never gotten married before," I say with a teasing smile.

William leans forward to cup my face in his hand, caressing my cheek with his thumb. "I want so much to begin living my life with you, Anna—not the two separate lives that we live now, lives that barely intersect. I need you as my partner and my most charming asset in this crazy world of finance that I'm part of."

I think of how tightly Mother currently controls my social calendar, filling it to the brim with activity, and I wonder if my obligations as William's wife will keep me even busier. I begin to feel trapped—which is silly, since my life has never been my own to do with as I please.

"In fact, I would be happy if we could be married tomorrow," William says. "Is four months enough time? We could be married as we usher in the New Year."

I reach to take his hand, squeezing it. "We can get married whenever we want. It's our wedding, after all. Our life. Starting the New Year together sounds wonderful." My words please him, and he lifts my hand to his lips and kisses it.

"You're so beautiful, Anna." I know he means it, but I can't help picturing Clarice Beacham and her glorious auburn hair. Compared with her, I am merely pretty.

The waiter returns with William's drink and the first course of our meal—asparagus soup. For some reason, I think of the Dutch pea soup that Oma Geesje made, and I remember how Derk and I had laughed and laughed as we ate it—although I can't recall why. I miss Derk. He and William are as different as salt and pepper. William is handsome and elegant, a proper gentleman in his tailored suit and starched white shirt. He keeps himself as tightly locked as his father's bank vault, and it would be so out of character for him to laugh out loud over a bowl of soup. Derk, on the other hand, is as simple and unsophisticated as salt, as honest and open as the blue sky above Lake Michigan. It's as natural for him to share his thoughts and feelings as it is to breathe.

"We need to decide where we'll live after we're married," William says, breaking into my thoughts. I scold myself for comparing the two men. After all, I'm going to marry William. "We need to decide if we're going to build a new house or renovate an existing one. Either way, it will take time and planning, so the sooner we begin the process, the sooner our home will be ready. Although I doubt if any home will be ready by the time we marry in January. What do you think?"

Some women may care about details like silk draperies and Turkish carpets and crystal chandeliers, but I'm not one of them. The very thought of deciding how to fill room after room of an enormous mansion with furnishings makes me feel as though I can't breathe. I lay down my soup spoon and push away the bowl. "I think . . . I think I would prefer to let you make all the decisions about the house. I trust your judgment completely." I hope my answer pleases him, but I can tell by his furrowed brow that it doesn't.

"I thought choosing a house was something we could do together."

I search for the right words and get a reprieve when the waiter appears to remove our soup bowls and serve the fish course. The fillet has a strong, fishy smell that catches in my throat. "It's all too much for me to think about right now," I say when the waiter leaves again. "I have so many wedding plans to make, and I'm right in the middle of learning about my real parents' past and finding out who I am." I gesture to the detectives' report.

"Is your past as important as who you are right now? And who you're going to be very soon—my wife? Why should the past matter at all when we'll have our entire future together? Besides, it isn't even your past. You grew up here in Chicago, with the Nicholsons—the parents who raised you."

I can see he is growing irritated, as Mother had earlier today. I need to be careful not to allow this obsession, as Mother called it, to come between me and the people I love. "You're right," I tell him. "If you already have some houses or building lots in mind, maybe we could drive past them on Sunday afternoon and at least see them from the outside."

"I would like that," he says, smiling. I'm struck all over again by how handsome William is, and I recall Clarice Beacham's remarks from this afternoon. She might still be scheming to win him back, but William is mine and I am his. The thought brings a smile to my face.

William wraps his arms around me on the carriage ride home and holds me close. Did my mama feel happy and content when she was with Jack Newell? She loved him enough to run away from home with him and marry him. Once again, my thoughts turn to the landlady who thinks she remembers my parents. How will I ever wait until next week to meet her and learn more?

CHAPTER 2

Geesje

I don't know how to answer my son Jakob. I've been digging in
my flower gardens all morning on this warm fall day, cleaning
out the dead leaves and vines until next spring, and his question
has taken me by surprise. I wipe sandy dirt from my hands as
I ponder how to reply. If I say *yes*, my quiet, contented life will
be tossed upside-down. I've already weathered enough changes
during my sixty-seven years to make another one unwelcome.
Yet I have no reason to refuse his request except pure selfishness.
I don't want my life to be disturbed; it's as simple as that. It's
not a very Christlike attitude, I know.

Jakob's buggy is tethered out front, and the mare stamps
the ground impatiently. She and her owner both want to be on
their way, with many other tasks to accomplish before the day
ends. "I thought the girl, Cornelia, could stay in your spare
room, now that Anneke has returned to Chicago," Jakob says,

filling the silence. "Anneke isn't coming back for a visit anytime soon, is she?"

"No . . ." I say with a sigh.

"I'm sorry to impose on you, *Moeder*, but I've asked everyone in my congregation that I could think of, and no one else is able to help. So many people are already sponsoring friends and relatives from the Netherlands, and every spare room in the village is filled. My parsonage is filled, too. Besides, neither Cornelia nor her grandfather, Marinus Den Herder, speak English. You're one of the few people able to converse with them and perhaps teach them some English."

"How old is Cornelia again?"

"I think they said she's seventeen. She lost her parents and two brothers in a house fire, and the only family she has left is her grandfather. She could use some motherly care."

Jakob is making it harder and harder for me to refuse. I was also seventeen when I left the Netherlands to settle here in Michigan with my parents. They died of malaria less than a year after we arrived, leaving me as alone as this poor girl. "What about her family back in the Netherlands? Was there no one there she could turn to?"

"Her grandfather, who is a widower, wanted to give Cornelia a new start in a new land, away from the painful memories."

"Where is he going to stay? I don't have room for him here."

"I know you don't. Pieter Vander Veen offered to let him stay next door with him and Derk until he can find a place of his own. Pieter knows what it's like to lose his wife, and Derk lost his mother at an early age. I thought of you as soon as Pieter offered Mr. Den Herder a place. It would be perfect if Cornelia could stay right next door with you."

"For how long?" I ask, scraping some of the garden dirt from beneath my fingernails.

"It's hard to say. We're taking a collection at church to help pay for their board. And I'm sure Cornelia will be willing to help you out with cooking and cleaning and so forth. We're trying to find Mr. Den Herder a job, but it's difficult. He's sixty-eight and doesn't speak any English. Once he finds work, we'll help them find a place to rent."

"So this arrangement will only be for a short time?"

"That's the plan. Just until they get settled. Mr. Den Herder is very protective of his granddaughter and didn't want to be separated from her at all. This arrangement is the best I could come up with. Few people have room for one boarder, let alone two."

I know Jakob wouldn't ask such a favor of me if he could find another solution. With more and more immigrants arriving in America every day, many of his parishioners' homes are crammed with relatives who are making a new start. It's exciting for little Holland to be growing this way. When the town was first being settled, it was common for two or more families to live together in a tiny one-room cabin until more housing could be built. Then after the malaria outbreak that took my parents, we were left with so many orphans that we had to build an orphanage for them all. It was never put to use, though. We all opened our hearts and adopted the little ones as our own. My husband and I adopted two young brothers, Arie and Gerrit. It's what any good Christian would do. So is it just my age that makes me hesitate now?

"I know I'm asking a lot of you, Moeder," Jakob says. "But—"

"But you also know I won't refuse you. . . . *Ya*," I say with a sigh. "Ya, Cornelia can stay with me."

"Thanks, Moeder. They're currently staying at the hotel. I'll bring them over to meet you later this afternoon."

"Tell them they're welcome to have dinner with me."

And just like that, my life has changed. I watch Jakob drive away, marveling at how much he is like his dear father. Maarten wouldn't have hesitated for a moment to help Cornelia and her grandfather.

I see the mailman coming up the street and wait to see if he has brought me anything. He hands me a letter from my granddaughter Anneke in Chicago. I tear it open and start reading as I return inside.

Dearest Oma Geesje,

I have wonderful news! The Pinkerton detectives who have been searching for more information about Mama gave me their first report today. They found a record of Mama's marriage to Jack Newell! They were married in a town near Chicago two weeks after they ran away together. I know you've always wondered, as I have, if Jack took advantage of Mama, but it seems he did the right thing after all. Which means I have a legitimate father.

The detectives also found a former landlady of theirs at a boardinghouse who may remember Mama. I'm going to talk with her next week to see what she can recall. I'll write again when I have more news.

That's all for now, but I knew you would be happy to hear what I have learned so far.

All my love,
Anneke

I am so excited to learn that Christina was legally married when Anneke was born that I walk all the way downtown to share the letter with my son Arie at his print shop. He and Christina had always been close, and he was as devastated as the rest of us when she ran away twenty-six years ago. "I can't even describe how happy I am to know that she stayed true to our Christian principles about marriage," I tell Arie.

"Doesn't Scripture say, 'Train up a child in the way he should go: and when he is old, he will not depart from it'?"

"Yes. But I think that proverb is meant to be more of a wise observation than a promise from God. He also gives us free will, ya?"

"And Christina had a very strong will."

"That she did!" Arie has never married or had children, so he can't know the guilt and sorrow I've wrestled with over the years, blaming myself for making mistakes while raising my daughter. Was I too strict? Too lenient? Could I have done something different to keep Christina from running away with a man who wasn't a Christian? Arie can't know how much I treasure each little nugget that I learn about Christina. She was married! Perhaps I didn't do such a terrible job as a mother after all.

The September day is warm, and I'm so tired by the time I walk home from the print shop that I decide to eat a light supper in a few hours and go to bed early. Then I remember that I'm expecting company. I want nothing more than to sit down in my chair with my cat on my lap and take a nap, but I go to the kitchen to see what I can prepare for my guests' dinner.

I have chicken soup and dumplings bubbling on the stove by the time Jakob arrives with Cornelia and Marinus Den Herder. It isn't a fancy dinner, but I hope it will help them feel at home. Marinus has to duck his head as he enters the door of my tiny house. He looks around as if the house is for sale and he's trying to decide if he will buy it. "Welcome," I greet them in Dutch as Jakob introduces us. "It's so nice to meet you."

"Thank you." Marinus studies me from head to toe, as if determining if I will measure up. He is a very handsome, distinguished-looking man with light brown hair that is turning silver above his ears. He carries himself with the rigid posture of royalty. He doesn't return my smile, and his expression is one of a man who has been squinting into bright sunlight all his life. I try not to judge by appearances, but his downturned mouth and deep frown don't leave a very good first impression. I turn to his granddaughter.

"Welcome, Cornelia. It's so nice to have you staying with me for a while." I'm surprised by how angry she looks. Her temper seems to be boiling just beneath the surface, ready to spill over at the merest spark, like my pot of soup that is simmering on the stove. From everything Jakob told me about her, I expected to see grief. But what I also see is anger. Perhaps she and her grandfather had an argument before coming here and their tempers haven't had a chance to cool.

"Will you stay and eat dinner with us, too?" I ask Jakob.

"I'm sorry, I can't. But I'll help with the trunks and other baggage before I go." The men go outside to retrieve them, and I take Cornelia to see her room.

"I hope it will be suitable," I tell her.

She seems afraid to move past the door for fear of damaging something, even though the room is plain and simple.

"This room will be yours for as long as you need it." She is a very pretty girl, slender and delicate, but her beauty seems to be deliberately shrouded beneath a drab, shapeless dress the color of mud. Her light brown hair, the same color as her grandfather's, is pulled into a severe, unflattering bun on the back of her head. She is about the same size as my granddaughter Anneke, and I make a note to ask her to send Cornelia some skirts and shirtwaists that she no longer needs.

A moment later Derk arrives, carrying Cornelia's things. "You and your father are welcome to come back and eat dinner here," I tell Derk. "We'll be seeing a lot of each other in the coming weeks, so we may as well all eat together tonight."

"We would love to." He sets down the trunk and turns to Cornelia. "Hello, Miss Den Herder. I'm Derk Vander Veen from next door." She hasn't understood him, and she looks to me to translate. How lonely she must be with no one her age to talk to. For the first time, I'm glad I agreed to have her stay with me.

When the trunks are moved and everyone has had a chance to settle in, Derk and his father return with Mr. Den Herder and sit down around my table. Cornelia has remained in her room until now, and she slips into her seat as silently as my tabby cat. She is still wearing the dowdy brown dress.

"How are you related to the Vander Veens, Mrs. de Jonge?" Marinus Den Herder asks me after Derk says a blessing over the food.

"We're not related. But Derk has been like a son to me ever since his mother died. Both he and Pieter have become like family. . . . And please, call me Geesje."

"No, thank you," he replies. "I would prefer not to be so personal." His refusal brings a chill over the meal as if the newcomers have ushered in a snowstorm. I wonder if Derk and Pieter understand enough Dutch to know what just happened. Mr. Den Herder has been here for less than an hour, but I'm already regretting my dinner invitation. He seems to occupy all of the space in the room.

As we eat our soup, Derk attempts to talk to Cornelia, but his knowledge of the Dutch language has grown rusty over the years. He turns to me. "Please tell her that I would be interested to know what she thinks of America so far." I translate his question, and Mr. Den Herder's frown deepens. He replies before Cornelia has a chance to.

"We were told in the Netherlands that America is founded on freedom of religion." He speaks very loudly, as if volume alone will help him be understood. "But it seems to me there is much more *freedom* than religion here. I see too much silliness among the young people I have met. And a lack of respect for their elders and for God's holy sanctuary."

I turn to Derk, unwilling to translate his disapproving remarks. "He isn't impressed with America," I say.

"So I gathered." Derk hides a smile.

"What was your occupation in the Netherlands, Mr. Den Herder?" I ask.

"It's *Dominie* Den Herder, if you don't mind. I was a minister."

Now, why didn't my son mention that important fact? I give up and let Pieter try his hand at conversing with him in his stumbling Dutch. As the dinner proceeds, I begin forming an opinion of Dominie Den Herder as a man who is stern and strict and very old-fashioned, the sort of husband who never allows his wife to speak or voice an opinion. He looks shocked and annoyed whenever I try to add to the conversation—let alone when I dare to ask a question. If he's here for very long, he'll soon learn that I have plenty of opinions and I'm not afraid to speak them.

"The dominie is going to have a lot of adjusting to do here in America," I whisper to Derk in English. He grins in reply.

Meanwhile, Cornelia hasn't spoken a single word throughout the entire meal. She lays down her spoon and folds her hands in her lap after barely finishing half of her soup. I notice how skeletal her hands are before she hides them and wonder just how thin she is beneath the baggy dress. Is homesickness adding to her grief, I wonder? My heart aches for her.

The dominie thanks me for the food when everyone is finished eating, then says, "And now if you have a Bible, Mrs. de Jonge, it is my custom to read a Scripture passage aloud after the evening meal."

"I have a Dutch Bible right here," I say, reaching for mine. "It is my daily custom, as well." The passage I open to from the Gospel of John is about love, but he reads it with the fire and diction of an Old Testament prophet of doom. I'm relieved when he says good night and leaves to go home with the Vander Veens. "Good luck," I whisper to Derk as he bends to kiss my cheek.

31

"We'll need it," he replies, and his blue eyes sparkle with laughter.

Cornelia has filled the dishpan with water and is already washing the dishes when I rejoin her in the kitchen. I watch her for a moment, searching for a sign that she has begun to relax now that her grandfather is gone. I see no change. I have been clenching my teeth the entire evening, and I can't imagine crossing the Atlantic Ocean in a tiny steamship cabin with him. I'm glad that it has worked out for Cornelia and her overbearing grandfather to live apart for a time. I would like her to know that she can be herself with me, and that I'm not as rigid as her grandfather, but I can't seem to find the right words. Instead, we chat about the warm fall weather, and I ask her again what she thinks of America.

"It is very big," she replies.

"Yes, that was my impression, too, when I first arrived."

"I would like to go to bed now, please," she says when we finish the dishes.

"Of course. You must be tired." I turn out the kitchen light and walk with her to Anneke's room. "My granddaughter stayed in this room this summer," I tell her. "It's a long story, which I'll share with you another time, but Anneke and I just met in July even though she is twenty-three years old." Cornelia doesn't reply. "There will be a nice breeze if you leave this window open," I add. She merely nods. "Good night, then. Let me know if you need anything." I leave her and go to my own bedroom.

Cornelia is carrying secrets, I can tell. She is surely mourning her family and perhaps her life in the Netherlands. But right now, her anger seems more overpowering than her grief. Maybe once she learns to trust me she will unpack the heavy load she is struggling to carry.

I fall asleep wondering what I have gotten myself into.

CHAPTER 3

Anna

I am out of bed before the maid arrives with my breakfast tray, searching through my wardrobe for something suitable to wear to the boardinghouse in Cicero this afternoon. After anticipating this day for more than a week, it has finally arrived. This afternoon, Agents Albertson and Mitchell will accompany me on my visit to meet Mama's former landlady. I'm trying not to get my hopes up that she will remember much, since nearly twenty-six years have passed since Mama and Jack Newell boarded with her, yet I can't help feeling excited.

I'm on my hands and knees, searching for a pair of shoes, when I hear plates and silverware rattling as the maid arrives.

"You may set the tray on my writing desk," I tell her.

"May I help you find something, Miss Anna?" she asks.

I straighten up and brush the dust off my hands. "I'm looking for an older pair of brown shoes I used to have, but I don't see them."

"If you please, miss . . ." She offers me an awkward and totally unnecessary curtsy. "I took several pairs of your shoes downstairs to give them a good polish. I'll bring them up to you right away." She darts toward the door and nearly trips over her own feet.

"Wait . . . there's no hurry. I won't need them until this afternoon. Tell me your name again?"

"It's Lucy, miss." She curtsies a second time.

"Thank you. You may go, Lucy."

I barely have time to finish my breakfast before Sophia arrives to pin up my hair and help me into my gown for this morning's meeting. I long to skip the event altogether, but I can't. Mother and I are being inducted into the Women's Literary Club today.

I never would have been invited to join this exclusive women's club if not for my engagement to William. His mother is the president this year, and she is eager to sponsor Mother and me as new members. "This is a huge honor," Mother assures me as we drive to the event. "The finest women in Chicago are all members." She may as well have said the wealthiest women in Chicago. She is thrilled to be invited to join. William's mother explained that the club's goals are to read and discuss works of literature, poetry, and history in order to broaden our perspective and improve our minds. I'm not enthusiastic about spending my free time reading poetry when I barely have time to read the Bible Derk gave me. And joining a new club will mean selecting new dress patterns and choosing fabric and consulting a seamstress for fittings since Mother insists that we need new gowns to wear to the meetings.

I am also uneasy because today's event is being held at the home of William's former girlfriend, Clarice Beacham. She is waiting in her grand, marble-lined foyer to welcome us, her glorious hair swooped up in the stunning Gibson girl fashion again. "You are going to adore this club, Anna," she assures me. "We learn such interesting things. Do you enjoy poetry?" Before I have a chance to reply, she links her arm through mine as if we are best friends and tows me into the conservatory. A group of young ladies our age stand in a tight circle, their heads bent together as if telling secrets. "Do you know everyone, Anna? Or shall I introduce you?"

"I believe I know everyone." They are the cream of young Chicago society. Part of my training in the social graces has been learning how to remember important people's names. It would be a serious breach of etiquette to forget someone's name once we've been formally introduced.

The other girls scrutinize me from my hat to my shoes, but I'm accustomed to these inspections and am confident that I will measure up, thanks to Mother's diligence. We exchange a few pleasant compliments before one of them turns to me and says, "I hear that you and William have begun searching for a home." I'm so startled I can't reply. Last Sunday afternoon William and I drove past three houses that are for sale, but that has been the full extent of our search. I find it unsettling that they already know about it.

"Um, yes . . . we have just begun to look," I say when I find my voice.

"It must be such fun to decorate an entire house," Clarice says, "especially with all of William's money to spend. Imagine being able to choose the very finest furnishings! I envy you, Anna." The mention of William's wealth shocks me. It simply isn't done. I'm guessing Clarice did it intentionally, to throw me off-balance.

"We're in the very early stages of the process," I say, ignoring the rude remark.

"If I were you," another woman says, "I would ask William

to build a room just like this one." She gestures to the conservatory, a magnificent, many-sided room with a soaring ceiling and walls made entirely of window glass. The light-filled space is embellished with lush green plants, including an orange tree with real oranges and a flowering gardenia bush that fills the air with its exotic perfume. Dainty bamboo chairs that have been painted white are lined up in rows for the club meeting.

"Which decorator will you be working with?" Clarice asks.

"We haven't chosen one yet."

Thankfully, Mrs. Beacham begins ringing a little silver bell, so I am spared further questions. "Ladies, if you would take your seats, please. It's time to begin."

Clarice's mother starts the meeting by reading a poem. Everyone claps politely when she finishes, our applause muffled by our gloves. Then Mrs. Wilkinson calls Mother and me to the front and presents us as the newest members, although I am certain we have already been discussed and dissected before our membership was approved and we were ever invited to join. I am pleasantly surprised when Mrs. Wilkinson introduces me as her son William's "charming and delightful fiancée." A little ceremony follows as we are inducted into the club and presented with a small diamond pin in the shape of a book, along with a packet detailing the history and goals of the organization. Then we take our seats again for the program.

I find my mind wandering as one of the members gives a review of the latest book the club has read, followed by a dignified discussion. I hope the presentations aren't this boring every time. Before the meeting adjourns, Mrs. Wilkinson reads the announcements. One of them involves a trip to Racine, Wisconsin, but I'm no longer paying attention, my thoughts already on my trip to Cicero this afternoon.

Clarice is by my side the moment I rise from my chair to mingle and enjoy tea and *petit fours*. "You must sign up for the steamship excursion to Racine next month, Anna. We always have such a grand time on our club outings. The boat voyage on Lake Michigan is certain to be the highlight of our year."

I stare at Clarice, unable to disguise my fear. I don't need to consult my social calendar to know that I will not be going. Having survived a shipwreck as a child and a terrible storm on my voyage across Lake Michigan this summer, I cannot bring myself to board another ship. I fumble for a reply. "I-I don't think—"

"Oh, Anna, I forgot! I'm so sorry!" The expression of shock on Clarice's face seems genuine. She lowers her voice as if to speak confidentially, but I know the others can hear her. "Mrs. Wilkinson told me the story of your tragic past. But don't worry, I won't tell a soul. She swore me to secrecy, and I agreed. It's no one's business but yours that you were a shipwrecked orphan when the Nicholsons adopted you."

"My father saved me from drowning," I say. I want her and everyone else to know that he is a hero.

"So I heard! Mrs. Wilkinson also told me you've hired detectives to learn more about your family. How exciting! It's like something from a novel."

"The Pinkertons have already found the record of my parents' marriage," I tell her. I'm so relieved to know that my birth was legitimate, and so excited to be meeting Mama's former landlady today, that I have tossed discretion aside. If there's going to be gossip, I want Clarice and everyone else to know that I have nothing to hide. My birth wasn't shameful.

Clarice leans closer. "And what have you learned about your father and mother?"

"Nothing yet. Just the date of their marriage. They moved to Chicago right after the Great Fire."

"Well, you must let me know the moment you discover something more. This sounds so exciting!"

"I will." Clarice is the only person who has shown any interest at all in my search. I have longed for a close friend to share confidences with for some time. Yet I also remember Jane's warning that Clarice wants William back. Time will tell if her offers of friendship are genuine.

The Pinkerton agents arrive right on time, and I climb into their carriage for the journey to Cicero. The road runs alongside the railroad tracks, offering me views of rumbling freight trains, busy factories, and sprawling working-class neighborhoods. I have never been to this part of the city before and didn't know that neighborhoods like these even existed. When we halt in front of the aging boardinghouse, I'm grateful that the two detectives accompanied me here and not Mother. She never would have crossed the decaying front porch, let alone stepped inside.

Mrs. Marusak greets us at the door, and we introduce ourselves. "Come in and have a seat," she says, with the faintest trace of a foreign accent. She seems unwell. Deep creases in her sallow face make her look as though she has lived a hard life. She leads us inside, walking as if all her leg joints have fused.

"Thank you so much for agreeing to talk with me today," I say as I take a seat on the sofa. She sits down alongside me with a grunt. The odor in the front parlor threatens to overwhelm me, smelling of years' worth of onions and cabbage and boiled meat, along with the musty stench of old furniture. The carpeting on the wooden floors is tattered and unraveling in places. Cobwebs that Mrs. Marusak is probably too nearsighted to notice festoon the corners of the room like lace. I can't begin to imagine what the bedrooms are like. "The detectives tell me that you might remember my mother, Christina de Jonge."

"Well, I wasn't sure when they first asked about her—I've had so many boarders over the years, you know. But now that I've met you, I'm positive. You look just like Christina." She points to a plate of cookies on the table beside me. "Help yourself."

"Thank you," I reply, but considering my nervous stomach and the room's odor, I don't think I can eat. I clear my throat and say, "I would be grateful to hear anything you can remember about my mother, Mrs. Marusak. I was only three years old when she died."

"They told me she drowned in a shipwreck?"

"Yes, that's right. On her way home to Michigan."

"Such a tragedy. And to think, I always urged her to go home." She clicks her tongue as she settles into the sofa cushions. "Christina certainly knew how to work hard, even though she was just a tiny little thing—and very young. I figured she had lied to me about her age. She didn't look twenty years old when she showed up at my door asking for a job."

"Mama worked for you?"

"Yes, for about a year. I remember Christina because she was very different from the other young women who have worked for me over the years."

"In what way?"

"She was kind to all the boarders and treated everyone, including me, with respect. I was reluctant to hire her at first. But my cook up and quit one morning, and so I hung a sign in the front window advertising for a new one. Not an hour later, Christina and her scoundrel of a boyfriend came knocking on my kitchen door. . . ."

CHAPTER 4

Mrs. Marusak

The girl stood outside my kitchen door, her golden hair shining like sunlight. She was neatly dressed and well-groomed but so tiny I mistook her for a schoolgirl. "I'm here about the job as a cook," she told me. "My name is Christina de Jonge."

"Don't waste my time. You're a child and I have a house full of boarders to feed." I went back inside, but she opened the screen door and followed me.

"I'm twenty years old. And I grew up with three older brothers and a hardworking father, so I know how to cook for hungry men. I have work experience, too. Back in Michigan, I worked as a maid in a very large house for a busy family."

I was frazzled, trying to get dinner ready on time without any help, and I didn't see that the pot of potatoes was about to boil over. Christina grabbed a kitchen towel and moved the

40

pot to a cooler part of the cast iron stove. "Please, just give me a chance to show you what I can do," she begged.

Meanwhile, the boyfriend hung around in the kitchen doorway, smoking a cigarette. "Close the screen door," I hollered to him. "You're letting all the flies in."

Christina picked up a fork and stuck it in one of the potatoes to test it. "They're done," she said. "Would you like me to drain off the water?"

I needed help. It was a few days after the Great Chicago Fire, and my boardinghouse was stuffed to the rafters. I usually boarded only single men, but I had rented three of my largest rooms to families with children who had no place to go. Every bed in the attic dormitory was filled, and more young working men slept on the floor. They all needed to be fed. "Very well. I could use your help today, but I'm not making any promises. The sign stays in the window, and if someone more experienced comes along, I'll have to let you go."

"I understand."

Christina put on an apron and set to work right away, plucking chickens out on the back stoop. I don't know where the boyfriend went, but he disappeared while we made supper. Christina helped me serve it to a dining room full of hungry boarders, and she did a good job of it, too. The men all perked up when they saw a pretty young girl serving their dinner, and I began to wonder if I could charge more for rent with Christina brightening up the place.

"So, may I have the job?" she asked when she finished scrubbing the pots and pans after supper.

"For now. There's a spare room behind the kitchen where my last cook slept. Your pay includes room and board."

"What about Jack—my fiancé? Do you have a job or a spare bed for him?" He had reappeared around dinnertime, but I made him stay outside, and I didn't offer him any food.

"The boardinghouse is full. I don't even have a closet he can sleep in." I had been boarding young men for nearly ten years and liked to think I was a good judge of character, but I didn't like the looks of that young man from the very first time I saw him. He was a handsome devil, and he knew it. It was more than self-confidence, it was cockiness—as if the world owed him a lot more than it owed most people.

Christina fixed herself a plate after the dishes were washed, and she shared it with him outside on the back step. I could hear them talking through my open bedroom window, and I couldn't believe he had the nerve to give her a hard time after she had worked at a demanding job all afternoon. "Why didn't you fight harder to get me room and board in this place?" he growled.

"I tried, Jack, but Mrs. Marusak says that every bed is full. Some men are even sleeping on the floor."

"You should have told her I was your husband, not your fiancé. Now where am I supposed to sleep?"

"Not with me," she said firmly. "Not until we're married."

"Come on, Christina. You know I'm going to marry you as soon as we get settled. You have a job now, and—"

"And you still don't."

"Why did you run away from home with me if you don't want to be with me? Don't you love me?" he asked in a wheedling voice.

"I didn't run away from home. I came with you because I love you, and I want to spend my life with you—and we both know that my parents never would have let us get married."

"Right. Because I'm not religious like them. I thought Christians were supposed to be kind to strangers. What a bunch of hypocrites."

"Don't call them that. And they might have gotten used to you if you had tried a little harder."

"There was no future for me in that dingy little town."

"I know, and none for me, either, except to marry a suitable Dutch boy from church and have dozens of children. I want to see something of the world. I only wish we had known that Chicago had been destroyed, too. Everything is in such chaos. I was lucky to find this job."

"Come here, beautiful. . . ."

It got quiet for several minutes and I assumed they were kissing. I was afraid I would have to fire her because I couldn't have a servant in my household who engaged in immoral behavior. It was hard enough to keep tabs on a house full of young men, let alone my servants. But then I heard her say *no* in a very loud voice and then, "Good night, Jack. I have to get up before dawn to start the fires and make breakfast for the boarders."

"Where am I supposed to sleep tonight?"

"Back where we've been staying, I guess."

I was impressed with her character, and I decided then and there to take down the sign and hire her.

Christina was a hard worker, I'll give her that. For someone as young as she was, she knew how to handle herself in the kitchen. As we worked together, I noticed that she pronounced certain words differently than most people in Chicago. "Where did you say you're from?" I asked.

"I grew up in Michigan. My parents emigrated from the Netherlands."

"From where? I've never heard of such a place. It sounds made-up, like a land from a storybook—the *Netherlands*."

"You're right," she said, laughing. "It does." She said no more about her family, and it was none of my business to pry.

The boyfriend showed up at the back door around suppertime the next day, looking as though he'd worked in a coal mine. "I got a job clearing away rubble from the fire," he told Christina. "It's the only work that's available right now, but the foreman says if I work hard, he'll eventually put me on a building crew." She moved into his arms for a kiss, hugging him tightly, not caring that she would be smudged with soot.

While the boarders ate their dinner, I let Christina fill a basin with warm water and give Jack a sliver of leftover soap and a mirror so he could clean up outside in the summer kitchen. Chicago was in ruins, and I'd heard stories of how workers had to load all the charred bricks and burned timbers and twisted metal onto wagons and haul it to the edge of Lake Michigan to dump it in. Later, city officials would fill in the new shoreline with dirt and grass and trees, and make it into a nice park. But cleaning up after the fire was a terrible job! Every day Jack would come home all black and filthy, and Christina would haul hot water for him so he could wash up. He expected her to scrub all his dirty work clothes, too, yet she did it willingly because she loved him. I've never seen a girl so crazy in love with a man. Or so totally blind to the way he stood in front of that mirror, admiring himself as he preened like a dandy. Every night he pressured her to sleep with him, and every night she said no. She insisted on getting married.

On her first half-day off, Christina left with Jack in the morning and came back waving a piece of paper. "We got married today, Mrs. Marusak. Here's the paper to prove it."

"Congratulations. I hope this doesn't mean you're going to quit."

"Not at all. We're trying to find a place of our own to rent, but I need to ask for a favor in the meantime. May Jack please stay here with me until we do?"

"That bed is hardly big enough for one person, let alone two."

"We don't mind," Jack said. I didn't like the way he grinned. "I tried to find a hotel room for our wedding night, but every place we could afford was already full."

"Well . . . as long as it's only temporary. And I need you to promise not to leave me and go work someplace else without giving fair notice like my last cook did."

"I promise, Mrs. Marusak. I like working here."

"Good. Then I suppose Jack can stay." But I would have to keep my eyes open for another cook, knowing that Christina might soon get pregnant.

About a week later, she told me they'd found a one-room apartment to rent a dozen blocks from here. The owner had chopped up his regular apartments into even tinier spaces so he could rent to more people. But Christina was so crazy in love with Jack, I doubt if she even cared what the place looked like. She walked all the way here to cook for me every day, in all sorts of weather, arriving before dawn to fix breakfast for my boarders and staying until the last of the dishes were washed in the evening. She worked so hard I decided to let Jack eat here at the end of his workday so Christina wouldn't have to go home and cook another meal for him on their tiny potbellied stove. That was all they had in the way of a kitchen, and there was no running water at all.

At first Christina would watch for Jack through the kitchen window every afternoon, and she would run outside to throw herself in his arms when he arrived, even when the weather was cold and snowy. I couldn't get over the way she looked at him, like he was royalty or something. But he was just too handsome for his own good. And very hot-tempered, as it turned out. It seemed like he was always changing jobs and always running out of money. "Jack is working his way up in the world, Mrs. Marusak," Christina told me when he quit working at the docks and started working for one of the railroads. "He'll be president of the railroad company one day, you'll see." All I could do was nod my head and wish her well. He might have been making a good living, but I could tell by the way he staggered into my kitchen at suppertime that he was drinking a lot of it away. Some nights he didn't show up for dinner at all. I had experience with men like him, and I knew it was only a matter of time before he broke Christina's heart.

The change in Christina happened so gradually that I don't suppose I took much notice of it until it was too late. It was like watching a flower slowly fade and wilt and droop, until the petals started falling one by one. By the time a year had nearly passed, Christina had changed into a different person. I remembered how sweet and cheerful she was at first, how feisty and full of life. But it was as if Jack had pulled a stopper from a sink full of water and drained all the life from her. She no longer smiled or hummed while she worked. And Jack no longer came to the boardinghouse for his dinner after work. Instead, Christina would pull off her apron and hurry home to cook for him the moment she finished her work.

Chicago had just commemorated the first anniversary of the Great Fire when Christina arrived at work one morning with a huge purple bruise beneath her eye. She tried to keep her face turned away so I wouldn't see it, but I couldn't help noticing. "I tripped and fell," she told me, "and struck the edge of the table." I knew better. I tried to guide her closer to the window so I could get a better look at the bruise, and she gasped as if I had punched her when I touched her rib cage.

"Christina, what's wrong? Are you hurt?"

"No, I'm fine." She slid away from me and started cracking eggs into a bowl for the boarders' breakfast.

"Listen, I'm fond of you, Christina. You're a sweet girl and a good worker. I know it's none of my business, but if your husband did that to you, you need to leave him and go back home to your family."

"I would never leave Jack. He's my husband."

"Any man who lays a hand on a woman doesn't deserve her loyalty. Tell me, did your father ever treat your mother that way?"

"I told you, I fell down." She hurried out the back door to bring in another load of wood for the fire.

I let it go the first time. But I noticed that she had a lot more "accidents" in the weeks after that. I even saw a set of deep bruises on her upper arm that looked exactly like a man's handprint. Then one day she limped into work as if she ached all over. She had another black eye and her left wrist was so swollen and bruised she couldn't hold on to anything. I sent for the local doctor, and he came and put a splint on it. He thought her wrist might be broken.

"Enough is enough, Christina," I said after the doctor left. "Just because you stood in front of a justice of the peace with Jack Newell doesn't give him the right to do this to you."

Christina fell into my arms, weeping.

"I don't know what to do to make him love me again."

"He's not worthy of your love. Jack Newell is a brute, and he isn't going to change. You're only what—twenty years old? My advice is for you to leave him and go back home."

"I can't go home."

"Why not? No decent parents would want their daughter to be treated this way."

"You don't understand. I'm from a very tight-knit community, a very religious one. Everyone knows each other's business. I defied the church's teaching and went against everything my parents taught me when I ran off with Jack. I'm too ashamed to go home. Besides, I don't even know if my parents would take me back."

"Well, then. Even if you don't want to go home, it doesn't mean you have to stay with Jack."

"But what else can I do?"

"Go pack your clothes right now while he's at work, and move in here. There's still a bed for you in the back."

"He'll come looking for me. And he'll be furious." I saw fear in her eyes where there was once adoration, and I could have murdered that man myself.

"I'll hide you here. I have a couple of boarders who will be happy to help you get rid of him. They all love you, Christina. You brought sunshine into this place, but Jack Newell has stolen all the life from you."

In the end, Christina agreed. She left everything behind in the apartment except her clothes and moved into my back room again. That night Jack came looking for her, and he was roaring drunk. I locked all the doors and didn't answer him or let him inside. At first he stood outside Christina's window and pleaded with her to come back. "It will never happen again, Christina, I swear. I'll never take another drink, either. Please! I love you! I can't live without you."

I was afraid she would give in, so I asked two of my burliest boarders to go outside and kick him off my property. What followed was a terrible scene with Jack cursing and raging and threatening to club the men with a chunk of firewood. "She's my wife! She belongs with me!" he yelled.

By now several of my boarders had joined the first two in the shouting match. One of them had a brother who was a Chicago policeman, and he threatened to send for him if Jack didn't leave. He finally left, but he returned on several more nights after that, drunk and bellowing. He had the whole neighborhood in an uproar, not to mention my boarders.

"I'm scared all the time," Christina told me. "One of these nights he's going to break through my window and kill me." I feared she was right.

As luck would have it, my niece Vera had just been hired as a maid in a big mansion somewhere in Chicago. "I think they're still looking for maidservants," I told Christina. "I would hate to lose you, but I'll ask Vera to help you get a job there, if you'd like. I'll give you a good recommendation, too. Jack will never find you."

And that's what we did. I was happy that it all worked out for Christina when she was hired on as a housemaid. But I had grown very fond of her and hated to see her go. I paid her a little extra and hugged her good-bye. "Come back, now and then, and let me know you're all right. Promise?"

"Yes, I promise." She hugged me in return, but she didn't keep her promise. That was the last I ever saw of Christina Newell.

Anna

CHICAGO, ILLINOIS
1897

I feel exhausted by the time Mrs. Marusak finishes her story. I ache for my poor mama. And I hate my father for the way he treated her. I can only sit in stunned silence for a moment after she finishes. Her story leaves me with so many questions, and when I can finally speak, they start pouring out. "Do you know if my mother was expecting a baby when she left Jack?"

"If she was, she never said a word about it to me."

"Might she have gone back to him, in spite of everything he did?"

"It's hard to say. I know she was crazy in love with him at first. But she was scared to death of him in the end."

"Maybe Jack changed. Maybe he won her back."

"Experience tells me that men like Jack don't change. But who knows?"

"Do you remember which family Mama went to work for? Or where in Chicago they lived?"

"Not after all these years. Vera might be able to tell you."

"I would love to talk with her. Would that be possible?"

"She lives in Chicago on the Near West Side. She's married now and no longer works as a maid. I can give you her address." She struggles out of her chair and limps into a back room, returning a few minutes later with a piece of paper with her niece's address on it. Agent Albertson copies it down, as well.

"Thank you so much, Mrs. Marusak," I say as I rise to take my leave. "I'm grateful to you for taking the time to help me learn a little more about my mama."

"You're welcome." She reaches to take my hands in her gnarled ones. "Are you married, my dear?"

"No. Not yet."

"You seem like a sweet girl—just like Christina. I hope you won't make the same mistake she did and marry the wrong man. Don't be fooled by good looks and charm. Make sure your sweetheart values the same things you do." She squeezes my hands tightly before letting go again.

I climb into the carriage feeling shaken. Not only was Mama's story upsetting, but the timing was all wrong. Mama married Jack in 1871, and Mrs. Marusak said she left him a year later in 1872. But I wasn't born until 1874. "She must have gone back to Jack after all," I tell Agent Albertson on the drive home. He and Agent Mitchell took notes the entire time that Mrs. Marusak was telling her story, so they must have figured out the timing, too.

Unless Jack isn't my father.

"We're still searching for a record of your birth," Agent Mitchell replies. "And we'll start looking for a record of their divorce."

"But even if you do find a record of their divorce, that still won't solve the problem of who my father is."

Agent Albertson closes his notebook and looks at me with

sympathy. "Now that we know that Jack Newell worked for the railroad, we can check the union records for his name. If the information is out there, we'll find it."

I arrive home still upset by my mama's story. It has raised more questions than it has answered. I am horrified to learn that my real father was not an honorable man, and that he treated Mama so shamefully. I can imagine Clarice Beacham gloating if she ever heard that tidbit of gossip. William's mother and Clarice's mother are close, so once I tell William what I've learned about my father, Clarice is certain to hear about it, too. For the first time I understand why Mother has been insisting that I let go of the past and not risk dredging up something unpleasant. I can see how it might reflect badly on William if it was discovered that his wife is the daughter of such a brute. And what about my grandmother? I promised Oma Geesje I would share any news I learned with her, but how can I tell her the truth about what happened? She will be brokenhearted to know how her daughter suffered. And even more upset to learn that Mama was afraid she would be judged and condemned if she returned home.

"You look glum," Mother says when I join her and Father at the dinner table that evening. "Am I to assume that the meeting with the landlady was not a success?"

"She remembered a few things," I say. "She told me I resemble Mama. But twenty-six years is a long time to try to recall past events. The afternoon was disappointing."

"It's just as well," Father says, unfurling his napkin on his lap. "Knowing the past won't change anything in the present."

We fill our plates as the maids serve the meal. I picture Mama in their place, working for a wealthy family while living in fear that Jack will find her. Or maybe Mama loved him so much she forgave him and returned to him. Either picture is unsettling.

By the time we finish eating, I have made an important decision. "I'm going to stop investigating the past," I tell my parents. "It's taking up too much of my time, and I have wedding plans to make." My parents look relieved. And although I still have questions that will never be answered, I'm relieved, too. Surely this is the best thing to do, for everyone's sake.

CHAPTER 5

Geesje

HOLLAND, MICHIGAN

I set a plate of scrambled eggs and toast in front of Cornelia several minutes ago, but she hasn't taken a bite. "You need to eat something, dear, or you will simply waste away to nothing," I tell her. "A strong wind will blow in from the lake and sweep you away with the fall leaves." I watch for even the tiniest smile, but she looks up at me and nods, as if she knows that is exactly what will happen. As if she is planning on it. "I can fix you something else for breakfast if you don't like eggs. Just tell me what you're used to eating."

"I'm not very hungry, Mrs. de Jonge."

"Can we agree on a better name to call me, something less formal? How about *Tante* Geesje? I know I'm not really your aunt, but that's what Derk calls me, and it will make us seem more like friends."

She shrugs and says, "Yes, ma'am."

Her plate is still half full when she starts to get up to clear away her breakfast dishes. "Sit down, Cornelia, and let's talk while we finish our tea," I say, stopping her. She sits down again, her hands folded in her lap, her head lowered. "I don't intend to pry for information about your life before you came here, because it's none of my business. But I understand that your grandfather came to America to get a new start, so maybe we could begin there. I would love to hear what some of your hopes and dreams are for your new life in Michigan. Maybe I can help you. If you feel like sharing, I'd be happy to listen."

Cornelia runs her slender finger around the rim of the teacup. "I don't have any dreams. Coming here was Grandfather's idea."

"Well, then, we already have something in common. Coming to America fifty years ago was my parents' idea, not mine. I was only seventeen years old and too young to remain behind on my own, although I wanted to. I was in love with someone back in the Netherlands, you see."

She looks up at me and tears pool in her eyes. She quickly looks away again, and for a brief moment her expression is one of exquisite pain, as if she has just bitten down on a throbbing tooth. Did her grandfather force her to leave someone behind? Someone unsuitable? I want to tell Cornelia that I know what that kind of grief is like, to be separated from the man you love. But it is too soon. She doesn't know me well enough to trust me with her secrets.

"I understand that your grandfather is looking for work—will you be looking for work, as well, or just keeping house for the two of you?"

"I'm not sure. We didn't talk about it."

I find that very strange. How could they set out for a new country and travel together for several weeks without talking about the future and making plans? I recall Cornelia's anger when they arrived at my home yesterday, and I wonder if she refuses to discuss it with him. I decide to continue chatting, hoping she'll eventually warm up to me.

"Well, around here the young ladies your age can often find work with a large family that needs help with cooking and washing and tending the children. My daughter, Christina, worked for the Cappon family across town and seemed to enjoy it very much. I know she liked having her own money to spend." I feel a stab of guilt and sorrow the moment the words are out of my mouth. Christina had met Jack Newell while working in that house, which was very close to the factory where he was employed. There were so many things I would do differently if I could live my life over again. But would it have been right to keep Christina locked up and under guard all the time?

"I don't think I can work for anyone unless they speak Dutch," Cornelia says. She nibbles on her fingernails, chewing them down to the quick.

"Of course, of course. Would you like to start learning English? There are still many older people here in Holland who speak Dutch, but most of the young people your age don't know it very well. You'll be able to make new friends once you learn the language."

"I would like to learn." It is the first sign of enthusiasm she has shown since arriving.

"Good. We'll start with a few simple words. I'll fetch you some paper and a pencil so you can write them down." I rise from the table to collect the paper and we begin our first lesson with common kitchen items like *fork* and *chair* and *table*. Later I decide to walk with her to Van Putten's Dry Goods store on Eighth Street to pick up a few items and show Cornelia around Holland. I thought she might like to choose some of the foods that she enjoys eating, but she refuses to select anything at all.

"Whatever you cook is fine," she says. It's a beautiful fall day, and the leaves are putting on a glorious show of color, especially the maples. But Cornelia walks with her head lowered, looking up only briefly whenever I point out something to her, such as the new clock tower or Pillar Church, which I attend. I try to teach her a few new words, but she is unenthusiastic.

We are nearly home again when we meet a young mother from my congregation who is out for a stroll, pushing a baby carriage with her newborn inside. I take a moment to introduce her to Cornelia, explaining that she doesn't speak English yet. "Do you speak any Dutch, Mrs. Visscher?" I ask, hoping Cornelia can make a new friend.

"Please, call me Lena. And no, I'm sorry, but I don't speak Dutch. My mother-in-law does, and my husband learned a few words because his parents spoke it at home—especially when they didn't want their children to understand what they were saying."

We share a laugh and then I peek inside the carriage. "Oh, look at this precious little one. He's beautiful."

"We named him Willem after my grandfather."

"Come and look," I say to Cornelia in Dutch. "Isn't he sweet?" She glances at him and quickly turns away. I'm surprised to see her wiping her eyes. "We'd better be on our way," I tell Mrs. Visscher. "Enjoy your walk." We are nearly home, so I don't speak again until we're inside. "I'm sorry if I did something to upset you, Cornelia—"

"It doesn't matter," she interrupts, shaking her head. "May I go to my room?"

"Yes, of course." She remains there until I call her for lunch—another meal that she barely touches.

"May I go for a walk?" she asks when we finish. "By myself, please?"

"Of course. If you walk in that direction," I say, pointing, "you'll come to a road that leads up the hill to the cemetery.

It's very peaceful up there with lots of trees, and you'll be able to see the town from the top of the hill."

"Thank you." She leaves a few minutes later through the back door. I watch her go, walking with her head lowered, her back bent, chewing her fingernails.

I have no idea what to make of Cornelia. How terrible it must be to feel all alone in a strange country. Yet she seems afraid to accept my offers of friendship. I whisper a prayer for wisdom, then tell myself to give her more time.

I am standing in my kitchen, thinking about what to fix for supper, when someone knocks on my front door. I find Cornelia's grandfather standing on my little porch. "Good afternoon, Dominie. Won't you come in?" I open the door wider, but he takes a step back.

"No, thank you. I would like a word with Cornelia, please."

"She isn't here. She left about forty minutes ago to go for a walk."

"What!" He fairly shouts the word. "Who is with her?"

"No one. She wanted to go by herself."

The color rises in his face as if he is about to boil over. "I trusted you to keep watch over her! Why didn't you do that?"

"Please stop shouting at me," I say, trying to remain calm. I am unaccustomed to being yelled at, nor do I understand why he is so furious with me. "No one told me that I had to watch over Cornelia every moment of the day. She is a grown woman and entitled to her privacy. I'm sure she didn't go far."

"You cannot be certain of that. This arrangement will not work unless you agree to keep an eye on her."

"No, Dominie. It will not work unless you explain to me why such constant attentiveness is necessary."

He gazes into the distance as if deciding how much he should say. I dislike this man more and more every moment I am with him. "Because she will run away," he finally says.

"I find that very unlikely. Cornelia is in a strange town with no money and no place to go. Besides, there is a huge lake in one direction and nothing but farmland or woods in the other three. And she doesn't even speak the language."

He folds his arms across his chest and lifts his chin. "She has run away before."

"You mean since coming to America?"

"No . . . but I have kept a close eye on her since we came to this country."

I find this man so infuriating that I can't help sighing in frustration. "It may help if you could explain why she would want to run away."

"Because she is rebellious! Unruly! She won't listen to anyone!" The words explode from him with such force that I take a small step back. My heart goes out to Cornelia in that moment, and I'm determined to find a way to help her, to bring healing and peace to her and her grandfather.

I recall her tears when I spoke of leaving behind the man I loved in the Netherlands and summon my courage to ask, "Was there a young man involved?" He glares at me without replying. "You see, I also had a daughter who ran away. The young man she was in love with talked her into it. Love is a very powerful emotion. It can cause a young girl to abandon all sense and—"

"Enough! There is no young man. Her reasons for running away are none of your business."

"They will be if Cornelia chooses to tell me about them." I'm trying to sound brave, but I'm starting to feel very uneasy as this angry man glares down at me. I suspect that his anger and unreasonableness were at least partially to blame for Cornelia's decision to run. I want to run from him myself. "While she's under my roof," I continue, "I will try not to give her a reason to run away from me."

"Now, you listen. The arrangements I made with your son

consisted of a place for Cornelia to stay, not prying into our business."

"I'm not prying, but I refuse to become Cornelia's jailor unless you give me a very good reason why it's necessary."

"We are wasting time. Tell me which direction she went so I can find her."

"I didn't watch her go. I don't know where she went." It's the truth. I suggested the cemetery, but I don't know for certain that she went there. I can see the dominie's mounting frustration, but I'm determined not to let him bully me.

"Then I have no choice but to wait here for her to return— that is, if she ever does return."

"As you wish." I leave him on my front porch and return to the kitchen. My hands are trembling from our encounter, and I have to wait for them to stop before doing any work. It is impossible to imagine Marinus Den Herder as a pastor, caring for the needs of God's people with grace and sensitivity. I feel sorry for his congregation and even sorrier for Cornelia.

An hour passes, and she still doesn't return. I'm beginning to worry that he is right and that she has run away when I finally see her coming through the gate into my backyard. "Thank you, Lord," I whisper before going to the door to greet her. "Did you have a nice walk, dear?" She nods and pulls her sweater tightly around herself. "Listen, your grandfather is waiting for you on my front porch. He is very angry with me for letting you go off on your own. He was worried about you."

Cornelia looks up at me with such a look of despair that I drape my arm around her shoulder and pull her close. She doesn't flinch or move away from me. "Would you like me to come with you to talk to him?" She nods. I take her hand in mine. I think I know a little of how she feels as we walk outside together to face him. "Cornelia is back from her walk," I tell him. I battle to keep the note of triumph out of my voice.

59

"So I see." His anger seems to have cooled while he waited. "Did you have a nice walk, Cornelia?" he asks as he rises to his feet.

"Yes. I like it here."

"Well, I don't think we will be staying much longer." Cornelia drops my hand and stares down at the floor. Her grandfather turns to me. "Tomorrow I will let your son, Dominie de Jonge, know that this living arrangement will not work for us."

"But . . . but you only just arrived," I sputter. "We've hardly had a chance to—"

"My mind is made up. Good day."

Cornelia and I watch him walk down the steps and go next door to the Vander Veen's house. "Why does he want us to leave?" she asks. "I don't understand."

"I'm so sorry, Cornelia, but it's probably my fault. He was angry with me for letting you go off on your own. He was worried that you might run away."

"I don't want to leave here. If I promise not to run away, will you let me stay?"

"Yes, of course. If it's up to me, you may stay as long as you need to." We go back inside the house, but I stop her before she heads to her bedroom. "Listen, Cornelia, if your grandfather is mistreating you in any way, I can speak with my son and make sure you don't have to go with him—"

"He has never mistreated me." I see the sincerity in her eyes and hear it in her voice. I believe her. "That's not why I ran away."

I wait, hoping she will trust me enough to confide in me, but she doesn't. We return to our long silences as she helps me fix supper and we sit down to eat it. I decide to fill the awkwardness with more English lessons, adding phrases such as "My name is Cornelia. It's so nice to meet you." We spend the evening in my front room, each reading a book. My tabby cat has taken a liking to Cornelia and curls up on her lap. I teach Cornelia the word *cat* and how to say good night as we each retire to our room.

I awaken later that night to an odd sound. I listen in the darkness, my heart pounding, before I realize what it is. Through the wall that separates our two bedrooms, I can hear Cornelia weeping inconsolably. I get up and go to her door, fearing she is having a nightmare. As I stand in her doorway, wondering what to do, she sits up in bed.

"Go away and leave me alone!"

I hesitate, then take a step toward her. "I can't do that." I slowly cross the room and sit down on her bed. After a moment of hesitation, I wrap my arms tightly around her and hold her close.

"Go away," she says again, but softer this time. She doesn't resist my embrace.

"God hears you weeping, Cornelia. He counts every tear that falls. He longs to comfort you, and the only arms He has are mine." She leans into me then, accepting my embrace. I stroke her soft hair and gently rock her in my arms as she sobs.

When she finally runs out of tears, I hear her say softly, "Tante Geesje?"

It's the first time she has called me by that name, which is an encouraging sign. "Yes?"

"I ran away before because I wanted to die. I tried to end my life. Grandfather is afraid I will try again."

I'm so stunned I stop rocking her for a second. "And do you still want to end your life?" I ask.

"I don't know. . . . Some days I do."

I can think of nothing to say. I pull Cornelia into my arms and hold her tightly while she weeps.

CHAPTER 6

Anna

CHICAGO, ILLINOIS

I wake up to a cold, gray morning that perfectly matches my mood. I reach behind me to pull the cord, signaling the servants downstairs to bring up my breakfast. My room is so dark and dreary that I rise and open the curtains myself to try to dispel the gloom. Below my window, the leaves have lost their color, and they lie on the branches and along the road in soggy, wet clumps. Rain slides down my windowpane like tears. I'm deep in thought when I hear a light knock on my door. It's the new maid, Lucy, with my breakfast tray. "Put it on my desk for now," I tell her.

"Yes, Miss Anna. . . . Oh, and another note arrived for you."

I recognize the imprint of the Pinkerton Detective Agency on the envelope she holds out to me. I have forgotten to notify the agents of my decision to abandon my search.

"Wait a moment, Lucy, while I see if I need to reply." I slit open the flap with my letter knife and read the memo:

From: The Pinkerton Detective Agency
  Agents R. J. Albertson and M. Mitchell

To: Miss Anna Nicholson
  We have found additional information concerning Jack Newell that will be of interest to you. Please advise us of a convenient time to call upon you with our findings.

I back up a step and sink down on the edge of my bed, wondering what to do. I'm not sure I want to know anything more about Jack if it's bad news. On the other hand, maybe they've learned whether or not he is my father. I don't want him to be, but the alternative seems even more upsetting.

"Is something wrong, Miss Anna?" the maid asks.

"It's nothing. Is the courier who brought this still waiting downstairs?"

"I believe so, Miss Anna."

"Then wait a moment. I'll need you to deliver my reply." I sit down at my desk and pull out my stationery. Several minutes pass as I decide what to say. The smell of the steaming, soft-boiled egg on my tray makes my stomach turn. My mouth has gone dry. I lift the teacup and take a sip, then scribble a reply, inviting the agents to call today at three o'clock. I am meeting William for lunch, which should only take an hour or so. And Mother has an afternoon appointment that should keep her away until after the agents have gone. "Take this down right away, Lucy."

"Yes, Miss Anna."

I'm just finishing my breakfast a short time later when I hear another knock on my door. "Come in."

63

It's Lucy again. "I gave the messenger your note, Miss Anna. Is there anything else I can do for you?"

"Not at the moment. I'm nearly finished with my breakfast, but the chambermaid will collect the tray when she comes up to make my bed. You're excused." Lucy backs up a few steps but hesitates in the doorway instead of leaving. "Was there something else?" I ask her.

"If you please, Miss Anna," she says with another little curtsy. "I noticed that you share a lady's maid with Mrs. Nicholson, and I-I would be very pleased to help you the way Sophia does— making sure your dresses are laid out and pressed and your silk gloves are clean and your shoes all polished. I'm good at pinning up hair, too. I used to be a lady's maid like Sophia in the last house where I worked."

"Why did you leave?" I ask.

"Well . . . because I heard that your mother, Mrs. Nicholson, was hiring help and—" Lucy curtsies again. "If you please, Miss Anna, she pays more money than my last employer."

"Doesn't our housekeeper need you as a maid downstairs?"

"I can do both jobs, Miss Anna. That is . . . I would like to try doing both."

I don't know why, but I want to give Lucy a chance. Maybe it's because Mama was once a housemaid, or maybe it's because Mother can be so demanding with our servants. Either way, I decide it can't hurt to give Lucy a chance. "I'll speak with our housekeeper about borrowing you as my lady's maid from time to time. I'll let you know what she says."

"Oh, thank you, Miss Anna," she replies, and curtsies twice.

I turn away to hide a smile. "You don't need to curtsy to me, Lucy. I'm not a queen. You may go now."

The rain is coming down hard by the time Mother and I leave home for another Literary Club meeting. Our carriage drives along the lakeshore, where the water is the same smoky gray color as the sky. More than a week has passed since I visited Mrs. Marusak and learned Mama's story. The knowledge of how Jack Newell abused her has settled on my heart like a heavy stone. I go through my days finding no joy in the routines of a wealthy woman's life—the hours of dressing and primping, the endless social functions where it seems as though all we do is gossip about the women who aren't there. No one dares to miss an event for fear she will be the next subject of gossip.

We arrive at the home of Chicago's former mayor, George Bell Swift. "I'm surprised Mrs. Swift offered to hold the meeting here after so recently losing the election," Mother whispers as uniformed footmen race to our carriage, bearing umbrellas. I was aware that both Father and William were upset with the recent election results, but I pay little attention to politics since women aren't allowed to vote. Mrs. Swift greets us in her foyer and directs us to her spacious drawing room, where extra chairs have been set up. We take our seats after everyone arrives and, just like last time, I can think of nothing but my afternoon appointment with the detectives throughout the entire ninety-minute meeting. The poetry readings are uninspiring, but at least today's presentation on ancient Greece is a little more interesting than the last one. Even so, it's at times like this when my days feel so meaningless that I can't help wondering what God's purpose is for my life. I'm wealthy and have everything a woman could wish for—yet I feel restless and dissatisfied. I long to use my position in society to serve Him, but how do I do that?

When the presenter finishes, we are assigned our reading selection for next time—a Greek tragedy by Euripides—and dismissed for refreshments. "Anna," Clarice calls to me. "Come and join us." She has gathered near the buffet with a group of six other young women my age to nibble on refreshments. She looks stunning, as always, with her auburn hair piled high, and she's wearing the very latest fashion accessories—a pleated frill on the front of her gown and a pleated belt and bow around her narrow waist. "How is your search going with the Pinkerton detectives?" she asks without preamble. Since they have been on my mind all morning, it's as if she has been reading my thoughts. I have forgotten that I foolishly confided in Clarice. But why would she speak about such a private matter in front of all the others? She promised to keep my search confidential.

I am speechless as the women await my reply, so Clarice fills the silence. "The last time Anna and I spoke," she tells the others, "the detectives had just found a record of her real parents' marriage. Have you learned anything more about your real family since then?"

"Um . . . I believe the detectives have reached a dead end," I mumble.

"I didn't know you were adopted!" someone says. "How interesting!" The ladies move closer as if expecting me to divulge secrets. My cheeks feel warm, betraying my embarrassment as I fumble for something to say. Why, oh why didn't I heed Jane's warning not to trust Clarice? I feel foolish and naïve.

"I heard that you've recently recalled some memories of your real mother," one of the women says.

My heart races. I am stunned that my private life is common knowledge. "Only a few," I reply. "I was very young when she died."

"But now you've met your real grandmother—an immigrant!" Clarice says. "What was she like?"

"Um . . . She's a lovely woman." How do they know all of this? And how do I make them stop questioning me? I don't have the nerve to tell them to mind their own business and then walk away. Besides, that will make it seem as though I'm hiding something.

"What about your father?" Clarice asks, pretending to whisper. "Do they think he might still be alive?"

"I-I don't know. I suppose it's possible, but I—"

"If he is, maybe the detectives will able to locate him. Then you would have two fathers." Two of the other women begin to giggle. They couldn't possible know about Jack, could they?

I clear the knot from my throat and hope they don't detect a tremor in my voice. "As far as I'm concerned, I have only one father—the one you all know, Arthur Nicholson."

"Is it true that he rescued you from a shipwreck?" one of them asks.

"Well, yes . . ."

"Tell us what that was like!"

"It . . . it was horrifying, as I'm sure you can imagine. It's not something I care to relive by talking about it." I am desperate to change the subject. I reach for another tea cake and say, "I've been meaning to ask you, Clarice, how does your lady's maid manage to dress your hair so beautifully? I would love to wear mine like that, but I fear that my hair is much too curly."

She smiles, and I can tell by the look of satisfaction on her face that she knows I'm embarrassed and uncomfortable. "It takes hours," she says. "And there are hundreds of hairpins holding it in place. It's such a bore to sit still for so long every day."

"Well, it looks lovely on you, Clarice."

"You're kind to say so. By the way, have all of you heard the latest about the Kirkland family? It's turning into quite a scandal. Lavinia's fiancé has called off the wedding." Her face is alight with glee.

"No!"

"Did he really?"

The women huddle closer, talking in stage whispers, but it's clear from their expressions that they find the scandal a delicious source of gossip.

"Why would he end the engagement?" someone asks. "It's not Lavinia's fault that her father went bankrupt."

"Didn't you hear? The authorities are talking about filing criminal charges against Mr. Kirkland. Something to do with some shady investments he made. The shame of something like that reflects on his entire family, so naturally Lavinia's fiancé was quick to distance himself from the whole affair."

"I heard that Mrs. Kirkland has already left town with Lavinia and Emeline and their two younger brothers."

"Well, of course they had to leave town after the bank foreclosed on their house," Clarice says. "They aren't allowed to live there anymore."

"Poor Lavinia," I say. "Is there anything we can do to help her and her family?" Everyone ignores my question.

"It was bound to happen," Clarice says. "Mr. Kirkland was always buying something new and showing it off. He spent well beyond his means, especially on that enormous house."

"Emeline and Lavinia are part of our circle," I say, trying to halt the slaughter. "They seem like such sweet girls. They did nothing to deserve this."

"What's it to you, Anna? You weren't close friends with them."

I decide to close my mouth. Over the summer I overheard Father talking about the financial problems he was experiencing and how he needed me to marry William in order to secure a loan from William's bank. If I had called off the wedding, these women might be gossiping about my family. My home might be the one that was in foreclosure. My parents would never survive such a scandal. Now, hearing about the Kirklands, I am more determined than ever to help Father by marrying William.

The women continue their malicious gossip. "The Kirklands always acted as though they were too good for us," someone says. I feel sick inside and long to leave and go home, but I can't. I have a luncheon date with William at his club, and it would take too long to go all the way home and then turn around and come back. Besides, Mother has a luncheon date someplace else, and we are sharing a carriage. I have no choice but to stay a little longer. I don't dare to walk away as the ladies continue gossiping, fearing they will misjudge my motives and begin gossiping about me. For the second time that morning, I find myself wondering if this is how God wants me to spend the rest of my life.

I allow my thoughts to wander to last Sunday's church service. I always draw comfort from worshiping in God's house, but the sermon subject reminded me that I have been neglecting my Bible since returning home from Michigan. I did manage, however, to read a little from the Gospel of John on Sunday afternoon before William arrived to take me for a drive through the park. William and I have been together three times since my trip to Cicero, and it occurred to me as we drove last Sunday that he never once asked me about my interview with Mama's landlady. Did he forget? Was he uninterested? Or was he being sensitive to how morose I've been and didn't want to upset me further? Perhaps he is waiting until I mention it. I can't complain because I decided not to tell him, my parents, or anyone else what I learned about Jack Newell. At the same time, holding such a terrible secret inside makes me feel ill. I long for someone to talk to about how brutal my father was—that is, if Jack Newell truly is my father. But the only friend I've ever been able to share my heart with is Derk Vander Veen, and he lives far away in Michigan.

The interminable socializing finally ends, and I leave the former mayor's home. William is waiting to greet me at his club downtown. He smiles and kisses my cheek, but my thoughts are miles away, worried that everyone in Chicago is gossiping about my personal business with the Pinkerton detectives. What new information have they discovered about Jack Newell? "You seem very glum, Anna," William says as we sit at a quiet corner table. "You haven't changed your mind about marrying me, I hope."

"No! Not at all! Please forgive me for being moody, William. This weather is so cold and dreary. It seems as though the sun hasn't shone in days."

"Well, I have a surprise for you after lunch that should cheer you up."

I chastise myself for not giving him my full attention and say with a smile, "How can I wait that long? Can't you give me a teeny hint? Does it have something to do with our wedding?"

"No hints, my dear. You're much too clever for me. You'll guess it right away."

The waiter arrives, and as William orders for us, I notice Clarice Beacham enter and sit down at a table on the other side of the room. She is with her father and another man his age that I only vaguely recognize. I watch her from where I'm sitting, and she is so beautiful and graceful that I'm mesmerized. I can't imagine why William or any other man isn't completely entranced with her. I turn my attention back to William when the waiter departs, and for the life of me, I can't think of a single thing to say to him.

"What have you been up to this morning, my dear?" he asks before I can think of something.

"Oh, you know . . . just the usual ladies' events. Today it was a meeting of the Women's Literary Club. Your mother kindly arranged for Mother and me to become members. Today's meeting was held at the mayor's house."

"Mayor Swift?"

"Yes, but I understand he's no longer the mayor."

"True. And that's extremely unfortunate. Carter Harrison is certain to bring trouble as our new mayor."

"Why is that? Didn't we used to have a mayor named Harrison?"

"That was Carter's father. The new Mayor Harrison and his brother used to run the *Chicago Times*, the only newspaper in the city that came out in support of the Pullman strikers a few years back." William continues talking about his displeasure with the election results, and two things occur to me as I listen: the first is how little I know about politics; the second is that men seem to have their own pet topics of conversation and gossip just as women do.

The lunch is much too filling, especially after tea and refreshments earlier this morning, and I leave the club feeling like an overstuffed chair. William and I pause to speak briefly with Clarice and her father on the way out, and I sense William's coldness toward her. Then he calls for his carriage, and we're off to see his surprise. We cuddle close together as we ride through the chilly rain, and William feels strong and warm beside me. After a few minutes, we halt in front of an enormous three-story building made entirely of stone, facing Lake Michigan. "Is this an apartment building?" I ask.

"No," William says with a laugh. "It's all one house. The owners built it right after the Great Fire, and no money was spared to make it fireproof." His driver helps us from the carriage, and William walks with me to the front entryway, taking a key from his pocket. The main hall takes my breath away with its marble floors, columns, and graceful statues. Everywhere I look I see intricate woodwork and plasterwork. Paneled ceilings soar above me. I glimpse extravagant rooms on each side of the hall, but I'm so overwhelmed by it all that I'm afraid to move. I have visited some very beautiful homes in Chicago, but this . . . this is simply too much!

William seems to sense my hesitation. He takes my hand in his and begins leading me through the rooms on the first floor, each more elaborate than the last one, with carved walnut paneling and stained-glass windows. They're all furnished in the newest European fashion and decorated with exquisite paintings and statues. One of the formal dining rooms could seat fifty people at its enormous table. "What do you think?" William asks. "We could move right in, and we wouldn't need to change a thing. Do you like it?"

I weigh whether or not to tell him my true feelings—that it is too flamboyant and overdone for my taste. Too big, too cold. He's clearly enthralled with the house, and I would hate to hurt his feelings. "It's a beautiful house. But do we really need so much space for our first home? And so many huge rooms? I'm afraid I'll feel lost inside it."

"You'll soon get used to it, I'm sure."

"Shouldn't we start with something smaller? We'll need to buy so much furniture!"

"I understand that most of this furniture will be sold with the house."

I can't begin to imagine what all of this would cost. As we continue to wander through the rooms, I keep hoping that he has brought me here to glean ideas for our own home and not because he truly plans to purchase this mansion. It's a show-piece, a work of art—not a home.

We end up back in the main foyer just as I begin to fear that we're lost. I'm certain we haven't seen everything on the main floor, but William leads me up the imposing staircase to the second story. I quickly lose count of the numerous bedrooms and sitting rooms and bathrooms. I fumble for a way to tell William that it's all too much for me. "But . . . but won't we need an army of servants to take care of all this?"

He laughs again. "You let me worry about hiring servants."

I am reminded of my mama, who went to work as a servant after leaving her husband. Did she work in a house as huge as this one, or something much smaller like my parents' house? "I want to know if you like it, Anna," William says as we descend to the foyer again. We never made it to the third floor.

"Who wouldn't like it? It's magnificent!"

"Good. Then I'll tell my grandfather you approve. He wants to help us purchase it as his wedding present to us."

"Oh, my." I feel weak for some reason, and since there are no chairs nearby, I take a step backward and sink down on one of the steps.

"Anna, what's wrong?"

"You've truly surprised me, William. I can't . . . I can't imagine living here." Nor can I imagine Oma Geesje ever feeling comfortable if she came to visit me. Her entire house in Michigan would fit inside this grand foyer.

He offers me his hand to help me stand, then takes me into his arms. "I would be happy to live anywhere, as long as it's with you. You deserve a palace like this one, Anna. And if the paperwork goes through as I hope, we can hold the wedding reception for all our guests here." He cups my face in his hands and bends to kiss me. I feel weak all over again, but this time it's from his kiss. "We can come back and finish exploring another day," he says when our lips part, "but I need to return to work now."

We board his carriage, and the bits and pieces of everything I've heard today begin to fall into place. George Kirkland went bankrupt, and the bank foreclosed on his home. A very large, extravagant home. William's grandfather founded the bank where William and his family work. "Did . . . did the Kirkland family live in that house?" I ask as our carriage splashes through the rain-soaked streets.

"I suppose you've heard the rumors going around?"

"Gossip is more like it. People are saying that George Kirkland went bankrupt, and his family was forced to leave town in shame."

"It's true. Kirkland did go bankrupt. Unfortunately, these things happen in the business world. Fortunes can be made or lost overnight."

"I knew his daughters, Lavinia and Emeline. It seems like such a tragedy for the entire family."

William squeezes my hand. "That's one of the things I love about you, Anna—you have such a warm, tender heart. But I hope you won't allow others' unfortunate circumstances to spoil your enjoyment of our home. Think of the happiness that we'll be able to bring back to those rooms."

I don't reply. In truth, I don't know how I could ever enjoy such an overwhelming house. It's too much for a newly married couple. In fact, it could serve as a small hotel. "Were the Kirklands really forced to leave all their furniture behind, too?"

"I'm afraid so. George Kirkland's creditors might repossess some of it to cover his debts, but our bank is his biggest creditor. If you and I buy the house, we can go through the rooms and choose which furnishings we want to keep and which will be replaced. I'm sure Mother and her decorator will be happy to help you."

"That would be very kind of her." I wish I knew how to convince him that it's too much for us. But William isn't asking for my opinion. In his mind, the decision has been made, and we will live in this house after we're married in a few short months.

William's driver takes me home after dropping William off at work. I arrive with plenty of time to spare before the detectives are expected. My parents' home is large and very tastefully decorated, but it could fit inside the house William wants to buy two times over. I find myself hoping that the deal will fall through and William's grandfather won't buy it after all. My lunch lies in my stomach like a brick as I wait in the parlor, watching for the Pinkerton agents to arrive. I have stopped worrying about the house and have begun to worry about what the detectives have discovered.

The cobblestone street is slick with rain, and it sprays up behind the carriage wheels as vehicles roll past. At last, one of them halts in front of my house, and I watch the agents get out and come to our door. Our butler leads them into the parlor. Once again, Agent Albertson hands me a typewritten page after we've greeted one another and taken our seats. My heart is racing.

"I'm sorry, but we learned that Jack Newell died in a railroad accident in November of 1872. We found union records of the incident, as well as a newspaper account."

I take a moment to scan the written report, feeling shocked. Jack died only a month after Mama left him. Now I know for certain that he couldn't be my father, unless I am older than everyone thought. Our family's doctor examined me after the shipwreck and guessed by my height and weight and baby teeth that I was approximately three years old. While I'm relieved to learn that Jack isn't my father, this news opens up a new set of problems.

Agent Albertson hands me a second page. "According to the records we found, his widow, Christina de Jonge Newell, successfully sued the railroad company for causing his death and was paid a small sum of money in a legal settlement."

She knew she was free from him. Did she remarry? And if so, to whom?

"We have started looking for a second marriage certificate," the agent says. "And we'll continue searching for a record of your birth. But keep in mind, there was a great deal of chaos and confusion as Chicago was being rebuilt after the fire."

I read the second page, noting the modest amount of money Mama was awarded after her husband's death. She couldn't have lived in Chicago for very long on such a sum, but it would have purchased a steamship ticket home to Michigan. Oma would have welcomed her with open arms. I lay the pages on my lap when I finish. A cold chill shivers up my spine when I remember how many details of my story Clarice and the other women knew. I must make certain that they never learn about this. Didn't Mother warn me that once the truth is uncovered, it seldom remains hidden?

"Listen, I've decided not to continue searching," I tell the agents.

"That's entirely up to you, Miss Nicholson. But let me add that we have spoken with Mrs. Marusak's niece, Vera. She thinks she may remember working with your mother. We're willing to make arrangements for you to meet with her, if you'd like."

I stare down at my folded hands, trying to decide what to do. So far, the only gossip that my parents and William and everyone else knows about is that Mama married Jack. They believe I am his legitimate daughter. If I bury these latest reports and end the search right now, the truth will stay buried. The gossip I listened to today was disturbing, and I would never want to subject the people I love to such wagging tongues.

"I don't think I care to meet Vera," I say at last. "You may stop your investigation for now. I'll let you know if I change my mind." I rise to signal that the meeting is over. "Thank you for the work you've already done, gentlemen. Kindly send my father an invoice for your services."

As much as I would love to know more about my family's past and who my real father is, I believe it's wrong to unearth information that could fuel gossip. I need to marry William in order to help Father with his financial problems, or we could end up like the Kirklands. The truth about my real father— whoever he is—must remain buried.

I rise to see the men out and am surprised to find Lucy standing just outside the parlor door. "Oh, Miss Anna! I was waiting to see if you and your guests needed anything."

"No, thank you. They're just leaving." I'm tempted to scold her and explain that I would have rung the bell to summon her if I needed anything. Besides, it's the butler's duty to stand at the ready, not hers. But Lucy is new and still learning her way around. I know how eager she is to win my favor. A scolding would only make her more nervous than she already is.

I have trouble falling asleep that night, thinking about everything I learned today. One question haunts me: Why didn't Mama go back home to Holland after Jack Newell died? She would have had enough money from the settlement. I climb out of bed and take the copy of Oma's story from my desk drawer. I turn on a light so I can read it, then scurry back beneath the covers where it's warm. I page through it until I find the part where Mama said she was unhappy and wanted to leave tiny Holland, Michigan.

"Church is boring," Christina told her parents. *"I'm tired of all the rules and laws, I'm tired of being told I'm a sinner just because I can't possibly obey all of them. Nobody lives a perfect life, and if anyone says he does, he's a hypocrite."* I skim ahead to where her parents asked to meet Jack. Mama refused to introduce him. *"I know you would judge him and condemn him and try to make him feel guilty because he isn't religious like you. You would start preaching to him and telling him he was a sinner."* When asked if Jack believed in God, Mama replied, *"Of course he believes in God. But he thinks it's wrong to scare people into conforming to a bunch of old-fashioned rules and morals with stories of floods and whales swallowing people alive. Especially when the people who teach those rules are such hypocrites. We can live good lives without all the false guilt the church tries to scare into us."*

Mama's words and her attitude toward Christianity must have broken her parents' hearts. But after hearing the gossip today at my club meeting, I wonder if Mama was afraid to return home for the same reasons that the Kirkland family left Chicago. Maybe she feared the gossip and condemnation she might face after running away with a man who wasn't a Christian.

I close Oma's memoir and lay it aside, chiding myself. Once again, I have been obsessing about the past after deciding to let it go and move forward with my future. I reach for my Bible on the nightstand instead. It falls open to a marker I placed in the Gospel of Matthew. I have marked the verse where Jesus said, "Let your light so shine before men, that they may see your good works, and glorify your Father which is in heaven." I remember reading that verse during the summer, and it made me determined to let Christ's light shine in my life once I returned home to Chicago. I'm ashamed that I haven't done that. I should have walked away today when the other women began to gossip, refusing to take part in it.

I also recall Oma's words of advice to me before I left Holland. She believed I could do a lot of good for women like Mama who were being taken advantage of and had no place to turn. Might that be God's plan for my future, rather than attending silly meetings or wasting time and money chasing shadows from my past?

I shut off the light again and try to sleep. But something else Oma said pricks my conscience as I think of the extravagant home William plans to buy for us. She said that if I continued to draw close to God, my faith could have a good influence on William. Then she said, "*Imagine all the good that a wealthy man like William could do if his heart was surrendered to God.*" At the very least, he would see what a waste of money it is for us to buy a house like that.

I think about our wedding in a few short months and remember how Oma cautioned me not to rush into marriage. She advised me to talk to William about my faith more often and see how he responds. I haven't done that, either. I finally drift off to sleep, aware that I need to make some important changes in the way I'm living my life.

CHAPTER 7

Geesje

I returned to bed last night after Cornelia cried herself to sleep in my arms. But I lay in the dark worrying about her for quite some time before I finally had the good sense to pray for her and entrust her to God's care instead of worrying. Now it's morning, and the gloomy sky seems to be raining tears along with Cornelia. I've just finished my breakfast and am sipping my tea when Cornelia wanders into the kitchen. Her eyes are swollen and red-rimmed from crying. She hasn't yanked her hair back into a bun yet, and it hangs around her pale face in soft waves, making her look like the child that she is.

"Good morning, dear. What would you like to eat?" I rise to get a cup and pour her some tea. She drops into a kitchen chair as if she has just walked a hundred miles.

"I'm not hungry." It occurs to me that not eating might be another way to try to end her life.

"How about a little porridge? It's what I like to eat on rainy days like this. I left some for you in the pot. Shall I fix you a bowl?"

She doesn't answer my question. Instead, she gazes up at me with a pleading expression. "I want to stay here, Tante Geesje. I don't want to go back to the hotel. Will you please talk to my grandfather and ask him to let me stay with you? Please?"

I bend over her chair and give her a hug. "I'll do my very best, *lieveling*. Your grandfather and I got off to a bad start, I'm afraid, but I'll do what I can to make things right." I add some honey, cinnamon, and chopped apple to the porridge, hoping to tempt Cornelia to eat. I serve it to her with thick cream. She has just taken the first meager spoonful when through the kitchen window I see Dominie Den Herder standing in the Vander Veens' backyard. "There's your grandfather," I tell Cornelia. "Finish your breakfast while I go talk with him."

It's raining lightly outside, so I grab my coat from the hook by the back door and put on the hat I wear when working in the garden. The dominie stands like a statue, staring at nothing, the rain shining in tiny beads on his dark wool coat and cap. He is such a handsome, distinguished-looking man that I can easily picture all of the widows in his congregation bringing him pots of soup after his wife died—unless he was as gruff with them as he has been with me. He strikes me as a very unhappy man. But he has also suffered loss. When Cornelia's family died in the fire, he lost his son, daughter-in-law, and two grandsons.

The dominie was as much to blame for our argument yesterday as I was, but as I approach him, I'm determined to make amends for Cornelia's sake. "Dominie . . . may I have a word with you, please?"

He turns as if startled. "Yes? What is it?"

"I want to tell you how sorry I am for arguing with you yesterday. You were concerned about your granddaughter, and I spoke out of turn. Please forgive me."

He grudgingly accepts my apology, so I muster the courage to continue.

"I feel as though we haven't gotten off on the right foot. Can we begin all over again? If you haven't spoken to my son yet, about making other living arrangements, I hope you'll reconsider and allow Cornelia to stay with me."

"I haven't spoken with him. I expect to see him this morning."

"Cornelia told me that she likes living with me, and she begged me to ask you about staying. Please allow her to, Dominie. She and I are just becoming friends, and I feel that I am winning her trust."

"What is that supposed to mean?" His anger erupts so easily it startles me. Is he this quick-tempered with everyone, or do I especially irritate him for some reason?

"I didn't mean anything by it. Just that Cornelia is starting to feel comfortable with me. I heard her weeping in the middle of the night, and when I went to comfort her, she told me that she once tried to end her own life. If only I had known about it when she asked to go for a walk yesterday, I never—"

"I knew this would happen!" he shouts. "How can we ever get a new start if everyone knows our private business? No, Mrs. de Jonge. No. This arrangement will not work." He turns and heads toward the back door, but I chase after him. Once again, after only a few short minutes of conversation, he has caused me to lose my temper.

"Wait just a minute, Dominie. I would never dream of sharing the things that Cornelia tells me in private with anyone else. It's insulting that you assume I would! I'll excuse you this time because you don't know me very well, but how could you even think that I—"

He whirls to face me. "This is what always happens when

81

church women meet together! Oh, sure, it's veiled behind a screen of concern, and the need to pray for the poor soul. But those prayer concerns always become fodder for gossip, plain and simple. Women love to spread news like this until the entire community knows!"

His words infuriate me. I pray for help in controlling my anger as I try to answer calmly. "Perhaps that has been your experience in the Netherlands, Dominie, but I refuse to take part in gossip. It's one of the things God hates, and so do I."

His anger doesn't diminish. "Don't you know that people are already wondering and whispering about us? Cornelia's past will be all over town before we can blink an eye. No. I won't put her through that experience again."

"Nor will I! She is a deeply wounded girl who needs time and love and a place to heal. I want to help her do that. In fact, I believe God is asking me to help her. The last thing I would ever do is share her confidences with other people."

He reaches for the knob and opens the back door. "I'll think about it."

"Wait!" I grab his coattail to stop him. "Let me explain why I think God arranged for Cornelia to live with me, out of all the homes in Holland." I draw a deep breath. "My daughter, Christina, ran away from home when she was seventeen." I see his reproving expression and say, "Yes, I know you're shocked. You'll probably assume that my husband and I were terrible parents. Believe me, in the months after she left I agonized over what I might have done wrong in raising her, or what I should have done differently to prevent her from leaving. I also know what it's like to live with gossip in a town that's so small everyone knows each other's business. Yes, there was gossip about Christina. But there were also dear friends who didn't judge me. Who prayed for my daughter as if she was their own. Friends who prayed for me and for the grief and worry I had to endure, wondering where Christina was and if she was all right. And God answered those prayers. I never saw Christina alive again, but I learned only recently that she returned to God and to her Christian faith before she died. And now her beautiful daughter, Anneke, has come into my life to prove that God can redeem even the most difficult situations. He will bring joy from our sorrow if we let Him. Please, Dominie. Let me help Cornelia find joy again."

I can't tell if I've convinced him or not as I wait for his reply. "I would like to speak with Cornelia in private," he finally says. "Ask her to come out here."

"Of course. But there's one more thing I would like you to consider. I believe Cornelia would benefit from being with other young people her age. Perhaps Derk could introduce her to some of his friends when he has time off from his studies. You know, of course, that he is going to be a pastor soon. He understands the need to hold confidences in sacred trust."

"I will think about it. Now kindly send Cornelia to me."

I go back inside, taking a moment to shake the water off my jacket and hat and hang them up before talking to Cornelia. My shoes are soaked from the wet grass, and I slip them off, as well. Cornelia is still sitting at the table, biting her nails. She has barely touched her porridge. "Did he say I can stay?" she asks, looking up.

"He promised to think about it. Right now, he would like you to go outside and talk to him. Wear my jacket and hat. They're already wet."

Cornelia rises from the table as if she is about to face Judgment Day. It's damp and cold outside, but she walks out my kitchen door without a coat or hat or even a sweater, as if she welcomes the idea of catching a deadly chill. I watch her and her grandfather talk on my neighbors' back steps and wish I knew what they were saying. I see Cornelia shake her head, her chin lowered to her chest. Her grandfather talks some more, and she finally lifts her head again and nods. He is probably making her promise not to confide in me or share any more details of her life. The man infuriates me. How can I help Cornelia if I don't know what's wrong?

I hear a horse and buggy pulling to a stop out front and see that it's my son Jakob. I call to him from my front doorway. "Jakob! Would you please come inside for a moment?" He ties his horse to my post and dashes through the rain. He carries a small pile of books in his arms.

"How is everything going with your guest, Moeder?" he asks as he kisses my cheek.

"There have been good moments and hard moments. May I ask you something?" I switch to English in case Cornelia returns. "You don't have to answer if you're uncomfortable—but since you've asked me to share my home with Cornelia, I feel as though I need to know."

"Of course, you may ask."

"Cornelia is a deeply troubled young girl who is still grieving all of her losses. She barely eats anything, and last night I heard her weeping in the middle of the night. I want so much to help her, and so I wondered if there was any more information you can share with me about her situation. You know that I would never share it with anyone else."

"Yes, I do know that." He thinks for a moment. "They are distantly related to the Den Herder family from my church, which is what led them to settle here in Holland. The local Den Herders are farmers, as you know, and already have a houseful of children. The only information they gave me is that Cornelia's family died in a house fire. She wasn't at home when the fire broke out, but was helping a mother with her newborn baby. Cornelia's parents and two younger brothers all died."

"How long ago was that?"

"About four years, I believe. Cornelia would have been around thirteen years old at the time."

"That poor child. I can imagine how guilty she must feel for surviving. When my parents died of malaria and I lived, I remember thinking it should have been me."

"Arie has told me the same thing about surviving the war when so many of his comrades were killed."

I decide not to tell Jakob that Cornelia tried to end her own life, aware of my promise to her grandfather. "Did Dominie Den Herder's wife also die in the fire?"

"No. I believe she had passed away a short time before. Cornelia went to live with him in the parsonage. His church was in a different town from where she lived, quite far away, I understand."

"So she lost touch with all of her friends, too?"

"I assume so. Marinus found it difficult to meet the needs of his church while raising a young granddaughter all alone. He told me he felt he wasn't doing a proper job with either one, so he resigned from the pastorate and came to America to make a new start."

I don't say so aloud, but it seems to me there has to be more to the story. Most ministers consider their work to be a calling from God, not an ordinary job they can easily resign from. And why is he so stern with Cornelia, treating her so coldly, if he loves her enough to leave the ministry? For Cornelia's sake, I wish I knew the answers. "What sort of work is the dominie looking for here?" I ask Jakob.

"That's the problem. He doesn't seem to be qualified for the jobs that are available in the local furniture factories. He has been a minister all his life and has no experience working with his hands. Not understanding English makes it even more difficult. That's what these are for," he says, handing me the pile of books. I brush the raindrops off the top one as I look them over. They are schoolbooks, the kind a teacher would use in the early grades. "I wondered if you would be willing to tutor Marinus along with Cornelia?"

I smile. "I'm to be a teacher now? At my age? I don't have very much experience, you know."

"You'll do just fine, Moeder."

The thought of spending more time with Dominie Den Herder gives me a knot in my stomach. I decide not to tell Jakob about the arguments he and I have been having. "I would be willing, but you'd better ask him what he thinks first. He doesn't seem very comfortable around me."

"I'm sure he'll agree. He knows his lack of English is costing him jobs. I'm taking him to see about one this morning, but there isn't much hope."

I hear my back door open and close. Cornelia has returned. "I'll do what I can, Jakob. Thanks for the books."

CHAPTER 8

Anna

I have decided to speak with Mrs. Dunlap, our housekeeper, about giving Lucy a chance to serve as my lady's maid. She reluctantly agrees. "As long as I can have her back as a maid when I need her."

"Yes, of course." Mrs. Dunlap seems to have something more to say, so I wait.

"If I may ask, Miss Anna—was this your idea or Lucy's?"

"Hers, I suppose. She noticed that Mother and I share Sophia as our lady's maid and offered to help."

"Hmph. I'll warn you, Miss Anna. That gal might be getting too uppity. She's always bragging to the other servants about one grand plan or another for leaving service and getting rich."

Her words surprise me. "Lucy? She seems so timid. She's very nervous when she serves at the table or brings my breakfast tray. The dishes are always rattling in her hands."

"I wouldn't know about that. But when we're eating our meals downstairs, she brags that she's going places. She isn't always going to be a maid, she says."

"Well, I would still like to let her try being my lady's maid. If she doesn't do well, she can always return to her other duties." In truth, I admire Lucy for having ambition and trying to better herself instead of remaining a housemaid all her life. I decide to let her dress my hair on Saturday morning before Mother and I set out to do errands for my wedding.

"I know how to pin it up in the style of those Gibson girls," Lucy tells me as I sit at my dressing table. She has a nice, gentle touch as she pulls the brush through my thick curls. "I learned how to do it at the last place I worked."

"Let's start with something simpler for today," I tell her. "We'll save that look for a grander occasion. Besides, I'll be wearing a hat this morning. The one that matches my gray fitted jacket and skirt." Lucy does a nice job for her first time. I'm pleased with the way my hair turns out. She handles my clothing and other accessories competently, as well.

Mother and I spend the morning with our dressmaker, discussing my wedding gown. I have very little patience with fashions and frills, but I know how much Mother enjoys choosing fabrics and keeping up with the latest styles. I pretend to enjoy the process for her sake, but I can't help recalling how the Lord said we shouldn't worry about what we'll wear, but we should seek His kingdom first and foremost. I wish I knew how to do that.

Our seamstress has laid out a beautiful selection of fabrics to choose from as well as examples of fancy beadwork and delicate imported laces. But first we page through an array of pattern books to decide on the gown's features. "I notice that these new gowns aren't as full-skirted as last year's fashions," Mother says. I hadn't noticed at all.

"You have a very keen eye, Mrs. Nicholson. What you can't

see in these pictures are the petticoats and bum rolls that support the flared design. And lucky for her, Miss Anna has a tiny waist, which all of these dresses demand."

"I like the sleeves on these new formal gowns," Mother says. "They are much fuller and puffier this season."

"Yes," she replies. "It's almost as if the extra fabric that was taken from the skirt has gone into fuller sleeves."

"I don't care for those new sleeves," I say. "They look like they're stuffed with balloons. And I don't care for dresses that are as showy as these. Can't we keep my wedding gown simple?"

Mother looks at me as though I've spoken blasphemy. "My dear, you will be the center of attention on your wedding day. As William Wilkinson's bride, you're marrying into a very prominent Chicago family. You'll want to make William proud as he presents you to his guests."

The thought of being showcased makes me cringe, but I remain silent. We decide on a V-shaped neckline with a beaded bodice and lots of lace and pleats. And ridiculous puffed sleeves. It's all too much for my taste, like the extravagant house William wants to buy. When it's time to choose the fabric, Mother says, "It must be white, of course."

"Why is that?" I ask as my resentment toward all these expectations and excesses bubbles to the surface. "I know I've seen white gowns at the weddings I've attended recently, but I didn't realize it was a requirement. Besides, a white gown won't be very practical if I want to wear it on another occasion. The hemline will become filthy, trailing through the streets—especially in January."

"It isn't intended to be practical," the seamstress replies. "And it's more of a tradition than a requirement. Ever since Queen Victoria of England wore a white gown when she married Prince Albert, everyone has wanted to copy her."

"Well, I don't." But there's no room for my opinion in these matters, so I hold my tongue while Mother makes the final choices for me. I'm her only child and I'll be married only once in my life, so I'll let her enjoy this moment.

After submitting to countless measurements from head to toe, I finally emerge from the dressmaker's shop into the cool fall air. I breathe deeply, trying to ignore the feeling that I'm suffocating. "You'll need new white gloves," Mother says as we wait for our driver to bring our carriage around. "Above the elbow, I should think, since we chose short sleeves for your gown. And which would you prefer, soft kid gloves or silk ones?"

"It doesn't matter to me," I say, stifling a sigh. "Whatever you think is best." We climb into the carriage. I would prefer to leave the windows open for fresh air, but Mother closes them against the draft. Our next stop is the Wilkinsons' mansion, where we will plan the wedding dinner with William's mother over lunch. "I truly don't care to plan any of this wedding," I say as we drive there. "You and William's mother can choose whatever you'd like, and I'm sure it will be fine with me."

Mother purses her lips and raises her chin, a look that I've come to recognize as extreme displeasure. "A woman's wedding is a major event in her life, Anna. You need to take part in planning it. It will provide good experience for all of the formal dinners and receptions you'll be hosting as William's wife. It's important that you learn how to choose the food and décor and arrange the rooms in keeping with the occasion." I recall the vast dining room in the house William wants to buy and feel sick inside. Is this truly God's purpose for my life?

I make a sincere effort to push aside my unrest and greet William's mother and sister with a smile. We sit down to lunch in the smaller of their two dining rooms, and Mrs. Wilkinson's housekeeper takes notes as we discuss the wedding. "I originally planned to hold the dinner reception here at our home," Mrs. Wilkinson begins. "But William tells me he would like to have it at your new home on Erie Street if the purchase is finalized in time. I understand that you've seen the house, Anna?"

"Yes. It's . . . it's . . ." I fumble for a word that won't reveal my true feelings and yet won't be a lie. "It's like a palace."

"As it should be," she replies with a smile. "Our William is rising in the business world, and it's important that his home reflects that. This reception will be a wonderful opportunity to cement the social, political, and business connections he'll need."

I nearly say, *I thought this reception was a celebration of our marriage*, but I stop myself in time.

We go over the guest list, which seems to include everyone in Chicago who is either wealthy or important. Then we spend a great deal of time choosing the multi-course menu. Mrs. Wilkinson insists that we serve quail, but given the size of the guest list, it's going to require a flock of biblical proportions to feed everyone. With the menu settled, we discuss the types and numbers of flowers needed for decoration while a servant clears our plates. I can't imagine where we'll find red roses in Chicago in January, but Mrs. Wilkinson doesn't appear to be worried as she imagines filling the room with them. I'm beginning to wonder if I lack the extravagant imagination and the inclination toward excess that I will require as William's wife.

The process of planning this reception exhausts me. While it's true that I was raised in this wealthy social world and should be accustomed to such extravagance, I also glimpsed a different world during the time I spent at Oma's house in Michigan. I saw how simply my grandmother lived and how she shared what she had with families who had even less.

We retire to the sitting room for tea and dessert. I long to ask Mrs. Wilkinson and my mother what they make of Jesus' words, "For what is a man profited, if he shall gain the whole world, and lose his own soul?" Or what He meant when He said it was hard for a rich man to enter His kingdom. Verses like these have disturbed me ever since I read them.

I am home again and still full from lunch when William arrives to take me to dinner that evening. It doesn't help that Lucy has yanked my corset laces so tightly I can barely draw a deep breath. I allowed her to swoop up my hair in the Gibson girl style, but I can tell from William's expression when he sees me that he doesn't care for it. I wonder if it's because Clarice wears her hair this way. "I like the way you usually wear it better," he says when I ask him about it.

William and I dine at the Palmer House before attending a symphony concert with the Chicago Orchestra. His parents are big supporters of Maestro Thomas and the new orchestra, who presented their first concert a mere six years ago. But as I take a bite of the minted lamb that William ordered for me—one of the most expensive entrees on the menu, and one I don't particularly care for—I make up my mind to begin speaking up for myself. All day long I have allowed myself to be pulled along by the current of others' opinions like a barge behind a tugboat. I've lacked the nerve to speak out against the waste-fulness and excesses that others seem to take for granted. Not to mention standing up to Clarice and her friends when they gossiped about other people and their misfortunes. I want to talk about things that are important to me, and who better to discuss them with than William, who will soon be my husband? I long to have a good influence on him when it comes to spiritual matters, as Oma suggested.

I wait for William to finish tasting the sample of wine the waiter has chosen, then I plunge ahead. "William, dear . . . since we're going to spend the rest of our lives together, I think . . . that is, I hope . . . we will become accustomed to discussing things that are important to each other. I know I will need to take more interest in the news and especially in what is happening here in Chicago, since those things are important in your life. And maybe . . . I mean . . . well, perhaps you'll want to talk with me about my interests."

His gaze locks with mine, and the intensity of it makes my insides feel as though they are melting. "I would love to know what is going on inside that beautiful head of yours," he says.

It's difficult to concentrate when he looks at me that way, but I need to try. "Well, for example . . . when we were in Michigan, you said you didn't understand my sudden 'religious fervor,' as you called it. But you said you were willing to listen more closely to my thoughts on such matters. You said you didn't want my faith to come between us again."

"I believe I recall saying something like that." He has stopped eating and is studying me as if he would like to devour me instead of his steak. It's unnerving.

"Well, it's my habit to read a passage from the Gospels every night before I go to bed, and I find our Lord's words so challenging. I just wish I knew how to put them into practice a little better in my everyday life, but—"

He looks away and returns to his dinner. "Perhaps reading and understanding the Bible is best left to the ministers and other experts. It's their job to interpret it for our times, isn't it? And to show us how it pertains to our lives?"

I refuse to close the discussion. "What do you think about the Lord's miracles?" I ask. "I was just reading last night about how He healed a man who had been blind from birth, and—"

"Jesus was divine, so I suppose anything is possible."

"Yes, I agree. I have decided to read some of the Old Testament stories, too, like the story of the Exodus from Egypt, and—"

"The Old Testament? I can understand why you would read about Jesus," he says before pausing to sip his wine. "But what difference does the Old Testament make for our current times?

The Bible was written a long time ago, Anna. For people who were very different from us."

"I guess it doesn't make any difference, really. But I enjoy reading it, and I wondered what you thought."

He chews a piece of meat as he thinks it over. "I admit that I haven't given the Bible much thought at all. I don't like talking out of turn about subjects I'm not qualified to address."

I recall the words I recently read in Oma's memoir and say, "I heard someone express the opinion that Bible stories like Jonah and the great fish were intended to scare people into believing in God and to conforming to His rules. Do you think—?"

"Perhaps that's true. Why don't you ask Reverend Lewis some of these questions?"

"Because I would like to talk with you about them, William. The Lord is very important in my life, and so are you."

His smile seems strained. "I'm happy to hear that I haven't been completely replaced by Jesus."

I wish Derk were here. He loved talking about the Bible. And he might even have some answers to my questions. Derk has been on my mind a lot lately. I stifle a sigh and decide to approach the subject of my faith and beliefs from a different angle. "William, I've been thinking about the house we looked at, and—"

"That's wonderful! So have I. I've been meaning to tell you that my grandfather has been negotiating with George Kirkland's other creditors." My stomach does a slow turn every time Mr. Kirkland is mentioned. My father's business might have suffered bankruptcy, too, if it weren't for my engagement to William. "It looks as though the house may soon be ours," William continues. "We should know for certain by the end of the month."

"But don't you think that house is too big for us? Jesus was the Son of God, and He didn't even have a place to lay His head at night."

He smiles at me as if indulging a child. "You are so sweet and modest. Of course it isn't too big. Listen, can I let you in on a little secret? We won't keep any secrets from each other once we're married, I hope."

I nod, even though I'm not certain I want to hear his secret. I'm keeping a big secret from him—the fact that Jack Newell probably wasn't my father and I don't know who was.

William leans toward me, lowering his voice. "My father has been interested in politics for some time now, and has even considered running for public office. But this latest mayoral election has tipped the scales for him."

"He wants to be mayor of Chicago?"

"He's thinking of even bigger things—like Illinois state senator and eventually United States senator. The thing is, he's very busy at the bank and with our other investments, and so . . ." He smiles and makes a dramatic gesture as if rolling out a royal carpet. "He decided that I should be the one to run for office instead."

"Oh, William!" I try to sound thrilled, but in truth, I'm horrified. "I had no idea you were interested in politics."

"President McKinley is going to be good for the nation. He plans to impose a tariff to protect our industries from foreign competition. I want to be part of directing the future of our state and our country. So, you see? We will need that house to entertain properly in the future."

And as William's wife, I will be in the public eye. In the political world, no less. There can't be any scandals or indiscretions in either of our families. I breathe a sigh of relief that I called off the search for more information about my parents.

We eat in silence for a while. William finishes his steak, then pulls out his pocket watch and checks the time. "We had better finish quickly if we're going to make it to the concert on time."

"I'm finished," I say, resting my fork on my plate. William

signals the waiter and pays for our meal. A short time later, we're back outside in the cold and on our way to the Auditorium Theater. Tears fill my eyes when I think of all the decisions that have been made for me today: the ridiculous wedding dress in which I'll be shown off as William's bride; the huge reception that has little to do with celebrating our marriage; the oversized house that I neither want nor like but will be forced to accept; and now William's decision to take the public stage as a politician, dragging me into the spotlight along with him. Doesn't anyone care what I want? But maybe the bigger question is, why can't I stand up for myself? Even the timid little housemaid Lucy was able to express her opinions and convince me to give her the job she wanted. My life feels like a top that someone else is spinning, and I can't control what happens to it. But from now on, I'm determined to figure out a way.

CHAPTER 9

Geesje

HOLLAND, MICHIGAN

It is Sunday morning, and I have invited the Den Herders to attend church with me. "You'll find that many people here in Holland still speak Dutch," I tell them as we walk down Tenth Street. The fall leaves rustle beneath our feet. "And with so many new immigrants coming to town, you may find someone new to talk to besides me. If not," I finish with a smile, "you can always practice your English."

"Your son is the minister, I presume?" Marinus asks.

"Well, no—"

"You don't attend the church where your son is the dominie?" His critical tone strikes me like a slap in the face.

I stifle a sigh. "Jakob's church is in the village of Graafschap. We would need a horse and carriage to get there. Besides, my husband, Maarten, and I have been members of Pillar Church ever since our congregation first built it years ago. It's where

97

my church family attends. And I can easily walk to it." I decide not to say anything else for the rest of the way. Marinus has a knack for raising my ire, and I don't want to begin the Lord's Day nursing a grudge. I slow my pace to match Cornelia, who is walking behind us, dragging her feet as if her ankles are chained together. Her head is lowered as if she is afraid to face her Maker. Or maybe she's as wary of vexing her grandfather as I am.

My spirits lift immediately when I see my friends making their way inside with their families. My son Arie is waiting for us on the front steps, and I introduce him to Cornelia and Dominie Den Herder. As we find a pew that will fit the four of us, Arie pulls me aside to whisper, "You're going to have tongues wagging, Moeder, showing up for church with a handsome stranger."

I laugh out loud. "We are like milk and vinegar together, Arie. I'll let you imagine which one of us is the vinegar." But Arie is right—I see plenty of curious glances as we take our seats for the service. The sermon on the verse "Tribulation worketh patience" seems tailor-made for me this morning.

After church I introduce the Den Herders to another Dutch-speaking family, and as they converse, Derk bounds over to greet me with a smile and a kiss on the cheek. "I haven't had a chance to talk to you in a while, Tante Geesje. I wondered if you've heard from Anneke lately. I'm curious to know how her search is going with the detectives."

"Didn't I tell you? They found a record of Christina's marriage to Jack Newell, the man she ran away from home with. It pleased me to no end to learn that Jack and Christina were married almost as soon as they arrived in Chicago. Now Anneke knows who her father is."

"She must be happy about that."

"She is. In her latest letter she told me that she's content with that knowledge and won't be investigating further. Besides, she's all wrapped up in wedding preparations. She and William will be married in January, so she doesn't have much time for anything else."

Derk closes his eyes for a moment, unable to disguise his emotions. His cheerful grin has vanished. It's plain to see that he still has feelings for Anneke.

"So soon?" he says. "I thought you advised Anneke to take it slow and not rush into marriage."

"I did. But this is what she decided. Her life in Chicago is very different from ours, Derk. Probably as different as the life I once lived in the Netherlands is from my life today. I'm not certain I'm qualified to offer her any advice."

"She's marrying him to solve her father's financial problems, isn't she?"

"Perhaps. But I truly hope that isn't the only reason. She wants me to come to Chicago for the wedding in January, but my instinct is to say no. I'm just a simple immigrant, and I know I'll feel horribly out of place among all those wealthy people. Yet I've grown to love Anneke, and I know she'll be disappointed if I don't come. I've been praying for the courage to go and celebrate with her."

"You're going by train, I assume? There won't be any steamships crossing the lake in January."

"Yes, by train. I thought I'd ask Arie to come with me, although I know it's hard for him to travel on crutches, especially with snow on the ground."

"I'll come with you if Arie doesn't want to. I don't have any classes over the holidays."

"That's sweet of you, Derk. I may take you up on your offer. I know Anneke will be happy to see you." He nods and looks away, but not before I see sorrow in his eyes. "How are things going with your houseguest?" I ask Derk. "Are you and your father getting to know the dominie a bit better?"

"Fine, I suppose. I'm not home very much these days except to sleep. I hear you're giving English lessons."

"Yes. We're making progress. I thought I'd bring the Den Herders here today to give them some practice." I glance over at them and see that Marinus is speaking Dutch with another family, and Cornelia is standing all alone. "So much for that," I say with a smile. "I guess I should help her out."

"No, let me, Tante Geesje. I'll introduce her to some people I know."

"Thanks, Derk."

I watch him trying to have a conversation with Cornelia in his rusty Dutch and her scant English. Derk is so friendly and easy to talk to, even with the language barrier, that Cornelia manages a smile. I notice how out of place she looks compared to the other girls in our congregation with her dark, shapeless dress and her hair in an old-fashioned bun. I will have to do something about that this week. Maybe a few changes will cheer her up.

"Good morning, Geesje." Someone hugs me from behind, and I turn to greet two of my friends, women I've worked beside and prayed with and laughed with for many years. "I see you brought your new houseguests with you this morning," one of them says.

"Now, don't start any rumors," I say, wagging my finger in jest. "Cornelia is the only one who is staying in my spare room. Her grandfather lives next door with the Vander Veens."

"Do you know for how long?"

"Until the dominie finds work and a place of their own—"

"He's a minister? I hadn't heard that."

"He was one, back in the Netherlands. Cornelia came to live with him after her family died in a fire. Neither of them speak English, so Jakob asked me to give them some lessons. Can you believe it? The blind leading the blind."

"He's very good-looking, isn't he?" My friend gives me a little nudge in my ribs.

"Don't get any ideas," I say, shaking my head. "Neither one of us is looking for a spouse." I resist the urge to gossip about how disagreeable the dominie has been, knowing it would be unkind. "The Den Herders could use our prayers. We all know how hard it is to adjust to life in a new country."

Neither of my friends asks nosy questions. We discuss a needy family we are helping and talk about our clothing collection to provide warm coats for local children before winter. These friends are very dear to me, and it irritates me when I remember how Dominie Den Herder judged all of us as gossipers before he even knew us.

I invite Marinus and the Vander Veens back to my house for Sunday dinner. My son Arie joins us, as well. The men talk in a mixture of Dutch and English as the dominie explains his efforts to find a job. "Why don't you come down to the print shop on Monday morning and help me out?" Arie says. "I can't afford to pay very much, but I can keep you busy until something more in your line of work comes along."

"Thank you," Marinus replies. "I would be grateful. I am willing to work and very uncomfortable with charity."

My son's offer sparks an idea. "Arie, maybe the dominie could work for the Dutch-language newspaper, editing or proofreading or something. You know the publisher quite well, don't you, since you print his newspaper every week?"

"That's a great idea, Moeder. I'll speak with him about it tomorrow."

I can't describe the mixture of emotions I see on the dominie's face—hope and relief, certainly. But unless I'm mistaken, I also see resentment. Is it because the idea was mine and he doesn't want to feel indebted to me? There seems to be little room for kindness or grace in Marinus's world, and they seem especially unwelcome when they come from a meddling woman like me. Not for the first time, I wonder what kind of a pastor he was to his parishioners.

After Derk and his father leave, the dominie asks for a few minutes alone with Cornelia. "Of course," I reply. "Why don't you make yourselves comfortable in my sitting room while I clean up the dishes?" But Marinus takes his granddaughter out to my front porch, even though the October afternoon is chilly, as if he wants to discuss secrets that no one else is allowed to hear. When Cornelia comes inside again, I can tell she has been crying. "The dishes are all done," I tell her. She excuses herself to her room. I wish I knew how to help her. All I can do is pray for wisdom.

Marinus comes for an English lesson early Monday morning, then leaves to walk to Arie's print shop an hour later. We have finished the first lesson book and have moved on to the next. Cornelia isn't nearly as attentive or diligent about memorizing her new English words as her grandfather is. She seems listless much of the time. Lifeless. Her confession that she sometimes wishes to end her life continues to haunt me. I see her sitting at my kitchen table in her drab, brown dress, and an idea comes to me.

"Do you like to sew, Cornelia?" She shrugs as if her shoulders are weighed down by a very heavy coat. "I was thinking we could walk down to Van Putten's Dry Goods store this morning and buy some fabric. We could make a new skirt and shirtwaist for you. What do you say?"

"I need to ask Grandfather first." I was afraid she would say that. It's on the tip of my tongue to ask *why* when she adds, "He's worried about money."

"The new clothes would be my gift to you."

"He doesn't like to accept charity."

I take both of her hands in mine. "Cornelia, when friends do kind things for each other, it isn't charity. It's just what friends do. Your grandfather can't object to us being friends, can he?" I receive another weary shrug in reply. "Come on, let's at least go and look. I need to buy a few other things while I'm there, anyway."

We dress in warm jackets and head out. "Do you feel that chill?" I ask as we walk. "Winter will soon be here. You'll find it gets colder here than back home in the Netherlands. And we get a lot more snow. But everything looks so lovely when it's all clean and white and snow-covered."

"I like snow," she replies. I take her enthusiasm as a good sign.

I introduce Cornelia to Mrs. Van Putten, and we chat for a moment in Dutch. Then she shows us several bolts of flannelette, twill, and wool to choose from. Cornelia runs her hand over the soft material as if caressing it. "This would look so pretty on you," I tell her, holding up a flowered print. "The blue flowers match the blue in your eyes."

"I agree," Mrs. Van Putten says. "You know, it won't be long before we won't need to sew our own clothes by hand anymore. The latest things in all the big cities are ready-made dresses."

"I can't imagine that. How would they ever fit? People come in all sizes—short and tall, thin and plump."

"The clothes come ready-made in all different sizes. We're going to order some for the store and see how they sell. We have to keep up with Sears, Roebuck and Company, you know. They let you order dresses and skirts from their catalogue, right from your home. Then they're delivered right to your door, too. Here, take a look."

She pulls a thick catalogue from under the counter and lets Cornelia and me browse through the ladies' clothing section. I'm surprised to see everything from corsets and petticoats to skirts and jackets. Even hats. "What will they think of next?"

I say. "It will save time and work, I suppose, but I still like the satisfaction of making something with my own two hands."

We buy two yards of the pretty blue-flowered flannelette for a blouse and some matching gray twill for a skirt. I notice that Cornelia's mood has lightened a bit now that we're out of the house and talking with other people. I must think of ways to get her out more often. But on the way home, her head lowers again and her shoulders slump. She clutches the package of fabric close to her chest. "Are you worried about what your grandfather will say?" She nods and doesn't look up from the dusty street. I want to tell her that he scares me, too.

"He'll say it's too colorful. And that we should be content with the used clothing that people give us."

"That makes no sense. If he doesn't like to take charity, why does he expect you to wear donated clothes? Besides, what about the nice, new suit he wore to church yesterday?"

"A tailor in his congregation made it to repay my grandfather for helping him."

My conscience pricks me. I shouldn't be sowing discord between Cornelia and her grandfather. He has a right to raise her as he sees fit. "I'll ask him about the new skirt and blouse tonight. If he gets upset, I'll give the finished clothes to charity."

Cornelia clutches the package a little tighter. "I hope he says yes. It's so pretty."

"Does he decide how you should fix your hair, too?" I ask. She glances at me with a frightened look, then nods. "At church yesterday, I was noticing how some of the girls your age wore their hair. If your grandfather agrees, we could ask one of them to show us how they pin it up. In fact, my son Jakob is a minister, and his daughter Elizabeth is a modest young lady. Maybe she could help us." Cornelia nods, but there is no hope in her expression.

I clear off my kitchen table after lunch so we can spread out the new fabric and start cutting it. "Have you given any more thought to what you would like to do once you're settled here in Holland?" I ask as we work. "If you'd like to earn a little money, I know a few families from church who could use a helping hand."

"Grandfather doesn't want me to work in a stranger's home."

"They aren't strangers to me."

She doesn't reply. It's as if she has constructed a towering dam between her and the rest of the world to hold back all her thoughts and her grief. Yet the only way her sorrow can ever heal is if she releases it. I long to make a small crack in her wall so her emotions can flow, but to do that, I'm going to have to risk hurting her. "You must miss your family," I say softly as I cut into the twill for the skirt. "Your mama and papa . . . your two brothers."

Cornelia bites her bottom lip. The only response I get is a nod.

"I was very close to my two older sisters and their babies," I continue. "But they stayed behind in the Netherlands when I came to America. I missed them terribly. Writing letters just isn't the same as being with someone. Both of my sisters have passed away now, and their children are all grown. It's hard to imagine. I keep picturing them the way they were when I left home—my sisters still young, holding their chubby little babies in their arms." I glance at her and see a pained expression on her face. I whisper a prayer and continue. "I thank God for the happy memories of our time together. Remembering is a wonderful way to hold our loved ones close in our hearts, don't you think? Even when we're far apart."

I wait for Cornelia to respond. When she doesn't, I refold the cloth to cut the next piece and continue talking. "I know how it feels to lose both parents. My mama and papa died of malaria our first summer here in America. I was seventeen years old, and I didn't understand why they died and I lived. I was furious with God for taking them and leaving me all alone when I still needed them so badly."

Cornelia meets my gaze. "But you still go to church."

"Yes. I don't fully understand why God allows good people like my parents to die. But I know that He has His reasons—and I know I can trust Him. I've discovered that it's okay to be honest with God and let Him know when I'm angry. He knows how I feel anyway. And He is always faithful to send someone to console me when I'm upset and hurt."

I pause and hand the cut pieces to her. She is looking at me with surprise and shock, as if I'm speaking heresy and she's afraid to believe what I'm saying. "I don't think it was an accident that God arranged for you to live here with me, Cornelia. I believe He wants me to offer you His love and comfort." She looks away. I wish I knew what she was thinking. I rearrange the cloth so I can cut the skirt's waistband. "Sometimes it helps when we talk about the people we love. It's a way to keep them alive in our hearts while they are away from us in heaven." I make the final cut and hand the piece to her. "What are your brothers' names?" I ask.

"Johannes and Jacobus." She answers as if she has been holding the names inside for much too long. "They were pesky, you know? Always bothering me and teasing me. I used to get so mad at them—" A sob catches in her throat.

"You loved them very much, didn't you?" She nods. "I'm sure they knew that, Cornelia." She looks up at me with tears in her eyes.

"Johannes liked to carve things out of wood. I still have a little bear that he gave me for a Christmas present." She reaches into the pocket of her skirt and shows me the little wooden figure, no bigger than a walnut.

"What a lovely gift to carry with you to remember him." When she has been silent for a moment, I ask, "What are some other things you remember about your family?"

"Papa was a schoolteacher. My grandfather wanted him to be a dominie because all of the other ancestors in our family were. But Papa loved to teach. He was always telling my brothers and me things about history or nature, like how flowers grow. His students all loved him."

"You must have enjoyed spending time with him."

"Back then I didn't know . . . I didn't think it was . . . special. You know? And now . . ." She doesn't finish, but I can well imagine what she doesn't say. Her father and grandfather sound like two very different men.

"It sounds like you had a wonderful father," I tell her. "And he was a very wise man for following his own dreams and interests."

"He would be disappointed with me," she says in a voice I can barely hear.

"Why would you think that, Cornelia? You're a lovely young woman."

"You don't know me." She has turned her back to me, and I can barely hear her words. "You don't know what I've done."

"That's true. But you can't really know how your father would feel about it. My daughter, Christina, broke my heart when she ran away from home, but I never, ever stopped loving her. In spite of everything that happened, her father and I would have gladly welcomed her home again."

Cornelia stares out my kitchen window, sadly shaking her head.

"Tell me about your mother," I say. "What do you remember about her?"

She doesn't reply. When I rest my hand on her shoulder, she shakes her head and says, "I-I can't . . ." I pull her into my arms and hold her for a moment. I brush a stray piece of hair from her forehead after I release her.

"Here," I say, handing her my pincushion full of straight pins. "You can start pinning the skirt pieces together while I cut out your blouse." She sinks down on a kitchen chair like a flower wilting beneath the sun, then starts pinning the front to one of the back pieces. I gather up all the scraps to use in a quilt and spread the flowered fabric out on the table. "Our first summer here in Michigan, my parents and I all became sick with malaria," I tell Cornelia. "I got better but they didn't. When Mama and Papa died, I wondered why I didn't die along with them. You must have felt the same way."

I pause, and eventually she says in a soft voice, "I would have died if I had been home that night."

"But you weren't home. You lived, and so did I." I grip my scissors and cut into the fabric. "After I finished being angry with God, I realized that there must be a reason why He wanted me to live. And the same is true for you, Cornelia. In a world that has been created by a loving God, nothing happens by chance or coincidence."

She props her elbow on the table and covers her eyes with her hand. "You don't know me," she repeats.

I sit down in the chair beside hers. "Cornelia, look at me." I wait until she does. "I've made some terrible mistakes in my life. I convinced a wonderful man whom I didn't love to marry me for all the wrong reasons. But God used my mistake and my marriage for good. He gave us our son Jakob, whose life as a dominie has blessed many, many people. Don't ever think your life is over before it is. God can use even our greatest failures for His glory." Her expression is filled with longing . . . but also with grief. I am certain she is about to dismantle her barriers and confide in me when someone knocks on my front door. The moment is gone. Cornelia resumes her work while I go to answer it and find her grandfather standing on my porch.

"Hello, Dominie. Would you like to come in and have some tea with us?" He surprises me by agreeing. I take his hat and coat and lead him into my kitchen. Cornelia looks guilt-ridden when she sees him, as if she needs to roll the fabric into a ball and hide it beneath the table.

"Cornelia and I were just working on a little sewing project," I tell him as I add a stick of wood to my kitchen stove and poke the coals. "She has been such a big help to me around the house that I would like to return the favor by helping her sew a new blouse and skirt. Would that be agreeable to you, Dominie?"

He hesitates as if analyzing my words, then surprises me by saying, "That's very kind of you. I'm not much help to Cornelia when it comes to things like clothing. My late wife and I raised only one child past infancy, Cornelia's father."

I try not to show my surprise as he reveals the losses he has suffered. How tragic that the only family member he has left is Cornelia, who tried to end her own life. I should know that when someone reacts with anger and bitterness, there is usually a root of deep pain at the bottom of it. "Please, have a seat, Dominie," I say. "It's going to take a few minutes for the water to boil. Maybe you can tell us about your day at our print shop while we wait."

He has folded his hands on the table where I can see them, and there is no printer's ink in the creases or beneath his fingernails. Arie must not have put him to work with the presses just yet. "My day has been good," he says after clearing his throat. "Your son is very kind to hire me for what he calls, 'odd jobs.' Tomorrow we will speak with the editor of the Dutch newspaper to see if he has something for me."

"I'll pray for a successful meeting, then." I say nothing more as I rinse out the teapot and the strainer and wait for the water to heat. I've seen how quickly the dominie can go from friendly to fierce if I say something I shouldn't.

"How was your day, Cornelia?" he asks. "Did you practice your English while you were out shopping with Mrs. de Jonge?"

"I didn't have to. The woman at the dry goods store speaks Dutch."

"Yes, it seems a lot of people in town do. But not the young men and women your age. You will need English to talk with them."

I see my chance and take it. "If it's fine with you, Dominie, I would love for Cornelia to meet my granddaughter Elizabeth. She's my son Jakob's daughter. I've noticed that American girls wear their hair differently than we did back home. Would you mind if she spent a day with Elizabeth at my son's home so Cornelia can fit in better with other girls her age?"

"If that's what Cornelia would like to do."

I look at Cornelia, and she manages a tentative smile. I am stunned that he has agreed. We have made progress today, and I'm happy for Cornelia. But why do I get the feeling as I pour the tea that her grandfather is plotting something?

CHAPTER 10

Anna

I have asked my maid, Lucy, to bring my breakfast tray every morning at seven o'clock sharp and to make sure that I'm awake. My Oma Geesje takes time first thing every morning to read her Bible and pray, and I know that if I ever hope to have faith as strong as hers, I need to follow her example. My goal is to read a section from the Gospels slowly and carefully and see what I can learn from it. Each morning since I began this practice, I have found a thought to carry with me for the rest of the day.

This morning's passage is about standing before the Lord on Judgment Day. He will commend the person who has given food to the hungry, something to drink to those who are thirsty, and who offer shelter and clothes to wear. Jesus' words seem to leap from the page: "Inasmuch as ye have done it unto one of the least of these my brethren, ye have done it unto me." Those who fail to help the needy "shall go away into everlasting

111

punishment." It seems clear that the Lord wants us to help the needy for His sake. If we turn away when we're able to help, we'll face condemnation.

I'm still thinking about what I read after I'm dressed and am sitting in the morning room downstairs reading the newspaper. This is another daily habit I'm trying to develop so I can stay informed of the latest news for William's sake. This morning I find an interesting article about the Hull-House settlement here in Chicago. A shiver of excitement races through me as I read. The work they're doing coincides perfectly with what I just read in Scripture about helping the poor.

According to the article, two wealthy young women, Jane Addams and Ellen Gates Starr, wanted to do something about the terrible living conditions among Chicago's working-class immigrants but found the usual charities lacking. They decided to live among the poor and develop relationships with their neighbors in order to learn firsthand the problems they faced, then work together to find solutions. The ladies rented a slightly run-down mansion on Halsted Street, right in the middle of Chicago's overcrowded Near West Side neighborhood. The Hull-House settlement opened its doors eight years ago in July of 1889, and since then, other like-minded social reformers have moved into the settlement house to join the two women. Their efforts are a resounding success, with new programs and opportunities being introduced to the community every day as they tackle the causes of poverty among Chicago's immigrants.

Mother joins me in the morning room, interrupting my reading. I'm so intrigued and inspired by the innovative idea of Hull-House that I nearly blurt out everything I've just learned. Mother's frowning expression makes me hesitate. "Make sure you wash the ink off your fingers when you're done," she says. "I don't know why you're even interested in reading the newspaper. It's all bad news anyway."

"I want to be able to discuss local and world events with William," I reply. "He takes a keen interest in them." I'm eager to read more about Hull-House, but not in front of Mother. Instead, I decide to check my calendar to see when I can sneak away and visit the settlement house in person. "You're right about the messy ink," I say as I rise and refold the paper. "I think I'll wash up."

Aside from the usual, boring social calls, my afternoon is free. It's so rare for that to happen, especially with the added preparations for my wedding, that I do a little dance in the middle of my bedroom. I see this opening as another heavenly sign along with the Bible verse and the newspaper article.

I do my best to be patient and agreeable all morning as Mother and I shop for hats, gloves, and the other accessories we'll need for my wedding. When we return home for lunch I ask, "Would you mind if we went our separate ways this afternoon? I know you're eager to call on Mrs. Wilson, and I would like to go in a different direction. I'll hire a carriage when it's time to part ways."

She eyes me with suspicion. "Where do you intend to go, dear?"

I have been planning my reply all morning, unwilling to tell a lie, yet armed with the information I read in the newspaper. "I hope to call on Miss Jane Addams this afternoon. We've never been formally introduced, but her father, John Addams, is a wealthy businessman and an Illinois State Senator."

Mother takes a moment as if mentally scrolling through a list of approved acquaintances. "I've never heard of either of them. If Miss Addams is new to our social circle, perhaps we should call on her together."

I smile, aware that I'm treading a delicate path. "That's not necessary. You've taught me well, Mother, and now I need to start fulfilling my social obligations on my own. After all, I'll be in charge of my own social calendar in just a few short months when I marry William."

"I suppose you're right." Mother's eyes glisten, and I can see she is growing emotional. "It's hard, sometimes, for mothers to accept that their children no longer need them."

Mother asks our driver to hail a hired carriage for me after lunch. I give the driver the address for Hull-House on Halsted Street, and he stares at me as if I've made a mistake. "That's not a very nice neighborhood, miss. You sure you got the address right?"

"Yes, quite sure." I begin to see what he means as we meander through unpaved streets lined with dreary tenement houses. The buildings are crammed so tightly together that I wonder how the occupants can breathe. Trash fills the streets where raggedy children play. Laundry flaps in the breeze on lines strung between the buildings. The world in this part of town looks dull and gray and treeless. We halt in front of a large brick house with a wide front porch that seems to have been dropped there from a different city. It's sandwiched into place between a huge, awkward addition and a livery stable reeking of horses. "Kindly return for me in two hours' time," I tell the driver.

As soon as I step onto the porch, I hear children's voices and the sound of activity inside. Several minutes pass before a middle-aged woman who is clearly not a servant replies to my knock. "Sorry about the delay," she says, puffing slightly. "Come in, come in."

"Good afternoon," I say as I step into the foyer. "My name is Miss Anna Nicholson. I read about the work you're doing here at Hull-House in this morning's newspaper, and I was inspired to come and see it for myself. I realize I should have made an appointment, but I didn't know when I would have another free afternoon."

"Of course. Welcome, Miss Nicholson. I'm Mrs. Smith."

She is sizing me up and can probably discern from the way I'm dressed that I'm from a wealthy family. "This way, please. I'll see who's available to give you a tour."

I expected the interior to be as run-down as the exterior, so I'm very surprised when Mrs. Smith leads me into a lovely parlor filled with gracious furnishings, shelves of books, delicate artwork, and fresh flowers. The squeals and giggles I overheard are coming from the drawing room, where two women are herding a noisy group of children dressed like ragamuffins toward the back of the house.

"The kindergarten children are going out to play now," Mrs. Smith says. "Please, have a seat, and I'll fetch someone to guide you." I look around as I wait and notice that the rooms seem to have been decorated with family heirlooms. This isn't a sterile institution but a home. I can't imagine Mother or any of our acquaintances opening their homes to working-class children. Yet I was born into a poor, working-class family just like those children. Rich or poor, we are all the same on the inside, with the same needs for food and shelter and a family to love. Only our material circumstances differ. How wonderful it would be if I could work to correct some of those differences.

My excitement continues to grow as a pleasant-looking woman named Mrs. Pelham conducts me on a tour of Hull-House. "Everything you see here began when Miss Addams and Miss Starr simply opened their door to the people of this neighborhood and invited them in. The working-class children were especially in need of a place where they could learn and play and grow up safely. So we set up a kindergarten for them right here in our drawing room. As the children grew, our work also grew to include a variety of children's clubs, including my own pet project, a theater group."

We move into the adjoining building, the Butler Gallery, which I'm amazed to learn houses an art gallery, classroom space, and even a branch of the public library. "The families in our neighborhood come from a variety of ethnic backgrounds," Mrs. Pelham explains. "We share our lives and our experiences with them, and they are eager to share their heritages with us. And so we host ethnic nights to enjoy the food, music, and folk dancing that celebrate our neighbors' heritage. In fact, tonight is German Night. You are welcome to come back and join us, Miss Nicholson."

I am reminded of my own Dutch heritage and the fascinating glimpse of it that I saw while visiting Oma in Holland. "What a wonderful idea. I thank you sincerely for the invitation. And although I would love to join you, I'm sorry to say that I'm already engaged this evening."

"Perhaps another time." She shows me the Hull-House Men's Club, a large room furnished with card and billiard tables. "We want to offer the young men a better place to socialize than the saloons. And you may want to join our Women's Club, comprised of reform-minded women from the neighborhood and all over the city. We work to find solutions to sanitation and public health issues as well as other social ills. We're also fighting to enact laws to end child labor and promote compulsory school attendance. Education is an important avenue out of poverty."

"How fascinating! I would love to join your club, Mrs. Pelham." My excitement grows. I can scarcely imagine attending a meeting with a purpose other than eating petit fours and discussing Greek tragedies.

Mrs. Pelham points out the children's public playground that Hull-House created across the street. "It's the only one of its kind in Chicago," she explains. "All children should have a place where they can run and play in safety, don't you agree?"

"I do." But my heart truly quickens when Mrs. Pelham points out the resources for women who are alone and struggling in the city—like my mama once was. "This is our Jane Club," she explains. "A safe, cooperative boardinghouse for single working women. It's also a place where they can support each other during union strikes. For married women, our kindergarten and day nursery provide a refuge for their young children while they are at work."

I can feel the Lord nudging me into action. *"Inasmuch as ye have done it unto one of the least of these my brethren, ye have done it unto me."* When Oma Geesje advised me to return to my privileged life in Chicago, she said, *"Think of all the young women like Christina who are trapped in Chicago, poor and alone in a huge city with no family to help them."* I want to be part of the work that Hull-House is doing. It's what Jesus would want me to do.

The two hours fly by, and much too soon it's time for me to leave. Mrs. Pelham provides me with information about the Women's Club as well as a variety of other volunteer opportunities. I can't wait to share my excitement with William this evening. We will be attending a political fund-raising dinner in the home of one of Chicago's aldermen, a first step for William into the world of politics.

"I had the most fascinating day today," I say as soon as we're seated in his carriage.

"Tell me all about it, darling."

"First I need to back up a little and tell you about the Bible verse I read this morning." His smile seems to dim. Or am I imagining it? "The Lord said that when we feed and clothe the poor, it's as though we are doing it for Him. And then right after I read those words, I happened to read an article in the newspaper about a place here in Chicago where people are doing those exact things. It's called the Hull-House settlement, and—"

"Is that the place that Jane Addams founded?"

"Yes! You've heard of it, too?"

"I certainly have." His smile has vanished completely. "Stay away from that place, Anna."

"But . . . but why? When I visited there today and saw the wonderful work—"

"You went there?"

"Yes, they gave me a tour, and I learned all about the work they're doing. They have classes and cultural events and a safe place where hardworking mothers can leave their children and—"

"Those people call themselves progressives, but they are socialists in disguise. You can't have anything to do with them."

I couldn't be more stunned if William had slapped me across the face. "I don't understand. Don't we have an obligation to help the poor? What difference do their political views make?"

"Jane Addams is not only a social progressive, she's anticapitalism. Those people support trade unions and women's suffrage. You cannot be associated with them and their outrageous ideas, Anna. Does your father know you went there?"

"I haven't had a chance to—"

"Make sure you tell him. I know he will agree with me. He won't want his daughter affiliated with that place."

My disappointment is overwhelming. I turn away from William to stare out of the carriage window at the wide, gas-lit boulevard and handsome stone houses we're passing. This clean, tree-lined street might well be in a different world from the neighborhood I visited this afternoon. I struggle to control my tears so I won't arrive with red eyes and a running nose. I hesitate to argue with William, yet I must make him see the benefits of the settlement house and why I feel compelled to be part of it. "Why is it so wrong to help immigrants and poor, working-class people, William? My mama was a cook in a boardinghouse, and her husband was a railroad worker. My grandma Geesje and her family were all immigrants. How can it be wrong for me to spend my time helping people like them instead of attending tea parties and luncheons?"

"There are plenty of acceptable charities here in Chicago that you can volunteer for and contribute to. But you aren't an immigrant or a poor, working-class woman, Anna. Your true family is the one that raised you—the Nicholsons. Your social obligations are to them, not to the people who gave birth to you. And you will become part of my family after we're married."

I pull a handkerchief from my reticule and dab the tears from my eyes. William is right, I suppose. But I can't escape the feeling that what I read in Scripture and saw in person at Hull-House was the true path I should be taking if I want to follow Jesus. William lifts my gloved hand and kisses the back of it.

"I'm sorry if I sounded brusque, darling, or if I upset you. But those sorts of people are some of our harshest critics. They dismiss the hard work of men like my grandfather, who started with nothing and worked hard to succeed. They treat us as if we're the enemy. Anyone in America can get ahead and make something of himself if he's willing to work hard, even if he's an immigrant."

I swallow the lump in my throat and ask, "Have you ever seen the tenements where they live?"

He kisses my hand again and says, "Of course I have. Listen, I admire your tender, generous heart, Anna dear. I will ask Mother to give you the names of the wonderful charities she supports. But please don't ever mention Hull-House again, especially at the dinner tonight."

The subject is closed and sealed. But it leaves a hollow place inside me, and I don't know what will replace it. I stay by William's side for the remainder of the evening and fill the role that's expected of me. But I feel like I'm playacting, reciting lines that someone else has written in a drama that I no longer enjoy.

I am still hurt and confused the next morning when I open my Bible. I'm almost afraid to read it, afraid that I'll learn of another command that I won't be able to fulfill. Today these words of our Lord stand out: *"But I say unto you, That every idle word that men shall speak, they shall give account thereof in the day of judgment. For by thy words thou shalt be justified, and by thy words thou shalt be condemned."* The full import of what the Lord means doesn't hit me until later that day when I'm at a meeting with Clarice Beacham and the other women in our club. We're discussing ways to raise funds, not for charity but to build a permanent home for our Women's Literary Club. I can think of more deserving causes to donate my time and money to, but I remain silent. Have any of these ladies ever visited Chicago's Near West Side?

After the meeting ends and we're having refreshments, the other ladies begin to gossip. They slice into an acquaintance of ours named Dorothea as if dissecting a botanical specimen, criticizing everything from her hair and facial features to her fashion taste and her family's financial status. I recall the Lord's warning about being accountable for our words, and I feel an arrow of guilt.

"No one of any importance will ever court her, you know," one of the ladies says. "I heard—"

"Please stop." I am as surprised as the others when I finally say aloud what I've been thinking. The ladies stare at me as if I've tossed my cup of tea in their faces. My heart is racing, but I simply can't bear to hear any more. Might I be held accountable for remaining silent?

"What did you say?" one of them asks.

"I'm very uncomfortable talking about Dorothea behind her back this way. It isn't kind. Can we please talk about something else?" They all look to Clarice as if she is the leader. They will tailor their response to match hers. I wait, wondering what will happen. Clarice could gracefully change the subject and all would be well, even if she doesn't admit any wrongdoing.

"Do you think you're better than we are?" Clarice asks instead. My heart pounds harder.

"No, of course not. But we're supposed to be kind and compassionate to one another. The Bible says we will have to give an account, someday, for all the idle words we speak."

Clarice laughs as if I've told a joke. The others follow her lead, smiling and smirking. "I heard all about your religious conversion, Anna," she says. "But I didn't realize you've turned into a preacher."

My cheeks feel as though they are on fire. "It was never my intention to preach. I merely asked if we could change the subject." I want to ask why it's so controversial to do what the Bible says, but my courage is quickly draining away.

Clarice takes a challenging stance, hands on hips, and although she continues to smile, I see contempt in her eyes. "Who are you to dictate what we talk about?"

I set down my teacup, fearing I might drop it. "I think it would be best if I leave now." My legs feel as if they may not support me much longer as I make my way to the door. The butler fetches my coat, and I ask him to tell my mother that I have already left. I can't even imagine what she will say. Probably that I have humiliated myself and her.

Outside, I find our driver and ask him to hail a cab for me. Once I'm safely inside and heading home, my tears begin to fall. I'm not even sure why I'm crying. Is it because Clarice and the others are certain to shun me and gossip about me next? Or because, once again, I tried to do what the Lord commanded and to stand up for what's right, and it ended all wrong?

I long to talk to Oma Geesje. I know she will listen while I tell her about Hull-House and about William and Clarice and everything else that has happened these past two days. Maybe she can help me figure out what I'm doing wrong. I want to serve God, but I'm obviously not going about it the right way. The carriage slows to a halt near the river, and I hear gears grinding as the swing bridge opens to let a sailing vessel and a tugboat with a long string of barges pass through. The longer I wait, the more I realize how badly I need to get away and take time to pray and to think. I need to figure out how the lessons I'm learning in the Bible can fit together with my life here in Chicago.

I'm not used to making decisions for myself, but I make one now. I rap on the window of the carriage to get the driver's attention. "Take me to the nearest Western Union office, please. I need to send a telegram. Then take me to Union Station."

I'm in my bedroom later when I hear Mother return home. Sending the telegram has halted my tears, and I decide to face Mother directly with the truth. She is in the foyer, pulling out her hatpins, but she pauses as she sees me descend the stairs, as if watching a stranger.

"What in the world happened after the meeting, Anna? You stirred up a hornet's nest. All the ladies are buzzing about your unusual behavior."

"I expressed my opinion, and the others misinterpreted it. Listen, Mother, I've decided to go away for a few days and—"

"You can't run from your problems."

"I'm not running, but I need some advice, and—"

"Tell me the whole story." She removes her hat and places it on the hall table for the maid to attend to. Then she starts pulling off her gloves, one finger at a time. I've seen Mother do this countless times, but today I recognize it as her way of stalling for time as she controls her temper. I admire her forbearance, knowing how upset and embarrassed she must be.

"The other girls were spreading gossip about Dorothea, and

I asked them to stop. They were being very unkind. I merely asked if we could please talk about something else. Clarice became offended."

Mother lifts her chin. "I'll see what I can do to mend fences. There are ways to remedy this. I'm sure Mrs. Wilkinson will help you—"

"Please don't interfere, Mother." She looks startled, so I hurry on. "I need to learn how to fight my own battles. Besides, I'm not sorry for asking them to stop, because they were wrong to gossip that way. The Bible says—"

"You didn't quote the Bible, did you?" she asks in horror. I nod. "No wonder they were offended. I thought you knew better than to discuss religion or politics in polite society."

I'm getting nowhere. This is an argument I cannot win. I draw a deep breath, steeling myself. "I'm going to take the train up to Michigan for a few days."

"You're doing what? All by yourself?"

"Yes, unless you would like to come with me."

"I can't spare the time. I have too many obligations. And you do, too, with your wedding in a few months."

The reminder of the dwindling time until my marriage causes me to shiver. "I'll only be away for a few days. I need a chance to think. And maybe it will give everyone else time to see that they were unkind to gossip that way."

"Let's discuss it with your father first."

"Please don't be angry with me, Mother, but I already sent Oma Geesje a telegram to tell her I'm coming. My train leaves tomorrow morning."

Mother closes her eyes. "This is a fine mess you've made."

She may be right, but I still don't regret any of the decisions I've made today. I go upstairs to my room and ring the bell to summon Lucy to help me pack.

"Where are you going, Miss Anna?" she asks as I choose a

plain skirt and shirtwaist from my closet. "Will you need jewelry and eveningwear?"

"I'm going to visit my grandmother in Michigan. I won't need anything fancy because it's a much simpler way of life up there."

"I would be happy to come along, Miss Anna, and help with your hair and tend to your clothing."

I release a sigh. Dragging along a maid would defeat the purpose. I want to be free from all the fuss, if only for a day or two. "Thank you, but that won't be necessary."

"As you wish, miss," she says with a little curtsy. "I suppose your family up there has plenty of servants to help you."

I look at her in surprise. "Not at all. My grandmother lives in a very modest house and does all the cooking and washing herself. She even grows vegetables in her own garden."

Lucy looks doubtful. "Hardly the life you're used to, is it?"

I don't reply. Oma's life is very different from mine, it's true. I wouldn't know how to get by if I had to cook all my own meals and wash my clothes and do all the other chores that our servants perform for us. Yet I can't deny how content I was when I stayed with Oma and how unhappy I am with the direction my life is taking now. Once again, I make up my mind to regain control of it, somehow. I'm hoping that Oma will help me figure out how to do it.

Chapter 11

Geesje

Cornelia and I have nearly finished sewing her new skirt and blouse. We are working on them in my kitchen, where the afternoon light is better, when a messenger comes to my door with a telegram. I stare at the words in surprise. "It's from my granddaughter Anneke," I tell Cornelia. "She's arriving for a visit tomorrow by train." I can barely comprehend it. Anneke is coming! She doesn't say why. I am delighted but also befuddled. She must not have received my letter, telling her about my houseguest. But it doesn't matter. We'll make room for her.

Arie lets me borrow his horse and buggy so I can get Anneke at the train station the next day. Cornelia offers to drive the carriage, and she turns out to be quite good at handling the reins. I can barely contain my joy when I hear the train whistle in the distance and watch the locomotive hiss to a halt in the station in a cloud of steam and dust. The conductor helps Anneke step down, and she runs into my arms. I hold my granddaughter tightly, inhaling her soft, sweet scent and thanking God for this unexpected gift.

Cornelia gapes at Anneke in her elegant traveling suit as if she is royalty. I introduce them to each other. I have already explained Anneke's story to Cornelia, but I take a moment on the short drive home to tell Anneke about my guest. "She and her grandfather recently emigrated from the Netherlands. She is staying with me, and her grandfather is staying next door with Derk while he looks for work." I decide to leave out any details about Cornelia losing her family in the fire or about her suicide attempt.

"I'm so sorry for barging in when you already have a guest," Anneke says. She looks guilt-stricken. "I never should have presumed that I could arrive without any warning. I'll gladly find a hotel room."

"That isn't necessary. There's space for both of you in my spare bedroom if you don't mind sharing it. Cornelia is trying to learn English, so it will be good for her to get some practice. She could use a friend."

Anneke's smile returns. "I don't mind sharing. I've always wished I had a sister."

"Maybe you could also show Cornelia how American girls dress and fix their hair. It would help her fit in a little better with other young people her age."

"I'll be happy to try, Oma. My maid offered to come, but I didn't want her to."

How different our worlds are. Wealthy young women like Anneke don't have to pin up their own hair or sew their own clothes. I long to ask her why she has come, suspecting that she didn't endure the long train ride without a reason. Something must have happened back home in Chicago to upset her. But I'll give her time to settle in before we talk.

Cornelia ties the horse to my post when we arrive home and helps Anneke with her bags. She didn't bring much, so it doesn't look like she'll be staying long. "If you would like some time to rest up after your trip," I tell her, "please feel free to do so. I need to run an errand for my church while I still have Arie's carriage, but I won't be long."

"For your church?" she asks.

"Yes, we've been collecting winter clothing and knitting mittens and hats for some needy children here in town. I want to deliver them, and Cornelia offered to drive."

For some inexplicable reason, Anneke's eyes fill with tears. "May I go with you, please?"

"Of course, but don't you want to rest?"

"I would rather help you. Give me a moment to change my clothes." She hurries into her room, and I hear her rummaging around.

"Are you able to understand anything we're saying?" I ask Cornelia while we wait. She shakes her head, staring at the floor and nibbling her fingernails. "Anneke is going to come with us on our errands," I explain.

Cornelia nods, still studying the floor. "I'll wait for you outside by the carriage," she replies.

"Wait . . . I'm sorry that I neglected to ask if you mind sharing your room with Anneke for a few days."

"No, ma'am. I don't mind. It's her room." The fact that Cornelia calls me *ma'am* instead of *tante* is a bad sign. She is distancing herself from me again. She turns to me as she reaches the front door and says, "She's beautiful, isn't she?"

"Yes. And Anneke is beautiful on the inside, too. I hope you'll become friends."

Anneke comes out a few minutes later wearing a plain gray skirt and a white blouse with tiny pleats down the front that would be considered her "Sunday best" by Holland's standards.

She puts on the jacket from her traveling suit and the three of us squeeze onto the carriage seat with Cornelia in the middle, driving for us. Two of my friends are waiting at Pillar Church, and they help us load the bundles of clothing into the carriage. I give Cornelia directions in Dutch to the home of the first family, and we're on our way.

"You get along with this horse very well," I tell Cornelia. "I know from experience how ornery and disagreeable she can be, which is why I don't ask Arie if I can borrow her very often. How did you learn to handle horses so well?"

"I had a mare back home." Cornelia's voice is so soft I strain to hear it above the clomping hooves. "Her name was *Suiker*. She was like . . . like a friend to me. I would ride her bareback sometimes, and we'd wander for miles past fields and farmland. . . ." Cornelia gazes down the road as if looking into the past. It's hard to visualize her as a carefree girl on a galloping horse, her brown hair streaming in the wind. "I wanted to take Suiker with me after the fire, but Grandfather didn't have a stable."

"I'm so sorry. The small losses can be just as painful as the big ones. Since you seem to get along so well with Arie's horse, I'm sure he'll let you borrow her whenever you'd like." As soon as I say this, I wish I hadn't. Cornelia's grandfather will never allow her to wander off by herself on a borrowed horse.

We drive down a street of small, working-class houses near the basket factory and halt in front of one that is little more than a tar paper shack. The fall afternoon is chilly, but there is no plume of smoke rising from the chimney. "I don't think you saw this part of Holland," I tell Anneke. "The Murphy family lives here. They need our help because Mr. Murphy has been ill and unable to work. My heart goes out to these poor souls. I know what it's like to struggle to get by."

"Then it would break your heart to see how poor the working

families in Chicago are," Anneke says. "Hundreds and hundreds of families are packed together in rickety tenement buildings with no running water and only one reeking outhouse that a dozen families have to share. The garbage just piles up in the streets where the children play, and—" Her voice catches.

I reach to take her hand. "Your church in Chicago must feel overwhelmed trying to meet so many needs."

"That's the problem, Oma. My church isn't doing anything like this." Her blue eyes glisten. She has Christina's eyes. "That's one of the reasons I had to get away. The need is so great, yet it frustrates me that I can't find a way to help. An acceptable way, that is."

"What do you mean?"

"One that William approves of. This is what I wanted to do," she says, gesturing to the house as we climb down. "I wanted to give clothing and food to the poor, but it all went wrong." A stream of children flow out of the door, and I see that two of them are without shoes. It's too cold on this autumn day to be barefooted. We gather the bundles from the back of the carriage as a young, weary mother comes to stand in her doorway holding a squalling baby. I suspect from the mother's disheveled appearance that we interrupted the baby's feeding time.

"Good afternoon, Mrs. Murphy. I'm Geesje de Jonge, and this is Anneke and Cornelia. The ladies at Pillar Church have gathered some things that we thought you and the children might need for the winter months."

"That's kind of you." Her eyes and voice are flat, her expression lifeless. The children take the bags from us, clamoring to see what's inside. As they begin pulling out clothing and mittens, I'm happy to see a few pairs of shoes in the bags, as well.

"If there is anything else we can help you with, Mrs. Murphy, I hope you'll feel welcome to come to the church and ask."

She nods and shifts the fussy baby to her other shoulder. I

move closer to take a look at him. The child can't be more than a month old, with fuzzy red hair and a pink face. The blanket is threadbare, and I make a mental note to knit him a warmer one for winter.

I rest my hand on Mrs. Murphy's shoulder. "God loves you and your little ones, Mrs. Murphy. That's why He sent us here." She nods, her woeful expression never changing. I return to the carriage and climb onto the seat, where Cornelia and Anneke are waiting.

"That's all I wanted to do," Anneke says after I direct Cornelia to the next house. "I just wanted to help feed and clothe the poor like the Lord told us to do. But it seems like every time God leads me in a new direction, William opposes it. I was learning so much at the church on La Salle Street, but William didn't want me to attend there anymore. And the other day I read about a wonderful organization in Chicago called Hull-House, where they help poor mothers who need a safe place to leave their children while they work. I thought of Mama and how a place like that could have helped her when I was little. I wanted to volunteer there, but William forbade it. He says I must never go back there."

Her words worry me. William seems very controlling. But I don't really know if his behavior is unusual in her circle or not. Some people believe it's a husband's right to make decisions for his wife, but I believe there should also be room for her personality and her gifts to grow and shine. I'm thankful that my husband considered me his partner, and that we made decisions together. "Have you asked William to explain why he forbids it?"

"Yes, and he got quite upset about it. He thinks Hull-House is trying to make a political statement, and that they have an agenda beyond merely helping the poor. But I guess . . . I guess I still don't understand. I'm trying so hard to find God's purpose for my life, and I thought it would be wonderful to help women like Mama. I can't bear to live a useless life, Oma. Hull-House would give me a purpose and would be a way to obey the Lord's teachings. Now I don't know what to do. Even worse, I'm letting Him down by not following His commands."

"Be patient, sweet Anneke. God knows your heart, and He knows you want to serve Him. He'll answer your prayers and show you the perfect place He has for you, in time, even if Hull-House wasn't it."

We arrive at the O'Dells' house next, near the tannery. Thick smoke and soot blackens everything and leaves a layer of grime in the air that I can feel. The O'Dell children run outside to greet us while Mrs. O'Dell remains inside, peeking through the tattered curtain. I speak to the oldest child, a girl of about twelve, while her younger siblings collect the parcels and carry them inside. "What's your name, dear?" I ask.

"Nellie."

"That's a pretty name for a pretty girl. Please tell your mother that if she needs anything else, to visit us at Pillar Church. It's the big, white building on Tenth Street with the pillars in front. We would be happy to help you." I climb onto the seat again, and we drive to the next house. "God sees your desire to serve Him, Anneke," I say, continuing our conversation. "Maybe for now, He simply wants you to share His love with the people around you."

"I'm a failure at that, too!" She lifts her hands in a helpless gesture, then lets them flop onto her lap. "I tried to share the Lord's words with the ladies in my circle yesterday, but they interpreted them all wrong."

"What happened?"

"They were gossiping about a friend of ours, and I asked them to stop. I told them that the Lord holds us accountable for every idle word we speak. They were furious with me."

I hide a smile, imagining how the women I know would react to such advice, especially if they were caught in the act. But I'm also reminded of Dominie Den Herder's accusation about gossiping women. "You're right, Anneke. God does hate gossip. I suspect that the women became angry because you struck a nerve. We don't like to have our faults brought into the light."

"I'll have to socialize with those women again when I go home. I'll see them at all manner of events. I can't avoid them."

"Hold your head up high and don't back down, dear. I'll be very surprised if they gossip right in front of you again, so that's a victory."

"Mother thinks I should apologize."

"Well, she knows more about those women and why they were offended than I do. Maybe you can find a way to say you're sorry for offending them without apologizing for what you said. Pray about it and ask the Lord to guide your words when the time comes."

We arrive at the last house near the furnace factory and see Mrs. Ramsay taking her laundry down from the clotheslines. She walks out to the street to meet us, nodding mutely as I tell her who we are and why we've come. Her children gather around to see what we've brought, as excited as on Christmas morning. The littlest boy asks to pet our horse, and Cornelia lifts him up to stroke its muzzle.

"No one seemed particularly grateful today," Anneke says on our way home. "I don't think anyone even said thank you."

"You're right. But I know how humbling it is to be unable to provide for your loved ones, and to be forced to accept charity. My family lost nearly everything we owned when the fire destroyed Holland years ago, including our home and our print shop. We had to live on handouts for quite a while. When that happens, people sometimes put up a wall of indifference to preserve their dignity."

"I guess I can understand that," Anneke says.

"Of course, it would be wonderful if our gifts had an immediate effect on these families and they decided they would like to learn more about Jesus, but that rarely happens. Yet even though it seems like we're not making a difference, God sees the long-range picture that we can't always see. For now, it's enough that these families know that God loves them and that He's taking care of them through our hands."

I glance at Cornelia and notice that she seems more downcast than usual, as if our errand has had a negative effect. "I'm sorry for leaving you out of the conversation, Cornelia," I say in Dutch. I explain a little bit of what Anneke and I have been talking about, sensitive to the fact that Cornelia also was left with nothing when fire destroyed her home. "Can you understand any of what we've been saying?" I ask again. She shakes her head.

"Oma, how did you know that this was the work you were supposed to do—collecting clothes for families like these?" Anneke asks.

"I'm not doing this alone. The other women at my church are also involved. But we decided to ask ourselves, what work would Jesus be doing if He were here? Where would He go? Who are the people He would reach out to?"

"That's exactly what they're doing at Hull-House!" I can hear the frustration in Anneke's voice. "A group of wealthy people like me decided to live right in the middle of an overcrowded immigrant neighborhood so they would get to know the people as neighbors and learn what their needs are. I think it's precisely what the Lord would do if He came to Chicago. The immigrants are able to keep their dignity because they're giving back to each other, and everyone shares what they have."

"It sounds wonderful. Are the people who started Hull-House from a particular church?"

The question seems to surprise Anneke. "You know, I never realized it before, but it isn't affiliated with a church. God was never mentioned when I toured there."

"It's wonderful to help meet people's physical needs. But what they need even more is to be restored to our heavenly Father. That's true for rich and poor alike."

"I never thought of it that way."

"Jesus had a heart for the poor, certainly. But He also spent time with wealthy people, and He loved them, too. He invited a wealthy tax collector named Levi to become His disciple. Then Levi hosted a dinner with all his fellow tax collectors because he wanted them to meet Jesus, too. And you probably know the story of the rich young ruler who came to Jesus. The verse says that Jesus looked at him and *loved* him. I have always treasured that verse . . . Jesus *loved* him, even though the man decided he couldn't give away his riches and follow Him. I want to be able to look at people the way Jesus did, and truly see them and love them."

Anneke is quiet as we ride home. When we turn onto my street, she looks over at me and says, "I think it's harder for my rich friends to admit they need God than it is for the poor families we saw today to accept charity. We don't want to admit that there's something missing in our life or that we have any needs. We're accustomed to relying on ourselves for everything, and we try hard to pretend that we're perfect—but we're not."

"That might be why your friends reacted so strongly when you pointed out their faults."

"Yes. I think you're right."

We halt in front of my house, and I notice Anneke gazing at Derk's house next door as if hoping he will run out to greet her. "I haven't seen Derk in over a week," I tell her. "I didn't get a chance to tell him you were coming." I see her disappointment. She and I climb down and walk toward my door. But Cornelia doesn't follow us.

"I can drive the carriage back to the print shop," she says. She has barely spoken all afternoon. "You and Anneke can have time alone. I'll walk back with Grandfather when he is finished working."

I hesitate, and I hate that Cornelia notices me doing it. But she could travel a long way with a horse and carriage if she decided to run away again. I promised her grandfather that I would watch over her. "I don't mind going with you," I tell her. "Anneke might want to take a little nap while we're gone."

Cornelia meets my gaze, something she doesn't do very often, and the sorrow I see in her eyes breaks my heart. "I promise I'll come back," she says. She looks so forlorn that I go to her and take her into my arms. She stands with her arms at her sides, not returning my embrace.

"I believe you, Cornelia," I murmur. "And it would be a big help to me if you returned the carriage. Thank you. And thanks for helping us today." I watch her climb onto the seat and drive away. I wish I knew what was going on in her heart.

I make tea, and Anneke and I sit in my front room to sip it. I soak up the sight of Christina's daughter—my Anneke—the way a thirsty man guzzles water, thrilled to have her with me again, never dreaming that I would see her again so soon, even if it's a short visit. She is so beautiful—and so troubled. "Tell me about your William," I say. "I imagine you're knee-deep in all the plans for your wedding."

"Those plans have spun completely out of my control, Oma. Not one thing is as I would have chosen it. My gown is too gaudy for my taste. The wedding dinner is going to be a huge, extravagant affair. And the house that William is buying for us is . . ." She pauses, gazing up at the ceiling as if to keep her tears from overflowing. "I hate that house. It's bigger than the hotel we passed in downtown Holland today. I hate that we got that house because the lovely family who built it and cherished it were evicted when they ran into financial problems. But William insists that it's the perfect house for us, and I . . ." Her voice grows quiet. "I go along with whatever he wants to make him happy."

"So the changes you saw in William after the hotel fire didn't last?"

Anneke shakes her head. "He said he wanted to take more interest in spiritual things and hear about what I've been learning, but he hasn't done it. I know he loves me, and he treats me very well, but every facet of his life is carefully planned and tightly controlled, and some of the things I want—like to grow in faith—don't fit into his plans."

"Is it the same way for the other wealthy couples you know?"

She takes a moment to think it over. "Yes, I suppose it is. Husbands make all of the important decisions and most couples live separate lives."

"But you want more."

"Is that asking too much?"

"I don't think so. Even though the husband is the head of the household, I think it's important that he and his wife value the same things and share the same faith. It's one thing to give in to your husband's wishes on decisions such as where you'll live. But it's never right for him to ask you to compromise your beliefs. Have you had a chance to explain to William just how important your faith is to you?"

"I've tried . . . but I can tell it doesn't interest him. William has his own hopes and dreams at the moment. He wants to go into politics and run for office. He wants to be a United States senator someday."

"Keep trying, dear. Don't give up. Perhaps the repetition will get through to his heart." Anneke nods, but I can tell she thinks it's hopeless. I lean forward in my chair, drawing closer to her. "Anneke, do you feel trapped? Do you wish you weren't marrying him? Because there is still time to change your mind."

Again, I see that she's fighting her tears. "I try to imagine what my future will be like, living in that enormous house and supporting William's ambitions, and . . . and I wouldn't have chosen that life for myself. But none of us really knows what our future holds, do we? And it is too late to call off the wedding. My parents are depending on me. Besides, I do care for William, and I know he cares for me."

The life she describes isn't one I would wish for Anneke, but I can't interfere. I whisper a silent prayer, asking God to stop the wedding before it's too late if this marriage isn't His will for Anneke. "Listen, when you get home, lieveling, I urge you to find a way to let William know how important your faith is to you. He needs to be fully aware that you plan to live your life by the Lord's teachings. You need to stand firm on that point so he won't ask you to compromise or give in to his wishes."

She nods, but I can tell that we have talked enough for today. "I need to start cooking supper," I tell her. "Why don't you come out to the kitchen and keep me company?"

"I would love to. And maybe I could help."

I give her a knife and some carrots to scrape and chop. I see how awkwardly she handles the knife and hope she doesn't cut herself. We talk while we work just like we did during the summer. "Cornelia seems very sad," Anneke says. "Is she homesick?"

"That's part of it. She lost her parents and two brothers in a fire a few years ago. She's lonely and grieving. Now she has to deal with all the challenges of moving to a new country."

"I wish I could talk to her. I would like her to know that I want to be her friend. It's so hard, though, with the language differences."

I am relieved when Cornelia returns in time for dinner, as she promised. A few hours later, we are just finishing up the dishes when Derk ducks through my kitchen door. He lights up like the dawn on a summer day as he greets Anneke. "It's great to see you again, Anneke! Welcome back!" I can tell that he longs to embrace her, but he holds back. "Did you know she was coming, Tante Geesje?"

"Not until I received her telegram yesterday afternoon."

"How have you been, Derk?" she asks him. Her cheeks have turned pink as if sunburned by his glow.

"Great! How about you?"

I listen to them make small talk and see that the embers of their feelings for each other are being stirred into flames all over again. And while a warm fire on a cold day can be a good thing, I've also seen fire's destructive side. I don't want either of these precious children to get hurt. If they were to fall in love, I don't see how Anneke could possibly survive in Derk's world as a pastor's wife. Yet I'm glad she can compare William to a wonderful man like Derk before she makes a mistake she may regret.

"I came to Holland to ask Oma for some advice," I hear her saying. "I would value your advice, too, Derk."

"Hey, I have an idea," he says. "Since tomorrow is Saturday, how about if I borrow a horse and carriage and take all three of you ladies for a ride out to the lake? The hotel isn't busy this time of year. And I don't think Cornelia has seen Lake Michigan yet, has she?"

"That would be very nice of you, Derk. Thank you," I say. "Arie might let you use his rig. Cornelia handled his horse very expertly today." I translate his words into Dutch for Cornelia, and everyone seems enthused by the idea. I don't tell Derk, but I already know that I won't be going along. He can advise Anneke in ways that I can't, and say things she needs to hear that I can't say. I fear she is making a mistake in marrying William, but she needs to reach that conclusion herself, not through my meddling.

"Great!" Derk says. "Let's get started right after lunch."

CHAPTER 12

Anna

HOLLAND, MICHIGAN

I wish I could communicate better with Cornelia. She lay so still in the bedroom we shared last night that I wondered at times if she was even breathing. She is six years younger than me, yet she seems twenty years older. I've been so caught up in my own problems that I've barely considered how my arrival has inconvenienced her. I must do better at including her.

She sits between Derk and me as the three of us drive out to the Hotel Ottawa on the lakeshore. I'm grateful that Cornelia serves as a buffer. I didn't realize until Derk walked through Oma's kitchen door last night how strong my feelings are for him. Even now I can feel my heart thumping beneath my ribs whenever he looks at me.

"I understand that congratulations are in order," he says as we cross the bridge over the Black River. "Tante Geesje tells me you're getting married in a few months." The reminder makes my stomach flip. The trees are shedding their leaves, which means that winter is coming. So is my wedding in January. I'm not ready.

"Yes, everything is happening so fast," I tell him. "I would love for you to come to Chicago with Oma for the wedding if you can get away in January." And yet I hope that he doesn't come. I try to picture Derk in the grand dining room of William's new house, and I wince at how out of place he will feel among the other guests in their gowns and tuxedoes.

"I'm glad you and your fiancé were able to work out your differences," he says. "I hope you'll be very happy together."

"I'm sure we will be, even if happiness in our social circle looks a little different from what a happy marriage looks like to you."

"That's probably true." Derk glances at me, and I'm aware that my heart is keeping rhythm with the horse's hooves on the hard-packed road. "I guess what I really want to say is that I hope you and your husband will find God's grace and peace and accomplish all His purposes for both of you."

"Thank you." My throat closes with emotion, and the words come out so softly I'm not sure Derk hears me. I clear away the lump and say, "Oma assures me that I'll find His purpose if I keep asking, but I'm not certain she realizes that my life isn't my own to control. My parents have made decisions for me all my life, and William will make them once he becomes my husband. I will face countless expectations and obligations as his wife, and my time won't always be my own to control as I please."

"We all have expectations placed on us, Anneke, no matter what our job is. I'll also face a host of obligations as the pastor of a church. I guess the key is to let God be in control of our lives instead of other people. For example, I know it's God's will for me to be a pastor, so even with a congregation full of expectations, He's the voice I should listen to because my life is ultimately under His control. The same is true for you. If it's God's will for you to marry William, then you can know that God is ultimately in control."

I feel my body relax as Derk's words bring a measure of relief about my future. "Thank you. It helps to think of it that way. I know my marriage will rescue my parents from the same financial disaster that befell another Chicago family I heard about. And I'm certain that God would want me to honor them by helping that way. Perhaps it's also His will that I support William's political future. Not only can he accomplish a great deal of good in that role, but maybe I can become an advocate for Chicago's poorest families."

"Good," he says, smiling again. "I'm very happy for you, Anneke."

I turn away from Derk, fighting the attraction that I feel for him, knowing that it's wrong when I'm engaged to another man. I concentrate on the journey, which offers little glimpses of Black Lake along the way. We both try to talk to Cornelia, but it's hard for all three of us to break through the language barrier. At last the view opens up, and I see the sparkling water and the sprawling hotel where I stayed. The cottages on the hill in the distance look tightly shuttered. The large hotel across the lake looks nearly empty. There are no huge steamships from Chicago anchored near the docks. Derk ties our horse to the hitching post and helps Cornelia and me down from the seat. His hands feel warm and strong on my waist as he lifts me. "Want to walk down by the water?" he asks.

"Yes, let's do that." He says something to Cornelia in Dutch, pointing and gesturing, but her puzzled expression tells me she doesn't understand.

We walk along the shore of Black Lake, passing the place where Derk and I first met. The boats and canoes that were tied up near the dock all summer have been stored away for the season. Cornelia walks a few steps ahead of us as we follow the shoreline and the edge of the channel that leads out to Lake Michigan. Three fishermen are casting their lines into the water, and Derk pauses to talk to them and ask what they've caught. The lighthouse stands sentry across the channel, and whitecaps dot the waves on Lake Michigan in the distance. But I'm not here to sight-see. I desperately need advice, and I trust Derk to be honest with me.

"What bothers me the most about my life," I say when we start walking again, "is that it's a life of excess when others have so little. I feel very guilty about it."

"How much of your wealth is truly yours to give away?" Derk asks after thinking for a moment. "And how much of it belongs to other people—to your parents or your fiancé?"

"I suppose none of it really belongs to me."

"Then you have no reason to feel guilty. You can be generous with what you own, but you can't force others to be generous. We'll each give an account one day for the way we've used what was entrusted to us. And while you may not have your own money to give away, you can distribute kindness and compassion wherever you go."

I gaze up at him, my heart full. "Thank you, Derk. You'll make a wonderful pastor."

He takes a deep breath and lets it out with a sigh. "Well, as your friend and not as a future pastor, I want to add that I hope you and William truly love each other."

In an instant my peace vanishes, replaced by unease. I'm not at all certain that I love William or that he loves me. Yet I feel the need to defend my decision to marry him. "We discussed this over the summer, Derk, and I explained that love isn't important in the world I live in."

"Love is important in everyone's world," he replies. He seems very certain.

"William and I are very fond of each other. He treats me very well. And I'm confident that our love will grow over time if we nurture it. Romantic love isn't nearly as important as a lifetime of commitment to each other."

"That's probably true, but you deserve to spend your life with a man who truly loves and cherishes you. A man who believes that your hopes and dreams are just as important as his own. Someone who encourages you to pursue them. The Bible says that husbands should love their wives the same way that Christ loved the church and gave Himself up for her."

I have no answer to that. I don't think William will ever be that kind of husband. "How about you, Derk?" I say, trying to take the attention off myself. "Is there someone special in the picture for you?"

He waves away the question. "I've been much too busy with my studies to meet anyone. But I know that time is short, and many churches won't even consider calling a young pastor who isn't married."

"Why not? That seems unfair."

"Well, for one thing, they think I'll be too distracted if I'm focused on finding a bride instead of the needs of my congregation. But the main reason is because a pastor's wife plays such a huge role in the church. It's important that she fits in with the congregation, too."

We stop walking for a moment and stand facing each other while Cornelia continues on. When she is some twenty feet away from us, she suddenly turns toward the water and steps forward as if she doesn't realize that she is dangerously close to the edge of the shipping channel. She is about to fall in.

"Cornelia, look out!" I shout. But she doesn't stop. I watch in horror as she drops into the deep water with a splash. "Derk!" I scream. "Cornelia fell in! Help her! She fell in!"

Derk whirls around and we run to where Cornelia stood a

moment ago. She has disappeared beneath the dark waves. "Go get help, Anna!" Derk says as he shrugs off his jacket and kicks off his shoes. Then he jumps over the edge into the water to save her.

For a terrible moment I stand motionless as fear paralyzes me. Derk's head briefly appears above the surface as he draws another breath, then he goes under again. He needs my help! I remember the fishermen we just passed, and I lift my skirts to keep from tripping over them as I race back, shouting to them. "Help! Our friend fell into the channel! Help us, please!" The fishermen lay down their poles and follow me to where Derk dropped his shoes and jacket. I peer over the edge, and I'm relieved to see that Derk has found Cornelia. He paddles frantically with one arm while holding Cornelia's head above the water with the other. Then they vanish as a wave washes over them, swallowing them up. Cornelia's heavy skirt and coat are probably dragging them both down. In an instant, I relive the shipwreck and the terrible feeling of being pulled under the icy water, unable to breathe beneath the cold waves. I recall how the water seemed to grab Mama and me and drag us to the bottom. I feel like I can't breathe.

One of the fishermen lies down on his stomach and stretches out his hand to try to reach them. The distance is too far. "Run up to the hotel and get more help," the other fisherman says. "Tell them to bring warm blankets."

I race across the grass to the hotel, shouting for help. By the time I stumble up the steps and yank open the main door, I'm panting so hard I can barely speak. "Help us, please!" I say to the desk clerk and a porter. "Someone has fallen into the channel and my friend jumped in to save her. We need help pulling them out. And bring warm blankets!" I remember the weight of the quilt that one of my rescuers wrapped around my shoulders after the shipwreck, and the warmth of the fire they built for us on the beach. *Please, Lord! Don't let anything happen to Derk and Cornelia*, I pray.

It seems to take forever, but four hotel workers drop what they're doing and gather supplies to race back with me. We're in time to help the fishermen pull Cornelia out of the water and onto dry land. We quickly wrap a blanket around her. She is shivering violently and coughing. Her face is deathly white, her lips purplish-blue. They pull Derk out next and drape a blanket around him. The men are talking to Cornelia, asking if she is all right. "She doesn't speak English," Derk tries to tell them, but he is shivering so hard he can barely talk. The hotel clerk lifts Cornelia in his arms and carries her up to the hotel, which seems miles away.

Two of the porters support Derk and propel him along, too. "What happened?" one of them asks. "Did the girl slip and fall?"

"I guess so," Derk says. "I didn't see it happen."

But I did, and I know that Cornelia didn't slip. I can't erase the terrible image of her walking forward as if there was an invisible bridge across the channel that only she could see. I watched Cornelia deliberately step off the edge and plunge down into the water. What I don't understand is why.

Everyone is exhausted by the time we reach the lobby. Someone adds more wood to the fire, and we stand around the lobby fireplace enjoying the warmth. The porters find some spare clothes for Derk and Cornelia, and they change into them in the back office. They drape their wet ones in front of the fire to dry. Cornelia is still coughing up water. "You might want to see a doctor when you get back to town," one of the workers advises. Everyone is discussing how she might have slipped, but I remain silent—and baffled. I know it wasn't an accident.

"I don't suppose you know how to drive a carriage?" Derk asks me when he and Cornelia are finally warm and dry.

"I'm sorry, but I've never driven one before. I don't know how to handle a horse." Cornelia says something in Dutch, but Derk shakes his head. "What did she say?" I ask.

"She says she can drive us, but I think I'd better do it. She's pretty weak." She and Derk are still swaddled in blankets as we unhitch the horse. We huddle on the seat with Cornelia between us for the ride home. Once again, she mumbles something in Dutch and Derk answers her.

"Now what did she say?" I ask. I'm wondering if she is going to confess what she did.

"I think she's trying to apologize for causing trouble. I told her the accident wasn't her fault."

But it wasn't an accident. Should I tell Derk what I saw? He risked his life to save her, so he deserves to know the truth. I hesitate, but in the end I decide to confide in Oma first, leaving it up to her whether or not to tell Derk. Either way, he's a hero.

"That was a very brave thing you did today," I say. "You risked your life for her."

"Anyone would have done the same. Fortunately, I'm a strong swimmer."

"You could have frozen to death."

"That's why I had to act fast, or Cornelia would have frozen to death, too."

She grips Derk's arm all of a sudden and talks rapidly to him, shaking her head as if pleading with him. Derk doesn't seem to understand. "Can you figure out what she's saying?" I ask.

"Something about her grandfather. I don't think she wants him to know what happened."

I think I know why, but I remain silent. Cornelia has seemed sad, but I can't imagine despair so profound that she would choose to die in such a horrible way. My problems seem trivial in comparison, and I'm ashamed for complaining about them. I wish I could communicate with Cornelia so she would know I want to be her friend. But all I can do is hold her hand in mine as we ride home. Her slender fingers are as cold as ice.

CHAPTER 13

Geesje

HOLLAND, MICHIGAN

I'm watering my plants by my front porch when Arie's horse and carriage pulls up in front of my house. I'm surprised to see Anna, Derk, and Cornelia returning so early—but I quickly see that something is wrong. Derk is driving, not Cornelia, and the two of them are damp and bedraggled and swaddled in blankets. All three of them look pale and frightened.

"What happened?" I ask as I hurry toward them.

"Cornelia fell into the channel," Derk replies. My heart plunges. Was it an accident or another suicide attempt? Guilt floods through me. I should have been there to watch over her, even if it was an accident. I wanted the three of them to have time alone together, but I should have gone along to keep a close eye on Cornelia as I promised her grandfather I would do.

Derk jumps down first, the blanket slipping from his shoulders as he ties up the horse. He helps Cornelia and Anneke down. Cornelia is shivering and coughing. "You poor girl!" I say as I try to take her into my arms. She wiggles free. She looks as though she wants to run and hide.

"Please don't tell my grandfather what happened," she says, glancing at Derk's house next door. "I don't want him to know. He'll be angry with me."

"I can't imagine him being angry because of an accident. He cares about you."

"I don't want him to worry. Please?"

"Go sit by the fire in the kitchen, and I'll be there in a moment to make tea." I turn to see about the others as she hurries into the house.

"I'll drive the carriage back," Derk tells me.

"No, let it wait. Go home and change your clothes and warm up. A hot bath will help take off the chill. We'll worry about the carriage later."

He nods and picks up the blanket that has fallen from his shoulders. "I'll be back in an hour or so," he says. "Take care of Cornelia, Tante Geesje. And Anneke is pretty shaken, too."

"I will." I'm in a hurry to get inside and build up the fire, but Anneke stops me on the front porch.

"Oma Geesje?" she whispers. "Can I tell you something?"

"Of course."

"I saw what happened and . . . and it wasn't an accident." My heart plunges again as I wait to hear more. "Cornelia walked right off the edge into the water as if . . . as if she knew exactly what she was doing. I shouted for her to stop, but she just kept going. Derk and I weren't paying attention to her and . . . and it happened so fast I couldn't stop her. I'm so sorry."

"You have no reason to be sorry. Come inside and warm up

with a cup of tea. You've had a terrible shock. We'll talk more about it later."

"I didn't tell Derk what I saw," Anneke says. "He doesn't know the truth. He was a hero to jump in and save her that way."

"Thank goodness they're both okay."

We go inside, and I shove more wood into my kitchen range, letting it heat until the flames roar and the water in the tank and in the teakettle is boiling hot. None of us says much as we sip our tea. Anneke helps me haul buckets of hot water to fill my bathtub. Cornelia seems too weak to move, so I lead her into my little bathroom and help her undress. Her clothing smells rank and fishy like the lake. Her slender body looks skeletal as she slips into the hot water. I sit beside her on a stool, holding the soap and towel and a cloth for washing.

"It wasn't an accident, was it, Cornelia?" I say softly. She doesn't admit it or deny it, but her eyes fill with tears. "You can trust me with the truth, lieveling."

"I don't want my grandfather to know. Please don't tell him."

"I can't make that promise until you tell me more. He's responsible for you and has a right to know what's going on in your life." She sinks further into the water, her lips quivering. "Can you tell me why you did it?" I ask. When she finally replies, her voice is whisper soft.

"Grandfather wants me to marry Derk." I bite my lip to keep from reacting. His plan infuriates me for Cornelia's sake as well as Derk's. I wait, hoping she will continue. "He doesn't want Derk to know the truth about my past. But today when I saw Anneke and Derk together . . . I couldn't understand what they were saying, but I saw how much they love each other. . . . It's not right to trick Derk into marrying me without telling him the truth. Or to trick any other man into it, either."

"Derk will make up his own mind about who he marries, no matter what your grandfather wants or thinks. And I doubt very much if Derk will marry Anneke, either. She is engaged to a gentleman in Chicago. Her wedding will take place in a few months. She and Derk aren't a couple."

Cornelia sinks lower in the water. "They should be."

Her words dismay me. I'm not the only one who recognizes their feelings for each other. They are plain to see, in spite of the fact that Cornelia couldn't understand their conversation. I only hope that Anneke doesn't leave here even more confused than when she arrived.

"That still doesn't explain why you did what you did today, Cornelia. Won't you please tell me? I can't imagine a secret so big that it's driving you to end your life."

She shakes her head. "Grandfather doesn't want me to tell anyone. He made me promise."

"Well, he was wrong to do that. The story of your past is yours alone to share or to keep secret. It's not up to him to make that decision for you, especially if holding it inside your heart is driving you to despair. I would do anything to help you change your mind about killing yourself. Your secret is safe with me, Cornelia." She leans forward and ducks her head beneath the water for a moment. When she lifts it out again, her hair is streaming. Water and tears wash down her face.

I recall the timid little chipmunk that once dug a hole beside my back steps. With time and patience, I was able to coax it to trust me, and if I sat very still it would scurry up to feed from my hand. It's that way now with Cornelia as I wait for her to decide if she will trust me.

At last her story pours out like water that has been held back for much too long. . . .

150

Cornelia

I was in my bedroom, drawing a picture on my sketchbook, when Mama interrupted me. "It's time to go, Cornelia. Is your bag packed?"

"No. I told you I don't want to go." The drawing was a birthday present for my school friend, and I needed to get it just right.

Mama crossed the room, her hand raised as if preparing to slap my face. "Don't you dare tell me no! Your father is waiting to drive you into town. And the meal I made for the Vander Werfs' supper has finished cooking. Like it or not, you're going. Right now!"

I didn't move. The Vander Werfs already had seven unruly children, and Mrs. Vander Werf had just given birth to another one. "Why do I have to go? Why can't someone else help her?"

Before I could blink, Mama snatched the drawing book from my hand, then grabbed my arm and yanked me to my feet. "You're going. Don't make me take the switch to you!"

"But I don't want to go! I don't like doing other people's dirty work!"

"And I don't like having a daughter who is selfish and lazy." Mama dragged me into the front room of our farmhouse and shoved me toward the door. "Put your shoes on. And mark my words, Cornelia, God will punish you if you don't change your ways." She had told me that before—whenever I hid behind the barn instead of coming when she called me, or when I snuck off to ride our mare instead of finishing my chores. This time Papa heard her, too, as he came inside to get the food Mama had prepared.

"Don't tell her that," he said. "God isn't vengeful. He doesn't punish us for things like that. I won't raise our children with guilt and shame the way my father raised me."

"Well, it's time for Cornelia to grow up. She needs to be responsible and show some concern for others."

"I'm sure she will grow into a lovely woman. But right now, she's still a child. We can't expect her to act like an adult. There will be plenty of time for her to grow up."

"I promised Mrs. Vander Werf that Cornelia would come and help. She needs to obey me."

Papa smiled as he tilted his head toward the door, motioning for me to go outside where the wagon was waiting. "Yes, I also expect her to go. But she didn't volunteer for this task, so we can hardly expect her to be cheerful about it." I climbed onto the seat while he set the pot in the back of the wagon, wedging it next to a basket of apples so it wouldn't spill. "I know you don't want to go," he said. "But it would please your mother and me if you did this kindness. The Vander Werfs need our help. And it's only for two nights."

"May I drive?" I asked as he walked around to the front and untied the reins.

He handed them to me as he climbed up beside me. "Of course, lieveling." We lived a mile outside of the village on a little plot of land with a garden, a chicken coop, and a small barn for our cow and our mare, Suiker. I often fought with my mama, who had very strong opinions about how I should behave. But Papa took my side and let me be myself. He knew that I liked to draw, so he gave me paper and drawing pencils for my thirteenth birthday. "The Netherlands may be a tiny country," he said, "but we've produced some very fine artists. Perhaps you'll be the next one."

The Vander Werf children ran out to greet me when I arrived, shouting and bickering and tugging on my hands. I didn't ever want to get married if it meant having this many children. Mrs. Vander Werf seemed happy to see me. I hated all the work and the noise, but Papa was counting on me, and I didn't want to disappoint him. I went inside and got to work.

During the night, the entire household woke up when the village church bell started clanging. "There must be a fire somewhere," Mr. Vander Werf said. He pulled his trousers on over his nightclothes, grabbed a bucket, and left. I put all the children back to bed while their mother nursed the baby. Then I went back to sleep, too.

I was stirring a pot of porridge for breakfast the next morning when Mr. Vander Werf returned. He wasn't alone. Our dominie and his wife were with him. The expressions on their faces made my heart race. They asked me to come outside with them, and the dominie's wife took my hands in hers. "It was your house that burned last night, Cornelia. I'm so sorry, but all is lost."

"What do you mean? Where's my mama and papa?" I felt like I was in a dream. Any minute I would wake up and everything would be okay.

"I'm so sorry. . . . They didn't escape in time. They're in heaven now. Your brothers, too."

"No!" I screamed. "I don't believe you!" I felt so dizzy I feared I would fall over. I remembered Mama's warning that God would punish me for being selfish, and I screamed again. Why hadn't I listened to her? Why hadn't I been nicer to her? Mama had been angry with me when I left, and I had been angry with her. Our last words to each other had been sharp ones. I pulled my hands free and turned to run. I wanted to race all the way home and untangle the mess I had made yesterday. I would tell Mama I was sorry for talking back to her. She would smooth my hair from my forehead and tell me she forgave me.

I took only a few stumbling steps before the dominie grabbed my arm, stopping me. He held it so tightly I couldn't leave. "We contacted your grandfather, and he is on his way here. You can come home to the manse with us while we wait for him."

"But I need to stay here and help Mrs. Vander Werf. Mama promised her I would stay." I was convinced that everything would be different if I stayed and worked hard. They would find out they had made a mistake. It wasn't my house that had burned after all. God would change His mind about punishing me. But the dominie's wife wrapped her arm around my waist and made me walk with her to her house beside the church. I couldn't seem to breathe, as if my lungs were filled with water. I was drowning in guilt.

Late that afternoon my grandfather arrived, a man I barely knew. He had never visited our farm because he was always busy with his church in a different province. I remember visiting him a few times when Papa was on holidays from school, but after we moved to the farm a few years ago and had animals to care for, it was hard for our family to get away. Even as a young child, I could tell that Mama didn't like my grandfather. My kind, gentle papa seemed to shrivel up and grow smaller when he was around him, which made me wary of him, too. I remembered an argument I overheard between them one night that woke me from a sound sleep. I couldn't hear what Papa was saying, but Grandfather's voice and his mocking tone had been loud and clear as he mowed Papa down like a field of grain.

Grandfather and our dominie conducted the funerals two days later. As we gathered in the church hall afterward, Mrs. Vander Werf put her arm around my shoulders and said, "Would you like to come and live with us, Cornelia? Our children adore you, and although we couldn't pay very much, we could give you room and board." It was the very last thing I wanted to do. But it would be a fitting punishment for defying my mother. I knew I deserved it. "That way, you could still attend the village school where all your friends are," she added. And where the memories of my family and our home would surround me. I was about to say yes, but Grandfather had overheard her, and he replied first.

"Cornelia is coming to live with me," he said. "All we have left, now, is each other." It seemed like an odd thing to say. But neither Mama nor Papa had any relatives who were able to take me in.

The people from our church collected some clothes to replace the ones I'd lost, and the dominie's wife packed them in a bag for me. My favorite books, my sketchbook, and all my drawings were gone forever. I never finished the birthday present for my friend. "What about our animals?" I asked, panicked at the thought of leaving them behind. "And our mare, Suiker?"

"They will all be sold," Grandfather replied. "There is no place to keep them where I live."

"Please let me keep my horse. Please!"

Grandfather shook his head. "It isn't possible."

The night before I left the village forever, I begged Dominie's wife to take me back to see our farm one last time. I needed to make certain it was really gone, and that everyone had died. She agreed to take me, but Grandfather wouldn't allow it. "It would serve no purpose," he said. "Cornelia would be left with a horrible image that she never could erase. Much better to remember everything the way it once was."

Instead, what I remember is the fight I had with Mama. How she called me lazy and selfish and said God would punish me if I didn't change.

In the morning we traveled by train to the next province where grandfather lived. I hated it there. A housekeeper came during the day to clean and wash our clothes and cook simple meals, but Grandfather was always at the church. I hardly ever saw him. I had no friends in the new school, and I wasn't interested in anything the teachers had to say. They were terrible teachers, not at all funny and interesting like my papa had been.

I should have died in the fire that night, not my family. I'm the one who was lazy and selfish. It wasn't fair that God killed good people like my parents and my little brothers just to punish me.

I wished I was dead, too.

Geesje

"God isn't punishing you, Cornelia," I say as her story ends and her voice fades into silence. She looks up at me for the first time since beginning. "Didn't your grandfather or anyone else explain to you that God doesn't do things like that?"

"Then why are they all dead and I'm alive?"

"We may never know the reason until we get to heaven. But I'm certain that God isn't punishing you for not wanting to take care of those children. Our heavenly Father isn't like that."

"He isn't good and loving like people say He is, either. At least not to me." The bitterness in her voice makes me cringe.

"Please give Him another chance to show you His love, Cornelia. Let Him show you that you're wrong about what happened. And in the meantime, please don't try to end your life again."

A shudder rocks through her. "I'm tired of talking," she says.

I swish my hand through the water to test the temperature. "Yes, your bathwater is growing cold. It's time to get out." I hand her the towel, and she stands to climb out. She is alarmingly thin.

When she's dressed in clean clothes again, she comes into the front room where Anneke and I are talking and sits on my sofa. I bring her an extra shawl and another warm blanket, but her lips still have a bluish tinge to them. I pick up my tabby cat and place her on Cornelia's lap.

"I'm going to ask you a question, Cornelia, and I would like you to think about the answer. If you could talk to your mama and papa right now, do you think they would wish you had died in the fire that night along with them? Or do you think they would be happy that you lived when everyone else was lost?" Cornelia closes her eyes as if the light in my front room is too painful to bear. I wait a moment, then say, "I know I would gladly give up my life if it meant that my children or grandchildren had a chance to live a long, full life."

She opens her eyes again and begins stroking the cat, making him purr like a little motor. "I'm sorry Derk had to jump into the water for me. Will he be all right?"

"I'm sure he will be. He's young and strong. But do you think he would have risked his life to jump in and save you if he didn't believe that you were worth saving?"

"I'm sorry I ruined your visit with Anneke." She looks over at Anneke, then quickly looks away.

"You didn't ruin anything, lieveling." I take Cornelia into my arms, but she doesn't return my embrace.

"I think I'll rest now," she says, pulling free.

Anneke and I go into the kitchen, and I get out flour and eggs to mix up a batch of *pannenkoeken* for our supper. Tomorrow is Anneke's last day with me, and we talk about what we would like to do together before she has to leave. I can tell she is worried about Cornelia and disturbed by what she witnessed. "Do you need to talk about what happened today, lieveling?" I ask her.

"I've never seen anything like it," she says. "Do you know why Cornelia did it, Oma?"

"I don't know all of the reasons, and there's not much I can say without betraying Cornelia's confidence. But I'm very sorry she put you and Derk through that. It wasn't fair of her to involve you. Even so, I'm glad you were there to rescue her."

"Are you going to tell Derk the truth?"

"When the time is right, yes." I recall Marinus's plan for Cornelia to marry Derk, and I feel angry with the dominie all over again. As if marriage and a houseful of children would make all of Cornelia's problems vanish. How little he understands her.

Later that night I lie in bed, trying to put all the pieces of Cornelia's story together, and there is one piece that doesn't seem to fit. Her grandfather called her rebellious and unruly, but nothing in Cornelia's story confirms that. She is obviously angry with God, but she sat quietly beside me in church last Sunday. Marinus said they had to leave the Netherlands because of the gossip, but were people talking about her suicide attempt? How did they learn about it? And why didn't she mention her first suicide attempt when she told me her story?

Marinus abandoned his calling as a minister to immigrate to America, and I wonder if he was trying to make amends for ignoring Cornelia's grief and pain for so long. Yet if he's trying to show his love to her now and convince her of God's love, he certainly isn't doing a very good job of it.

I can't talk to him about any of this because then he'll know that Cornelia broke her promise not to tell me about her past. But should I tell him what she tried to do today? He has a right to know that she is still thinking of killing herself. Yet I fear what his reaction may be. I'm alarmed that Cornelia sees death as the only way to end her pain and guilt.

I asked Cornelia to give God another chance, but I have no idea what part I should play in the process. I fall asleep praying for wisdom.

CHAPTER 14

Anna

CHICAGO, ILLINOIS

Our carriage and driver are waiting for me at the train station in Chicago when I return. I'm weary from traveling, but at least some of my questions and concerns have been laid to rest after talking with Derk and Oma. Cornelia's brush with death continues to haunt me.

"Thank you for understanding that I needed to get away for a few days," I tell my mother. I find her sitting in our little morning room with our social calendar and a pile of correspondence spread out on the table in front of her. She has drawn the curtains closed, shutting out the sunlight on this lovely fall afternoon. "I'm ready to resume all my social engagements this week. Don't we have a Literary Club meeting tomorrow? I was catching up on my reading for it on the train and—"

"Anna, sit down." From the expression on Mother's face, I

can only assume that someone has died. My heartbeat throbs in my ears as I perch on the edge of a chair.

"What's wrong? What happened?"

"Some disturbing rumors are being circulated about you, and your hasty trip out of town has only added fuel to the fire."

"What rumors? I haven't done anything wrong. Whatever it is I'm being accused of has to be a lie." I can't remain seated as my anger rises. "Clarice and those other women started it, didn't they? They're being spiteful because I scolded them for gossiping."

"The rumors aren't about your behavior, Anna. The scandal is about your background."

"My background?"

"It's all over town that your mother was a harlot who gave birth to you in disgrace."

"What?!"

"They say there is proof that her husband died a few years before you were born."

I sink down on the chair again as my knees go weak. "But . . . but no one knows about that except me."

Mother catches her breath. "The rumors are true?"

"Well, yes. . . . Jack Newell died in a railroad accident and probably isn't my father. But how did everyone find out?"

"I tried to warn you not to dig up the past. I knew something like this would happen." The color rises in Mother's cheeks. She picks up an envelope to fan her face. I've rarely seen her this upset. "Mrs. Wilkinson is appalled, as she has every right to be."

"But I didn't tell anyone what I'd learned—not even you or William or Father."

"Your father doesn't know anything about the rumors, nor do I want him to find out. He has enough to worry about without this."

"I don't understand how this could have happened unless the Pinkerton agents told somebody."

"If you could hire them, someone else could, too."

"Who would be spiteful enough to do something like that?" As soon as I ask the question, I think of Clarice Beacham. William's sister warned me that Clarice would do anything to win William back.

"What difference does it make where the story came from?" Mother asks. "Everyone has heard it by now, and the fact that we can't deny it makes it even worse. The Wilkinsons were hoping we could disprove the rumors."

"My mother was not a harlot!"

"Can you prove it?"

"No, but maybe if we rehired the detectives, they—"

"And let even more rumors out of Pandora's Box? Absolutely not!"

I take a deep breath, struggling to calm myself. "Is William angry with me? Is he calling off the engagement?"

"I haven't talked to William. But his mother is demanding to know if there will be any more revelations that could taint his name, and this time she wants to hear it from you before the rest of society learns about it."

"But I don't know anything else! I did what you said and called off the search. And I never told a soul what I learned about Jack Newell's death. I still don't understand how someone found out about it."

"You can explain that to Mrs. Wilkinson when she pays us a visit tomorrow. You need to apologize to her for stirring all this up. In the meantime, you and I will be staying home for the rest of the week until this blows over. Let's hope people lose interest or that a better scandal comes along before it's time to send out the wedding invitations."

I go upstairs to my room, angry and frustrated and sick to

my stomach. I wish I never had to see those other women again or attend another silly event with them. How small-minded of them to spend time and energy trying to ruin me when there are so many more important problems here in Chicago.

I do my best to offer my sincere apologies to William's mother the next day, as Mother advised me to do. It feels like I'm apologizing for the circumstances of my birth, even though Mrs. Wilkinson must realize that I had no control over it. I tell her how sorry I am that I went against everyone's advice and raked up the past. And that I'm sorry the news was leaked—even though I still can't understand how it could have happened. Mrs. Wilkinson graciously accepts my apologies.

"Is William angry with me, too?" I dare to ask.

"You'll have to discuss that with him, dear. But he agrees with me that the two of you shouldn't be seen in public together until this blows over."

I fight back tears. William should be over here consoling me and letting me weep on his shoulder after my reputation has been tarnished so unfairly. Even if my birth does turn out to be shameful, I have never behaved disgracefully. What do my birth parents' actions have to do with me? They weren't the people who raised me. If William truly loved me, he should be taking my side, standing up to Clarice and anyone else who would dare to spread gossip about me. Instead, he's distancing himself from me as if his good image matters more to him than my feelings. I find myself hoping he does call off the wedding—that is, until I recall Father's financial problems.

Once my apologies have been offered and accepted, Mrs. Wilkinson says, "We feel it would be best if everyone forgets that you're adopted, Anna. It's already unfortunate that so much information is known about your background—which is one of the reasons why most adoptions are kept secret. Since we would rather not remind everyone at your wedding about your circumstances, we won't be inviting your birth mother's family to attend."

"But . . . but my grandmother—"

"We feel it would be best if she doesn't come. It would be difficult to explain to everyone who she is and how you are related to her. Besides, from what I understand, she doesn't have the means to buy a suitable gown for the occasion."

I'm so stunned I can't speak. Tears sting my eyes. They're telling me I can't share one of the most important events of my life with my dearest Oma?

"I agree with Mrs. Wilkinson," Mother says. "You have allowed enough unsavory information to be leaked already."

"But I didn't—!"

"We can't take a risk that your grandmother or any other relative will provide even more fodder for gossip."

"Oma would never do that!" The two women exchange looks.

"Do those people in Michigan know how wealthy William is?" his mother asks.

"They don't care about money."

"Don't be naïve, Anna. Anyone can be bought if the price is right."

I don't believe it for a moment, and I'm furious that they do. But what if William also believes it and refuses to allow me to see Oma after we're married? Fear makes me desperate. "Listen, let me rehire the detectives to find out who my real father is. It's possible that Mama remarried and that my birth was legitimate after all."

"Absolutely not!" Mother says. "This ends here and now."

"Who knows what else they might turn up?" Mrs. Wilkinson adds.

I can't recall ever being angrier. I return to my room after Mrs. Wilkinson leaves, and I'm too furious to even weep. I pace the room, then pull off my shoes and throw them across the room at my wardrobe with all my might. I hear a knock on my door a moment later and fear it's my mother. I don't want to talk to her right now. When I don't reply I hear a second knock.

"Miss Anna? It's Lucy. I-I heard a noise and I wondered . . . is there anything you need?"

"No. Just go away."

When I've calmed down enough to think clearly, I realize that the only way to resolve this mess so Oma will be welcome at my wedding is to clear Mama's name. But I will have to find another way to do it besides rehiring the Pinkerton detectives. Could I search by myself? After all, I have nothing else to do all week, since I'm banished from society until the scandal blows over.

I retrieve all of the agents' reports from my desk and pore over them for any details I might have missed, looking for a place to start. The reports raise more questions than they answer. According to the last one, Mama sued the railroad and was awarded a sum of money for her husband's death. But how did she learn that Jack Newell had died if she was hiding from him? How did she know that she was entitled to compensation as his widow? And where did she find the legal help she needed for a lawsuit? Hull-House didn't exist back then to help women like her. I study the report again and see that she was assisted by an attorney named James Blackwell. Might he have more information about Mama in his files and records?

The name Blackwell sounds familiar to me, and I recall that one of the wealthy young women in the Literary Club is named Florence Blackwell. I'm fairly certain that her father is a judge. Aren't judges usually attorneys? If Florence's mother is also a member of the club, I can find out what her father's given name is. I rummage in another desk drawer for the club directory— and there it is. Her mother's name is Mrs. James Blackwell. My heart skips a beat. Could he possibly be the same attorney who once helped my mother?

A small voice inside me tells me to let it go before I make everything worse. Florence Blackwell and her mother have surely heard the rumors about me by now, along with the rest of society. And how would I go about making an appointment to speak with Judge Blackwell? I put all the papers away and pick up my neglected Bible and try to read.

But I can't let it go. If I can find out which wealthy family Mama went to work for after she left the boardinghouse, maybe one of the servants there will know if she ever remarried. That's when I remember that Mrs. Marusak from the boardinghouse mentioned her niece—what was her name? I dig in my drawer again and find the paper Mrs. Marusak gave me with the name and address of her niece, Vera. I need to pay her a visit. She might know if Mama was pregnant with me at the time she left her husband, and then we could prove that Jack really was my father. Perhaps I'm older than everyone thought. Vera's address is in Chicago, but I have no idea where her street is located. I'll ask our driver to take me there tomorrow. Or perhaps I should take public transportation to avoid being recognized and stirring up even more gossip. I'm hesitant to go by myself, yet I don't want to involve the Pinkertons again. Could I ask one of our servants to accompany me? A very discreet servant?

I will be disobeying Mother's orders if I start digging for the truth again, but I need to clear Mama's name and salvage my reputation. I close my eyes and whisper a prayer, then ring the bell to summon Lucy.

"Do you know your way around the city?" I ask her after closing my bedroom door behind her. Her eyes go wide as if I'm locking her in jail.

"Most parts of it. Yes."

"And do you know how to use the public streetcars?"

"Yes . . . I guess so."

"Would you be able to help me find my way to this address tomorrow?" I show her the paper, and she studies it for a moment before nodding.

"I think so."

"Good. I could use your help. But you can't tell anyone—especially my mother."

We leave through the rear servants' door the following afternoon while Mother is resting. She is so distressed over this scandal that she is eating and sleeping poorly. I hope to discover some good news today for her sake. Lucy lets me borrow a shawl so I won't look too conspicuous, and we ride a streetcar and then a train. Mrs. Marusak's niece, Vera, lives in a working-class neighborhood near the stockyards. The air reeks of manure, and I can hear the distant lowing of cattle. Vera's apartment is above a saloon, but we find her in the basement scrubbing laundry. She is a frowsy-looking woman in her early forties who might have been pretty at one time. I'm surprised to realize that Mama would be about the same age if she had lived. Vera's fading brown hair spills from beneath her kerchief, and the front of her apron is damp and stained. She tells me that her husband manages the saloon and that she sometimes works there, too.

"Would you be willing to answer a few questions about my mother, Christina de Jonge Newell?" I ask her.

"As long as we can talk right here," she replies. "I need to get this laundry washed and hung up to dry, and it's already late in the day."

"Yes, of course." I pull Lucy's shawl a little tighter around my shoulders. The basement is damp and cold and smells of lye soap and bluing. There is no place to sit down.

"Christina and I were good friends, right from the start," Vera begins. "You resemble her, you know. She had the most beautiful golden hair I've ever seen. Like yours."

"Is there any chance that she was expecting me when you met her?"

"No." Vera snorts as if my question is ridiculous. I glance at Lucy, wishing she wasn't overhearing this. "Christina had just left her bum of a husband and was hiding from him. I helped her get a job in the same place I worked, and we shared an attic bedroom in the servants' quarters for over a year. I would have known about it if she was in a family way."

My hopes for proof that Jack was my father are dashed. I watch Vera work for a moment while I think what to ask next. Sweat runs down her face as she cranks the hand-wringer with one hand and feeds the cloth between the rollers with the other. It has never occurred to me to wonder how our servants wash my clothes. My garments simply reappear in my wardrobe and bureau drawers, clean and mended and neatly pressed.

"Um . . . do you recall the name of the family you and Mama worked for?" I ask.

"Certainly. The Blackwells." I freeze when I hear the name. "Herbert Blackwell was a big-shot judge, but the money to rebuild their new mansion right after the Chicago fire came from his wife's side of the family. Bessie Rockport Blackwell was a society matron."

"Were . . . were they any relation to James Blackwell?" I ask with my heart in my throat.

"He's their only surviving son. Their other two sons died young. The Blackwells also had two daughters a little younger than James."

"Was James a lawyer?" Vera looks up at me.

"How did you know?"

"An attorney named James Blackwell helped Mama win a settlement with the railroad after her husband was killed." Vera stops cranking for a moment and pushes a strand of sweaty hair out of her eyes.

167

"That's right. I remember now. Christina did come into a little pot of money, thanks to Mr. James."

"Can you remember anything else? What was he like?"

She gives a little laugh. "He was a very peculiar fellow who seemed to enjoy chatting with the servants more than with his rich society friends. Christina thought the world of him for helping her."

I scarcely dare to breathe. "Please tell me everything else you can remember."

Vera sighs and feeds another garment through the wringer. "Well, it all happened a long time ago, you know. . . ."

CHAPTER 15

Vera

CHICAGO, ILLINOIS
1872

I first met Christina early one Sunday morning when my aunt, who owned a boardinghouse in Cicero, brought her over to the mansion on Lakeshore Drive where I had just started working. "Christina needs our help," my aunt said. She told me all about Jack Newell and why Christina needed to hide from him. It so happened that Judge and Mrs. Blackwell had just moved into their grand new house, and they needed to hire a boatload of servants to keep it running. Christina went by her maiden name, de Jonge, back then, and of course she came with a good recommendation from my aunt after working at the boardinghouse for about a year. They hired her right away.

"Both of you girls will start at the bottom," the housekeeper, Mrs. Philips, told us. "You'll be beneath all of the other servants, but if you work hard and do what you're told, you can

169

earn your way up to a better position and more pay." Mrs. Philips wasn't really married, but she went by that name so the servants would respect her. She was like a little hornet, buzzing in and out of rooms and able to be everywhere at once. She had a pointy nose and a sharp tongue, and she carried a sting, too, if we didn't do exactly what she said as speedily as possible. Anna and I did all sorts of jobs—cook's helpers, scullery maids, dusting and cleaning and polishing the silver— whatever needed to be done. We were grateful for a job and a roof over our heads.

Our work kept us downstairs and out of sight most of the time, but not too long after we started working for the Blackwells, the judge called for someone to come up and build a fire in his study, where he was having an important meeting. The housekeeper sent Christina and me to do it. The fireplace burned coal, so we carried a scuttle full of it upstairs along with matches and kindling. The judge, his son, James, and five other gentlemen wearing dark suits and equally dark expressions were gathered around the table in the study, smoking cigars and talking in somber voices. We tiptoed into the room, trying hard not to draw attention to ourselves, but I was so nervous that I accidently dropped the coal shovel onto the stone hearth. The judge was sitting with his back to us, and the loud *clang* nearly made him jump out of his trousers. Christina tried to grab the shovel, but in the process, she knocked over the rack with all the brass fireplace implements and they fell onto the stone hearth with a terrible racket. "Stop that infernal noise!" Judge Blackwell shouted.

"We're sorry, sir . . . so sorry . . ." Christina said. Both of us were upset and eager to finish and get out of there. Neither one of us remembered to open the fireplace flue before lighting the fire. Smoke poured into the room. We tried desperately to douse the kindling, but the thick smoke caused a storm of coughing and shouting from the judge and his cronies. Christina and I scurried around like ants, opening windows and fanning the smoke with newspapers as we tried to undo the damage, but of course the men had to move to a different room.

"I suppose we'll both be looking for new jobs now," Christina said as we slunk back downstairs to the servants' quarters, our faces smudged with soot.

"And we won't be getting good references from Mrs. Philips, either," I added.

"No one is going to get fired," a voice behind us said. We turned, and there was the judge's son, Mr. James, following us downstairs. And he was laughing! "Do you have any idea how comical you girls looked, trying to chase out the smoke while my father shouted and sputtered? I've never seen a funnier sight!"

"We're so sorry—" Christina tried to say, but Mr. James stopped her.

"Don't worry about it. You already apologized. Tell me your names."

"I'm Christina, and she's Vera."

"Well, Christina and Vera, I'm sorry if my father frightened you. My parents are very old-fashioned, and they believe that servants, like children, should be invisible. In fact, my mother wanted to build secret passageways throughout this house so her servants could appear and disappear wherever they were needed without being noticed. She'd seen something like that in a castle over in Europe somewhere. I reminded her that this is America, not Europe, and that we aren't royalty. Our servants deserve to be treated with dignity and respect like other men and women."

It worried me that Mr. James had followed us all the way down to the servants' level, but I found out in the months that followed that he liked to spend time down there with the hired help. It made his parents furious, which is probably why he did it. He claimed that ordinary folk like us were more honest and trustworthy—and much more interesting—than his society friends. He was not much older than Christina and me, with a head of thick, wavy hair the same mahogany color as the woodwork throughout the mansion. Mr. James was good-looking, and he knew it. He loved to flirt with young servant girls like us and get us giggling. According to one of the parlor maids, James Blackwell was highly sought after as a future husband in society circles.

"If you two girls ever need anything, just let me know," he said with a wink that day, and he strolled outside through the back door to smoke a cigarette with the carriage driver.

We got so used to having Mr. James downstairs in the kitchen with us that we hardly noticed him after a while. He happened to be down there one morning, having a cup of coffee, when a messenger arrived at the back door. "I'm looking for Christina de Jonge," the man said, holding up an envelope. I was washing the breakfast dishes and Christina was drying them, and I saw her face turn pale. I knew she lived in fear that her husband would find her—she rarely left the house, even on her half-days off.

"Who is it from?" I asked.

"I don't know," the messenger said with a shrug. "Mrs. Marusak from the boardinghouse in Cicero asked me to deliver it." Christina set down the bowl she was drying and hurried to take the letter from him. Mrs. Philips appeared out of nowhere just then, so Christina stuck the envelope into her apron pocket to read later. Mr. James stopped her.

"Wait. I'm sure the letter must contain important news if it came all the way from Cicero this early in the day. Mrs. Philips won't mind if you take a moment to read it, will you, Mrs.

Philips?" The housekeeper shook her head—but I could see by her tight grimace that she did mind.

"The rest of you get back to work," she barked. "The Blackwells aren't paying you to stand around and gawk." I returned to my sink full of dishes, keeping one eye on Christina as she opened the envelope and pulled out a typewritten page. She looked it over, then let out a little cry before stumbling backward and slumping onto a kitchen chair. Mr. James was beside her like a shot.

"What is it? Are you all right, Christina?"

"No . . . I mean . . . I-I will be. I'm sorry." She started to rise, but James insisted she remain seated.

"Take a moment. I can see that you've received some bad news."

"Yes . . . There's been a death. . . ."

"Someone fetch her a glass of water," Mr. James said as he squatted beside her. I hurried to obey, hoping to get closer to see what the letter said. I didn't know if it was Mr. James' kindness or the news, but something had brought tears to Christina's eyes. The page fell to her lap as she took a drink, and I saw that it bore the letterhead of the Illinois Central Railroad. Mr. James must have spotted it, too.

"May I see it?" he asked. Christina nodded. She seemed too numb to speak. I returned to my task at the sink while Mr. James silently read the letter. Mrs. Philips hovered nearby, too, as nosy as the rest of us. Mr. James let out a little whistle when he finished. "I read about this railroad accident in yesterday's newspaper. Three men were killed. According to this letter, one of them was . . . your husband?"

Now it was my turn to be shocked. My hands flew to my mouth to stifle a cry. I wasn't sorry that her bum of a husband was dead, but Christina's secret was no longer a secret. She would be fired for lying about being unmarried, and maybe I would be fired along with her.

"Your husband?" Mrs. Philips echoed. "You told me you were single when I hired you."

"Now, now . . . I'm sure there's an explanation," Mr. James said.

"Oh, there's always some sort of excuse," Mrs. Philips said. She seemed oblivious to Christina's tears of grief. "These girls lie about being single in order to get a job, and then they go sneaking off to be with their husbands on their days off. First thing you know they're having a child, and I've wasted all my time training them."

"But I left my husband," Christina said. "I'm hiding from him . . . that is, I was hiding from him." She paused, wiping her tears. "He used to beat me, so I had to leave. I would never go back to him even if he begged, because I know he'll never change. And now I can't go back."

The room fell silent. No one ever talked about what went on behind closed doors. Many people believed a husband had a right to slap his wife around if she defied him. Christina wiped her tears again and straightened her shoulders as if gathering strength. "I'm sorry for not telling you the truth, Mrs. Philips." She stood, untied her apron, and handed it to the housekeeper as if certain she was about to be fired.

"Don't expect a recommendation—" Mrs. Philips began, but Mr. James interrupted her.

"You aren't going to be fired, Christina. Besides, you may not need this job anymore if you let me help you."

"What do you mean?"

"The Board of Admissions just notified me a week ago that I've passed the requirements to practice law in Illinois. I'm an attorney now. And according to what I read in the newspaper, the union believes the railroad was entirely to blame for the accident. You may be entitled to a settlement as his widow."

"But I don't have any money to hire you."

"Don't worry about that. With a lawsuit as big as this one, I could make a name for myself in this city—if you'll trust me to handle your case, that is."

Christina agreed. What choice did she have? James Blackwell was her employer. She put her apron back on and returned to the pile of dishes waiting to be dried while Mr. James bounded up the stairs two at a time, whistling a tune.

A few weeks passed and nothing seemed to happen with the lawsuit. But I sometimes heard Christina crying at night after we turned out the lights. "I loved Jack and I thought he loved me," she said when I tried to comfort her. "I left my family and my home to be with him, and I know it broke my parents' hearts. I don't understand why Jack stopped loving me."

"Sounds like he was just no good," I told her. "An honorable man would have asked your parents for your hand, not run off behind their backs."

"It was my fault as much as Jack's. I loved him so much that he was all I could think about."

"Well, don't waste any more tears on him, Christina. There are plenty of better men out there. And you're still young and pretty."

Christina wouldn't be consoled. "I don't believe in second chances," she told me. "I won't marry again."

Then one day the lawsuit took off, with meetings and trips to the courthouse nearly every day and legal documents flying everywhere. Christina and Mr. James were together a lot for the next few weeks, which made Mrs. Philips grumble behind their backs. "How can I run a household with my servants taking time off to go here and there?" But she could hardly complain, since Mr. James was the one taking Christina away from her work.

One afternoon, Christina and I were polishing the silver together in the butler's pantry when Mr. James came bounding in, carrying on and on about some decision the judge made in their court case. I didn't understand a bit of it—but I did notice the way Christina's eyes sparkled as Mr. James talked. I watched more closely, and I could tell by the way she looked at him that she was falling for him. I warned her about it that night when we were alone in our attic room.

"Don't be a fool and go falling in love with Mr. James, Christina."

"I'm not," she insisted, but her face turned a pretty shade of pink in the lamplight. "He's helping me fight the railroad, that's all."

"I've heard plenty of stories about servants who have affairs with the rich folk, and they never end well."

"It's nothing like that. He's interested in this court case, not me. It's his big break, he says. Everyone will want to hire him if he wins." The more she denied her feelings, the prettier she looked.

"Mr. James is a handsome man, isn't he?" I asked to test her reaction. She didn't reply, but her cheeks turned from pink to red. "Ah, so you have noticed! I hope you won't listen to any of his sweet talk if he starts laying on the charm. The heir to the Blackwell family fortune would never marry someone like you."

"I know." She sounded a little sad, which worried me. But I had said my piece, so I let it go.

Late one afternoon, Mr. James came downstairs with a bottle of champagne and a huge grin on his face. "Time to celebrate!" he shouted. Christina was getting ready to take a tea tray upstairs, but he took the tray from her hands and set it aside, then picked her right up in the air, twirling her around. "We won, Christina! We won! The railroad agreed to our terms, and we've settled out of court. You'll be getting your money soon." He set her down again, then pulled her into his arms for a hug before finally releasing her. Those of us watching were shocked.

Who ever heard of an employer embracing his maid that way? Christina looked radiant, but I was certain it had nothing to do with winning the money.

Mrs. Philips came flying into the room a moment later. "The celebration will have to wait until our work is done, Mr. James. Your mother is waiting for her tea." She nodded to Christina, who picked up the tray again and headed for the stairs. She looked so rattled and thrilled and dizzy, I had no idea how she would be able to carry it. She was playing with fire, and I could only hope she wouldn't get burned.

Now that Jack Newell was dead, Christina didn't have to hide anymore. My aunt wanted her to come back to the boardinghouse, but Christina kept working for the Blackwells. Mr. James didn't spend as much time in the basement with all of us after the railroad hired him to work as one of their lawyers. "They want me on their side, not working for the union," he said when he told Christina the news. "Thank you for trusting me with your case."

About a year or so after Christina and I went to work for the Blackwells, I started going to dances at a little dance hall not far from the stockyards whenever I had a Saturday evening free. "Please come with me, Christina," I begged. "I know you'll have a lot of fun."

"I don't dance. I don't know how. We didn't go to dances in the town where I grew up."

"You like music, don't you? Just come along and have a lemonade or a beer and listen to the music. You never go anywhere or do anything, even though you don't have to hide from Jack anymore."

I convinced her to come. She was such a pretty little thing that I knew I would get a lot of attention if she was sitting alongside me. We were all dressed up and about to leave through the servants' door that first night when we ran into Mr. James, who was chatting with the stableboys and carriage drivers outside. "Don't you girls look pretty all dressed up! Where are you going?"

"Vera talked me into going to a dance with her over by the stockyards, Mr. James. I've never been to one before."

"It sounds like fun. Have a good time, you two."

It turned out that we did get a lot of attention that night, sitting at our little table together. A lot of men asked Christina to dance, but she turned them all down, insisting she didn't know how. Then I nearly fell off my chair when I looked up and there stood Mr. James, holding out his hand to Christina. "May I have this dance?" he asked. She was so surprised and flustered—and pleased—that for a moment she couldn't speak.

"I-I don't know how," she finally stammered. "I just came to hear the music."

"I'll teach you. It's easy. Come on." He took her hand and pulled her to her feet, and she didn't dare refuse. Nor did she want to. I watched them move around the floor in each other's arms, laughing as Christina kept stepping on his toes until she got the hang of it. Once they got started, neither of them seemed inclined to stop. Mr. James held her closer and closer as the evening wore on, and when they finally grew tired of dancing, they sat down at a table all by themselves. I saw them whispering and laughing and felt sick inside for Christina's sake. And more than a little jealous.

Mr. James drove both of us home in his carriage when the dance ended. The driver had been waiting outside for him all that time. Christina and I bid Mr. James good night by the back door, and I quickly pulled her by the arm all the way upstairs to our attic room so she wouldn't be tempted to linger with him. She had made a huge mistake when she married Jack Newell, and I needed to convince her not to make another one.

"You're playing with fire," I said as we got ready for bed.

"It was just a silly dance. One night of fun. It doesn't mean anything."

And maybe Christina was right. I don't recall seeing Mr. James at any more dances, nor did he spend time hanging around downstairs with the servants after that night.

Anna

CHICAGO, ILLINOIS
1897

As Vera tells her story, Lucy and I follow her out of the basement and into the weedy backyard where the clothesline is. The weak fall sunlight feels good after the damp cellar, but I want to cover my mouth and nose with my handkerchief to block out the overpowering odor of cattle drifting on the breeze. Vera doesn't seem to notice it. She continues talking as she pins clothes on the line to dry.

"Christina never came to another dance with me again, but I met my husband there on one of those Saturday nights and married him a few months later. Christina stood up with me before the justice of the peace, and I know she was happy for me. We hugged and said good-bye and promised to visit each other, but we never did."

"Did she keep working for the Blackwells after you left?" I ask.

"She did. She had worked her way up from scullery maid to parlor maid by then."

"Do you know when my mother stopped working there?"

"No, we lost touch. I was a giddy new bride, and Christina

179

insisted she wanted nothing to do with marriage after what happened the first time. I offered to set her up with one of my husband's friends, but she wasn't interested." Vera pauses and looks me over from head to toe as if seeing me for the first time. "So, you really are Christina's daughter. I can see the resemblance. I guess she found someone and got married after all. Who was the lucky man?"

"That's just it—I don't know. I was hoping you could tell me. My mama died when I was three years old, and I was adopted by a wealthy family. I don't have any information at all about who she married. Is there anything else you can recall that might help me find my father?"

Vera shrugs. "I told you everything I can remember. It all happened more than twenty years ago, you know."

I feel even more frustrated than when I arrived, and I have even more unanswered questions. Did anything ever come of her brief attraction to James Blackwell, or is that another dead end? "Do you know of anyone else who worked for the Blackwells who might remember Mama?"

Vera thinks for a moment. "The housekeeper, Mrs. Philips, might. But who knows if she still works for them after all these years. She would be in her seventies by now." The back door to the saloon opens, and a man hollers Vera's name. "Coming," she calls back. She pins up the last few clothes, hanging her wet apron on the line last of all, then bends to lift the empty laundry basket. "He needs my help in the saloon."

"I appreciate your taking time to answer my questions," I say as we walk across the tiny yard.

"Not at all. It was fun remembering those days before marriage and children and all this hard work." Vera smooths back her hair and reties her scarf. "I'd invite you in, but the saloon is no place for the two of you. It fills up pretty fast once the whistle blows and the men at the stockyards get out of work."

"Thanks again for your time, Vera." I hand her one of my calling cards. "If you remember anything else that might help me find my father, please let me know."

The trains and trolleys are crowded on the way back, the streets bustling with workers on their way home. I'm tempted to hire a cab rather than squeeze in alongside dozens of sweaty men, but I need to return home through the back door, not the front, so Mother doesn't see me. I stop Lucy as we finally reach the alleyway behind my house and say, "Please don't tell anyone where we went today or what you heard."

"Oh, I would never do that, Miss Anna. You can trust me." Lucy pretends to fasten an invisible button on her lips, sealing them closed. The gesture makes me smile, and I feel some of the tension from today's events begin to ease. I've learned some interesting things about Mama's life, and I'm starting to picture what those years must have been like for her after she left her home in Michigan. But I'm no closer to learning who my real father is. Tomorrow I'll pay a visit to the Blackwell mansion and see if Mrs. Philips is still the housekeeper there. Maybe she can point me in a new direction.

CHAPTER 16

Geesje

HOLLAND, MICHIGAN

Cornelia seems listless after her ordeal at the lake on Saturday. I have been praying about what to do to raise her spirits, and one detail of her story keeps coming to mind—the fact that she once enjoyed drawing. Maybe tomorrow we'll walk over to Eighth Street and buy a new sketchbook and some drawing pencils together. But right now, the warm afternoon is beckoning to me, and I think it would do Cornelia good to get out of the house.

"You and I are going for a walk," I tell her, not giving her the option of refusing. "The fall afternoon is too beautiful to miss." She puts on her shoes and jacket without complaint. I stop in my backyard to snip off the last of my hydrangea blooms, which have dried to a lovely shade of dusty rose on the bushes. She helps me carry the bouquets as we head up the hill to Pilgrim Cemetery. I'm out of breath when we reach the top.

"I always enjoy the view from up here, especially when the leaves begin to change colors. It's lovely, isn't it?" I turn to Cornelia, but she isn't looking down at the town. She's staring at all the gravestones. The sorrow in her eyes tugs at my heart. Have I made a mistake in bringing her here? Is she seeing herself in one of these graves? I try to distract her by pointing out where the Log Church once stood. "We worshiped here every Sunday until Pillar Church was completed, and—" She isn't listening.

"Who are these flowers for?" she asks.

"My loved ones are buried here. I'm going to put the bouquets in the urns on their graves." I quicken my pace as I walk through the graveyard to our family plot. I usually like to linger and recall happy memories of my loved ones, but I'm regretting my decision to bring Cornelia here. I point out the gravesites, as if offering a quick introduction to my family. "My mother and father are buried right here, side by side. This is my son Gerrit's grave—he died while fighting in the Civil War. My daughter, Christina, is buried here—she's Anneke's mother. And this one . . ." My breath catches. "This is where my husband, Maarten, is buried."

Cornelia looks at me, and the only way I can describe her expression is that it's one of sympathy and kinship. It's as if she finally believes that I understand and share her loss. "May I put the flowers on them?" she asks.

"That would be very sweet of you." She crouches down to arrange her bouquets in the urns, then takes mine and adds them, as well. Before I can thank her, she drops to her knees and curls forward, weeping as if she may never stop. Her primal cry of grief shudders through me. I kneel beside her with my arm around her huddled body and let her sob.

As I close my eyes and pray for her, I realize that Cornelia never had a chance to mourn at the graves of her parents and two brothers. The day after their funerals, she moved away from the village where they were buried to live with her grandfather. There was no opportunity to put flowers on their graves and honor them by remembering. No chance to mourn and grieve. Now, in the shared kinship of our losses, it's as if the graves of my loved ones represent her own. I don't coax her to stop crying. She needs to weep.

When her grief is spent, we sit on the grass and hold each other for a long time. "Jesus promised that if we believe in Him we will live, even though we die. Death isn't the end, Cornelia. We'll see all of our loved ones again." She leans back and wipes her tears with her fists, drying them on her skirt. "We'll come back again soon," I tell her. She helps me to my feet and holds my hand as we walk home together.

I'm puttering around my kitchen after supper that evening when Derk comes through my back door. "Hello, dear," I say as he kisses my cheek. "I'm happy to see you haven't suffered any ill effects from your plunge into the channel on Saturday."

"I'm fine," he says. "Is Anneke still here?" He looks around with a hopeful expression on his face.

"No, she left on the train yesterday morning."

His shoulders slump, and his grin disappears. "We hardly had a chance to talk."

"I know. Her visit was a quick one, but she seemed more at peace by the time she left than when she arrived. With all the excitement, I never asked if the two of you had a good visit."

"We had just started talking about serious things when Cornelia had her accident. I was really hoping to spend more time with Anneke."

"She leads a very busy life."

Derk releases a sigh. "How is Cornelia doing?"

"Why not go into the front room and ask her yourself? I'll translate if you need me to, but she needs to practice her English."

"Thanks. I will."

But before Derk gets to the door it occurs to me to speak with Dominie Den Herder about buying the sketchbook. It would be much better if he gave it to Cornelia as a gift, instead of it coming from me. The story she told me about their relationship was a sad one, and they could use a chance to heal. "Is Dominie Den Herder over at your house right now?" I ask Derk. He nods. "Will you keep Cornelia company for a minute while I go over and talk to him?"

"Sure." He continues through the door, and I hear them greeting each other in Dutch a moment later. I feel nervous as I shove my arms into my coat sleeves and walk the short distance to the Vander Veens' house. I'll need to be careful not to betray any of Cornelia's confidences, yet I believe her grandfather has a right to know that she tried to end her life last Saturday.

Marinus is in the kitchen adding wood to the stove, and he answers my knock. "Could we talk for a few minutes, Dominie?"

He opens the back door for me to come in. "Is this about what happened on Saturday?"

"Well, yes—"

He gives a grunt of disdain. "I was wondering when you would get around to telling me about it." He folds his arms across his chest as if preparing for a fight.

I'm taken aback by his gruffness. "What do you mean?"

"Derk told me about the incident but only after I saw his wet clothes all piled up, waiting to be washed. Imagine my surprise when I learned that Cornelia had fallen into the lake and nearly drowned. And that it had happened two days ago!"

"I wasn't there at the time, I'm sorry. But I thought—"

"Does the fact that you weren't there excuse you from telling me what happened to my granddaughter when she was in your care? Or at least sending Cornelia over here to tell me herself? Surely you found out about it on the day it happened, didn't you?"

"Cornelia asked me not to tell you. She was afraid you would worry."

"And her wishes are more important to you than mine? Even though the child is my granddaughter and my responsibility? It makes me wonder what other secrets the two of you are keeping from me."

"I wasn't keeping it a secret. I merely thought she should be the one to tell you about it when she was ready."

He huffs again. "Did Cornelia really slip and fall, or did she jump?"

"You should ask her that question yourself."

"Send her over, then. Good day, Mrs. de Jonge."

"Wait. I'm not finished talking with you." I have been standing all this time, since Marinus hasn't asked me to sit, but I pull out a chair and sit down on it now. The kitchen has become very warm, so I unbutton my jacket. "I came over because I want to help Cornelia, and there are some things I think we should discuss. She is still grieving the loss of her family and—"

"Nearly five years have passed. It's time she stopped dwelling on it."

It takes every ounce of willpower I possess not to blow up at this man. "Kindly stop interrupting me and let me finish." I pause a moment. "You can't put a time limit on grief, Dominie. The fact that Cornelia may still want to end her life must surely tell you that she hasn't recovered from the loss of her family. What she needs more than anything else right now is a reason to go on living."

"She has a new life here in America. She will get married and have children. Those are reasons enough."

"That may be what you want for her, but do you know what Cornelia wants?"

"I'm sure you can't wait to tell me."

His sarcasm threatens to ignite my temper. I struggle to tamp it down. "I don't have any idea what Cornelia wants. She hasn't told me. And you made it very clear that you resent me for prying into her life." I pause to take a breath and lower my voice. I don't wish to get into a shouting match with him. "What I'm trying to say, Dominie, is that you need to talk to your granddaughter and really listen to what she has to say."

"And you need to stop being a meddling busybody and mind your own business."

I swallow my pride and ignore the name-calling for Cornelia's sake. "I care about Cornelia, and I will gladly listen to her hopes and dreams if you aren't interested in hearing them. But you ordered her not to confide in me, so the only person she has is you. Please talk to her. Let her know you love her."

"How dare you lecture me about what I should do?"

I don't answer his question as I hurry to finish. "I know you're working at the newspaper part of the time now, but I would like to invite you to come over for dinner sometime this week or in the evening if you wish, so you can spend more time with Cornelia. Find out what her interests are and what she wants for her future. She needs to know that you love her, Dominie. How will she believe that God loves her if you don't show her your love?"

"Show her my love? I gave up everything! My country, my work—everything!"

"Did you do it *for* Cornelia or *because* of her? There is a difference."

"Get out!" He points to the door, then turns and strides from the kitchen. I scramble to my feet and follow him.

"One more thing, Dominie. I understand that Cornelia once

loved to draw. I think she would be very grateful if you bought her a new sketchbook and some charcoal pencils as a gift." He walks straight through the living room and starts up the stairs. There is a door at the bottom of them, and he slams it behind him.

I let out my breath with a sigh as I stare at the closed door. I think I understand a little of how Cornelia must feel when she's with him. When Marinus doesn't reappear, I retrace my steps to the back door. The cold air knifes through me after the warmth of the kitchen stove, but I pause on the step for a moment, berating myself for not handling the conversation better. Nothing has gone the way I had hoped—to say the least! And while I didn't lose my temper and shout at him, even though I was sorely tempted, I did make him angry enough to shout at me, which almost seems worse.

Is he right? Am I a meddling busybody who should mind her own business? Perhaps. Yet I can't escape the conviction that out of all the homes where Cornelia could have stayed, God sent her to mine for a reason.

I return home to find Cornelia and Derk stumbling along in a mixture of English and Dutch. Cornelia has a piece of yarn and is trying to get my lazy tabby cat to play with it. We chat for a few more minutes before Derk returns home to study.

"Did you tell my grandfather about what happened?" Cornelia asks when he's gone.

"He already knew about it. He saw Derk's muddy clothes, so Derk had to tell him about the accident."

"Is my grandfather mad?"

"Not at you. He's mad at me for not telling him sooner."

"Then why hasn't he come over to see me?"

I can't answer her question. The man baffles me. I can only hope that when his anger at me dies down a little, he will think about some of the things I tried to tell him and reach out to Cornelia. She needs his love.

"Grandfather will know it wasn't an accident," Cornelia says. I wait, giving her time to find the words. "The first time I ran away from his house, I was gone for three days. I walked for hours and hours and caught rides on passing wagons and slept beneath haystacks at night until I reached Rotterdam. I followed the road right through the city until I came to the dock where all the ships were anchored. I reached the end of the road, but I just kept on walking into the water until it was over my head. One of the sailors saw me and jumped in to rescue me—like Derk did. Grandfather had people searching for me all that time, and when they found me in Rotterdam and he heard what I'd done, he was very angry."

I pray for the right words to say. "Cornelia, sometimes when we love someone our worry and fear come out as anger. But we don't really mean it—"

"*Nay*. He meant it." She sounds very certain. I remember today's confrontation with him, and I believe her. He asked me to send Cornelia over to talk to him, but I can't do it. Not when he's angry. Besides, he needs to take the first step and reach out to Cornelia, not summon her to stand before him in judgment. It occurs to me that even if Marinus does buy a sketchbook for Cornelia, I don't think she could bring herself to use it.

I recall her words just now—"*the first time I ran away*"—and feel a chill. Is this a pattern with her? Do I need to stand guard over her night and day as Marinus seems to think? I whisper another prayer for wisdom—I've been doing that a lot lately—and ask God to have mercy on all of us.

"Do you know how to knit?" I ask Cornelia as she continues to tempt the cat with the strand of yarn. She shakes her head. "Would you like to learn? Because winter is coming, and there are a few more families here in town who could use warm mittens."

She shrugs. A hopeless gesture. "I guess I could try."

It's a place to start.

CHAPTER 17

Anna

CHICAGO

According to my Literary Club directory, Mrs. James Blackwell and her daughter, Florence, still live on Lakeshore Drive, possibly in the same house where Mama once worked. It's not far from where I live, so I can walk there. I have tried in vain to think of a legitimate reason to speak with James Blackwell, who is now a judge like his father once was. I would like to ask him if he remembers helping my mama with her lawsuit, but I haven't come up with any excuse to see him. Surely he must remember her, since it was his first big case after becoming a lawyer. I decide to talk to his servants instead, in the hope that one of them will remember Mama. I will need to avoid Mrs. Blackwell and Florence, however. They will certainly recognize me, since I'm still the main subject of gossip.

Once again I ask Lucy to come with me on my secret expedition. I borrow a shawl and a plain straw hat from her. It isn't much of a disguise, but no one will be expecting a young woman of my social stature to arrive at the servants' entrance. "The best time to talk with the household staff," Lucy tells me, "is early in the afternoon. Everyone is in a rush in the morning when the gentlemen leave for work and the ladies are preparing to make calls. Then it gets busy again around suppertime, especially if they're expecting guests or getting ready to go out for the evening. But it usually gets quiet for a little while after lunch."

I take Lucy's advice, and we knock on the Blackwells' back door just after one o'clock in the afternoon. It's opened by a housemaid who is younger than I am and couldn't possibly have known Mama. "Good afternoon. Is Mrs. Philips still the housekeeper here?" I ask. My heart speeds up when the girl nods. It's too good to be true! "May I speak with her, please?"

"Who should I say is calling?" the maid asks.

"Um . . . Anna Nicholson." I can only hope that my so-called scandal hasn't filtered down through the servants' quarters, too. The girl leaves us standing outside and disappears. She returns a few minutes later and leads us to the housekeeper's room. I hide a smile when I meet Mrs. Philips, recalling Vera's apt description of her as a little hornet with a pointy nose and a sharp tongue. She is seated in a comfortable chair in front of her fire, and she tidies her white hair as if she has been napping.

"We're not hiring any help," she says when she sees us.

"We aren't looking for work, Mrs. Philips. I'm trying to find information about my mother, who once worked here as a housemaid. It was back when this house was newly built."

"Twenty-five years ago? We've had a lot of servants come and go in the years since then. I can't possibly remember them all."

"I understand. But my mama passed away not long after she worked here, and it's very important that I learn more about her for her family's sake. Her name is Christina de Jonge."

I watch Mrs. Philip's face, and I'm certain I see her react

to Mama's name—a slight widening of her eyes at first, then a frown and pursed lips. She looks me over from head to toe, and since I've been told that I resemble her, I'm hoping Mrs. Philips sees the likeness, too. "If you know anything about her or where she went after leaving here, it would be a great help to me. Or perhaps I could ask one of the other longtime servants about her?"

"I don't encourage gossip among our employees."

"No, of course not. You're right. But I'm here because of the terrible rumors that are circulating about my mother. I'm trying to clear her name, and the trail has led me here. I've learned that Judge James Blackwell once helped my mother win a lawsuit after her husband died in a railroad accident." Again, I watch Mrs. Philip's face, and she is unable to disguise her unease. I'm certain that she knows exactly what I'm talking about. It would have been highly unusual for the family heir to become involved in a court case for his servant. Mrs. Philips probably remembers the incident as clearly as Vera did. "Is there any way I could speak with Judge Blackwell to see if he remembers?" I dare to ask.

"I don't make appointments for the judge." Mrs. Philips stands, clearly agitated now, and I fear she is about to throw me out. Instead, she asks Lucy to leave, then closes the door behind her. My heart races. We are alone. "I know exactly who you are, Miss Nicholson, so let me ask you—would you want your servants whispering about your family and your hired help to anyone who asks? Or sneaking in through the back door trying to get an appointment with your father?"

"I'm asking for my parents' sakes, Mrs. Philips. The gossip has affected them, too, and I'm trying to clear their good names as well as mine. I need to find out where my mama went after leaving here, and who she married. I would greatly appreciate any help you can give me."

Mrs. Philips seems torn. I pray that I haven't reached another dead end. "Christina left without giving a reason," she finally says. "She didn't ask for references. However, I always ask for a forwarding address in case someone needs to get in touch with one of my people after they leave." She goes to a small desk and searches through the cubbyholes until she finds a notebook, old and wrinkled, the spine broken. Smaller pieces of paper are stuffed inside it. I hold my breath as I watch her page through it. At last she finds what she is looking for, and she turns the notebook around and hands it to me. "Christina gave me this address when she left. It's the best I can do." She offers me a pencil and a piece of paper so I can copy it down.

"Thank you so much, Mrs. Philips."

"I don't know what you'll find there after all these years. It's not in a very good part of town."

"I'm grateful for your help."

"Don't come back here again, Miss Nicholson. I'm going to warn the other servants not to speak to you or let you in. And since you know what it's like to be the brunt of gossip, I'll thank you to keep this family's good name out of the mud."

Lucy and I pass through the servants' dining room and the kitchen on our way out, and I try to imagine Mama working down here in the dim light, drying dishes and polishing silver and maybe wringing out laundry the way Vera did. What did Mama dream of back then after her failed marriage to the man she once loved? Did she miss her family in Michigan? Did she wish she could return home? She could have afforded the boat fare with the settlement money she received from the railroad. I wish for her sake that she had gone home.

"Now what, Miss Anna?" Lucy asks when we are back outside on the street.

"I don't know. Let me think." We should walk home again. I'm emotionally drained from the conversation, and I would like to lie down. Yet I need to follow this next clue while I still have the courage. "Would you mind hailing a cab for me, Lucy? I don't want to take public transportation today."

I show the cab driver the address Mrs. Philips gave me. "Are you sure about this?" he asks.

"Yes, and I would like you to wait there for me while I go inside. I'll pay you very well for your time." Twenty minutes later, we halt in front of a ramshackle, three-story tenement on a street that is filled with them. The wooden building seems vaguely familiar to me. Is it possible that I remember this place from when I was a child, or am I only imagining it? There are twelve apartments inside, four on each floor. Lucy and I climb to the top floor to work our way down, knocking on every door. Most of the people open their doors a mere crack and peer out at me through the tiny space. When I ask them if they lived here twenty years ago, they shake their heads. A few slam their doors in reply. The people in two of the apartments don't understand English. And one man on the second floor is so wild-eyed and scary-looking that I mumble, "Never mind, wrong apartment," and quickly retreat.

There are only two apartments left on the first floor when we meet a friendly young girl about ten years old who is carrying a child on her hip. "You should ask the O'Haras," she says. "They're the caretakers. Their apartment is in the basement." She points to a dark staircase leading down. I feel the chill of the dank basement as I descend. If the O'Haras have been living down here for the past twenty years, I pity them.

The tiny, wrinkled woman who answers the door looks like a character from a storybook. Her shaggy, gray hair spills from beneath a kerchief, and she's wearing several layers of clothes and shawls and socks. Her hands are gnarled with rheumatism, but the pleasant smile on her face gives me hope.

"Good afternoon, Mrs. O'Hara. I'm Anna Nicholson. I'm

looking for information about my mother, who lived here more than twenty years ago. By any chance, were you and your husband the caretakers back then?"

"We've been here since the place was built, right after the fire," she replies.

My hope rises. "I imagine you've seen a lot of tenants come and go since then."

"Oh yes. This isn't the sort of place where people stay very long. Although we've had to get the authorities in here to evict a few of them."

"Is there any chance at all that you remember my mother? Her name was Christina Newell, but she may have used her maiden name, de Jonge. She would have been in her early twenties, and I'm told I resemble her. I would have been a baby when we lived here."

My heart races as Mrs. O'Hara studies my face. I can tell she is searching her memory. But twenty years is a long time. "You'd better come in," she finally says, opening the door. It takes a moment for my eyes to adjust to the dim light inside, but when they do, the apartment is like nothing I've ever seen before. I recognize a sagging table piled with dishes, an ancient wing chair with a man asleep in it, and a bed layered with quilts. Narrow pathways lead to each of these destinations, but every square inch of space in between is stuffed with tottering piles of boxes, mounds of clothing and rags, and stacks of yellowing newspapers. The smell of mold and decay is appalling. I am about to excuse myself and leave when she says, "I think I remember the girl you're talking about."

She offers Lucy and me the only two empty chairs. It's like sitting in the middle of a garbage heap. I keep my eyes focused on Mrs. O'Hara, afraid I'll grow faint if I dare to look around. Mrs. O'Hara sits near me, perched on a pile of newspapers. If there was ever an avalanche from all this junk, no one would find her. Or Lucy and me, either. The man in the chair snores on.

"As I said, I've seen a lot of people come and go over the years, but if it's the young woman I think you mean, she was hard to forget. Sweet young girl. Told me her parents were Dutch. Hardworking. And very pretty. I was with her the night her baby was born. I sent for the midwife, but . . . what did you say her name was?"

"Christina."

"Yes. Well, Christina asked me to please stay with her, too. You say you're that baby?"

"Yes." My eyes swim with tears as I picture Mama giving birth to me in one of these dreary apartments with the little caretaker as her only friend. "Mama died when I was only three years old, Mrs. O'Hara." I swallow the lump in my throat and ask, "Was my father here with her, too?"

"She told me her husband was dead. Railroad accident, I think she said. Such a tragedy. I asked if she had family she could turn to, but she said no. She was all alone."

I struggle to hide my disappointment and shame. If Mama had married again, she surely would have referred to him as my father instead of implying Jack Newell was. My hopes for clearing Mama's name—and my own—grow dimmer.

"Can you remember anything else that might help me? Do you know where she worked? How she supported herself?" It's a risky question to ask. What if it turns out that she really was a harlot?

"She had some sort of factory job when she first arrived, but they let her go when it became obvious that she was expecting. After that, she couldn't go out to work with a baby to look after, so she took in piecework from the garment district to make ends meet. But she was barely making a living, and she worried about her little girl getting enough to eat. That's when she told me she was going away."

"Do you recall where she went?"

"She didn't say. Just packed a bag, took the little girl, and left. I never saw her again."

"Mama was taking me home to Michigan, where she grew up, Mrs. O'Hara. But our ship sank, and she drowned trying to save me. Another family adopted me."

"Oh my! I'm sorry to hear that. So sorry. No wonder she never came back. . . . Well, it's a real shame. Your mother was so young and pretty. I held the room for her until the end of the month and the rent came due, but then I had no choice but to clear out all her things and make way for another boarder. She didn't have very much."

"Do you remember what happened to her belongings?" The question makes Mrs. O'Hara bristle, so I quickly add, "It's understandable if you got rid of it all, it's just that I would love to have a picture or some other memento from her." I try not to imagine Mama's things buried in one of these piles beneath twenty years' worth of other tenants' abandoned belongings. From the look of things, Mrs. O'Hara never throws anything away.

"Well, time passed, you see. When she didn't return, I kept anything I could use and pawned the rest. But I may have boxed up her personal stuff in a crate, just in case she returned. If so, it would be in the storage room. You're welcome to see what you can find, if you want to have a look."

I tell her I do, and she lights a small kerosene lamp to light the way. It gives off a foul, smoky odor, and the glass is so grimy it doesn't offer much light. Mrs. O'Hara leads the way to a cold, windowless room next to the coal bin. The wind makes a whistling sound as it blows through the chute. Cobwebs dangle from the rafters above my head, sending shivers down my spine. I worry about spiders. And rats.

When Mrs. O'Hara unlocks the door to the storage room and opens it, any hope I had of finding something that belonged to Mama vanishes. The space is packed with junk, just like the O'Haras' apartment. It's stuffed from wall to wall, all the way to the rafters, without any passageways between the piles. I feel sick inside. It would take days and days to sort through everything. I hear Lucy groan.

"You know, it's getting late," I say, glancing at my little watch brooch. "I don't have time to search through all these boxes today. Would you mind if I came back another day?" I take a few dollars from my reticule and slip them into Mrs. O'Hara's hand as I ask the question, and she nods with enthusiasm.

"Oh yes. You come back whenever you want to, dear."

The sunlight and fresh air outside revive me. Thankfully, the cab is still waiting for us beside the curb. I give the driver my home address, and we climb in. "Are you really going back there to look through that mess, Miss Anna?" Lucy asks.

"I don't know. It would be such a daunting task. And who knows if I would even find anything."

"I've never seen anything like that before, Miss Anna."

"Me neither. But please, please don't tell anyone where we went today or what we saw and heard."

"Don't you worry, Miss Anna. You can count on me. Shall I draw you a hot bath when we get home?"

"That would be wonderful. Thank you."

Alone in the tub, I finally allow my tears of disappointment and shame to fall.

CHAPTER 18

Geesje

HOLLAND, MICHIGAN

Cornelia and I walk to Van Putten's Dry Goods, and I let her choose a few drawing supplies. She is so grateful that she manages a rare smile. I leave her to browse through the ready-made clothing that has just come in while I pay for the supplies and speak to Mrs. Van Putten. "I noticed you have a *Help Wanted* sign in the window," I say. "What sort of help do you need?"

"We're looking for someone to restock the shelves, sweep the floors, and straighten up. Maybe take money and make change if it gets busy. It's only a few hours a week. And I can't pay very much."

"I will need to ask Cornelia's grandfather first, but would you consider hiring her? Her English is getting better all the time. She's a good housekeeper, and I know she's bright enough to count money and make change."

"I could give her a try. It's been hard to find someone for only a few hours a week."

"Good. I'll talk with Cornelia and her grandfather about it." I dread the prospect of facing Marinus again. I don't enjoy being shouted at and called names. I decide to wait until after supper to visit him, and Cornelia and I walk up to the cemetery together instead. She doesn't sob as hard as she did the first time, and I can see that remembering her family and acknowledging her grief has brought healing.

We have just returned home from the cemetery when the dominie surprises me by knocking on my front door. "May I have a word with you in private?" he asks.

I send up a silent prayer for patience and wisdom. "Yes, of course. Let's sit out here on my porch." I choose one of my porch chairs while he perches on the railing. Anyone who saw him sitting with me—and who didn't know him as well as I do—would think he was a dignified, distinguished-looking man of God who had come to pay a pastoral call. But I have seen the man behind the façade, and I brace myself for what he might be about to say.

"I have come to apologize for the way I spoke to you yesterday, Mrs. de Jonge." My mouth drops open. I can't disguise my surprise. He hurries on. "I was upset to learn that Cornelia tried to kill herself again. I thought she was past all of that. I shouldn't have yelled at you or said the things I did. I'm sorry."

For a moment, I'm so stunned I can only nod. "Thank you," I finally murmur. I wait to see if he has more to say. I'm afraid to speak, afraid to unleash his anger again. Marinus is staring at the porch floor. He looks distressed. I'm guessing the apology hasn't come easy to him. When he remains silent, I summon the courage to speak. "Dominie, I would like very much to help you and Cornelia. Please tell me how I can do that."

"I don't know," he says, spreading his hands. "I'm at a loss about what to do. But I do need your help. I'm working more hours at the newspaper now and will be away from Cornelia. I know I can't leave her alone. I need you or someone else to stay with her until I can be sure she won't try this again."

"How many times has she attempted suicide?"

I can see he is reluctant to tell me. His words are offered like crumbs of bread. "Twice in the Netherlands. This was the first time here in America. When we were traveling on the ship I watched her night and day, always afraid she would jump overboard. She would stand by the rail, looking into the sea, and I feared for her. I can't understand her obsession. I don't know why she wants to do this."

"I will certainly watch over Cornelia as best I can. But unless we get to the root of her grief and help her manage it, we'll both spend the rest of our lives worrying that she'll attempt it again. Do you really want that?"

"No."

"Then I think . . . I think you'll have to give her permission to talk to me. About anything. You'll have to trust me to keep her secrets safe. I don't see any other way."

"I'll think about it."

His stubbornness frustrates me. "I can't imagine a secret so horrible that keeping it is worth the risk that Cornelia will end her life."

"It's nobody's business but ours."

"That's true. But I can't help her if I don't know what I'm facing." I can't get past his wall of stubbornness, so I decide to try a different approach. "If you don't mind my asking, I'm wondering how your faith figures into this? I've never heard you mention your Christian beliefs at all when we've talked about Cornelia."

"My faith is a very personal thing."

"Our relationship with God is certainly personal, but He

gives us a church family so we can help each other along life's journey. Even in Eden, God said it wasn't good for man to be alone. Other Christians are the only hands and feet that Jesus has."

"It seldom happens that smoothly in real life. People's 'concern' quickly turns into gossip."

"I'm sorry you've had that experience. But I don't know where I would be today without the prayers and support of my church family."

He's like a man on a frozen pond, trying to keep his balance as his control over his temper begins to slip for the first time. "Maybe it works that way for you, Mrs. de Jonge, but who can a dominie confide in? Who does he trust with his private concerns?" He faces me, and I see the pain behind his anger. I try to imagine him coping with Cornelia's suicide attempts without a wife or family to turn to. And he was unwilling to trust his congregation with his burden. No wonder the truth he tried to hide became a rich source of gossip once it leaked out. And Cornelia would have borne the brunt of his anger, since her actions were the cause of it.

"Do you believe that God can forgive Cornelia for wanting to end her life?" I ask. "Or has she committed an unpardonable sin?"

"Cornelia has no faith. She wants nothing to do with God. How can He forgive her if she doesn't repent?"

His words stun me. "Do you have any idea why she doesn't believe?"

"Because her father wasn't strict enough!" His temper begins to slip once again. "He let her get away with too much and didn't raise her in the faith the same way he was raised."

I close my eyes for a moment. *No. That isn't why.* I'll have to take a chance that sharing Cornelia's confidences with him will lead to change. "Cornelia blames herself for what happened to her family, Dominie. Did she tell you that she argued with her mother on the day before the fire? And that she thinks God killed her family to punish her?"

"She never talks about the fire or her family."

"Well, she needs to. Her grief and guilt are all bottled up inside, and the only way she can think of to stop the pain is to end her life." He looks at me as if he wants to ask what makes me such an expert. "I've lost members of my family just as you and Cornelia have. How did you explain the losses to her to help her through it?"

"I told her that the Lord giveth and the Lord taketh away. His ways aren't our ways. We can't understand His thoughts so we shouldn't try."

I stifle a sigh of frustration. "Answers like those didn't help me when I was grieving. They only infuriated me. My parents died of malaria when I was Cornelia's age. My son was killed in the war. My daughter drowned in a shipwreck on her way home to Michigan. My husband died a few months later. Each time I faced another loss, I wrestled with God the way Job did in the Bible. I dared to get angry with Him and shout at Him rather than walk away from Him forever, which is what Cornelia has done. And while I still don't have answers for why the people I loved had to die, the wrestling always brought me closer to God. He became very real to me when I was suffering, and I sensed that He understood. And during all that time, I knew that people were praying for me, and with me. I would like to ask some of them to pray for Cornelia, too."

"No. Then the gossip will start. I won't have it."

"I can't help her all by myself, Dominie. I'm not wise enough or strong enough. God doesn't want us to do it alone. He tells us in Scripture to bear one another's burdens. We have to trust each other. Suppose Cornelia had been all alone last Saturday? Suppose Derk and my granddaughter hadn't been with her?"

He rises to his feet. "I will think about it."

"One more thing," I say, stopping him from leaving. "Mrs. Van Putten is advertising for part-time help down at her store. I haven't said anything to Cornelia about it, but if she decides she would like to take the job, would it be all right with you? It might be good for her to get out of the house and meet new people."

"I already asked your son to find her a job with a family from his congregation. A family with young children."

"Oh dear," I say before I can stop myself.

"What?" he asks.

I know it would be the worst possible job for Cornelia after what happened while she worked for the Vander Werfs. Not only would she hate it, she would see it as further punishment from God. "Why don't we ask her which job she would prefer?"

He thinks for a moment. "I suppose we could do that."

"Good. I'm so glad we can work together, Dominie, instead of arguing. I know we both want what's best for Cornelia." I rise to my feet, as well. "And now, I'll take a little walk so you can go inside and talk with Cornelia alone."

"Thank you." I open the door for him to go inside, then set off down the street. The conversation has unsettled me, and I need time alone to think and pray about what to do before facing anyone else. But as I'm walking past the Vander Veens' house, Derk opens his front door and calls to me.

"Tante Geesje, wait!" He jogs down the steps and out to the street. "I was just coming to see you. I need to ask you a question."

My time to be alone vanishes. I have grown chilled while sitting on my porch with the dominie, and Derk is without a jacket. "Can we go inside your house?" I ask. "Marinus is talking to Cornelia in my house, and it's too cold to stand around out here." We go into his kitchen, which has always struck me as a bleak place, without the coziness of other kitchens. Derk and his father lived all alone after Mrs. Vander Veen died. They hire a housekeeper to clean once a week and do the washing, but the house could use a woman's touch. "What's on your mind, Derk?" I ask as we sit down at his table.

He runs his fingers through his hair, leaving some of it standing on end. He seems nervous, which is unusual for him. "After Cornelia had her accident, I never had a chance to finish my conversation with Anneke. I can't stop thinking about her, Tante Geesje. I'm worried about her. She admitted that she doesn't love her fiancé, and I'm afraid she's making a huge mistake."

"You and I have both talked to her about William. We advised her not to rush into marriage. There's not much more we can do."

"I need to try one more time. Can you give me her address?"

"Are you planning to write a letter?" He looks away as if afraid to face me. "Tell me the truth, Derk."

"I want to talk to her in person. I have a day off from my classes soon, and I want to take the train down to Chicago in the morning and come back the same day."

"Oh dear. That's not a good idea at all."

"Why not? Who knows when she'll be able to come back to Holland again? It's the only way I can see her."

"Anneke's life is very different from ours. You can't simply show up on her doorstep and expect her to welcome you. She has butlers and maids standing between her and the outside world—not to mention her mother. I'm sure you can imagine how Mrs. Nicholson will react when one of the hotel workers from last summer pays a call on her daughter. Besides, what would you say?"

"I would say . . ." He sighs, then turns to look me in the eye. "I want to tell Anneke that I love her."

"Oh, Derk."

"It's true. I can't stop thinking about her. I've tried and tried, but it's no use. When I saw her last week, I thought I would finally have a chance to tell her how I feel, but then Cornelia had her accident. I want Anneke to know that I love her, because I think she has feelings for me, too."

"I understand, Derk, but—"

"I can't just let her walk out of my life again and marry someone else for all the wrong reasons without telling her that I love her!"

"You will only confuse her, Derk. She's engaged to another man."

"Do you know if she feels the same way about me? Has she ever said anything?"

"Not in those words—"

"Has she ever said that she loves William?"

I scramble to find a way to talk Derk out of this wild idea. "Listen, I know what it's like to be lovesick. Believe me, I do—"

"Then give me a chance to talk to her, Tante Geesje. Just tell me where she lives. Please?"

"I don't think it would be wise for you to show up all alone on her doorstep without any warning."

"Then come with me. Please?"

"I can't leave Cornelia."

"Bring her along, too." Derk's ideas are getting crazier by the minute. I need to talk some sense into him.

"I believe you when you say you're in love with her, Derk. And that probably explains why you aren't thinking clearly. Even if Anneke admits that she loves you, have you thought about what it would be like to actually share a life together?"

"Yes! It's all I ever think about!"

"I mean practical things—like how ill-equipped Anneke is to be a pastor's wife. Do you honestly believe that one of our conservative Dutch congregations will welcome her with open arms, considering her background? She isn't one of us. She barely knows the Old Testament from the New."

"She wants to serve God as much as I do."

"Derk, she has never cleaned a house or washed her own clothes or cooked a meal in her life, much less plucked a chicken. You can't expect a woman like Anneke to do all those things. She has servants to wait on her hand and foot, helping her get dressed and even brushing her hair. You won't be able to afford a houseful of servants on your salary. You would be asking her to give up the only way of life she has ever known."

"Anneke told me she's sick of it all."

"That may be true, but I don't see how she could ever adjust to the way you and I live. Even if she does love you, it could never work."

"I want to let her know that she has a choice. She still might choose William, but I need to tell her I love her and that I want to marry her."

"Will you please think about this a little more first? I don't want to see you get hurt, lieveling. You must know in your heart of hearts that Anneke won't be able to marry you, even if she does have feelings for you. It would break her parents' hearts, for one thing. She is all they have."

"I want her to know that I love her."

I'm convinced that Derk's idea is a bad one, but I know him well enough to know that he won't let it go. He'll find Anneke's address one way or another. "I'll give you her address," I say. "But please use it to write her a letter. Don't go rushing down to Chicago in person. Anneke deserves a chance to think about your declaration before she responds to it. You can't simply knock on her door and spring the news on her while she's in the middle of making wedding plans."

"Thanks, Tante Geesje." He jumps up and gives me a hug. "Can we go over to your house now and get the address?"

"Write your letter first. Take your time with it. Besides, don't you have your studies to think about?"

"I can't concentrate on anything else until I get this off my chest."

I stand and reach up to caress his shoulder. "I'm worried about you, lieveling. Please take more time to think this through before you disrupt Anneke's life." He nods, but I know he hasn't heard me.

We talk about other things for a few more minutes before I wrap up in my shawl and walk home. The last thing I needed today was to add Derk to my list of worries along with Cornelia and Marinus and Anneke. For the hundredth time, I offer a silent prayer for wisdom. Then I open my kitchen door and go inside to see how Cornelia and her grandfather are getting along.

CHAPTER 19

Anna

A week has passed since I returned from Michigan and learned that I was the subject of gossip. Mother and I have now resumed our normal social activities as if the scandal surrounding my mama had never happened. On the surface, none of the other ladies behaves any differently toward me. In fact, Clarice Beacham has invited me and two other women from the Literary Club to a luncheon at her house later this week. I'm afraid to accept—and afraid not to. I don't want to turn my back on any of them when we're together, certain that I'll hear whispers and snickering.

William and his family invite me to sit with them in their pew on Sunday morning, as if to show the congregation that I have paid my penance and have been forgiven. Later that afternoon William invites me for a carriage ride to our new house to see how the sale of some of the furnishings is progressing. "I've missed you," he says as he snuggles close to me against the fall chill. "I'm glad that the scandal has died down and I have you back by my side. I dislike attending important events alone."

I'm unsure if I'm expected to apologize to William as I did to his mother. I don't want to. I still feel bruised after the way he kept his distance from me when I needed his support. I know I'm being stubborn, but I want him to know how I feel. "The gossip wasn't true, you know," I say. "Besides, I never told a soul what I learned from the detectives, not even you or my parents. I don't know how the rumors got started. It's almost as if someone has it out for me and wants to disgrace me." I'm about to tell him that I suspect Clarice Beacham, but he puts his fingers over my lips to stop me.

"I'd rather not talk about it anymore. The scandal is finally dying down, so let's not rake the coals. People are starting to forget about it, and you should, too."

How can I forget? It was my mother who was called a harlot, not his! It's on the tip of my tongue to tell him how much his lack of concern for my humiliation hurt me, but I hold back. Young ladies of my social class simply don't lose control and spew their feelings all over the place. Besides, I don't want to ruin my first afternoon back with William. "I'm trying to put it all behind me," I say instead.

"Good. I trust there won't be any new revelations between now and our wedding?"

I shake my head, wishing I had discovered something to salvage Mama's reputation. I would love to say "Aha!" to everyone who enjoyed the gossip and see their dismay when I prove them wrong. Instead, it appears that my discoveries at the tenement house have proven them right.

I can't stop picturing my mama dancing with James Blackwell, then polishing his family's silver in the servants' basement. Somewhere between her time with the Blackwells and the time she moved into the dreary tenement, alone and pregnant, she met someone and fell in love. Someone who abandoned her to give birth to me all alone, without any friends or family members by her side. No one must ever know that Mama may have been unmarried, not even Oma Geesje. And even if I wanted to continue searching for my father's identity, I've reached a dead end.

William smiles as he takes my hand. "Only a few more months and you'll be my wife." I try to smile back, but my stomach does a slow turn. I'm not ready. I need more time. I thought I was ready until I saw Derk last weekend and realized that I still have strong feelings for him. When he jumped into the channel to rescue Cornelia, I was terrified for his life.

"Is something wrong?" William asks.

"No," I say, shaking my head. "No, of course not."

We arrive at the mansion that will soon be ours, and I'm surprised when a butler opens the door to usher us into the foyer. "I've hired a few servants already," William tells me. "They'll be taking care of everything until we move in. But we'll need to hire more."

"I have a servant named Lucy who has become my lady's maid," I say. "I would like to bring her along to work for us after we're married. I'm sure my mother won't mind."

"Whatever you'd like, my dear." He leads the way through the rooms as if he already knows his way around the house. "You'll probably notice some bare spots here and there," he says. "We had to let some of the furnishings go to pay George Kirkland's creditors. But nothing that can't be replaced. Mother wants to hold our wedding reception in here," he says as we enter the enormous grand dining room. "Impressive, yes?"

Overwhelming is more like it. I can't imagine presiding over a roomful of Mrs. Wilkinson's pompous acquaintances, especially without Oma by my side. I take both of William's hands in mine as I look up at him. "William? Your mother doesn't want my grandmother from Michigan to attend our wedding. And while I understand her point of view . . . I-I really want Oma to be here."

"Mother is the consummate expert on Chicago society, Anna. I trust her judgment and so should you. She has excellent instincts when it comes to things like this, and she's as determined to launch my political career as my father and grandfather are."

I know I should nod and be agreeable and remain silent. But I recall how Derk once advised me to stand up to William and speak my mind. "It's just that . . . I already invited my grandmother to come, long before all those nasty rumors ever got started. It would be rude to tell her that she can't come now. Besides, I want her here on our special day."

William frowns and releases my hands. "I have enough to worry about without this, Anna. You need to talk to my mother about it, not me. You'll have to work something out with her."

That will never happen. I'm terrified of his mother.

William finishes our tour back in the stately foyer, and I can see how proud he is of his home, how important it is to him. I recall Oma's advice about letting William know how important my faith is to me, and I send up a quick prayer for the right words to say. "William? I-I think you should know that my faith means everything to me. If you marry me, it will be as though . . . as though you're marrying Jesus, too."

"What? Marrying Jesus . . . ?" He gives a short laugh, as if I've said something ridiculous. "What is that supposed to mean?"

"I read a Bible verse the other day that said when we place our faith in Christ, it's as though we've died and now Jesus lives in us. From now on, I'm determined to live by His teachings and follow what He says is right and wrong, instead of going by what other people say and think. That's why I had to speak up when the other ladies were gossiping. The Bible says gossip is wrong, and I needed to remind them."

"Aren't you being a little extreme, Anna?"

"I don't think so." I can see by the way his shoulders have tensed that I've upset him. But I'm determined to remain strong.

"Are you going to that radical church again?" he asks, making a face.

"Of course not. I promised you I wouldn't, and I'll keep my word. But I thought you should know how important my faith in Jesus is to me. It's the one thing I'll never compromise."

I have never seen William at a loss for words, but he is now. He looks around at the ornate walls, the marble floor, the grand staircase—anyplace but at me. "Thanks for telling me," he finally says. He makes it sound like I've just given him terrible news. "We should go." He speaks a few words to the butler, who opens the grand front door for us. I'm relieved to be outside in the fresh air again.

Later that night I'm lying in bed, trying to fall asleep and failing as thoughts swirl through my mind. William barely spoke on the way home, but that's not what's keeping me awake. Everyone says I should forget about my real mama, forget about the past, and look ahead to the future. But I can't. According to the caretaker, Mrs. O'Hara, Mama struggled and worked hard to provide for me. She worried that I wasn't getting enough to eat, so she swallowed her pride and decided to return to Michigan. She thought it was the best thing she could do for me. She loved me, and she died trying to save me. And while I'm curious to know who my real father is, I want to know for Mama's sake as much as my own. I want to clear her name and prove that she didn't behave shamefully, because I don't believe that she did. If she insisted that Jack Newell marry her after running away together, I believe she would have insisted on marriage the second time, too.

I can't stop thinking about the mounds of trash in Mrs. O'Hara's horrible storage room. What if there is something buried beneath all that garbage that could clear Mama's name? It would be well worth the trouble of digging through musty crates of trash if I could find Mama's belongings. Maybe I'll ask Lucy and one of the stable boys to help me. Lucy might know which boy I could trust to be discreet. I fall asleep, dreaming of spiders and rats and dark family secrets.

Mother and I spend Wednesday morning with the dressmaker to be fitted for our new winter gowns. The seamstress shows me the beautiful bolt of fabric that will become my wedding dress as I try on the muslin pattern she has created to see how it fits. "Have you lost weight, Miss Anna?" she asks as she adjusts a few dressmakers' pins.

"I may have." Not only have I gone a week without petit fours during my enforced isolation from society events, but I've been much too upset by the scandal to eat much.

"Don't alter the size," Mother says. "I'm certain Anna's appetite will improve soon."

I'm not so sure. I'm having lunch this afternoon with Clarice and two other ladies from the Literary Club, and my stomach already feels like I'm onboard the *Ironsides* again, right before it sank.

"I'm so happy that Clarice and the other girls have welcomed you back," Mother says as she and the carriage driver drop me off at the Beachams' house for the luncheon.

No other carriages are in the driveway. The house is quiet as the butler shows me inside. He escorts me all the way to the conservatory at the rear of the house, and there is no one else in sight, not even another servant. The conservatory is fragrant and green and filled with plants, while the trees beyond the windows look like bare sticks. The sky above the glass ceiling is wintery gray. It's about to rain. I find Clarice seated at a small table in the center of the verdant conservatory. I seem to be the first guest to arrive. She beckons me over, and I notice that only two places have been set at the table—hers and mine. "Where are the other ladies?" I ask.

"It will just be the two of us, Anna. Please sit down. We have some important things to discuss. In private."

I feel sick to my stomach. I should turn around and walk out, but I don't dare. Clarice takes her time unfurling her napkin, waiting for the footman to fill our water glasses, ordering him to bring the first course. Hours seem to pass as we wait for him to return with two small bowls of fish chowder and a basket of oyster crackers. Then we wait again for him to leave. I can feel the blood rushing to my face, and I see Clarice's delight in my discomfort. I'm unable to speak, even if I knew what to say. I pray for help.

At last Clarice picks up her soup spoon and takes a taste. "Last week must have been so difficult for you, Anna, enduring the scandal and feeling banished."

I don't give her the satisfaction of a reply. My food sits untouched. My hands are trembling so badly, I don't dare lift the spoon to my mouth.

"I would hate to see you and your family suffer through that experience again," she says, "not to mention William's family." She enjoys a sip of soup between each sentence, dragging everything out. "Mrs. Wilkinson and my mother have always been close, so I know firsthand how upset she was by it all. It would devastate her if an even bigger scandal were to surface." She takes a few more spoonsful.

"Were you the one responsible for starting the gossip, Clarice?" I'm dismayed that my voice is unsteady.

She smiles her dazzling smile. "Your mother created the scandal by the way she lived, Anna. I'm not to blame for that. And now it has come to my attention that there is even more proof that your birth was shameful."

I'm going to be sick. I swallow bile and push away the bowl of soup as the fishy aroma reaches my nostrils. Clarice seems to enjoy my distress.

"It seems a witness named Vera can testify before a court of law that you couldn't possibly be Jack Newell's child. Your mother was not pregnant when he died. But I wonder who your father is, then?" She pauses, smiling. I can't breathe. "And another witness named Mrs. O'Hara can testify that your mother was already pregnant when she moved into the tenement building. Christina was all alone, with no husband in sight. Your mother even lied to the landlady, claiming her baby's father had died in a railroad accident. But you were born a little bastard in that disgraceful place, weren't you, Anna?"

"Stop it, Clarice. Just stop." I see her smile of victory through my tears. The only way she could have learned all this information is from Lucy—whom I trusted! The cruelty of Lucy's treachery makes everything worse. I feel stupid and naïve and horribly betrayed. I'm deeply sorry that my search will put Mother and Father through another painful ordeal once Clarice tells everyone what she learned. "Why are you trying to ruin me and my family?" I ask. "My adoptive parents never did anything to harm you. What do you want from us?"

"It's simple. No one will ever need to know what I've learned, dear little Anna, on one condition." I wait, certain I know what she's about to say. "You need to call off the wedding. Now is the best time, before the invitations are engraved and delivered." I close my eyes to erase the sight of her smug smile. "If you don't break your engagement, the next scandal will be even bigger than the last one, and I know for a fact that the Wilkinsons will call off the wedding themselves when they hear about it. After all, William has political ambitions. He can't be married to a little bastard wife." She pauses, and when I open my eyes again, I see a smile of triumph on her beautiful face. "Either way, you and William are finished. The choice of whether you end the engagement quietly or it ends in your disgrace is yours to make."

"And you think William will marry you instead?"

"I don't want William. He hurt me, and now it's my turn to hurt him back. This isn't about you, Anna. I have nothing against you."

"Yet you're trying to destroy my life!"

"Not yours—William's. I'll never understand why he wants to marry you. But he stole my happiness, and now it's my turn to steal his. He'll find out what it's like to be jilted."

"If I tell William what you're trying to do and that you're behind all the gossip, he won't let you get away with it."

Clarice laughs. "You underestimate how important William's reputation is to him. And to his mother."

I recall how William treated me last week and suspect she is right. I'm astonished at the measures Clarice went through to get even with William, going so far as to hire my maid to spy on me and report back. Clarice must hate William more than anyone imagined. "How do I know you won't create a scandal even if I do break off the engagement?"

"Because you have my word."

It isn't enough. Clarice is as phony as this beautiful conservatory—seemingly green and lush and fragrant, when the cold reality beyond the glass is startlingly different. "I need a few days to think about it," I tell her. I won't leave here letting Clarice believe she has won. "I'll let you know what I decide." I push back my chair and walk out.

"Don't take too long," she calls after me.

It has begun to pour rain outside, and I'm soaked by the time I walk to the main street a few blocks away to hail a cab. The streets are jammed from the lunch hour rush, and by the time I finally find a cab and climb inside out of the rain, I'm shivering. My shoes and hat are ruined and probably my dress, as well. I close my eyes to stop the dizziness, still fighting the urge to be sick.

I'm in an impossible position. What Clarice doesn't know is that Father may lose his fortune, just like George Kirkland did, no matter who calls off the wedding. Mother will no longer be accepted in the Wilkinsons' social circles, which will devastate her. My parents will be ruined, and all because I couldn't let go of the past and stop searching for my real father. My foolish actions are about to cause a lot of suffering to two dear people who don't deserve it. I think about the elaborate wedding dress being sewn for me, the huge reception Mrs. Wilkinson is planning, the enormous home William has chosen. I once complained about all those things, but now they will be lost to me. I'm sorry for being so ungrateful. Who could have imagined that Clarice Beacham, a jilted lover, would devise such a wicked plan?

I struggle to compose myself on the ride home in case I run into Mother before I can retreat to my room. Thankfully our carriage is still gone, which means Mother is still making afternoon social calls. "Are you all right, Miss Anna?" the butler asks after opening the door for me. He appraises my ruined hat and soaked jacket.

"Yes. I got caught in the rain. Kindly send Lucy up to my room to help me." I intend to tell her what a horrible person she is for betraying me and then fire her on the spot.

The butler's face turns hard as he says, "Lucy no longer works here, Miss Anna. She walked out without so much as a thank-you or a good-bye."

Of course she did. Her task of spying on me was finished. I

recall how timid and fearful she seemed at first, and how I felt sorry for her. It was all an act.

I'm trembling so badly as I ascend the stairs that I have to keep a tight grip on the railing to maintain my balance. Once again, I fear I'm going to be sick. I kick off my soggy shoes and sink down on my bed.

What am I going to do? What in the world am I going to do?

CHAPTER 20

Geesje

HOLLAND, MICHIGAN

When I return home after talking with Derk, Cornelia and her grandfather are sitting in my front room. I feel a chill from the wall of ice that seems to stand between them. Both sit with their arms folded tightly across their chests. Cornelia had been sketching when I left, but I see that she has hidden her notebook and pencils beneath an afghan on the sofa beside her. The scene brings tears to my eyes. If I filled the stove with a forest full of trees, it wouldn't thaw the iceberg between them. And yet I do believe that Marinus cares for his granddaughter. She is all he has left.

"I'll make tea," I say. But Marinus rises from his chair.

"I can't stay. But thank you." He moves toward the door.

"Dominie, wait." I look from him to Cornelia and back again, trying to gauge if I'm interfering or helping. "I'm wondering if you had a chance to talk to Cornelia about the job down at the store, and if she made a decision."

"We didn't discuss it."

"Would you mind if I asked her?"

Everything about his rigid stance and thunderous expression tells me that he does mind, but after pausing for several tense moments, he surprises me by saying, "Go ahead."

"Cornelia, Mrs. Van Putten is looking for someone to help out in her store for a few hours a week. She's willing to hire you, if you're interested." Cornelia looks up at her grandfather. I look to him, too, giving him a chance to ask her about taking a job as a mother's helper.

He clears his throat. "You could try it. See if it works out."

"There's no need to decide right now, Cornelia," I say when I see the wary expression on her face. "Take time to think it over."

She looks visibly relieved after her grandfather leaves, and I have to admit that I breathe a little easier, too. "Let's go have some tea in the kitchen," I say. "It's warmer and brighter in there. This front room always seems dark to me, especially on cloudy days, because the porch blocks off so much light." She follows me to the kitchen and sits at the table while I stoke the fire and move the kettle to the warm side of the stove. I notice that she has brought her sketchbook with her. "May I see what you're drawing?" I ask.

She opens the cover and shows me a sketch of my tabby cat. Even half-finished, the picture is skillfully drawn and shaded. "Cornelia, it's wonderful! You're a very good artist."

"It isn't finished yet." She bends over the picture and continues sketching while I prepare the tea and add a spice cookie to each of our saucers. "Grandfather says I can talk to you now," she says without looking up.

"I'm glad. We all need someone to talk to and share what's

on our heart. I'm very grateful for the dear friends I have." I watch her darken the cat's eyes, leaving a tiny spot of white to make them seem alive.

"He's upset with me for . . . for last Saturday. He says it's a huge sin against God to try to end my life."

I squeeze my hands into fists in anger. I would like to shake some sense into that man. "Sin doesn't come in sizes, Cornelia. Suicide is no worse than any of the dozens of other sins we all commit every day—pride, gossip, unforgiveness . . ." *And anger*, I add to myself. "But it would be a terrible tragedy if you killed yourself. I know that God has a purpose for creating you. He designed a special place for you to fit into, just as all the different pieces of a blouse pattern each have an exact place and a purpose. The blouse would be incomplete if one of the pieces was missing. You can't see God's purpose right now because you're angry with Him for everything that happened, and that's understandable—"

"What about my parents? Was it their purpose to die?"

I release my breath with a sigh. My certainty wavers. "Only God can answer that, Cornelia. I was your age when my parents died. You've seen their graves. We were all sick with malaria, but they died and I lived, just like you. My parents loved God and believed that He wanted them to move to America. So they followed Him here to this dangerous wilderness where they died only a few months later. My mother trusted God right up to the end, even when she knew she was dying. She believed that He is completely loving and good. And so she trusted His will for her as she took her last breath. I miss my mother and father. And I know you must miss yours, too."

A tear rolls down Cornelia's face and drops onto the page. "My papa used to give the best hugs. I felt safe when he held me. And I knew . . ." She can't finish.

"That he loved you?"

She nods and blots the tear from the paper. "After he died, there was nobody to hold me anymore."

My heart breaks for her. I crouch beside her chair and enfold her in my embrace. Silent sobs shake her body, and I hold her tightly until they stop. "When I go into the water," she says, her voice muffled against my shoulder, "it's very cold, but I can feel it surrounding me. Holding me."

"I'll hold you whenever you need me to, Cornelia. But even my arms will never be enough. You need to feel God's arms around you the same way you felt your papa's arms—surrounding you, holding you tightly. Will you give Him a chance to do that?"

She pulls away and leans back in her chair, wiping her face. "How?"

"Start by opening your eyes to all the little ways that He shows you His love. Like that sketchbook. It gives you joy, doesn't it?" She tilts her head, a grudging *yes*. "It didn't come from me, it came from God. He's the One who urged me to buy it for you."

She picks up her pencil again, toying with it. What I need to say next will be risky. The last thing I want to do is turn Cornelia any further away from her grandfather. But she needs her vision restored. I decide to take a chance.

"Please don't picture God like your grandfather, standing in angry judgment over you. Imagine Him like your papa—loving you even when you misbehave, taking delight in you, wanting what's best for you. Will you try to do that?"

"My grandfather is a dominie. He must know all about God."

"Yes, but perhaps he hasn't seen God's love in a while. He lost his wife, all of his children, and his work as a minister. I think he's angry with God, but he hasn't admitted it yet. Or else he's afraid to admit it. I believe that he loves you, but he just doesn't know how to show it." I pause to give her time to think about my words. She brushes her hand across the paper.

"God shows us His love wherever we look, Cornelia. Only a loving God would think to create a tabby cat so we could enjoy the softness of its paws, the warmth of its fur, and the delight of its purring. Your life is also a gift from God. You're His beloved child. Please don't throw that gift away."

I have talked enough for today. Cornelia needs time to think about what she has heard. Marinus has allowed her to share her secrets with me now, but I need to be patient and wait until she's ready. And I'll need wisdom once she does.

The next week, Cornelia goes to work at Van Putten's Dry Goods store for the first time. She seems excited about it in her quiet, nearly invisible way. I give her a hug and whisper "good luck" as she leaves to walk there with her grandfather. I have something important to do while she's gone. I have invited three of my closest friends from church, including our pastor's wife, to come for coffee so I can ask for their help. We gather around my kitchen table, taking time to laugh and catch up on our lives before we get down to serious business.

"I need you to pray with me for Cornelia Den Herder and her grandfather Marinus," I tell them. "Not just today, but in the days and weeks and months to come. I won't go into their specific needs—not because I don't trust you, but because God already knows them, and that's all that matters. Both Marinus and Cornelia are far away from God right now—in different ways, perhaps—and I know God wants to draw them back. And we all believe that it's the church's job, our job, to help people find their way back to God. We can do it by praying, of course, and we will do that in just a minute. But in this particular case . . ." I pause as my tears well up. "In this case, Marinus and Cornelia see Him only as a God of wrath and judgment. We need to show them His love in every way that we can, every chance we get."

"Cornelia seems very shy," the pastor's wife says. "She barely responds when I speak to her after church, even if I speak Dutch."

"She is shy, yes. But her response also comes from shame. She feels as though she isn't good enough to face people. As if everyone else has led a perfect life."

We share a little chuckle at that idea, and one of my friends says, "If she believes that we're perfect, then it's our fault for giving a false impression by smiling and pretending everything is fine on Sunday mornings." We all agree that she is right.

"The few times I've tried to talk to Dominie Den Herder," another friend says, "his response has been cold and abrupt."

"He pushes everyone away," I reply. "He had a very bad experience with gossip in his church in the Netherlands, and he pushed his congregation away instead of allowing them to help him and Cornelia through their grief. I agree that he seems unlovable. But it's the unlovable people who need our love the most."

We take time to pray. I know that my friends will not only pray for the Den Herders in the days ahead, but will invite them to Sunday dinner and do other acts of kindness for them. By the time my friends leave, I already feel the weight of my burden being lifted from my shoulders, knowing that the load is being shared.

CHAPTER 21

Anna

I can't sleep. I spend the night tossing in bed, worrying and praying about what to do. Clarice has given me an impossible choice. Either way, my engagement to William will end. Clarice will win. And my father will lose everything. I decide it will be better if I end the engagement rather than expose my family to further scandal. I will need to give William a reason for calling off the wedding, but right now I'm too distraught to think of one. And deep inside, I suspect that even if I do call it off, Clarice won't keep her word.

I've walked around this dilemma a thousand times, viewing it from every angle. There's only one very slim hope of escaping from Clarice's trap—and that is to find my real father. If Mama were legally married to him, there will be no scandal, no need to break the engagement. If she wasn't, then all hope is truly gone. I could rehire the Pinkerton detectives to find him now that I know they weren't the ones who betrayed me, but that would take too much time. I don't know how long Clarice is willing to wait. And the wedding invitations will go to the engraver next week.

I try to get out of bed but can't do it. My bones ache. My body feels as though it weighs a thousand pounds. I continue to cry off and on, unable to stop. I want to burrow beneath my covers and stay there forever. The most I can manage to do is to ring for a maid.

The girl who comes is one I've never seen before. Is she another spy, sent to replace Lucy? I can barely control the rage that boils up inside me. I hate Clarice with an intensity that shocks me. And I hate that sneaky little traitor Lucy just as much. I want revenge.

"Yes, Miss Anna?" the maid asks. "Would you like breakfast now? A cup of tea?"

Jesus' words swirl among my vindictive thoughts like wisps of smoke: *"Love your enemies and pray for those who persecute you."* Impossible.

"Nothing, thank you. Please tell my mother that I'm feeling ill. I won't be able to make any social calls with her today."

"Yes, Miss Anna."

Mother comes in a few minutes later wearing her dressing gown. "What's wrong, dear? The maid said you were unwell." She presses her hand against my forehead to see if I'm feverish.

"My stomach has been upset all night. I don't feel well enough to go with you today."

"Did you forget that William's sister is hosting a tea this afternoon?"

Tears fill my eyes at the thought of sweet Jane being poisoned by Clarice's gossip. "Please offer Jane my sincere regrets. I'm just too ill to go."

Mother looks as though she wants to say something but

changes her mind. "Very well, dear. I hope you'll feel better tomorrow."

I try to pray, aware of how desperately I need God's help. Then I manage to doze for a while, catching up on my lost sleep. I'm awakened by a knock on my door. It's the new maid again. "I'm sorry to disturb you, Miss Anna, but there's a gentleman downstairs in the kitchen who's asking to speak with you. He says it's important. We told him you're indisposed, but he keeps insisting."

I can't imagine who could be at our back door. Nor can I bear more bad news. "Did he tell you his name?"

"Yes, miss—Derk Vander Veen."

I scramble to sit up in bed. Derk? Here in Chicago? Impossible. Someone is playing a cruel joke on me. "What does this gentleman look like?" I ask.

The girl gives a shy smile and her cheeks flush. "He's tall and fair-haired, miss. With blue eyes. Very nice and friendly. But he wants to speak with you and says he won't leave until we tell you he's here."

Derk is here. I don't know why he came or how he got here, but I know he's the answer to my prayers. "Have him wait in the morning room. . . . And ask if he would like tea or coffee or . . . or something to eat. Tell him . . . tell him I'll be down shortly." I dress as quickly as I can and brush my hair into a loose bun, too anxious to wait for a maid to pin it up. I waste several minutes searching for my shoes before recalling that I ruined them in the rain yesterday. My legs feel shaky as I make my way downstairs.

Derk looks out of place in our overly furnished morning room. I resist the urge to run into his arms when I see him. "Hello, Derk. What are you doing in Chicago?" I can't control the smile that spreads across my face. He grins in return, but he appears nervous as we both sit down. There are beads of sweat on his forehead, and he wipes his sweaty palms on his trousers.

"I needed to see you. We never had a chance to finish talking after Cornelia's accident, and there are so many things I still need to say. Is . . . is this a good time? Can you talk?"

Derk is solid and real, like one of the tall, white pillars that hold up the roof of his church in Holland. I'm so relieved to see him that I have to cover my face as I burst into tears. How I've needed someone strong to lean on! Derk jumps up and rests his hand on my shoulder. "Anneke, what is it? Have I done something wrong?"

"No, not at all! It's just that I needed a friend, and I prayed for help—and here you are! It seems like a miracle!"

He pulls out a handkerchief and hands it to me. His eyes are as blue as the lake on a summer day. "Tell me everything," he says as he sits on the sofa beside me.

I tell him about my search for my real father and how I learned that Jack Newell died long before I was born. I talk about meeting Vera and Mrs. Philips and seeing the Blackwell mansion where Mama worked. Then I explain how the trail came to a dead end with Mrs. O'Hara at the tenement house. "My mama gave birth to me all alone in that awful place. She told the caretaker that her husband had died in a railroad accident—but Jack isn't my father. That means Mama may have been unmarried."

"I can see why you're so upset."

"But that isn't the worst of it. I trusted one of our maids to go with me while I was searching, and all along she was spying for a woman named Clarice Beacham. Clarice wants to ruin William, so she is blackmailing me. She says the only way I can avoid a huge scandal about my birth is to end my engagement to William—but then my father's finances will be ruined and Mother will never survive the disgrace. Besides, I don't trust Clarice. I think she'll destroy my family and me even if I do call off the wedding."

"There's no way out for you? You're at this woman's mercy?" I can tell by the way that Derk's eyes flash that he's furious.

"I've been stewing over it all night, and the only possible way out of this dilemma is to find my real father. But even that would be risky, because he and Mama may not have been married after all."

"Then you have nothing to lose. If you find out who he is and that he never married your mother, you're no worse off than you are now. But if you can prove that they were legally married, then there's no scandal for this woman to use."

"But how do I find him? I've reached a dead end. My only hope is that Mama left a marriage license or my birth certificate among her belongings before she died. The caretaker says her things might be in the basement storage room at the tenement house, but I saw that storeroom, Derk. It would be like digging through a garbage heap."

"Even so, I think you should try. I'll help you." He stands and offers me his hand to help me up.

"You have no idea what you're getting into."

"Yes, I do. I'm helping a friend who needs me."

We gather up two kerosene lanterns from the carriage house and a pry bar in case the crates are nailed shut, and I ask one of our drivers to take us there. It no longer matters if he or any of our other servants are spying on me.

Derk appears moved when we pull up in front of the tenement house. "I can't believe that people are forced to live in such dreary places," he says. We tell the driver to return in a few hours, and we go downstairs to Mrs. O'Hara's apartment. She smiles when I introduce her to Derk.

"What a handsome couple you two are!" she says.

I feel my cheeks growing warm. "You did say I could come back and look for my mama's things?"

"I did. I'm glad to see you brought help. I don't think anyone has been in that storeroom in years, especially with my husband as sick as he is."

She gives us the key, and Derk lights our lanterns. I lead him through the basement to the storage room door. Shiny, dark insects skitter beneath the boxes as light enters the room. "Wow!" Derk breathes when he sees the task we're facing. "It's packed solid in there!"

"I know. Where do we begin?"

He exhales. "How about if I pull out the boxes, one by one, and put them here by the coal bin so you can search through them?" He finds two nails to hang up the lanterns. The rafters above our heads are covered with cobwebs. Derk lifts the first box from the top of a pile and sets it down in front of me, raising a cloud of dust. The lid opens easily without a pry bar, and I crouch down to riffle through it.

"I can barely tell what these contents once were," I tell him. "Old papers and matted, moth-eaten clothing, it looks like." I glance up and catch him staring at me. The expression on his face makes my heart race. It's the same expression William wore the first time we toured his enormous mansion. Derk blushes and turns to reach for another box. He passes down one after another, prying open the ones that are nailed shut. It's my job to search through the contents. I have never done such hard, disgusting work in my life, but desperation propels me to keep going. My skirt and shirtwaist will be ruined. I don't know how the servants will ever get them clean. Derk's shirt and trousers are being coated with filth, too. I hope he brought a change of clothing.

"We should have worn gloves," I say when I see how dirty and black our hands have become. "I don't know how I'll ever get the grime out from beneath my fingernails."

"Too late to worry about it now," Derk says with a grin. Our gazes meet and hold. I see the warmth and love in his eyes, and I can't look away. I don't want to. The powerful emotions I felt for him over the summer, the feelings I fought so hard to ignore, come rushing back in a huge wave, overwhelming me. I want nothing more than to run into his arms and lose myself there. "Do you need to take a break?" he asks, his voice soft.

I force myself to turn away. "No. We've barely begun." We return to work, searching through crate after crate, hauling each crumbling box out to the area in front of the coal bin and prying it open. We find nothing but broken, useless belongings, old papers, and worn-out clothing—items that should have been thrown into the garbage to begin with. It's grubby, disgusting work.

"Anneke, you have to come here and see this," Derk says when we've tunneled halfway into the room. His hand is warm and strong as he helps me to my feet. He takes down one of the lamps and shines the light between the boxes. "Look—it's a nest of baby mice."

"Mice!" A shiver runs up my spine. My instinct is to back away, but he tightens his grip on my hand to hold me in place.

"No, don't run. They won't hurt you. Aren't they beautiful?" I don't know how to tell him that I find mice repulsive, not beautiful. I'm also worried that their mother might crawl up my leg any minute. "Come take a closer look, Anneke." He tugs my hand, pulling me into the storeroom. Nestled in a bed of fur and shredded paper are six tiny, pink-skinned babies, their eyes still sealed shut. "Look how delicate and perfect they are," he says.

With my hand in his, I am able to see what he sees. "You're right. Thank you for showing me." Once again, I look up at him and feel an overwhelming urge to move into his arms. I long to kiss him.

This time Derk breaks the spell first by letting go of my hand. "Back to work," he says.

"What are you going to do with the nest?"

"I'll leave it. I can work around it."

I return to the piles of boxes, searching each one, finding nothing but trash. I can no longer deny my feelings for Derk, and I find myself staring at his broad back and strong arms as he works. He has rolled up his sleeves, and the golden hairs on his arms gleam in the lamplight. I will need to store away my feelings for him after we're done; they will have to remain hidden like the contents of this dark storeroom. I am watching Derk lift down another box when he suddenly gives a shout of surprise and backs up a few steps. I scream as I glimpse a huge brown rat slithering out of sight. I scramble on top of a wooden crate as fast as I can move.

"It's okay. It's gone," Derk says.

"It's not okay! That rat is still in the storeroom somewhere, isn't it?" Derk laughs, a glorious, uproarious sound that brings a nervous smile to my face. "What's so funny?"

"I've never seen anyone move as fast as you did just now. Look at you, balancing on top of that crate!"

"Well, you should talk! You jumped straight up in the air!"

He laughs again as he offers me a steadying hand so I can climb down. "Do you want to take a break and sit outside for a few minutes? I can keep searching by myself."

I draw a calming breath. "No, I have to do this. Let's keep digging."

Late in the afternoon when we've emptied three-quarters of the room, Derk pries open a wooden crate and I see a little white handkerchief with embroidered blue flowers lying on top. I gasp in astonishment. "Derk, that handkerchief was Mama's. I recognize it!" It has yellowed with age, but I clearly remember her using it when I was a child. I dig a little deeper and find a well-worn baby's blanket and two booklets from Moody Church. Tears of joy fill my eyes. "Oh, thank heaven! We found Mama's belongings, Derk! We found them!"

He pulls me into his arms and for that brief moment, I forget the dirt and filth of the afternoon's search. I feel safe. Loved. I'm sorry when he releases me again. "Let's look through a few of the boxes that were surrounding it," he says. "Maybe there's more." He lifts one of the lanterns from the nail and I follow him, too excited and relieved to worry about the rat we saw earlier. But none of the other boxes contains anything of Mama's. "I'll carry the crate upstairs into the sunlight for you, Anneke. You can start looking through it while I shove every-thing back in the storeroom." Derk looks tired and filthy. We both do. I check my watch in the lamplight and am stunned to see how late it is.

"Oh no! I need to go home. Mother will be worried. I'll help you put everything back, and we can look through the crate together after we get cleaned up. Either we'll find something that will help me, or we won't."

"What time is it?" Derk asks.

"Nearly four-thirty."

"It can't be that late. I'm all out of time!" He looks panic-stricken as he runs his fingers through his hair. "If I'm going to make all my train connections and get back home by morn-ing, I need to put this stuff back and leave for the train station right away."

"You're going back to Michigan tonight?"

"I have to. I can't miss any more classes."

"I'll ask my driver to help us." I offer the man a huge tip, and he and Derk are able to quickly put everything back into the storage room. I stop by Mrs. O'Hara's apartment to tell her what I found and to thank her. She seems happy for me.

"You take good care of that handsome young man," she says. If only I could.

We jump into my carriage and Derk asks my driver to take him straight to Union Station as fast as he can. "I don't understand why you have to leave," I say as the carriage begins to roll. "After all the work you did today, can't you at least stay long enough to see if we've found anything?" I feel shaken again. I'm about to lose Derk, my pillar of strength, and I can't bear it. But there is another reason why I don't want him to leave. I'm in love with him.

"I'm sorry. I would like to stay longer, but I can't. There were no direct trains between Holland and Chicago today, so I had to make all kinds of crazy connections to get here. I don't dare miss any of them on the way back."

Once again, I think of Clarice's ultimatum, and I feel sick inside. We ride in silence for a few minutes and the stench of mildew from the crate fills the compartment, adding to my nausea. I open a window to keep from being overwhelmed, and when I look out, I see that we're nearing the station. I'm nervous about what I might find—or not find—among Mama's things, and I wish I could talk Derk into staying by my side when I open it. "Why did you travel all this way if you could only stay one day?" I ask as a train whistle shrieks in the distance.

"Because I was hoping I would get a chance to see you and tell you . . ." He pauses, swallowing a lump of emotion.

"Tell me what? Is Oma Geesje all right? Does she know you're here?"

"Yes, yes, she's fine." He gives a crooked smile. "She'll be as mad as a wet cat when she finds out I came. She advised me not to. She tried to tell me how different your life is from mine, and that I shouldn't barge into it, but I wouldn't listen. I had to come."

"I'm glad you did. This crate might contain my last chance to help my family."

"I understand, now, how much they mean to you. I've seen your beautiful mansion and watched you dig through that mountain of trash when there was only a slim chance that you would find anything. I have a much clearer picture of how much is at stake if you don't marry William."

I gaze at this man who worked so hard to try to rescue me, and I can't help comparing him with William. Derk willingly dug through a mountain of trash to help clear my name, while William stayed away in my time of need, distancing himself from me and my "scandalous" past. The reminder of William's selfishness brings tears to my eyes. "Thank you for helping me, Derk. I couldn't have done it without you."

"You're welcome. Anytime." His smile breaks my heart.

The carriage slows to a halt in a long line of traffic. Derk peers out the open window. We can see the station beyond the knot of jammed carriages. "I'm going to miss my train if I don't go." He opens the door and jumps out. "I can run the rest of the way," he tells the driver. Then he turns back to me. "I'm sorry to leave you in such a hurry, without a proper good-bye. But I have to go."

"Derk, wait!" I shout as he turns to go. "You said you came here today to tell me something. What was it?"

He looks down at the ground for a moment, then back up at me. "I came to tell you that I love you."

I'm stunned. William has never spoken those words to me. I gaze at Derk, wanting to leap out of the carriage and into his embrace, longing to feel his arms around me again.

"I know you need to marry William," he says. "I see that now. I hope you find something in the box that will help. If not . . . if everything falls apart . . . well, I just want you to know that I'm willing to help you any way I can." He reaches for my filthy hand and squeezes it before he lets go and closes the carriage door. "I love you, Anneke."

I can see that he won't be able to hold back his emotions much longer and that he wants to escape with dignity. He starts walking away and is a few feet from the carriage when I throw open the door and call to him.

"Derk!" He turns around. "I love you, too!" I shout, not caring who hears me.

His smile breaks my heart. He gives a little wave, then turns and hurries away.

CHAPTER 22

Anna

CHICAGO, ILLINOIS

I ask our carriage driver to carry the musty crate upstairs to
my room when I get home. He has worked for our family for
many years, but after everything he has seen and heard today,
I can only pray that he will be discreet. "Is my mother here?"
I ask our butler.

"No, Miss Anna. She left to run errands and hasn't returned yet."

I feel a wave of relief. I can't face anyone right now. My
heart is still full after saying good-bye to Derk and hearing
him say that he loves me. I have finally admitted to myself
and to him that I love him, too. But once again, I will have to
stow away my feelings for him, out of sight, perhaps for the
rest of my life.

I have just finished bathing and have changed into clean
clothes when Mother knocks on my bedroom door. "I'm so

glad you're feeling better, dear." She kisses my cheek. "Now you'll be able to join your father and me for dinner at his club. . . .What is that dreadful smell?" she asks, wrinkling her nose.

"Um . . . do you smell something?" I ask. I need to find another place to stash the box.

"I'll send one of the servants up to sniff around," Mother says. She is about to leave when she turns back.

"By the way, I've been told that your little lady's maid has walked out on us. Any idea why? Did something happen?"

My anger at Lucy's betrayal returns in full force. "She never said a word to me before she left," I reply. It's the truth.

"She was such an odd girl," Mother says with a sigh. "And very unpopular with the other servants, so I'm told. They aren't sorry to see her go. I suppose I'll have to hire a new girl. Can you be ready to leave within the hour?"

"I'll be ready."

"William may be joining us," she adds. "Your father has a meeting with him this afternoon."

I cringe at the thought of facing William after spending the day with Derk. William would be furious—and rightly so—if he ever found out, even though I did it to save his family and mine from further scandal. I shove Mama's box beneath my bed, frustrated that I won't have enough time to dig through it before I go. I had to scrub my fingernails with a brush to get them clean, and I can't risk dirtying them again. Poor Derk has to ride all the way home to Michigan without bathing or changing his clothes.

Mother sends a maid upstairs to investigate the smell, and I give her my skirt and shirtwaist to wash. I don't owe her an explanation, so I don't offer one. This is the second time in as many days that I've arrived home in ruined, disheveled clothing, but the servants have been trained not to react or to ask questions. I can only imagine what the servants are saying behind my back about my strange activities. Will they tell my parents about Derk?

William greets me at the club and kisses my cheek. "You look lovely tonight, Anna."

"Thank you." I can barely look at him. I cannot imagine him digging through the tenement storage room the way Derk did today—and not simply because William is unused to manual labor. I still can't forget how he distanced himself from me when I was being shunned. Yet Derk willingly shoveled his way through a trash heap for me. He not only declared his love, he demonstrated it. And when I told him I loved him, too, I spoke from my heart. Is it wrong to marry William when I'm in love with Derk?

It doesn't matter. I have no choice.

The headwaiter seats us at a table, and we make small talk for a few minutes while we look over the menu. After the waiter takes our order, Father and William resume the conversation they'd been having before Mother and I arrived, while Mother tells me about the tea she attended today. I'm barely listening to either conversation. My stomach is in knots again as I ponder Clarice's ultimatum and everything that's at stake. My last hope lies in a smelly box beneath my bed.

I bring my attention back to the table in time to hear Father say, "I appreciate your bank's willingness to extend my credit once again." He looks worried; his smile seems strained. The threat to his finances must still be very real. I can't bear the thought of Father's world crashing down around him, especially if I'm the cause of it. He once fought with all his strength to keep me from drowning when the *Ironsides* sank, and I'll gladly do whatever I can to save him.

"It's not a problem," William replies. "We're practically one family now, aren't we? But let's not bore the ladies with business talk. How was your day today, Anna?"

I scramble to think of what to say without lying. I need to

erase Derk's image from my mind. "I had to miss your sister's tea, I'm afraid. I didn't feel well this morning." I hope everyone assumes my flushed cheeks are from embarrassment. It isn't proper to mention one's health in such a direct way.

The meal seems endless. I have no appetite, and I merely push the food around on my plate. "I'm still not feeling well," I say on the way home. "I think I'll retire for the night, if you don't mind." The stench of mildew fills my room. I change out of my evening dress and open a bedroom window, even though it's cold outside. I make sure to lock my bedroom door before pulling the crate from beneath my bed. Derk has loosely fastened the wooden lid back into place, and it takes me a few minutes to pry it open using a shoehorn and my letter knife.

The sight of Mama's handkerchief brings tears to my eyes again. I carefully lay it aside and lift out the next few items. Beneath a baby blanket that must have been mine and booklets from Moody Church, I find a cardboard legal file filled with papers. My heart races as I leaf through them, but they all seem to be related to Mama's lawsuit against the railroad and the final settlement. James Blackwell's name appears on nearly every one. My excitement turns to disappointment when I reach the last document without finding a marriage license or a birth certificate.

The next layer consists of Mama's well-worn work clothes, aprons, and a pair of woolen socks that are unraveling from moth holes. There are a few chipped dishes, a battered cooking pot, some eating utensils, and kitchen towels. I lift out a woolen blanket peppered with moth holes like the socks, cringing at the rough, grimy feel of it. Two dead moths flutter to the floor, as fragile and dry as tissue paper. And that's when I see it—a small, cloth-covered book that might be a diary. I'm afraid to hope, afraid I'll be disappointed. I pick it up carefully, worried that the pages will crumble to dust in my hands. I leaf through it, and my excitement grows when I see that page after page is

filled with beautiful handwriting written in pencil. It is a diary!
I turn back to the first page and see the words:

THIS BOOK BELONGS TO:
Christina de Jonge

My hands tremble as I turn the page and begin to read. . . .

Dear Diary,

*I'm writing my thoughts and feelings in this notebook
because there is no one in all the world who I can share
them with. Vera is my closest friend, but I know what she
will say if I tell her these things. And Mrs. Marusak was
very kind to help me break free from Jack, but I know that
she would also tell me I'm making a big mistake. My own
logic tells me I am, and my common sense confirms it.
But my heart won't listen to either one. People say love is
blind, and it's true. I was a blind fool to ignore my parents'
warnings and run away with Jack Newell. And now I'm an
even bigger fool for falling in love with James Blackwell.*

*It all began on the night of the dance. No, that isn't
true. I could feel myself falling in love with James during
those wonderful days we spent together when fighting
for a settlement from the railroad. It was such a glorious
feeling, like falling out of the sky through soft, lovely
clouds, with the whole world spread out beneath me, far
below. I knew how my fall would end and how much it
was going to hurt when I finally hit solid ground again,
but I was helpless to stop myself. I never felt this way
with Jack. I thought I loved him, but that romance was
all about him—what he wanted, how important he was,
and how lucky I was to be chosen by him when there were
so many other women who thought he was handsome. I*

was a silly fool who mistook his roughness for passion. Now I know better.

James is the complete opposite. On the days when we were together for the lawsuit, he treated me with dignity and respect and gentleness—the way I remember my papa treating my mother. James always asked how I felt about everything and how I wanted to respond to the railroad's offers, yet he was quick to take charge and stand up for me when I needed an advocate. He treated me as if I was a society lady and never like his lowly maidservant. James looked at me the same way that Jack looked at himself in the mirror.

So I fell in love with him in spite of Vera's warnings and my own good sense. I couldn't help myself. Handsome James Blackwell with his wavy mahogany hair fills my thoughts in the daytime and my dreams at night. I love the way his blue eyes sparkle when he laughs. I assumed that he was being kind to me because that was his job as my attorney. I believed that he treated me with respect because he was raised to be a gentleman. But I found out I was wrong on the night I went to the dance hall with Vera. I looked up from the table we shared—and there he was! James Blackwell! Asking me to dance with him!

I'll remember that night as long as I live. We talked and laughed, and James held me in his arms as he taught me to dance, cheerfully ignoring the dozens of times I stepped on the toes of his expensive leather shoes. It seemed like a dream, and I told myself to enjoy every moment because tomorrow I would wake up in this dreary attic room again, and he would be gone. The other servants and I all know that it is nothing more than a lark for Mr. James to spend time downstairs with us, pretending to be one of us instead of the wealthy gentleman he really is. But *on that wonderful evening in the dance hall, I fell deeper and deeper in love with him each moment I was with him.*

We barely left the dance floor. James held me closer as the night wore on, and then in a moment I will never forget, he bent his head to mine and whispered in my ear, "I'm in love with you, Christina." I felt his breath on my ear and a thrill shivered through me all the way to my toes. I think I forgot to breathe. "The more time I spend with you," he said, "the more I know that I want to be with you forever. Please tell me you feel the same way. Or else tell me what I can do to make you love me in return."

I held him tighter, savoring the joy of his strong, warm body next to mine. "You don't have to do anything," I whispered. "I love you, too." He caressed my back and sighed.

"Then it's settled. No one will ever keep us apart." I knew by the way he gazed at me and by the love I saw in his eyes, that he meant what he said.

We both know the tremendous opposition we will face. Only in children's fairy tales do servants turn into princesses. But I made up my mind that I would accept that night as a gift, savoring the love I felt at that moment instead of thinking about tomorrow or the next day.

Much too soon, the magical evening drew to a close. I could sense James' anxiety growing as we danced the final waltz together. "I won't let you go," he said. "I need to figure out a way for us to see each other again."

"How? We both know it's impossible."

"Don't say that. We could meet somehow . . . somewhere . . ."

"Without anyone knowing about it? Everyone in your household knows each other's business, upstairs and down. There will be gossip. Your parents are sure to find out."

"When is your next day off?"

"Next Sunday. A week from tomorrow. I'll have the afternoon off."

"I'll get a message to you. I'll tell you where we'll meet, and I'll give you money for the streetcar. Will you come, Christina? Please say yes."

"Yes! Of course, yes!"

We rode home together in his carriage, but we couldn't talk because Vera was with us. I longed for a good-night kiss from James, but Vera pulled me upstairs to our room and gave me a stern warning about how foolish it would be to let myself be charmed by Mr. James. I pretended that the evening had meant nothing to me and went to bed, wondering if James would really find a way for us to meet or if he would see the wisdom in forgetting all about me by morning. I want to believe that he'll find a way, but I'm afraid.

Thursday

James hasn't come down to the kitchen all week. I only glimpsed him twice—once when I was dusting the parlor and once when bringing tea to his mother. He acted as if I was invisible. My heart has begun to ache with loss.

Friday

A letter arrived for me in this afternoon's mail. The plain white envelope had no return address. In it were two streetcar tokens and a piece of paper with the words: Garfield Park. Washington Boulevard and Central Park Avenue.

I don't know how I will ever wait until Sunday!

Dear Diary,

I just returned home after spending a wonderful afternoon with James. If Vera were to snuff out the light in our attic room, I'm certain I would still glow with happiness. I had to lie to her when she asked how I spent my afternoon off. I wanted so badly to tell her the truth and share my joy with her, but James warned me not to trust anyone.

We spent the afternoon walking through the park and sitting close beside each other on a bench. We talked and laughed and held hands. "I want to take you everywhere with me," he told me. "I want the world to see what a beautiful, wonderful woman you are. But we can't be seen together—not yet, anyway. Not by the servants or my family or by any of my rich acquaintances. For now, we'll have to meet in public places like this where working-class people go, so I won't be recognized."

"I don't care where we meet," I told him, "as long as I'm with you."

When it was time to say good-bye, we snuck behind a little pavilion, and James kissed me for the first time. It was the most wonderful kiss I've ever known—tender and passionate at the same time. I savored the taste of his lips, the gentle way he cupped my face in his hand. Yet the kiss ended much too soon.

I know James wants to see me again because before we went our separate ways, he gave me enough money for six months' worth of streetcar fares. I could have floated home without the streetcar. I know there is a very real possibility that this is all an act on his part. That James will try to woo me into his bed, then discard me when *he is bored with me. My mind warns me that it might be true. My heart doesn't care.*

Dear Diary,

I had the afternoon off again today. Vera wanted to spend it together, and I think she became a little suspicious when I told her I had other plans. "What are you up to, Christina? Have you met someone new and you haven't told me?" We were in our attic room, changing out of our gray maids' uniforms and white aprons. I didn't have much choice of what to wear to meet James, but I put on my nicest skirt and shirtwaist.

"How could I meet anyone new?" I asked, avoiding Vera's gaze. "You and I work together all day. When would I have a chance to meet anyone?"

"You could meet a lot of great fellows if you came back to the dance hall with me again. There were several men who wanted to meet you the last time, but you wasted the evening with Mr. James."

"He was trying to teach me to dance. I wasn't very good at it, though."

"It looked to me like he was trying to do more than dance with you. I'm glad you listened to me and decided not to trust him."

"It's hard to trust any man after what happened with Jack. I'm not interested in getting married again."

"Oh, don't say that, Christina. You don't want to spend your life all alone like Mrs. Philips, do you? Don't you want to have a husband and children?" I shook my head, but in my heart, I was saying, "Only if my husband is James and my children are his."

I told Vera I was meeting an old friend from my days at the boardinghouse, then I traveled by streetcar to Humboldt Park on North Avenue and California to meet James.

We ran into each other's arms, not caring if the people passing by looked shocked. "I hate that I barely get to see you all week," *I told him.*

"I know. But I can't come downstairs to the kitchen anymore. Mrs. Philips is too nosy. She'll get suspicious when she sees that I can't take my eyes off of you. You're so beautiful, Christina. Not only on the outside, but your heart is so pure and genuine. You have no idea how phony and shallow the society women are in comparison— especially the ones my mother arranges for me to meet. I can't imagine spending my life with anyone but you."

"We both know how impossible that is. We live entirely different lives—yours is upstairs and mine is downstairs."

I feel torn in two. I want to believe that James loves me, but I also need to guard my heart. I'm afraid the time will come when he'll get tired of meeting this way. Tired of me. Yet until that time comes, I want to cherish every moment of our Sunday afternoons together. I know that doesn't make sense, but love seldom does.

"It isn't impossible, Christina," *James said.* "I've been working on a plan. If I can save enough money and make a big enough name for myself as a lawyer, I won't be dependent on my parents anymore. Then when they threaten to disinherit me, it won't matter. Once I do that and I find a place for us to live, will you marry me?"

My heart tripped and leaped. "Do you really mean it?"

"Christina, I would marry you today—right now—if I could." *I longed to believe him. Oh, how I longed to! But James is a hopeless romantic, and I don't think he understands what would happen if he married me.*

"You know all about my first husband, Jack," I reminded him. "But I never told you that I ran away from my family and my home in Michigan to marry him. My parents didn't approve of him, just as your parents would never approve of me. At the time I didn't care. But I cut myself off from them when I left home, and now . . . now I miss them very much. You say you don't care what your parents think, but someday you might regret being estranged from them. And you might grow to resent me for causing it."

"Never. I love you too much, Christina."

"And I love you. But what if that isn't enough someday?"

We both felt sad when we said good-bye. James promised to let me know where we'll meet the next time, but I wish . . . I almost wish he would end this right now before we make any more promises to each other that we can't keep. Do I want my heart broken now or several months from now? I'm powerless to tell James good-bye and end it myself. It would be like cutting out my heart.

I wish I could talk to my mother. I miss her so much. She would know what I should do.

Dear Diary,

I just returned home from another afternoon with James. We have been meeting in secret for more than two months now, and our longing to be together for more than a few stingy hours feels like torture. We can't keep it up much longer.

We're also worried that people are starting to suspect we're keeping secrets. "My mother was short-tempered with me when I said I wasn't available for one of her events," James told me today. "She wanted to know where I've been *going every week, and I had to tell her it was none of her business."*

"She wouldn't send someone to follow us, would she?" I glanced around at the people in the park as we walked together, worried I would see one of the other servants. James and I haven't cared who sees us holding hands or kissing, but maybe we should.

"I don't know," he replied. We stopped walking, and he rested his hands on my shoulders, caressing them. His touch sent shivers through me. "Listen, I'm worried that if my family does find out about us, they'll do something to break us apart. I'm their only heir, and they have the money and the means to control my life. I know I can't afford a place of our own yet, and I don't have enough money to support you once they disinherit me—"

"I don't need much. Just you." But even as I said the words, I remembered that James had been raised in a beautiful home with servants, elegant clothes and food, and all the finest things in life. Even if he was willing to give them all up for me, I couldn't ask him to.

His hands tightened on my shoulders. "Marry me, Christina. Let's not wait any longer. We would still have to keep it a secret for a few more months, but at least we could really be together every week, in a private hotel room somewhere instead of wandering around a park. And once we're legally married, my parents won't be able to stop us."

"They'll never accept me."

"I know. You'll need to be prepared for that. They'll probably reject both of us at first. But in the end, I'm their only heir. Please say yes."

"Yes, yes! Of course I'll marry you!" James pulled me close, and we stood in the middle of the walkway with our arms around each other, not caring if people stared.

"I'll see about a marriage license and find a justice of the peace in one of the little towns outside Chicago. The next time you have a full day off, we'll elope."

I thought I would burst with joy. But now that I'm back in my attic room, I feel as though I'm reliving a past mistake. Once again, I'm planning to sneak away to get married—only this time it's his parents who are opposed to the two of us, not mine. Am I making another mistake? The last time I married in haste, I had nothing but regrets. But I love James. And he is nothing at all like Jack Newell. I have to trust that James knows his family better than I do, and that somehow, some way, we will be together in the end.

Dear Diary,

Vera has met someone at the dance hall and has fallen in love. He is all she talks about. I want so badly to tell her that I know how she feels so we can share our happiness together, but I don't dare. James says to trust no one. My next full day off from work is in two days. I have been waiting with butterflies in my stomach for that day to arrive, wondering if James is having second thoughts about getting married. I haven't heard from him since he dreamed up the crazy idea of eloping, more than a week ago. I want to believe that it will really happen, but I'm afraid to.

Dear Diary,

This afternoon another plain white envelope came for me in the mail. I slipped into the butler's pantry, alone, to read it. The note inside said, "Take the train to Cicero. I'll be waiting at the station. We're going to do it."

It's really going to happen! James and I are going to be married!

All this time I've been afraid to believe that his love for me is real. I've worried about Vera's warnings and wondered if he is using me as a secret diversion from the life that has been carefully structured and planned for him, the same way he used to entertain himself by chatting with the chauffeurs and other servants downstairs. I know he likes to escape from his parents' overbearing control by doing things that irritate them. But if he is really waiting in the train station two days from now, if he really has found a justice of the peace to marry us, then I'll know that James Blackwell loves me every bit as much as I love him. And that even the threat of losing his family's fortune can't alter his love. But how will I ever wait two more days to become his wife?

Dear Diary,

I have no words to describe my joy! James and I were married yesterday!

Anna

CHICAGO, ILLINOIS
1897

There is more in Mama's diary, but I have to stop reading as tears flood my eyes. I now have proof that my birth was not disgraceful. Mama was legally married to James Blackwell. He is my father. I cover my face and weep with relief. An enormous burden has been lifted.

Yet even as I wipe my tears, I realize that the truth isn't going to end the nightmare of Clarice's blackmail scheme. Her goal is to shame me and end my engagement to William, and she won't think twice about dragging Judge Blackwell and his family into the mud along with me. I can clear my mother's name, but William's family will still be scandalized to learn that my father is a prominent Chicago judge who married his servant and then deserted her. I would be sinking to Clarice's level if I ruined the Blackwells' lives for my own selfish interests.

At the same time, I'm enraged with James Blackwell for abandoning my mother, leaving her all alone to give birth to me in a grim tenement house. How could he do such a thing to the woman he claimed to love? In the end, did he love his family's fortune more than Mama? I need to know the rest of the story.

I pick up Mama's diary and continue to read. . . .

CHAPTER 23

Christina

Dear Diary,

I have no words to describe my joy! James and I were married yesterday! We spent the first day of our new life together in a small hotel room in Cicero near the train station. Neither of us wanted the day to end. When it finally did, James rode the train home to Chicago with me and waited in the lane behind his mansion until he knew I was safely inside. "If anything ever happened to you," he said, "I don't think I could live without you."

I was certain that Vera would see my happiness and guess my secret, but she was in her own little world, madly in love with her new boyfriend. She didn't even ask where I had been all day. I can hardly believe that I am now Mrs. James Blackwell. Someday my husband will inherit this beautiful house where I'm working as his maid. But I don't even care about his wealth or his high-society family. I would be happy to live with him in a little home of our own, cooking his meals and washing his clothes. Tonight I'm so happy, I could burst with joy!

Dear Diary,

I haven't written in a while because so much has been happening. Vera has given Mrs. Philips her two-weeks' notice and is leaving to get married. She'll be moving into an apartment above a saloon where her husband works. How I envy her! If only James and I could live as a real married couple instead of keeping up this phony, secret life. It's so hard to see him when I'm working around the house and to pretend that he's a stranger. Whenever we are able to be together, the time always flies by much too quickly. But oh, the moments when I'm with him are among the happiest in my life! "Soon," he says. "Soon my plan will be complete, and we can come out of hiding and announce our love to the world."

We won't have any time together on my next day off. It's the first time that has happened since we got married. But I promised Vera I would stand up with her at her wedding. How surprised she would be if she knew that James and I were married! No one in the whole world knows the truth except the two of us.

Dear Diary,

Ever since Vera left, I've had this attic room all to myself. I mentioned it to James the other day, and he came up with a brilliant idea. Now, after everyone is asleep, he sneaks upstairs to be with me. I can't describe how wonderful it is to have my husband beside me every night! To be able to laugh and whisper in the dark and talk about what the rest of our life together will be like. I feel like I'm really his wife now, not merely someone he sees for an afternoon here and there. I have never been happier in my life!

Dear Diary,

I haven't written anything in more than two months, but now something terrifying and wonderful has happened. I'm expecting James' child. I can't wait to tell him tonight, because we share everything with each other—and yet I'm afraid to. We will have only three or four months at the most to decide what to do. After that, nosy Mrs. Philips is certain to notice my condition, and I'll be let go. James will be under pressure to find a place for us to live. And his family, who still don't know the truth about us, will certainly find out. I hate to turn his life upside-down this way, yet we're both growing tired of living a shadow life.

The moment I realized that I was having a baby, I thought of my mama. How I long to share the news of this miracle with her, knowing she would understand the joy and fear and wonder that I'm feeling. But I can't. She must hate me for leaving town with Jack the way I did. My parents must have been disgraced and humiliated when everyone in their church learned what I had done. If I returned now, it would only stir up a new round of gossip at their expense. I'm so sorry for what I did. I can't expect my parents to ever forgive me.

Yet I marvel at this tiny new life growing inside me

and wonder if Mama once felt the same way about me. If only I hadn't squandered the right to have Mama by my side when her grandchild is born.

Dear Diary,

James just went back downstairs to his room, and I'm writing this by candlelight. I told him about our baby tonight. I had to. He knows me so well that he could see I was anxious about something. "Please tell me, darling," he begged. "You look so worried. Let me help you if I can."

I took his hand and rested it on my stomach. "Our baby is growing inside here."

James pulled away from me and sat up. Even though the room was dark, I could see he was shaken. "A baby . . ." he said. "A baby . . . ?" He ran his hand along his jaw. "This changes everything."

"What do you mean?" I asked. He didn't reply. I wanted him to smile, to take me in his arms and tell me he shared my joy even if the news terrified us. But James kept shaking his head. He looked dazed.

"This changes everything," he repeated. The narrow cot squeaked as he rose and went to stand by the window. He looked out at the moonlit sky, not at me. My heart squeezed as I waited.

"James, please say something," I finally begged. I heard him exhale. He turned and came back to sit on the edge of the bed. His eyes looked blinded, as if he'd been staring at the sun instead of the moon.

"Christina . . ." His voice choked, and he had to clear his throat. "Christina, I—"

"No, stop! Don't say anything, James. Not yet." I was

terrified to hear what he might be about to say. "I needed time to get used to the news, and I know you must need some time, too. I shouldn't have sprung it on you so suddenly." He nodded and offered me the ghost of a smile before taking me into his arms again. But his embrace felt different this time. This time he held me as if I were made of glass and might break. When I remember the hollow look in his eyes, it seems as though he is the one who was shattered tonight.

I have no idea what to think.

Dear Diary,

The new maid that Mrs. Philips hired has moved into the bedroom with me. She is very young and seems homesick as she sits on the bed across from me, sniffling as she pretends to read a book. I know I should befriend her and make her feel at ease, but I have been moving in a daze all day, still devastated by the way James reacted to my news last night. And now that I have a new roommate, we won't have a chance to talk about the baby again until my half-day off next week. But maybe that's a good thing. Maybe James needs more time to decide what we're going to do.

Dear Diary,

I have been waiting all week for an envelope to arrive from James, telling me where to meet him. When it finally came this afternoon, I thought I was going to be sick. The note said, "I've been called away to New York on business.

I'll be gone at least two weeks." I don't know if the terrible nausea I'm feeling tonight is from my pregnancy or from fear.

Dear Diary,

It has been nearly two weeks, and James hasn't returned from his trip. But today a plain white envelope came in the mail for me. The note inside was typewritten: "Union Station. Sunday. 2:00 p.m." Maybe James has returned to Chicago but doesn't want his parents to know. Maybe he went to New York to find a new job and a place for us to live so we can start all over again in a city where no one knows us. Maybe we'll leave everything behind and get on a cross-country train on Sunday afternoon when we meet at the station.

I'm so eager to see him, so anxious to hear what he has planned for us, that every nerve in my body feels like it's on fire. For the first time since coming to work here, I dropped a tray I was carrying in my unsteady hands and shattered a crystal wineglass.

"The cost of the glass will be deducted from your pay," Mrs. Philips told me. It was all I could do not to laugh in her face.

Dear Diary,

I want to curl up and die. The only reason I don't is because of the baby I'm carrying—this child who is part of me and part of the man I love. I'm writing this now for my baby's sake, so there will be a record of what happened, and he will know why his father is gone.

*I went to Union Station on Sunday like the note said
and wandered around the cavernous hall for what seemed
like hours searching for James. At last I decided that he
may not have arrived yet, and I sat down on a bench to
wait, close to the stairs that led down to the tracks. I was
seated for only a few moments when a bearded gentleman
in an expensive suit approached me. "Miss Christina de
Jonge?" he asked.*

*"Yes." My heart raced so fast that I feared it would
burst. James had sent him! He was going to give me a
train ticket so I could go to New York to be with James.
The man sat down and rested the briefcase he was carrying on his lap.*

*"I'm here on behalf of Mr. James Blackwell. He has
recently become aware that he has made a foolish mistake,
as youths often do, and he has hired my law firm to help
him clean it up."*

*His words hit me with the force of Jack Newell's fists.
"A mistake?"*

*"Yes. Mr. Blackwell now realizes that his relationship
with you simply isn't worth the loss of his family's sizeable
fortune." The man reached into his briefcase and handed
me a small pile of papers. "He asked my law firm to take
the necessary steps to have the marriage annulled."*

I shook my head in disbelief. "What does that mean?"

*"It means the marriage is over, Miss de Jonge, as if it
never occurred in the first place."*

*I wanted to stand up and run, but I knew my legs would
never hold me. "I don't believe you," I finally said. "James
would have come here and told me himself."*

*"This is his signature on the annulment papers, Miss
de Jonge. I'm sure you'll recognize it." I did. I had seen it
dozens of times on the many documents James had filed*

*during my lawsuit. "Since the vows weren't spoken before
a clergyman," the lawyer continued, "and you haven't
lived together as husband and wife or established a legal
household, sufficient grounds exist for an annulment."*

*The stunned blow I felt was the same as when Jack
Newell used to knock me to the floor. A dull pain in my
chest grew and swelled. Yet, hadn't I worried all along
that this would happen?*

*"Neither your fellow servants nor Mr. Blackwell's family
know anything about your affair," the man continued. "And
Mr. Blackwell doesn't wish for them to ever find out. He is
offering you a very fair sum of money to leave quietly." He
pulled a thick, unsealed envelope from his briefcase and
set it on my lap. It was filled with cash. "You have the rest
of the afternoon to make travel plans. Then Mr. Blackwell
would like you to return to the house, pack your things, and
give Mrs. Philips notice that you're quitting as of tomorrow
morning. It would be best if you left Chicago altogether."*

*"What if I refuse to do what you're asking? If I refuse
to sign your papers?"*

*He smiled as if indulging a naughty child. "You don't
have the resources or the know-how to fight the Blackwell family. We will have you arrested for harassment
and blackmail if you try to make trouble. May I remind
you that Mr. Blackwell's father is a judge here in Chicago,
with the means and the legal connections to keep you in
prison for a very long time? Cook County Jail is a terrible
place, Miss de Jonge."*

*I couldn't imagine receiving worse treatment in jail
than the way James was treating me now.*

*The lawyer hadn't said anything about our baby. Surely
James would want to provide continued support for his
own child. How else would we live? He had to be aware of*

the shame and scorn I would face as an unmarried woman with a baby. Yet I remembered his unusual reaction when I told him about our child. It was as if the game he'd been playing suddenly had unexpected consequences, and he'd decided to end it.

My hand shook as I signed the annulment papers. The man closed his briefcase and left without another word. I don't know how long I sat on the bench in the train station, waiting to summon the strength to stand. When I did, I ran into the ladies' room and was sick.

I didn't count the cash inside the envelope until later that afternoon when I gave Mrs. O'Hara, the woman who manages this tenement house, my down payment for a month's rent. I gave Mrs. Philips my notice and moved out.

I think I knew all along that this day would come, but I still wasn't prepared for it. Or for the cruel way James rid himself of me, sending his lawyer to end our marriage instead of being courageous enough to face me himself. I feel battered and beaten down. The pain is far worse than any of the physical blows Jack Newell ever gave me.

Anna

That is the last entry in Mama's diary. After rereading the page for a second time, I still can't imagine the terrible pain she must have felt at such a cruel rejection. Was I the reason that my father, Judge James Blackwell, deserted her? Did fathering a child make the future too scary for him as he realized what he would be giving up for Mama and me? Had his little diversion with the chambermaid been nothing more than a lark all along? The only way I'll ever learn the answers is if I ask him. I'm determined to find a way to do that. I need to confront him with the truth and ask him why he acted so cruelly—but first I need to figure out a way to meet him. I add James Blackwell to the growing list of people I hate along with Clarice and Lucy. I didn't know I was capable of such strong, dark emotions. I find myself wishing I could plot a means of revenge that would be worthy of what they've done to me and to the people I love. Yet I know that God would not be pleased with the hatred that's in my heart. *"Love your enemies,"* Jesus said. *"Whosoever shall smite thee on thy right cheek, turn to him the other also."*

I can't do it. Was it only a week ago that I wanted so badly to follow Jesus?

I now have a weapon I can use to defend myself against Clarice's blackmail. My mama was married. My birth was legitimate. But if I use this weapon, I will destroy innocent lives just as Clarice is threatening to do, including James' daughter, Florence. And in the end, my father and mother may still end up ruined and bankrupt.

I am back where I started. I have no idea what to do.

CHAPTER 24

Geesje

HOLLAND, MICHIGAN

Dominie Den Herder knocks on my front door on this dreary, fall day, arriving to walk with Cornelia to work. "She is nearly ready," I tell him. "Come inside. It's too damp to stand outside."

"Thank you." He offers me a rare smile. "I hope it does not rain as we are walking," he says in English. He and Cornelia have been practicing their new language and are coming along nicely. Marinus has been more sociable lately, spending time visiting with his granddaughter at my house in the evenings. I have offered to let them be alone, but he insists that he wants me to join them. I do most of the talking. It's as if neither of them can summon enough warmth for the other to thaw the wall of ice that stands between them. Even so, it's encouraging that they both seem to be trying. Maybe our prayers for the Den Herders are beginning to be answered.

"I want you to know, Mrs. de Jonge," he says to me now in

Dutch, "that I have been looking for a place to rent. We have already stayed longer than I hoped to and have presumed too much on your hospitality."

I don't reply. I worry that he will be making a mistake if he uproots Cornelia again. It has been less than two weeks since she tried to end her life, and she still seems very fragile to me. "There's really no hurry," I say. "I enjoy having her live with me." Cornelia hurries into the front room as I'm speaking and takes her coat from the hook. I turn to her and say, "You're part of my family now, and I'm going to miss you very much when the time comes for you to move. I hope your new home is close enough that we can still visit." She smiles at me. I should mark this day on my calendar—a smile from each of them, and on the same day!

My house does feel very quiet on the days Cornelia is at work. She has been a big help to me around the house, and I've enjoyed having someone to talk with while doing my chores. I spend the morning making a pot of soup and baking bread for a woman from my church who has been unwell. Cornelia can help me deliver it when she comes home. The pleasant aromas fill my little house with warmth. After lunch, I sit down at my desk to write a letter to Anneke. I haven't heard from her since her visit, and I want her to know that I'm thinking of her. I have just taken out my stationery when I hear pounding hooves and the sound of a wagon thundering up my quiet street at breakneck speed. I jump up to look out my front window and see the delivery wagon from Van Putten's store screeching to a halt in front of my house. My heart pounds like the horses' hooves. Mr. Van Putten leaps down from the wagon and runs toward my door, calling, "Geesje! Geesje!"

I throw open the front door and hurry out. Dread washes over me when I see the frantic expression on his face. "What's wrong? What happened?"

"Is Cornelia here?" he asks.

My dread turns to panic. "No. Is she missing?"

Mr. Van Putten turns to the woman seated on his wagon and shakes his head. "She's not here!" he tells her.

The woman cries out and scrambles down from the seat. I recognize young Lena Visscher from church as she races toward me, her face white with fear. She is breathless as she asks, "Where's Cornelia? . . . She took my baby . . . She has my baby!"

"Your baby? I don't understand. Isn't Cornelia at the store?"

"I want my baby!" Mrs. Visscher lets out a heartrending cry, and I reach to catch her as her knees go weak.

"Tell me what happened, Lena."

"We're wasting time! We have to find them!" She is becoming hysterical. Mr. Van Putten takes over. "Lena was shopping at my store when her baby started to cry. My wife lifted him from the carriage and asked Cornelia to hold him for a moment. When we went to fetch the baby a few minutes later, Cornelia had vanished with him. Can you think of where she might have gone? We don't know where to look."

I cover my mouth as I envision Cornelia jumping into Black Lake with Lena Visscher's baby in her arms. I'm going to be sick. The town of Holland hugs the shoreline of Black Lake just a short walk from the store. I know I need to remain calm, but my heart races with fear. "How long has she been gone?"

"Maybe five or ten minutes. She couldn't have gone too far on foot, but we just don't know where to look."

"Let's try searching near Black Lake. Cornelia is fascinated by the water. I'll come with you."

Mrs. Visscher pushes free from me. "No, no! We need to spread out! We need to search in all directions!" The little town must seem enormous to her with her tiny baby missing.

"Take the carriage and head down to the lake, then," I say. "I'll run over to the church and get more help."

They climb back into the delivery wagon and head toward Black Lake at a gallop. I stumble up the steps into the house to fetch my coat, my feet clumsy with fear. I'm responsible for this mess. I never should have let Cornelia out of my sight. And I shouldn't have pushed for her to work in the store. *Please, God! Please!* I silently pray as I run out the door again, heading toward Pillar Church. *Please help us find Cornelia and the baby before it's too late!*

As I'm praying, I suddenly think of the cemetery. Might she have gone up there? I hesitate for a moment, wondering if I should go get more help or search up there first. The idea of Pilgrim Cemetery tugs at me. I quickly change direction and lift my skirts to race up the hill as fast as I can, praying all the way. *Please, heavenly Father. Please help us find her. Please let them be all right.*

I'm staggering from exertion by the time I reach the top. My chest aches with pain from my pounding heart. I weave through the gravestones instead of taking the road, and when I finally see Cornelia, I nearly collapse from exhaustion and relief. She is sitting on my parents' graves with her back to me, rocking the bundled baby in her arms. "Thank God! Thank God!" I whisper as I approach her.

Cornelia is singing a lullaby, so softly I mistake the sound for weeping at first. The baby is asleep in her arms. "Cornelia?" She stops singing. I kneel down beside her and caress her back. "Cornelia . . . everyone is looking for you, lieveling. Mrs. Visscher is worried about her baby. We need to take him back to her now."

She nods and wipes her eyes. "I'm sorry, Tante Geesje. . . . I just needed to hold him." I wait, sensing she has more to tell me. "They didn't let me hold my own baby, not even once. . . . My grandfather made them take him away from me right after he was born."

I cover my mouth to hold back a cry as my soul wails in grief for Cornelia. "You . . . had a baby," I say when I can speak. I make it a statement, not a question, struggling not to betray my shock and surprise.

Cornelia nods and holds the child closer. She is little more than a child herself. "They didn't even let me see him."

"Oh, lieveling." I wrap my arm around her shoulder and pull her close. "That was very cruel of them to take away your baby. Your arms must have felt so empty."

"Not just my arms . . . I felt empty everywhere. Especially my heart."

"You poor sweet child. I understand. I do. But this isn't your baby, Cornelia. You must know that. And now Lena Visscher's arms are empty. We need to bring him back to her."

"I know. . . . I'm sorry. I just needed to hold him for a little while."

I stand, my legs cramped and aching. Cornelia doesn't resist as I help her up. She clutches the sleeping baby against her chest as we start walking home. "I brought him here so I could say good-bye. . . . Like I said good-bye to my family."

"I understand. And I'm glad you had a chance to do that."

As we walk, I silently praise God for answering my prayers, grateful that I found her and that they were both safe. I thank God that Cornelia went up the hill to the cemetery instead of down to the lake. This day could have ended in tragedy.

When we reach my street, I'm not sure what to do. I'm uneasy about leaving Cornelia at home all alone, yet I hesitate to bring her back to the store to face all the nosy questions and stares—not to mention Lena Visscher's understandable anger. In the end, I gently take the baby from her arms and say, "Why don't you wait for me at home, Cornelia? I'll take the baby back to his mother, okay? We'll have some tea together to warm up when I get back."

She nods and bends to kiss the baby's forehead before I go. "Good-bye," she whispers.

My legs ache as I hurry to the store on Eighth Street, my skirts hindering my steps. The baby grows heavy in my arms. A crowd has formed in front of the store, but Lena breaks free and runs to me, snatching her son from my arms. "Thank God! Thank God!" she says as she clutches him to her heart.

People are shouting questions at me. "Where did you find him?" "Where's Cornelia?" "Why did she kidnap him?" I ignore them.

"Let's go inside and sit down," I say. I steer Lena toward the store, but she is weeping so loudly I'm not sure she hears me. "Please send everyone else away for now," I tell the Van Puttens. "Mrs. Visscher needs to sit down in the back of the store where it's quiet."

"Of course," Mrs. Van Putten replies. "Follow me." I hear her husband thanking everyone for their help and saying that the baby is just fine as I lead Lena inside to the storeroom. It's blissfully warm from the potbellied stove, and I sip from the glass of water Mrs. Van Putten offers me while we wait for Lena to stop crying.

I rest my hand on her shoulder. "I'm so sorry that this happened. But I hope you know that Cornelia never meant to worry you or to harm your baby. She was very gentle with him."

"Then why did she steal him and run away with him?"

"That was never her intention." I choose my words carefully. "Not too many people in Holland know Cornelia's story because her grandfather wanted to avoid gossip and give her a brand-new start here in America—but she has had a very tragic past. I'm telling both of you because I know I can trust you to keep it confidential." I pause and sip more water, considering how much to share. I decide not to mention Cornelia's baby, since I don't know the story myself yet.

"Cornelia was still a child when her mother, father, and two younger brothers were all killed in a house fire. She moved away to live with her grandfather right after their funerals, before she had a chance to truly mourn their loss. Dominie Den Herder meant well, but his wife had passed away, and he was a busy pastor who didn't know how to handle a young girl's grief. No one from the church stepped forward to comfort her when she needed it so badly. Today, when your baby started crying, Mrs. Visscher, Cornelia wanted to comfort him, and I don't think she knew how. So, she started walking with him, and after he stopped crying she just kept going. She took him up to Pilgrim Cemetery because that's where she goes with me whenever she needs to remember her own mama and mourn for her. . . . Am I making any sense?"

Mrs. Van Putten nods. "She's such a quiet girl. Never says a peep."

"More than anything else, Cornelia needs our understanding and love. She is still holding a great deal of grief and sorrow inside. Today, when she held your baby, she was able to let some of it pour out so she could begin to heal." I turn to Lena. "Cornelia will want to apologize to you herself, I'm sure, but I do hope you'll find it in your heart to forgive her. I know she never meant to frighten you. And she would never hurt your baby."

"I guess so . . ." she says. "Thank God I have him back." She kisses the baby's forehead just as Cornelia did.

"Thank you both for understanding. And I will thank everyone outside for helping us with the search. But for Cornelia's sake, please remember that we don't owe them any explanation except to say that she took the baby for a walk and lost track of the time, as young girls are apt to do. I think . . . I think the very best way we can help Cornelia is to let her return to work here as if nothing happened. Then the gossip and whispering will soon die away." Mrs. Van Putten begins to speak, but I interrupt her.

"No, you don't need to decide right now whether or not you'll let Cornelia come back. Take time to think about it and talk it over with your husband. You can let us know what you decide."

I'm exhausted by the time I walk home again, and greatly relieved to find Cornelia sitting at my kitchen table drawing on her sketchbook. I peer over her shoulder and see that it's a picture of the baby.

"Is everyone mad at me?" Cornelia asks.

"No, but I'm sure you can understand that the baby's mother was very worried about him. We need to walk over to her house tomorrow so you can say you're sorry for scaring her."

"I'm making this picture for her. Do you think she'll like it?"

The page blurs out of focus as tears flood my eyes. "I think she will love it."

Her voice grows softer. "Please don't tell my grandfather about today. He doesn't want anyone here in Holland to know about my baby—not even you. He'll be very angry with me for telling you."

"Well, I'm certain he's going to hear about what happened at the store. The entire town will be talking about it."

"I wasn't going to hurt the baby."

"I know you weren't." Cornelia's pencil makes a faint scratching sound as she sketches. I pray for wisdom, as I have so often since she came to live with me. "Will you tell me about your baby, Cornelia?"

"Nobody is supposed to know about him," she says, her voice whisper-soft.

"You can trust me with your secret, lieveling. Besides, I'm guessing that you need to talk about him, am I right? Otherwise, it's as if he doesn't exist. But he does." I wait, watching her draw, praying that she will let me help her lift this great weight from her heart.

She begins her story slowly, speaking in a halting voice. "There was this man in my grandfather's church. . . . Everybody liked him. He was my papa's age, with a wife and children of his own, but . . . but he was the only person who ever took time to listen to me, like my papa used to do. . . . Sometimes he would hold me when I needed it. But then he wanted to do more than hold me." She pauses, and I want to murder the man.

"I knew the Bible says it's wrong, and I squirmed away from him, at first. . . . But then I stopped caring if I broke the church's rules. God took my family in order to punish me, so what did I care if I broke His rules? Besides, the man made me feel . . . special." A rage begins growing inside me that will have no outlet. This evil man lives thousands of miles away in the Netherlands.

"When I felt my baby moving inside me it was like . . . like I finally had someone to love again. God killed all the people I loved, but now I had gotten even with God and made a new person to love. And my baby would love me, too. I ran away from home—not to kill myself, but so I could be on my own. Grandfather found me and made me come back. I told him that I was going to have a baby because I wanted him to throw me out of his house. He asked who the father was, but I wouldn't tell him. He could probably guess who it was, but he didn't want to admit it to himself. . . . Do you know what I mean?"

"I do. And it infuriates me! He never confronted the man?"

Cornelia shakes her head. "He said he couldn't accuse him unless I named him and testified against him, but I wouldn't do it." She lifts her chin, a gesture of defiance. I admire her strength and courage in holding on to her secret. It was the only thing in her life that she could control. But the cost was much too great, for everyone.

"My grandfather was furious with me. He said I had shamed him. He sent me far away to have the baby, and I was like a prisoner there. I made up my mind that as soon as the baby was strong enough, we would run away and hide where no one could ever find us." She stares into the distance for a long moment, as if imagining what her future might have been like. Then she shakes her head, erasing it.

"It took me all day and night to have him. I felt like I was being torn in two. Then at last, I heard my baby crying . . . and I heard someone say, 'It's a little boy.' I decided I would name him Willem after my papa. . . . I had no strength left at all, but I swore that as soon as I was able to, I would take Willem far away from there.

"The midwife wrapped me in a warm blanket because I was shivering, and she brought me some bread and cheese to eat. 'I want to hold my baby, first,' I told her. 'Where is he? Can I hold him now?'

"'The baby is with a family who will love him,' she told me.

"'But I love him! He's my baby and no one else's! Bring him to me!'

"The woman shook her head. 'Your grandfather arranged for him to be adopted by a family that isn't able to have children of their own.'

"I started screaming and trying to get out of bed, but they held me down. They told me he was already gone. I needed to see him and hold him, but nobody would listen to me." Cornelia pauses to choke back a sob as she relives that terrible day.

I take her in my arms and say, "Go ahead and cry, Cornelia. You need to cry." And I weep along with her.

"They didn't let me hold him!" she sobs. "Not even once before they took him away from me! . . . How will he know that I love him if I couldn't hold him?"

I rock her in my arms for a long time. "I'm glad that you had a chance to hold Mrs. Visscher's baby today. Glad that you finally had a chance to say good-bye."

When Cornelia is able to speak again, she leans back in her chair and wipes her eyes. "My grandfather sent me away to have the baby because he wanted to keep it a secret. But when I came back, everyone in his church was talking about it. The dominie's unmarried granddaughter had a baby! He was ashamed of me. And I had no reason to live anymore without my son. That's why I wanted to die."

"Let me help you find some new reasons to live. Will you let me do that for you, Cornelia? I would miss you so much if you died—just as much as I miss the rest of my family." I watch her, waiting for her reply. She shrugs and picks up her pencil to finish her drawing.

I can now see why Cornelia is so angry with her grandfather. And I understand that a man as proud and self-righteous as Marinus must have felt disgraced and shamed when his congregation learned of his granddaughter's moral failures. But I wonder if he even recognizes the part he played in the tragedy. By not showing Cornelia his love, he made her easy prey for a man who would. I also understand why Marinus had to give away the baby. The child deserved a chance to grow up without the stigma of being illegitimate. But Cornelia doesn't understand. No one explained it to her or sat with her and comforted her in her sorrow. Now neither of them is able to forgive the other. If there is a remedy for this terrible situation, I have no idea what it is.

The loud pounding on my front door startles both of us. "Stay right here!" I tell Cornelia before going to answer it. When I see her grandfather on my porch, I want to pummel him with my fists.

"Let me speak to Cornelia!" he bellows.

"No. Not right now. She needs—"

"Don't tell me *no*! She's my granddaughter!" He starts to move past me, but I push him backward as hard as I can to get him away from my door. Then I step outside onto the porch with him, closing the door behind both of us.

"You keep your voice down, Dominie! Getting angry and yelling at Cornelia is the worst thing you could possibly do right now."

"Everyone is talking about what she did today, snatching that baby. It's all over town! Tell her I said to pack her things. We're moving away. Everyone will think she's a crazy woman!"

My temper boils over. I have tried so hard not to lash out at him and to be kind and loving toward him, but I can't keep up the façade any longer. Not after the way he treated Cornelia. "The only crazy person is you!" I shout. "You tried to run from your problems in the past and they followed you here! How many more times are you going to uproot that poor girl and make her suffer before you decide to help her instead of running away with her?"

"I suppose she told you all about . . ." He waves his hand in the air as if avoiding a shameful word.

"About her baby? Yes, she told me."

"Everyone in town will probably know about it now."

"No, Dominie. I'm the only one. I'm the only person in town who knows that Cornelia's life was so bleak and loveless after her family died that she found consolation in the arms of an evil, married man. I'm the only one who knows how you ripped her child from her arms without any warning or explanation. And without even giving her a chance to hold him and say good-bye."

"It had to be done."

"Not in such a heartless way. No wonder she's still grieving. It's a terrible loss for any mother to lose the child she has carried inside her for nine months, regardless of the situation."

"She shamed me! Her behavior shamed me before my entire church!"

"Listen to yourself! All you care about are your own feelings! Why can't you see this tragedy from Cornelia's point of view?

Look at all the wreckage and pain in her short life! Where is your pity, your compassion, your mercy on a young girl who lost so much?"

"I lost everything, too! I resigned from my position in the church in shame! Because of her behavior!"

"Why wasn't your church willing to offer grace to you and Cornelia?"

"I didn't expect them to."

"And you didn't think to show Christ's grace and mercy to Cornelia yourself?"

"The law against adultery is very clear. It's one of God's Ten Commandments—"

"Grace and mercy are the hallmarks of Christ's Kingdom!" I say, outshouting him. "Remember the woman Jesus met at the well? Or the woman who was caught in adultery? Jesus told her, 'Neither do I condemn thee—'"

"Cornelia brought shame on me and on our family!"

I want to shake him. "Haven't you ever shamed our heavenly Father? I know I have. The psalm says that if God kept a record of our sins, who among us could stand? But with Him, there is forgiveness."

"How dare you preach to me?"

"I dare because you need to hear it. You've forgotten Christ's most basic teachings. Don't you remember His parable about the man whose huge debt is forgiven, and yet he refuses to forgive someone else's debt? The king casts him into prison! Our sins bring shame to our heavenly Father every single day, yet He shows us mercy. In fact, He piled all of our shame on His innocent Son. And right now, His love and grace are the only things that can convince Cornelia to live."

"How dare you—?"

"Where is your outrage at the married man who took advantage of a lonely girl?" I'm shouting now, unable to stop.

"She wouldn't name him. If she had, I would have excommunicated him."

"And so, instead of pursuing justice, you allowed this man to continue attending your church, where he is free to prey on other innocent girls? You both should be in jail!" I take a deep breath and say, "How God must grieve over the messes we create in His name! You should worry less about yourself, Dominie, and more about your granddaughter. You should ask God how you can help her so she'll decide her life is worth living. And you need to begin by asking her to forgive you for taking her baby away." He starts to speak, but I cut him off. "We've said enough for one day. Cornelia is not moving out of my house. I asked Mrs. Van Putten to let her come back to work so this will all blow over. And it will. Now go home and read what Jesus has to say about forgiveness and mercy and love. Good day, Dominie."

I go inside and slam my door so hard the windows rattle.

I watch from the front room as he leaves my porch and stomps home. I'm trembling so badly from head to toe that I need to sit down and catch my breath. When I do, I'm immediately filled with remorse. I shouldn't have lost my temper and yelled at him. I'm ashamed of the way I behaved. I'm supposed to be a good Christian woman, turning the other cheek, being patient and kind. I was none of those things. I close my eyes and ask God to forgive me. I've made such a mess of this.

When I open them again, Cornelia is standing in front of me. She kneels down and takes my hands in hers. "Thank you, Tante Geesje." I stare at her. I don't know what to say.

"For what?" I finally ask.

"Everybody is so afraid to stand up to him. He always gets whatever he wants. He's the dominie. He speaks for God, so he must be right. Nobody has taken my side since my papa died." She squeezes my hands and says, "You sounded just like Jesus did when He yelled at all those religious people and told them they were hypocrites. Thank you, Tante Geesje." She leans forward and wraps her thin arms around me, holding me tightly. "I love you," she whispers.

"And I love you, too, Cornelia."

I think back to the day my son asked me if I would let Cornelia stay in my spare room for a few weeks. I remember wishing I could refuse, unwilling to have my quiet, cozy life disrupted. I ask God to forgive my selfishness. And I wonder how many other times in my life I have refused to answer His call because it might inconvenience me.

CHAPTER 25

Anna

Ever since I learned that James Blackwell is my father, I have been trying to devise a way to meet him and confront him. It won't change the mess I'm in with Clarice, but I want him to know about the consequences that his cruel behavior had on Mama and me. And I admit I'm also very curious to meet my real father face-to-face, this man whom Mama loved so deeply. But James Blackwell is a busy judge whose life has no intersection with mine. I've thought about sneaking into his courtroom and sitting in the back row to watch him from a distance, but I don't even know where his courtroom is. I certainly don't dare approach him at his home, especially after Mrs. Philip's warning.

To make matters worse, I haven't been feeling well. I have a terrible sore throat, and I'm running a slight fever. I imagine it's caused by exhaustion from all the pressure I've been under. I'm not eating or sleeping well. I need to stay home until I have a chance to recover, but I'm running out of time with Clarice, who will want an answer soon. I still have no idea what to tell her. At least my illness has delayed my trip to the engravers with Mother and Mrs. Wilkinson to order the wedding invitations.

I spend my time in bed, alternating between praying for a solution to my dilemma with Clarice and rereading Mama's journal. I love hearing Mama's voice in the words she penned, but I'm also trying to form a clear picture of my father. The James Blackwell in the beginning of her diary is a romantic character who is charmed by the ordinary people who run his household and ignores the barriers between the two classes. Like a hero in a romance novel, he is quick to jump in and rescue Mama from the railroad company, battling them in a lawsuit to win the settlement she deserved. He found creative, romantic ways for them to meet and was willing to marry her rather than simply taking advantage of her. So how did he suddenly change into the cowardly man who ended their marriage in such a cold, unfeeling way? I long to ask him.

I am sitting up in bed with Mama's journal open on my lap when an idea begins to form in my mind of how I might be able to meet with him. What if I were to send him a plain white envelope like the ones he used to send to Mama? It could contain a cryptic message with only a place and a time to meet. Would he be intrigued enough by the mystery to keep the appointment? Perhaps some remaining guilt from his past actions would also draw him. He may even believe the message came from Mama, since he probably doesn't know she's dead.

The idea continues to grow and take shape until I feel a compelling urge to do it. I'm going to ask him to meet with me. I know there's a very good chance that he won't come, in which case I'm no worse off than I am now. But if he does show up,

I'm going to ask him why he rejected his own child and hurt the woman who loved him so deeply.

I climb out of bed and sit down at my desk, determined to follow through on my plan before I have a chance to change my mind. I choose the same time and place where James secretly met with Christina for the first time. I write: *Garfield Park. Washington Boulevard and Central Park Avenue. Sunday. 2:00 p.m.* I add a streetcar token to the envelope, left over from my travels around the city with Lucy, to further remind him of Christina. Then I wait, wondering what will happen.

I still feel ill on Sunday afternoon, my sore throat much worse, but I drag myself out of bed, tuck Mama's diary in my bag, and ask our driver to take me to Garfield Park. "Return for me in an hour," I tell him. The day is cold and gray. The sharp wind blowing off Lake Michigan knifes straight through my cloak, making me cough. I have a fever and can barely swallow, but anger and a hunger for revenge propel me to see this through. At ten minutes before the hour, I enter Garfield Park at the intersection of Washington Boulevard and Central Park Avenue and sink down on the first bench I come to. In truth, I feel too weak to wander the park searching for him. He'll have to find me—if he decides to come. A few people walk past me, mostly couples. None of them look like a wealthy judge.

I have just checked my watch at two minutes past two when I see a man in an expensive woolen overcoat and shiny leather shoes walking toward me. He is looking all around as if searching for someone. The man is tall and slender and carries himself with a gentlemanly elegance that I didn't see in the other passersby. My heart begins to race. I stand, my head spinning, and walk forward to meet him. We are twenty feet apart when

I pull off my hat so he can see my flowing, golden hair. The instant I do, he halts on the path. I continue toward him, my feet unsteady.

"Judge Blackwell?" He draws in a breath as if he has seen a ghost. I feel victorious. My instinct is to drive the knife deeper and hurt him the way he hurt Mama. I halt three feet from him. "Do I look familiar, Judge? I'm told I resemble my mother, Christina de Jonge."

"*Christina* . . ." he breathes. He looks shaken, and I'm glad.

I gesture to the wooden bench. "Let's sit down over there and talk, shall we?" We walk to the bench and sit facing each other, both of us perched on the edge. The mahogany hair that Mama once described has lost its luster with age, like old wood dulled from use. Wings of gray frame his temples, and his blue eyes have wrinkles at the corners. But he is still a nice-looking gentleman.

"Christina de Jonge is my mother, Judge Blackwell. My name is Anna, and I've been searching for my father. Now I believe I may have found him."

I draw a breath, preparing to launch into my scathing rebuke, when the judge interrupts. "I loved Christina. She broke my heart when she left me without even a word of good-bye."

His words knock the air from my chest. "When *she* left *you?*"

"Yes. Didn't your mother tell you what she did? She made an appointment with my father while I was away in New York on business and threatened to blackmail him with the truth about our marriage if he didn't pay her off. She was after our money from the very beginning, and she eventually agreed to accept a large payoff from my father to have our marriage annulled. By the time I returned from New York, she had left town."

I am trembling with fury. "You're wrong! That's not what happened at all! I know because I found her diary." I pull it from my bag and wave it at him. "You were the one who got rid of her after she told you she was expecting your child. I'm that child!"

"But . . . no. They told me there wasn't any baby. They said Christina lied about that, too, so she could extort more money. They had proof that she wasn't expecting at all."

"She was! And you left the two of us all alone! Here, read what she wrote." I shove the diary into his hands, open to the last entry. I watch his face as he reads how the lawyer met Mama at the train station—how he told her that James had made a foolish mistake and wanted the marriage annulled. When he looks up at me again, I say, "He handed her the annulment papers with your signature on them and threatened her with jail if she didn't sign them and go away quietly. What was she supposed to do?"

"None of this is true!" he says, pointing to the diary page. "I never asked for an annulment. It was Christina who—"

"Would the woman you fell in love with and married do something like that? Was she ever greedy for your money?"

He slowly shakes his head. "No . . . no, she was such a pure soul. That's why I was so shocked and hurt when she . . ." His voice trails away.

"How could there be two conflicting stories, Judge? One of us must have it wrong."

He looks up at me, and I see the same hollow-eyed gaze that Mama must have seen after she told him the news about their baby. "My family did this to us," he says. "That's the only explanation there can be. I was so careful to make sure that no one knew about Christina and me, but my family must have found out. . . . And they turned us against each other."

"My mother didn't leave Chicago right away. I think she stayed because she hoped you would find her and return to her. But three years later after all of her money ran out, she decided to take me home to her family in Michigan. On the way there, our ship sank in a storm, and she drowned. I was with her, but I survived."

"No . . . no!" Judge Blackwell shakes his head. He moans so loudly, I fear someone will come over to see what's wrong. "You're Christina's daughter?" he asks.

"Yes. And I'm also your daughter."

"My . . . my daughter! You're my daughter—and Christina's!" He closes his eyes in anguish, moaning as he comprehends the truth. Suddenly he leans toward me and pulls me into his arms. This isn't the reaction I expected, and it takes me by surprise. He holds me so tightly I can scarcely breathe, and I wonder if, in his heart, he is imagining I'm Mama. When he finally releases me, he has tears in his eyes. "Christina was the love of my life!"

"And you were hers. I'll let you read the entire diary, if you want to, and you'll see how much she loved you. Her friend Vera kept warning her that she was just a toy to you. That you would get tired of her and discard her. That's why, when the lawyer told her—"

"You're my daughter!" he interrupts. "I can't believe it! I mean, of course I believe it, but . . . but I was upset on the night Christina told me she was expecting because I knew I needed to act fast. I had to find a home for us and figure out a way to support her and our baby. I started making plans the very next day. I was so happy that I was going to be a father that I wanted to announce the news to the entire world, including my family. But before I could finalize my plans or even speak with Christina again, my father insisted that I go to New York to help him with an urgent business matter. And then my mother hired another servant who moved into Christina's room and . . . Oh, no, no . . . ." he says, moaning again. "I see it so clearly now! My family orchestrated the whole lie to break Christina and me apart!"

"And they succeeded."

"And now Christina is gone forever?"

"I was three years old when she died. I only have a few memories of her."

"You're her child—my child. I can't believe it! You're as beautiful as she was."

He is so much like the James Blackwell in my mother's diary that I know he is telling the truth about what happened. I like this man—my father. I arrived here intending to hate him, but I believe his version of the story. I believe that both he and Mama were duped. And I believe that he truly loved her and would have loved me, too.

"How can I make this up to you, Anna?" he asks. "For Christina's sake? And for your sake?"

"I don't need anything, Judge Blackwell. I was adopted by a wealthy Chicago couple, Mr. and Mrs. Arthur Nicholson, right after Mama died. I've had a wonderful life. And now I'm engaged to marry William Wilkinson."

"From the banking family?"

"Yes."

As I mention my marriage to William, it occurs to me that if there is a way to escape from the trap Clarice has set for me, perhaps the judge can find it.

"Maybe there is something you can help me with, Judge Blackwell. You see, I began searching for my father because I'm faced with an impossible situation." I tell him about Clarice, and how she has threatened to ruin me and my family if I don't break the engagement. His eyes flash with anger when I tell him how she accused Christina of being a harlot and me of being her bastard child, creating a ruinous scandal. "That's why I've been trying to find out who my real father is, so I can prove that Mama was married and that my birth was legitimate. Then there would be no scandal for Clarice to use to threaten me. But now that I've found you, I realize that the truth would cause an entirely different scandal. I'm in the Literary Club with your wife and daughter. You're a well-respected judge. I won't ruin your lives just to save my own. Besides, William wants to run for public office, and he and the Wilkinsons would be just as appalled by this scandal as the first one. But if you can help me think of a way to—"

"What's this blackmailer's name?"

"Clarice Beacham. Do you know her?"

"I know of the Beacham family. I believe they have ties by marriage to my mother's side of the family, the Rockports."

"Clarice is doing this to get even with William, and she doesn't care how many lives she destroys in the process."

"Let me give it some thought. There must be something I can do. How soon is your wedding supposed to take place?"

"The first of January. Clarice wants my answer within the next few days, before the wedding invitations are mailed."

"And you're in love with young Wilkinson and want to marry him?" I hesitate just a moment too long, and he notices. "Ah! You aren't sure. Are you in love with someone else?" I can't help thinking of Derk, and once again I hesitate too long. The judge shakes his finger at me. "I always knew when Christina was holding something back from me by the funny way she would chew her bottom lip. You did the very same thing, just now." I start to speak, but he stops me. "I haven't earned the right to ask about your secrets. But if there is someone you truly love, you need to move heaven and earth to be with him. I wish I had done the same with Christina." His eyes shine with unshed tears. "Don't get me wrong, I've had a good life with my wife and family, and I'm confident that young Mr. Wilkinson will treat you very well, too. But I loved Christina—" He stops when his voice breaks. He waves his hand as if impatient with himself for becoming emotional. "I'm sorry, Miss Nicholson, forgive me for . . ."

I open my arms and offer my father my embrace.

He walks me to the corner when my carriage arrives and helps me inside. "Are you unwell?" he asks. I assure him I'm fine, even though I'm shivery with fever again. "I'll help you find a solution, Anna, I promise. No one is going to accuse Christina of wrongdoing and get away with it. Tell Miss Beacham you need a few more days to decide."

"Thank you. You've given me hope."

I want to go to bed the moment I arrive home, but the butler hands me a letter on my way toward the stairs. "This came for you in the mail today, Miss Anna."

There's no return address. I don't recognize the handwriting. It must be a letter of warning from Clarice. I undress and climb into bed before slitting it open. But the letter isn't from Clarice— it's from Derk.

Dear Anneke,

I haven't stopped thinking of you since I left Chicago. I love you, and now I know that you love me. That's enough for me, for now. Your Oma Geesje kept telling me that it would be impossible for you and me to be together because your way of life is so different from mine, but I didn't want to believe her. Now that I've seen your beautiful home and the way you live with servants to do everything for you, I know that she's right. I would never dare to ask you to leave all of that when I have nothing to offer you in return. I also saw how much you love your parents and how important it is that you marry William, for their sakes. It makes me sad for you, but I understand now. We'll leave it at that. Please know that I'll never stop loving you. Never.

I'm wondering if our efforts in that dingy storeroom were all in vain or if you found something in your mother's

*box of belongings that was useful. I've been praying about
your situation with the blackmailer and hoping you will
be able to find a way out that won't bring ruin or scandal
to you. I don't understand how people can be so selfish
and evil.*

*I understand if you don't feel comfortable writing back
to me because you're engaged to another man. But maybe
you can send a quick message to me in one of your letters to your grandmother, just so I'll know that you're all
right and that you found a solution to your problem. I'm
curious to learn what was in that crate!*

*You can turn to me whenever you need help, Anneke.
Ask any favor. I love you more than you'll ever know.*

Derk

I tuck Derk's letter back inside the envelope and put it beneath my pillow. I will have to burn it in my fireplace so no one
will see it, but I want to read it a few more times and memorize
it first. I'm so glad that he knows I love him, too.

I drift off into a feverish sleep thinking of Judge Blackwell's
advice to me: *"If there is someone you truly love, you need to
move heaven and earth to be with him."*

Impossible.

CHAPTER 26

Geesje

Cornelia looks as though she wants to crawl into a hole in the
ground and hide as we knock on Lena Visscher's door. "Everything is going to be fine, lieveling," I assure her. "You'll see."

Lena smiles as she opens her door to us. She is holding her
baby, who gurgles and coos, his chubby arms flailing. "Won't
you come in?" she says.

"Thank you. We can't stay long. Cornelia is expected at work
in a little while." Mrs. Visscher's house is small but very neat
and tidy, the worn cushions on the settee inviting. The rocking
chair looks as though it has rocked many Visscher children to
sleep before this baby. The aroma of cinnamon fills the room.

"Please sit down. Would you like some coffee or tea?"

"No, thank you. We just had some at home. Cornelia has
something she wants to give you."

Cornelia wipes her palm on her thigh before opening her

sketchbook to remove the drawing she has made. She already tore it from the book before leaving home, but she has carried it there to keep it from getting wrinkled. I helped her practice what she wants to say in English, since Lena doesn't understand Dutch. I know Cornelia is nervous. She swallows before speaking.

"I am sorry that I take the baby. I know you are scared by me. Your arms are feeling empty yesterday. Will you please forgive me?"

"Of course, Cornelia. Of course. You meant no harm." I hope Cornelia hears the warmth in Lena's voice.

"This . . . this is for you. To say how I am sorry." Her hand trembles as she passes the drawing to Lena.

"Why, it's him!" she says in surprise. "This looks just like my Willem! Thank you, Cornelia!"

"You are welcome."

"She is a very gifted artist," I say. I had forgotten that the baby's name is Willem—the same name Cornelia gave her son.

Willem bats at the paper with his little fists, making baby sounds as he tries to grab it. "Hey, now! Don't you tear your pretty portrait," his mother says. She smiles at Cornelia. "Will you hold him for me while I put this someplace safe?"

I stop breathing. I can feel my heart beating as Cornelia gives me a questioning look. I nod, and she carefully lifts Willem from his mother's arms. Cornelia sits down with him on the settee and starts singing quietly to him in Dutch as he bounces on her lap.

I want to hug Lena Visscher in gratitude.

Cornelia seems happy as I walk with her to work at the store. I leave her at the door, and I can hear Mrs. Van Putten greeting her as she goes inside. I'm grateful that everything has worked out, yet I feel a lingering uneasiness at the harsh way I spoke to Dominie Den Herder yesterday, even though he deserved it. Besides, I don't think he really heard what I said.

Derk is just walking out of his front door as I turn onto our street, and he hurries toward me. "I need to talk to you," he says. "Do you have a minute?"

"Of course. Shall we go over to my house?" I'm wary of running into the dominie at Derk's house before I've had a chance to decide what I need to say to him.

I offer Derk a kitchen chair as I put another log in the stove and poke the coals, but he doesn't sit down, pacing the floor instead. "What's wrong?" I ask.

"I have a confession to make, and I'm afraid you're going to be mad at me." I wait, watching him rake his fingers through his hair. "I ignored your advice and I . . . um . . . I went down to Chicago to see Anneke."

"Oh, Derk." I sink onto a chair. "Was she home? Did you see her? What happened?"

"It turned out that she really needed my help that day, and she was very glad I came. She said I was an answer to her prayers. She's trying to find information about her father, and I was able to help her dig through an old storeroom and find a box of belongings that were her mother's. I don't know what was in the box because I had to race back to the train station so I wouldn't miss all my connections, and—"

"You went down and back in one day?"

"That's all the time I had." He finally sits down. "I know you've been telling me that it's hopeless to think about marrying Anneke, but I guess I had to see for myself. She lives in an enormous house, Tante Geesje, and has rooms full of servants to wait on her. Her life is so different from ours . . . and yet she dug through a dingy storeroom with cobwebs and rats and cockroaches because she loves her parents. Her father will lose everything if Anneke doesn't marry William."

I'm not following everything he says, not seeing the connection between the storeroom and Anneke's marriage. I can straighten out the details later, after I find out if he confessed his love to her. And if his heart was broken. "Did you accomplish what you went there to do, lieveling?"

He looks at me, and his smile could light up a room. "I did. It was well worth the long trip down there and back. I told Anneke I loved her, and . . . and she said that she loves me, too."

"She did?" My misgivings return.

"Yes. But I'm not going to interfere in her life anymore. I know she has to marry William. I see that now. But I'm glad I told her, and it's good to know that she . . ." He can't finish.

My heart breaks for both of them. I think of Derk's grandfather, Hendrik—my first love. I want to tell Derk that even though we can't always marry the person we love, life does go on. And love just might surprise us by showing up again, someday. But he doesn't want to hear any of that right now.

"I'm so sorry, Derk. For both of you."

"Yeah . . ." he says, sighing. "Thanks. I'd better get going." He pulls a knitted hat from his coat pocket and jams it on his head. "By the way," he says as he opens the back door, "do you know where Dominie Den Herder went?"

I feel a chill, and it doesn't come from the open door. "What do you mean?"

"Well, he never came home last night. Not for dinner and not to sleep. I just wondered if he told you where he was going."

"No, he didn't. I have no idea where he is." But I have a sinking feeling that I may have played a role in his disappearance.

CHAPTER 27

Anna

CHICAGO, ILLINOIS

I'm still not well. The weather is bitter cold outside, with a damp wind blowing off the lake. The first wet snowflakes sift down from the soggy clouds. Winter is starting early in Chicago. I haven't been out of bed since meeting with Judge Blackwell on Sunday, but I manage a smile when a plain white envelope arrives addressed to me. I think I know who it is from. I ask the chambermaid to light my bedside lamp, then I pull out the message to read it.

> *Anna,*
> *I have a plan that I hope will resolve your dilemma. If it's convenient, arrange a late-afternoon tea on Wednesday with you, Miss Beacham, and Mrs. Wilkinson in attendance. Your adoptive mother, as well, if you think it*

would be appropriate. I will join you. I can be at your home by 4:30.

J. Blackwell

"How can you host a luncheon when you're still feverish?" Mother says when I ask her to invite the two women. "Can't it wait until you're well?" I convince her that it's very important, and she makes the arrangements. Clarice will be overjoyed at the invitation, thinking I've arranged the tea to announce that I'm ending my engagement to William.

It takes every ounce of my strength to get out of bed and get dressed on Wednesday afternoon. My scalp hurts as Sophia brushes my hair in front of the mirror. My skin is as pale as paper, yet my cheeks are aflame. I grip the bannister as I make my way downstairs at four o'clock, the joints in my body aching with each step I take. I can't imagine what Judge Blackwell is planning to say, but I'm guessing that he will surprise all of us.

The servants have set up a tea table in our morning room with our best silver tea set and bone china cups. I'm seated there by four thirty with Mother, Clarice, and William's mother. The fifth seat is empty. "Who else are you expecting?" Mother asks. I give her a strained smile and a little shake of my head. We're sipping tea and making small talk when the butler ushers Judge Blackwell into the room. I make the proper introductions, and he charms the others as he greets them, gallantly offering a pleasant compliment to each woman. He seems completely at ease. The ladies, however, are baffled by his presence at my afternoon tea, especially my mother. If I gave them each a thousand guesses, they would never imagine that the charming judge is my biological father. He continues his easy chatter as he takes his seat, and the maid serves him from a platter of tiny cakes.

He turns to Clarice. "I believe our families are related by marriage, Miss Beacham. You may recall that my mother is Bessie Rockport. One of her older brothers married a great-aunt of yours."

"How interesting. I had no idea." Clarice is all smiles and genteel haughtiness as she plays the game with him, mentioning various cousins and second cousins to cement their kinship.

The judge turns to Mrs. Wilkinson next. "You and I have something in common, as well, Mrs. Wilkinson. My grandfather Rockport invested very generously in your father-in-law's bank years ago, when he was looking for start-up money. Grandfather served on the bank's first board of trustees. I would say that their partnership has benefitted all of us in the years since, wouldn't you?"

"Yes, certainly." She grows uneasy as the conversation turns to money—something that simply isn't mentioned in polite circles. Yet the judge has disarmed her by his easy manner. She must be dying of curiosity to know why he's here.

Judge Blackwell continues pouring on the charm, as if perfectly comfortable sipping afternoon tea with four society ladies. He turns to Mother last. "Mrs. Nicholson, I recently learned of a connection between myself and your family, too." He winks at me, and I feel a wave of dizziness. Part of it is caused by my stuffy head and fever, but most of it is caused by fear. I know what he is about to tell them, and I can well imagine how shocked they are going to be. "I understand that you and your husband adopted Anna when she was a child, Mrs. Nicholson."

"Yes . . . we did." I hear a note of caution in her voice.

"I'm sorry to say that for the past few weeks, my wife and daughter, Florence, have heard a great deal of gossip about Anna's past. I understand that the nasty rumors have been burning through our social circles lately. I know this must have had an unwelcome effect on your family, as well as on yours, Mrs. Wilkinson, since Anna is engaged to marry your son."

Mother and Mrs. Wilkinson have stopped eating. They are searching for something polite to say. They want him to stop. Clarice shoots me a poisonous look, her smile gone. Mother clears her throat. "If you don't mind, Judge Blackwell, this is hardly the time or the place to discuss rumors—"

"I know. I know. But putting a halt to these rumors is important to everyone at this table, am I right?"

"Yes, of course," Mother begins. "And yet this is—"

"You see, Mrs. Nicholson, I met with your daughter, Anna, a few days ago. She confided in me that ever since the rumors began, she has been trying to put a stop to them by secretly searching for her father. She feels compelled to prove that her mother, Christina, was a respectable married woman who hadn't given birth to her in shame, as the stories claim. And now I'm happy to say that she has found her father. Anna has the undeniable proof she needs to confirm that her mother was legally married. She wants the three of you to be the first to know who her father is." He pauses. The women look frozen, none of them daring to breathe. My eyes fill with tears as he reaches to take my hand. "Anna is my daughter. I'm her father."

Silence. His words have fallen with the force of an explosion that makes my skin tingle. We're all numb from the aftershock. Mrs. Wilkinson looks as though she may need smelling salts. The silence lengthens.

Clarice is the first to speak. "I don't believe it," she says flatly.

Her cheeks have turned very red. She must be worried about being exposed as the source of the gossip. She must also wonder if Judge Blackwell is about to inform the others of her blackmail scheme.

"Oh, it's quite true, Miss Beacham. Why would I lie about

it? I not only have a copy of our marriage license, I'm willing to swear that it's true in a court of law." He pulls a faded document from his inside pocket, unfolding it to lay it on the table in front of her. "There is no shame at all in Anna's birth. I was legally married to her mother."

"How is that even possible?" Mrs. Wilkinson asks.

"Anna's mother, Christina, worked as a servant in my family's household. She and I fell in love—and it was true love, the kind that's so very rare in our social circles. We were married in secret, and when my parents learned about it, they came up with a plan to separate Christina and me and deceived us into thinking the other one wanted the marriage annulled. We believed the lie when nothing could be further from the truth. Thanks to their devious plot, we each thought the other had fallen out of love and wanted to end the marriage. We both suffered a broken heart from the tragic misunderstanding."

Once again, silence fills the room. The etiquette books we live by don't offer advice for a situation like this one. I look up at my father and say, "Thank you." His honesty could cost him a great deal.

"You are quite welcome, my dear. Now," he says, turning to the ladies again, "because all of our families are interconnected— the Wilkinsons, the Beachams, and the Nicholsons—I think we all recognize the wisdom in keeping the truth under wraps. Why should any of us allow society to slander us? Not to mention attempting to defame our families' good names. It isn't helpful for any of us. But I thought it was important for the three of you ladies to know the truth in the event that people do start believing the gossip, or if another scandal should happen to arise. In that case, you can always contact me, and I'll gladly help you quash it with the truth."

The others remain speechless. What polite response can possibly follow such a shocking revelation? The ladies are clearly uncomfortable in this awkward situation, but Judge Blackwell knows how to make a graceful exit. He sets down his teacup and rises to his feet. "I'm sorry that I have to dash off, Mrs. Nicholson, but my wife has theater tickets for this evening. I can't truthfully say this has been a pleasure, but . . . more of a necessity, wouldn't you agree?" He bends to kiss my cheek. "Thank you for the tea, my dear. I'll see myself out."

It doesn't take long for Clarice and Mrs. Wilkinson to excuse themselves and hurry off, as well. Mother turns to me when we're alone, studying my face as if we're strangers. "What in the world? Why didn't you tell me, Anna? And to think you had to suffer all that shame . . ."

"I didn't know until a few days ago. You asked me to stop searching for my father, and I was afraid you would be angry with me for disobeying. Besides, I didn't know what I might uncover. I never dreamed that Judge Blackwell would be so gracious about admitting the truth."

"Let's hope this will be the end of the rumors."

"It will be. Clarice was the one who was spreading them."

"Anna, it's wrong to accuse someone—"

"It's true. She told me so herself. She was once in love with William, and she wanted to get even with him for rejecting her. She hoped to create a scandal that would end our engagement and ruin his reputation. She knows how concerned the Wilkinsons are with keeping up appearances."

"I'm glad it's over." Mother folds me into her embrace, then pulls back in alarm. "Anna! You're burning up with fever!"

"I need to go back to bed and sleep off this terrible cold. My throat feels as if it's on fire."

"I'm sending for Dr. Paulson."

"I'll be fine. It's just a sore throat."

I notice a strange rash on my body as I undress. By the time I've crawled into bed, I feel like I'm inside a furnace. I kick off all the blankets, but a moment later, I'm shaking with chills. I can't recall ever feeling so sick. My last thought before falling asleep is that the nightmare is finally over. Clarice's plan has failed, and everything is going to be all right. Thanks to Judge Blackwell.

My father.

CHAPTER 28

Geesje

Dominie Den Herder is still missing. Derk told me this morning that he hasn't come home since the day I confronted him. Cornelia doesn't know that her grandfather is missing, nor has she asked why he hasn't been coming over in the evenings or walking to work with her. Instead, Cornelia and I have been undertaking the enormous task of dealing with her grief and her anger at God for allowing her losses to happen. As we slowly move forward, I'm trying to convince her that she was the victim of the tragedies she has suffered, not the cause.

"It wasn't your fault that your family died," I tell her as we sit in my front room. I'm knitting a pair of mittens while Cornelia draws a picture of my cat playing with my ball of yarn. "It wasn't your fault that your grandfather was unable to show you his love. And it wasn't your fault that the man from church abused you. He is to blame for what happened, not you. He is the one who should be ashamed and made to pay for it. He is the one who deserves to be punished. God knows the truth about what happened, and He loves you and grieves with you."

Cornelia reaches to pull the cat away from my yarn before he makes a tangled mess of it. She holds him close, rubbing her cheek against his fur. "Do you ever have doubts, Tante Geesje? About God, I mean. . . . After your parents died, and then your children?"

"Of course, I do. We all have moments of doubt. But our faith allows us to bring our doubts to God and ask all those hard questions, like *Why?* and *Where were you?* and *How could you let this happen?* God would much rather have an honest wrestling match with us than have us keep our distance and pretend we don't have any doubts at all."

I see movement outside my house and stand to peer out. A young man leans his bicycle against my hitching post and walks toward my porch. He is wearing a Western Union cap. Telegrams rarely bring good news, and if something has happened to Cornelia's grandfather, I need to read about it before she does. She's too fragile to face another loss. I hurry to answer the door, then stand outside on the porch to tear open the envelope—but it isn't about the dominie at all. The telegram is from Anneke's mother, Mrs. Nicholson.

Anna is critically ill. STOP
She is asking for you. STOP
Please hurry. STOP

I stop breathing. I'm so stunned I can barely think, much less move. *Anneke is critically ill?* But she can't be! She was so vibrant and alive when I saw her a few weeks ago.

Cornelia comes to the doorway. "What's wrong, Tante Geesje? Who is it from?"

"I-I need to go to Chicago right away. This is from Anneke's mother. Anneke is very sick!"

"What's wrong with her?"

"It doesn't say. It just says *hurry*. I need to go to her!"

"Let me help you." Cornelia wraps her arm around my waist and gently leads me inside. I'm so distraught, I can't think what to do first. "I have to go to the print shop. . . . Maybe Arie will go to Chicago with me. . . . I can't ask Derk to go. He can't leave his studies, and besides, he . . . Anneke's mother said to hurry! Oh, what if I'm too late!" I'm babbling in a mixture of Dutch and English. Panicking isn't going to help, but that's exactly what I'm doing.

"I'll go with you," Cornelia says.

"To Chicago?" She nods. "But it's such a long trip. And you would have to miss work and—"

"Mrs. Van Putten will understand. You shouldn't have to go all the way to Chicago by yourself."

"But . . . you don't mind?"

"Not at all. You pack your things, Tante Geesje. I'll run to the print shop and tell Arie. He can drive us to the train station and help us with our tickets." She grabs her coat and is gone before I have a chance to reply.

I pack hastily, throwing clothes and toiletries into a small bag. I change into my best Sunday dress. And a warm coat. It will be cold in Chicago. I'm going through the motions of getting ready, but everything seems unreal, as if it's happening to someone else. I try not to imagine Anneke lying sick in bed—dying—but I've sat at too many bedsides watching too many loved ones die to erase the image. I need to fall on my knees and pray, and yet I know that God is sovereign over life and death. If it's His will for Anneke to die . . . Oh, I don't even want to think about it! I couldn't bear it! Was it only a few minutes ago that I was talking to Cornelia about my faith and about wrestling with God? Now my faith has flown away on wings of fear, and my only thought is that Anneke is critically ill. She is asking for me. I must hurry!

Lord, where are you? What are you doing?

The wait seems endless, but Cornelia and Arie finally return with the horse and carriage. Cornelia rushes inside and quickly packs a bag. "I stopped by the store to tell Mrs. Van Putten where we're going," she says as Arie helps us onto the wagon. "She promised to pray."

"Good. That was good." I wonder what else I'm forgetting in my haste to leave.

Arie drives us to the bank so I can withdraw the money I'll need, then to the train station, where he helps us buy our tickets. We will need to change trains at three different stations and the trip will take most of the day, but at least we will be on our way within the hour. The last time—the only time—I took a long journey by train was during the war when I went to the army hospital in Port Fulton, Indiana, to see Arie after he'd been wounded. Christina traveled with me, and I was grateful for her company—as I am now for Cornelia's.

Arie recovered, I tell myself. He didn't die. And I want to believe that Anneke will recover, too.

I leave Cornelia on the platform with our bags as Arie and I go inside the Western Union office to send a telegram to Anneke's mother, letting her know when our train will arrive and that Cornelia will be traveling with me. "Have you heard any word from Dominie Den Herder?" I ask Arie while we wait for a clerk. He shakes his head.

"He hasn't been to work in the print shop or the newspaper office for the past few days. He didn't tell anyone where he was going."

"I haven't told Cornelia he's missing. She has enough to worry about as it is. I feel responsible for his disappearance,

Arie. We had words the day he left, and I lost my temper. I said some pretty harsh things to him. But I felt like he needed to hear them."

"I can't imagine you being harsh, Moeder. Much less to a dominie. What was it all about?"

"It's a long story, and it will have to wait until I get back. Right now all I can think about is Anneke. I know Mrs. Nicholson is embarrassed by me with my old-fashioned clothes and foreign accent. She never would have sent for me unless the situation was critical." The telegraph clerk returns to the window, and I hand him the message I've printed out. Arie pays the fee.

"Will you feed my cat for me?" I remember to ask as the train chugs into the Holland station. "And get my mail?"

"Of course. Don't worry about a thing. Let Jakob and me know what's happening down in Chicago so we can pray for Anneke."

The train doesn't move quickly enough. Every time we stop at a station or sit on a side track waiting for a freight train to pass, I want to scream. I didn't remember to bring my knitting, so I have nothing to do with my hands except wring them.

Cornelia seems just as tense and worried as I am. "Tante Geesje?" she says.

"Yes, lieveling?"

She takes my hands, stilling them, and looks directly into my eyes, something she doesn't often do. "I believe you now."

"What do you mean, dear?"

"Even if something does happen to Anneke, I know it's not because God is punishing you. He would never punish someone like you, Tante Geesje. You do so much good for everyone, and you show us His love. He would never make Anneke die just to punish you."

In spite of my inner turmoil, I recognize the miracle. A tiny ray of light has shone in Cornelia's heart. "And He didn't make your parents die to punish you, either. Please believe that. We may have to wait until we reach heaven to understand why we lost our loved ones, but in the meantime, we can trust His goodness."

She is quiet for a moment. The clattering rhythm of the wheels along the tracks seems to say *Anneke, Anneke, Anneke . . .*

"But what if Anneke dies?" Cornelia asks. "You've already lost so many people in your family, and now . . . it would be terrible if you lost her, too."

I squeeze Cornelia's hands as tears fill my eyes. "I know . . . I know."

She leans against me, resting her head on my shoulder, and we ride like that for a time. I'm comforted by her presence and the love and concern she shows me. After a while, she sits up and faces me again. "Tante Geesje? I want to pray for Anneke. And for you. But . . . I mean, I don't really know how . . . or if God will listen to me after . . . you know . . . everything."

Tears fill my eyes at this second miracle. Cornelia wants to talk to God. "He is always ready to listen to us, lieveling, in spite of everything we've done. Just talk to Him the same way you talk to me. You can tell Him anything that's on your heart."

"Will Anneke live if we pray really hard for her?"

"Prayer doesn't come with guarantees. We can't change God's mind by pleading with Him. But praying will bring us closer to Him, so He can comfort us and let us know He loves us no matter what happens." My throat catches as I voice the unthinkable. Yet, I feel His warmth in my heart as I'm speaking, and it keeps some of my worry at bay. "I wish someone had prayed with you after your family died, Cornelia. Someone who could have led you into His arms."

"Ya . . . But now I have you."

She lowers her head and closes her eyes. We clasp hands as we pray.

It takes all day, but at last the train winds along the edge of the lake and into Chicago, where a cloud of gray smoke hovers over the distant buildings and factories. I have never seen such an enormous, sprawling city—and to think, it was all rebuilt after the fire destroyed it twenty-six years ago. The journey has exhausted me, not only because it was long and uncomfortable, but because of the added worry and fear that Anneke might die.

The Nicholsons' uniformed driver finds us on the station platform and carries our bags. I want to race all the way to his carriage and tell him to make his horses gallop. But we move at a snail's pace, the streets a tangled mess of carriages and horses and wagons. I have never seen so many of them all in one place. At last, we turn down an avenue lined with stately homes. We must be nearly there.

Another man in a uniform opens the front door for us. If I weren't so desperate to see Anneke, I wouldn't have the courage to step over the threshold of such a grand place. The spacious rooms on either side of the foyer are swathed in layers of fringed draperies and stuffed with furniture and statues and curio cabinets. There are potted palm trees and ferns, and thick, colorful carpets. Fires blaze on the hearths, but they can't drive away the chill I feel as I look around. Anneke's house is a mansion, but it isn't a home.

A middle-aged woman in a gray dress comes to greet us. I hope Cornelia doesn't notice the way she looks us over with mild disapproval. "You must be Mrs. de Jonge."

"Ya, and this is my friend Cornelia Den Herder."

"I'm Mrs. Dunlap, the housekeeper. I'll show you and Miss Den Herder to your rooms. I'm sure you'll want to freshen up and rest after your journey."

"No, thank you. I would like to see my granddaughter right away, please."

"Give me a moment to check with Mrs. Nicholson and—"

"Mrs. Nicholson asked me to come, and she said to hurry. Please take me to see Anneke."

Mrs. Dunlap turns and heads up the stairs without another word. I follow right behind her. I have never seen stairs like these, gracefully winding toward the second-floor balcony. A stained-glass window at the top spills sparkling colors across the polished floor like jewels.

The housekeeper turns down a hallway and knocks on one of the doors. When someone speaks from inside, she opens it a crack and says, "Mrs. de Jonge has arrived, ma'am. She is asking to see Anna."

There is a pause, then I hear Mrs. Nicholson say, "Let her come in."

"I'll wait here," Cornelia whispers.

"No, please come with me, lieveling. I need you."

She takes my hand. "I'm praying," she says.

I must remember to thank God for today's miracles— Cornelia, who was angry with God, is calling on Him in prayer. But all I can do at the moment is silently plead with Him not to take my Anneke.

I think of the fairy tale "Sleeping Beauty" when I see her lying in her elegant canopied bed, swaddled in blankets and linens. She is thin and pale but still beautiful, her golden hair spread in a tangle on her pillow. I want to wring all the life from my own veins and pour it into hers. *Heavenly Father, please . . . no . . .*

Anneke's mother stands to greet us. She looks haggard with worry, her eyes red-rimmed. Twice I've known the sorrow of losing a child, but Mrs. Nicholson has only Anneke. "Thank you for coming, Mrs. de Jonge."

"I left as soon as I got your telegram. How is she?"

"Still very ill. She has rheumatic fever. The doctor says it has affected her heart and weakened it."

"I'm so sorry."

"We should know within the next few days . . . if . . ."

"Ya. I see." I don't want to hear the words spoken out loud any more than she wants to say them. I consider comforting Mrs. Nicholson with an embrace, but I sense by the way she holds herself aloof that she wouldn't want that. Yet I see the fear and desperation in her eyes, and I know they must mirror my own. I remember falling apart after Christina died and after our son Gerrit was killed in battle, and I long for my husband's strength to lean on now as I did back then. I can't bear to lose Anneke, too.

"Anna will be so grateful you came," Mrs. Nicholson says. I can tell by her trembling voice that she is hanging on to her composure by a slender thread. "And . . . and I'm grateful, too. You see, I don't have any family here in the city whom I can turn to."

I know, then, that I'm here for Mrs. Nicholson as well as for Anneke and for myself. I pray that I'll be as strong as my husband was when I needed him. "I hope you'll consider Cornelia and me your family," I say, resting my hand on her arm. My touch breaks the slender thread of her control, and she drops onto her chair, sobbing.

"This is so hard. . . . I've never faced anything like this. I try to pray, but I don't have any words. . . ."

"Then simply pray without words. God hears the cries of our hearts."

"I don't have as much faith as you do . . . or as Anna does. That's why I wanted you to come here and pray. So God would hear you. . . ."

"He hears both of our prayers exactly the same, Mrs. Nicholson. Please believe that. He sees you and He hears you, just as He hears me."

"I don't know how I will bear it if . . . How did you . . . ? When you lost Anna's mother, how . . . ?"

I swallow, remembering. "It was one of the worst days of my life. My husband, Maarten, and I had each other, and we had the prayers of our church community, but there is no easy way to grieve for someone we love. Cornelia lost her entire family five years ago, and she still feels the pain every day." I glance at Cornelia to see if she's able to follow our conversation, and I see tears flowing silently down her cheeks.

"Then . . . you know?" Mrs. Nicholson says, looking up at Cornelia. She nods and swipes at a tear. Grief binds the three of us together.

"It does get easier to go through each day as time passes," I continue. "But I won't lie to you and say the pain goes away. It never does. What gives me the greatest comfort, Mrs. Nicholson, is knowing that my daughter, Christina, is still alive, even though her physical body has passed away. My separation from her is only temporary. The Bible promises that we will be together again with Christ for all eternity."

A sob escapes from Mrs. Nicholson's chest, and she lowers her head and covers her face. I go to her, crouching down so I can embrace her where she is seated. She clings to me as if to a life raft. "I'm sorry," she says. "Anna is all I have!" I let her weep for as long as she needs, then I stand again when she releases me to dry her eyes on her handkerchief. I stay near her with my arm around her shoulders, silently praying for her and for Anneke. And in spite of the words of hope I've just spoken, I don't know how I will get through the days ahead if Anneke dies. It will be as if I've lost Christina all over again.

When Mrs. Nicholson has composed herself, I step to the bedside and study Anneke's beautiful features through my tears, seeing a shadow of my lovely Christina. Then I reach for her hand and close my eyes, pleading with God to spare her life—

not only for Mrs. Nicholson's sake and for mine, but also for Anneke's. She has so many years left to live, and she wants so badly to live them for God.

When I open my eyes again, Anneke is awake. She looks up at me and says, "Oma . . . you're here. . . ."

I squeeze her hand, praying to be strong for her sake. "Ya, lieveling, I'm here."

Then her eyes fall closed once again.

CHAPTER 29

Anna

CHICAGO, ILLINOIS

I know I've been hovering close to death. I can hear the angels whispering in the corners of my bedroom. It would be so easy to put my hand in theirs and slip away. The fever and pain would finally end. But then I open my eyes and see Oma Geesje standing beside my bed, praying for me, and I want to be with her, not the angels. I want to live. She takes my hand, and I feel her strength flowing through me. I close my eyes and sleep again.

I don't know how long I've been drifting in and out of sleep, but it's comforting to see Mother and Oma here with me whenever I wake up. Sometimes Father is here, too. And Dr. Paulson or one of his nurses. They all look so worried. Today when I open my eyes, the Dutch girl, Cornelia, is sitting beside my bed.

She looks different from the last time I saw her. Her expression seems different, but I can't decide why. "How are you?" she asks in English when she sees I'm awake. I take stock, for a moment. My fever seems to be gone, and the ache in my joints has lessened. But I have no strength at all in my body.

"I think I'm getting better," I tell her. I wonder if she can understand my English. I look around but don't see anyone else in the room with us. "Where's Oma?" I ask.

"She goes for . . ." Cornelia mimics drinking from a glass. She looks nervous as she moves to the edge of her chair to talk to me. "I am wanting to say to you I am sorry."

I shake my head, puzzled. "What for?"

"I am wrong to go into the water that day . . . when you visit."

"I'm glad Derk was there to rescue you." I hesitate before asking, "Why did you jump, Cornelia? I saw you. I know you didn't slip and fall."

"Because I hurt. In here," she says, laying her hand over her heart. "I am thinking it will stop hurting if I die. . . . I am sorry."

"No, don't be sorry. I understand. I have felt the same way since I've been sick. But my pain has been in my body, not my heart."

"I pray and pray that you live, Anneke. Tante Geesje will be crying so much if you die. And she cries for me, too, if I die."

"She loves you, Cornelia."

She nods, her entire body moving and not just her head. "Yes. I am not feeling love until now." That's the difference I see in Cornelia. She knows she is loved. "To live or not to live is from God," she continues. She gestures as if holding an imaginary gift in her hands and then gives it to me. "I pray He gives life to you. And I tell Him I am sorry for not wanting it."

"I'm so glad, Cornelia. I would be sad, too, if you died. I hope we both live for a long, long time so we can be friends."

Oma smiles with delight when she returns and sees we've been talking. She is carrying a tray with a teapot and two cups on it. "Shall I get another cup for you?" she asks me.

"No, thank you. Not yet. But I do feel much better."

"I'll make a special drink for you when you're ready to eat, made from eggs and milk and a little vanilla. It will help you grow stronger."

Later, Dr. Paulson comes and confirms that I'm improving. "The nurses say that Anna hasn't had a fever for two days now," he tells Mother and Father. "I think it's safe to say she's out of danger." Mother falls into Father's arms, weeping.

Now that I'm awake for longer periods of time and able to sit propped against the pillows, I'm excited to share my mama's story with Oma Geesje. As wintry rain beats against the windows outside, I tell her about Jack's abuse and how he died in an accident, leaving Mama a widow.

"Oh, if only she had come home," Oma interrupts. "And yet I know why she was afraid to come back. We are such a tight-knit community that she probably felt ashamed to face us. If only Christians were as merciful as Jesus is. Then Christina wouldn't have felt so afraid."

"But she did return to you, Oma. She knew you would forgive her."

"Ya. At least that's a comfort."

I tell her about all the gossip I endured, and about Clarice's threats. I describe the path I took to try to find my father, and how my maid betrayed me. Oma shakes her head. "You went through so much, Anneke. You showed great courage to keep searching all alone."

"I did it for Mother and Father's sakes. I couldn't let Clarice ruin them. When the trail ended in a basement storeroom beneath the tenement house, I knew it was too much for me to tackle alone. Then Derk came at just the right time to help me. He was an answer to my prayers, Oma. And I found Mama's journal among her belongings. Open that drawer in my desk and you can read it yourself." I lay back against the pillows to rest while she does. Remembering the day I spent with Derk has brought a sharp pain to my heart—the kind of pain Cornelia talked about. I struggle to force all my feelings for him back into the box, but it's like stuffing too many treasures into an overflowing chest. I know my heart will heal in time, just as my physical heart will heal. But for now, I need to lock away my feelings for Derk and move on to marry William.

I'm talking with Oma and Cornelia after dinner that evening when Mrs. Dunlap comes to my bedroom to say that a visitor is asking to see me. She hands me a calling card: *The Honorable Judge James Blackwell.* "Shall I tell him to come back another day when you're feeling stronger?"

"No! Let him come up, Mrs. Dunlap. Please!"

Oma rises to her feet. "I'll leave," she says.

"No, please stay. I want you to meet each other. He's my father, Oma. The man you read about in Mama's journal."

Oma steps away from my bedside as the judge sweeps into the room with a worried look on his face. "I just learned that you've been unwell, Anna, and I had to come and see you. Is there anything I can do? Do you have the very best physicians? They said you were at death's door."

"Yes, I had rheumatic fever. But I'm much better now. The doctor expects a full recovery."

"Thank God!" he breathes, sinking onto Oma's chair. "There is so much I want to know about you, and I feared I had missed my chance. I hope you'll let me be part of your life—unless that would be too awkward for you."

"Not at all. I would like that."

"I shared your story with my wife and children. They know all about Christina now, and I hope they will get to know you, too—if you would like them to, that is."

"I would like that very much. My grandmother would, too." I gesture to her, and the judge turns and notices her for the first time.

"I'm sorry. Have I interrupted you?" he asks, rising to his feet.

"Judge Blackwell, I would like you to meet my grandmother, Geesje de Jonge. She's Christina's mother."

He takes her hand and gives a little bow. "Beauty is a strong trait in your family, Mrs. de Jonge. I'm so pleased to meet you. I want you to know that I loved your daughter very much."

"That's a comfort, Your Honor. My husband and I didn't know what became of Christina after she left home. I'm pleased to know she found happiness with a man who loved her."

"If only our story could have ended differently—" He's interrupted by shouts and the sound of a commotion in the downstairs hallway.

"What's going on?" I ask.

"A young man was causing a disturbance the same time I arrived. Do you want me to see what it's all about?" He moves toward the door, but before he gets to it, Cornelia comes rushing in. She hurries over to Oma, chattering frantically in Dutch.

"*Derk* is here?" Oma asks in English. "*Our* Derk?" Cornelia nods, waving her hands as she talks rapidly. "They're trying to send him away," Oma explains to me. "But he's refusing to leave."

"No! Don't send Derk away! Tell them to let him in, Oma. Tell Mother I want to see him." I try to climb out of bed, but Oma stops me.

"Don't excite yourself. Stay still." I don't have the strength to get up no matter how much I want to.

"I'll fetch him," the judge says. "If you want to see him, I'll make sure you see him."

Derk looks as though he was dragged behind the train all the way here, his hair rumpled, his clothes wrinkled and disheveled. He comes straight to my bedside, ignoring everyone else in the room, including my outraged mother, who hurries in behind him. "Anneke, are you all right?" Derk asks. "No, of course you aren't! What a stupid question! I found out you were sick last evening when I went to see Tante Geesje and learned she was here in Chicago with you. I've been so busy at the seminary that I didn't even know Tante Geesje was gone until your uncle came to feed her cat. He told me you might be dying, so I dropped everything and got on the first train I could find. I've been praying for you all the way here, Anneke. Please tell me that my prayers are being answered, and that you're getting better."

"I am getting better. I'm not going to die. But it may take a few more months for me to recover my strength."

"Thank God! Thank God!" He sinks down on the empty chair, his body limp with relief. I press my fist against my chest to ease the pain in my pounding heart. My carefully stowed box has burst open again, and the contents are pouring out.

The judge moves to Derk's side, offering his hand. "I don't believe we've officially met, young man. I'm James Blackwell."

Derk springs to his feet. "Derk Vander Veen. How do you do, sir?"

"Judge Blackwell is my father," I tell Derk. "I found him, thanks to you. Remember the crate you helped me dig out of that horrible storage room? It had Mama's diary inside, and it told the whole story of how they fell in love and got married. I never would have learned the truth if you hadn't helped me, Derk."

"I'm so glad. And I'm very pleased to meet you, sir."

"I think you should go now," Mother tells Derk. "Anna has had quite enough excitement for one day. She needs to rest."

"I'm sorry if I've upset anyone, Mrs. Nicholson, but I needed to see Anneke and—"

"I want you to know that it's highly improper for you to barge into Anna's bedroom this way, young man. You aren't a blood relative. Even Anna's fiancé knows enough to stay away."

Derk stares at her in disbelief. "You mean to tell me that William hasn't come to see her? I don't care how improper it is! He should be here by her side if he loves her!"

"Love compels us to leap the very highest hurdles, doesn't it?" the judge asks. He and Derk look at each other, and I see an understanding pass between them. "My dear," the judge adds, turning to me, "I believe I once advised you to move heaven and earth if you need to, remember?"

"Yes, but . . ." I can't tell him the reason why I must marry William. Not with my mother in the room. She is showing Derk the door.

"Where are you staying?" the judge asks Derk.

"Nowhere. I-I mean, I just got here from the train station."

"Come with me, Derk. I'm sure we can find an empty bedroom for you at my house. We'll visit Anna again tomorrow, after she's rested."

"I'll be praying for you," Derk says before he goes. He walks backward all the way to the door, as if reluctant to let me out of his sight, and nearly collides with the doorframe. Oma leaves with them, and I settle back against the pillows again. But my heart continues to race with joy, even after Derk is gone.

Mother smooths my blankets back into place and refills my water glass. "Wasn't he one of the workers at the Hotel Ottawa? Or am I mistaken?"

"Derk did work there for the summer, but he's also a seminary student. Remember?"

"I don't understand what he's doing here."

How can I explain that he's in love with me, and I'm in love with him? Love and marriage don't mean the same things in Mother's world as they do in Derk's. To her, marriage is a social institution, arranged for mutual convenience. Affection often grows over time, but it isn't a requirement. Judge Blackwell knows the perils of marrying outside one's social class better than anyone. He can explain to Derk the tremendous pressure my parents will exert in order to keep him out of my life. But for now, my mother is waiting for my reply.

"Derk is a good friend, Mother. He always will be. Where he comes from, friends visit each other when they're sick—and ministers come to comfort the sick and pray with them. Derk will be a minister when he graduates this spring."

"I hope that's all there is to it. We don't want any more scandals now, do we?"

"Has . . . has William asked to see me?"

"Of course not. It wouldn't be proper."

"Even though we'll be married soon? Surely one quick visit wouldn't hurt."

"I'm sorry to tell you this, Anna, but Dr. Paulson says the wedding must be postponed. He thinks it may take at least six months for you to fully regain your strength."

I don't know why, but the news brings enormous relief. "What about William's mother? And his sister? Have they asked to visit?"

"Anna, dear. I don't think you realize how ill you've been. They knew you wouldn't want to be seen in such a dire condition. I did give you the notes they sent, didn't I?"

"Yes. It was kind of them to send their wishes." There had been no note from William.

"Now, I think you've had enough excitement for one evening. Good night, dear."

Mother kisses my forehead and turns out the light, leaving me alone to sleep. I find myself wishing once again that my father's finances weren't in jeopardy. If it weren't for the specter of bankruptcy, I would gladly take Judge Blackwell's advice and move heaven and earth to be with Derk.

CHAPTER 30

Geesje

HOLLAND, MICHIGAN

There is an inch of snow on the ground in Holland and more is falling from the sky when we arrive home from Chicago, but my little house is warm inside. My friends and neighbors have taken good care of it for me while I've been gone. It's late in the afternoon and already growing dark, so I light a lamp in the front room. Cornelia picks up my cat, who is letting us know just how upset he was to be left alone all week. "I'm going to miss Anneke very much," I say, "but it's so good to be home again, isn't it, Cornelia?"

"Ya," she says with a sigh. "The city is too big and noisy and dirty. And I don't think I could ever get used to living in such a huge house." Indeed, Mrs. Dunlap gave us each our own bedroom to use, but Cornelia slept in mine all week, too nervous to sleep alone in a strange room.

Derk follows us inside, carrying our bags. "I hope you won't be in trouble for missing two days of classes," I say as he sets them down. He answers with a shrug, but I can tell he's worried. This morning he came to Anneke's house with Judge Blackwell for another brief visit with her, and I convinced him it would be best if we all bought train tickets and returned to Holland together. On the train ride home, I asked him what he and the judge talked about last evening. "He wanted to know all about me," Derk said. "He asked me hundreds of questions—where I grew up, what my life has been like, why I decided to be a minister. I like the judge a lot. He's wealthy and smart and high-class but very down-to-earth. I'm glad he'll be part of Anneke's life."

"I'm glad, too. My Christina once loved him."

"I have just enough time to run over to the seminary and talk to my professor," Derk tells me now. "Arie is going to give me a ride. I need to explain why I left town in such a hurry and had to miss an exam. I'm going to ask if I can still take the test and maybe do extra work over the Christmas holiday to make up for it." I keep my coat on and follow Derk outside so I can speak with Arie before he leaves. I haven't had a chance to ask him about Cornelia's grandfather. The cold, wet snow seeps through the soles of my shoes as we stand together near my hitching post. Flakes of snow dust the shoulders of my son's dark, wool coat, and I reach up to brush them off.

"Arie, did anyone hear from Dominie Den Herder while I was gone?"

"He came into the shop yesterday morning to tell me he'll be leaving town soon. He said he might have found a new job. He was looking for Cornelia, so I told him she went to Chicago with you, and that you were coming home today."

"Did he say where he'd been all this time?"

"I didn't ask. He said the new job is in Kalamazoo, so I assume that's where he went. He thanked me for letting him work in the print shop and asked if I would write him a reference."

"Oh dear. It sounds like he's going to rip Cornelia away from us and run from his problems again."

"I know he's been unhappy. He does good work, but his heart isn't in it."

"Arie, we have to do something to keep Dominie Den Herder from moving away. He has been at such a loss after giving up his calling as a minister, and I've been wondering if it might help him find himself again if our pastor invited him to be more involved at church."

"He hasn't shown much interest."

"I know. We should have made sure he was more involved right from the beginning, so he would have a chance to use his God-given gifts. . . . Listen, I know I'm probably meddling where I shouldn't, but will you do me a favor? Will you talk to our pastor and ask him to invite the dominie to preach at one of our Dutch-speaking services?"

"Preach?" Arie looks skeptical. "Why would you want someone as stern and opinionated as Marinus to preach? Who knows what he would say."

"I know the idea seems unwise considering how judgmental he can be. But whenever I pray for him, I'm always reminded of the calling he gave up and how he must surely be grieving that loss. Maybe it would help him—and Cornelia, too—if he could recover that important piece of his past."

"I understand what you're saying, Moeder, but . . . well, I suppose we could see what the pastor thinks."

"I've had it in mind for some time to ask him to give Marinus a chance to preach, even if there isn't a paid position for him in our church. But I'm sorry to say that I let my own disagreements with him get in the way of my instincts. Besides, I think the suggestion would be better received if it came from a man. And you're still on the consistory, aren't you?"

"Ya."

"You'll need to talk to the pastor about it soon, before Marinus and Cornelia move away."

"I'll go with you," Derk tells Arie. He has been listening to us all this time. "We can go right now."

"Don't you need to talk to your professor about your absence?" I ask.

"This is more important. Arie and I know Dominie Den Herder the best because he has been living with me and working for Arie."

"Bless you both. Let's hope this will be just what the dominie needs to convince him to stay." I watch Arie and Derk leave, praying that returning to the pulpit will help Marinus heal, just as grieving in the cemetery has helped Cornelia.

A few minutes after they leave, a friend from church comes to my door with a warm meal for Cornelia and me. "Your son told me you were coming home today, and I knew you probably didn't have much food in the house after being gone all week."

"You're right about that," I say, laughing. "Thank you so much."

"How is your granddaughter? Everyone at church has been praying for her."

"God heard your prayers. She's doing much better, which is why we decided to come home. The doctor says she's out of danger."

"I'm so glad."

I'm sitting at my kitchen table eating my friend's stew with Cornelia when her grandfather comes to my back door. My stomach does a nervous little flip when I see him, but I hurry to the door to invite him in. "It looks like it's still snowing, Dominie. Please come in out of the cold and have some dinner with us. Have you eaten?"

"No, thank you. I can't stay. I would like to speak with Cornelia."

"Why not sit down and join us? We just started eating." I know what he is going to tell her, and I'm regretting my decision not to warn her about what's coming. She has grown so much this past week while we've been away, learning about prayer and God's sovereignty over life and death. If he tells Cornelia they're moving, I fear he will destroy everything. I fill a bowl with stew for him and set it on the table along with a spoon, then pull out a chair and gesture to it. "Please, Dominie. I would like to ask for your help with something as long as you're here." He finally sits down and shrugs off his coat, leaving it on the back of his chair. His food remains untouched. I plunge in, hoping to at least distract him from any thoughts about moving away.

"Cornelia and I have had a lot of time to talk while we were in Chicago, and I've come to a decision but I will need your help. I would like to contact the church officials in the Netherlands and get justice for Cornelia. The man who abused her needs to be held accountable for what he did."

"She refused to name him."

"I know. But we've talked about it, and now she is willing. Can you help me contact the appropriate officials?"

"Why can't you just let it remain in the past?"

His indifference infuriates me. I struggle to speak calmly and not raise my voice. "Because Cornelia deserves justice for what that man did to her. He abused a vulnerable child in a horrific way. And the church needs to make sure it never happens to another young girl. We would be in the wrong if we looked the other way or swept it under the rug. The letter would carry more weight if it came from you instead of from me, since it was your church and your granddaughter. But whether you help me or not, I'm determined to see this through."

"Haven't you meddled enough in our lives? Are you going to reach into the past, now, to interfere?"

"You told me you came here so Cornelia could have a new

start. That doesn't happen by simply changing addresses. She needs to grieve for what she has lost before she can start all over again."

The dominie rises to his feet and reaches for his coat. "I've come to tell you to pack all your things, Cornelia. I may have found a new job in Kalamazoo."

"No! You can't do that!" Cornelia throws her spoon across the room. He manages to duck in time, but it hits the wall behind him and falls to the floor with a clatter. "Why are you doing this to me? I don't want to move away! I won't go!" The news has taken her completely by surprise, and I know I'm to blame for not warning her. I rise and stand behind her chair with my hands on her shoulders to keep her from leaping up and running away.

"I'm glad you found work, Dominie, but Cornelia can have a home here with me for as long as she likes."

"She belongs with me. I'm her grandfather."

"Does it matter to you what Cornelia wants? She's a grown woman now. Shouldn't she be allowed to make her own decisions?"

"And I don't want to move," Cornelia says. "I like it here. And I like working at the store."

"They still let you work there after you stole that baby? The gossip was all over town!"

"The fuss didn't last long, Dominie. Cornelia apologized to Mrs. Visscher, and the incident was forgiven and forgotten. That's the way love and grace work. Please let Cornelia stay and—"

"Why are you trying to break our family apart? You've been turning Cornelia against me from the very start."

"That's not true, Dominie. I've been trying to bring the two of you back together. It would be my wish that you both stay. Won't you please sit down and talk about this with her? She deserves to hear a little more about how and why you've made your decision."

"No arguments," he says. "My mind is made up."

"No!" Cornelia wails. "If you love me at all, please let me stay!" Tears roll down her thin cheeks. He doesn't reply. I long to unleash my tongue and tell this proud, stubborn man exactly what I think of him and his selfish decision. But my guilty conscience reminds me that when I spoke my mind a week ago, it led to this current mess. I pray for wisdom, and the only recourse I see is to swallow my pride and apologize.

"Dominie, I'm very sorry if anything I've said or done has influenced your decision to move away. I had no right to speak so unkindly to you last week. I need to ask your forgiveness."

"It won't change my mind."

In spite of my efforts to hold her down, Cornelia pushes back her chair and stands, her thin body rigid with anger. "I hate you! First you took my baby away from me and now you want to take me away from Tante Geesje! I won't go with you! I'd sooner die!" She is about to run, but I pull her into my arms to stop her. She leans against my shoulder, sobbing.

"I've heard enough," the dominie says.

"Please don't walk out that door." My voice is shaking. "You can't keep running from your problems. Remember what happened to Jonah when he tried to run from God? I believe God brought you to Holland for a reason. You need to listen to what the people He has put in your life are trying to tell you."

"I'm not the one who keeps running from God! First my wife, then my son, now Cornelia! The Bible is very clear about what's right and what's wrong. There are laws to be obeyed, rules for the correct way to live. No one in my family has wanted to listen!" He storms out the back door, slamming it behind him.

"Let's finish our dinner," I tell Cornelia after I soothe her tears. "Everything will work out. You'll see."

She sits down but pushes her plate away. "I'm not hungry."

"Don't go back to that dark place where you lived when you arrived here," I tell her. "You've worked so hard to move into the light these past few months. Trust God, Cornelia, and keep believing that He is able to work out all of the details of your life." She doesn't reply. She is chewing her nails again and nervously biting the skin around them. Naming her losses and grieving them has helped her move forward, and I believe it will help Marinus, too. That's why I'm so determined to get him back into the pulpit. But his final words before he left just now puzzle me. I sit down at the table again and take a few more bites of stew, even though I have lost my appetite.

"Cornelia, I'm trying to figure out what's hurting your grandfather so we will know how to pray for him. He keeps lashing out whenever we try to help him, like an animal that has been wounded too many times. I need your help. I don't understand what he meant when he said his wife and son and you were all running from God and from His rules. Do you have any idea what he meant?"

"I don't know. . . . My papa was never as strict about all the rules as Grandfather is," she says without looking up. "He told Mama that he refused to raise my brothers and me the same way he was raised."

"So in your grandfather's mind, your father was running from God?"

"I guess."

"And your grandmother? His wife? What was she like?"

"I barely remember her. She died before my parents did. Whenever we went to visit her, she always seemed so sad. It was like she was all alone, even in a room full of people. And she never laughed."

"Do you know how she died? Was she sick for a long time?"

"It was sudden. Papa was shocked. We traveled there for her

funeral, but we came home again on the same day. Papa barely spoke to Grandfather, and we never visited him again after that. I didn't see him until after my parents died."

"Cornelia, you told me once before that your grandfather was always busy with his church and never paid attention to you or showed you his love. Do you think it might have been the same way for your grandmother? Could that be why she seemed sad to you?"

"Maybe . . ." She's still chewing her fingers and staring at her lap, but she looks up at me suddenly, and I see a light of understanding in her eyes. "I just remembered—I once overheard some of the women in Grandfather's church talking. It was right after I tried to kill myself, and the women were supposed to be watching me so I wouldn't run away again. They thought I was asleep, but I heard them talking about me."

"Go on."

"One of them said that I was just like my grandmother, and that I must have inherited her bad blood. The other one said she felt sorry for Grandfather because he had to go through this nightmare all over again, with me."

"What do you think they meant? Do you think your grandmother might have tried to kill herself, too?"

"I don't know. . . . I didn't remember what the women said until just now." There is no one we can ask about it, either.

"Your grandfather mentioned God's laws and rules. Were they important to him?"

"He was always talking about them and preaching about sin and what would happen if you disobeyed His laws." I hear the bitterness in her voice. "One time he sent me to bed without supper because I played with a ball on the Sabbath. When he found out I was going to have a baby . . ."

She doesn't need to finish. I've seen the dominie's fury unleashed and can well imagine what Cornelia endured. But I can also see how badly shaken a man of such unbending principles must have been when his orderly world began to topple. Unless grace has been built into the structure, it is doomed to collapse. I exhale to keep from spouting my outrage, then reach across the table to push Cornelia's plate closer to her. "You must eat, lieveling, or this wintry weather will make you sick. . . . And will you promise me something?" I wait until she looks up. "Promise me that you'll read the Gospels with me, and see for yourself what Jesus has to say about God's laws? Yes, the Bible has laws and rules, and they teach us the best way to live—we shouldn't kill or steal and so on. Resting from our work on the Sabbath day is also one of God's laws because He knows our bodies need to rest. But in the Gospels, Jesus also teaches us about God's love. And that's what your grandfather has been missing—love."

"How can we read the Bible together if he makes me move away?"

"Do you believe God answers prayer?" Her shoulder rises in a small shrug. "Then we're going to pray that your grandfather will change his mind about moving."

"Can we pray right now?"

I reach across the table and take her hands.

It's after seven o'clock and still snowing when Derk returns. "I can only stay a minute," he says when I offer him our leftover supper. "Arie and I went over to the church and explained the whole story to the pastor. He was concerned when he heard Dominie Den Herder was leaving town and said he was sorry for not asking him to help out sooner. He's going to try to arrange for him to preach at one of the Dutch-speaking services."

"Let's hope Marinus says yes, and that he decides to stay.

Cornelia doesn't want to go with him, so he'll be all alone if he does leave."

"I also went to talk to my professor, and he agreed to let me take the exam and do extra work over Christmas to make up for being absent."

"That's good news. And from the looks of the weather outside, Christmas will soon be here."

Now that it's being arranged for the dominie to preach, I'm having misgivings. I know he would accuse me of meddling in his life again—and I am. I can only pray that this time, my meddling ends well for everyone.

CHAPTER 31

Anna

CHICAGO, ILLINOIS

Dr. Paulson holds his listening device to my chest to check my heart. "Tell me what you are hearing, Doctor. I want to know the truth." He glances at Mother, who nods, then looks directly at me.

"Very well. You're a brave young woman. . . . The rheumatic fever caused your heart to become enflamed, and the muscle was damaged. It also caused what we call a heart murmur. Your heart valves are no longer functioning properly. Unfortunately, this kind of damage is almost always permanent. You will recover, but your heart probably never will."

"What does that mean for my daily life?"

"You can resume your normal social activities once you feel strong enough, but nothing too strenuous. And nothing that puts added strain on your heart. You shouldn't do physical work of any kind. Fortunately, your station in life won't require you to."

"What about volunteer work? I've seen how my grandmother helps the very poorest people in her town, and when I'm well again, I hope to find a way to do the same thing in Chicago. The conditions in some of those tenement houses are horrible, and I want to do what I can for those people."

"My dear, the diseases that sometimes sweep through those areas of town would be the death of you. Your heart would never survive an illness like diphtheria or dysentery or typhus. If you want to remain healthy, you must stay far away from those places."

His warning means the death of my dreams. I tell myself not to complain. I'm lucky to be alive and to have servants to do all my work. I was able to afford the finest physicians during my illness. A less fortunate woman would have died. I have escaped death's clutches for the second time in my life, and I should be grateful.

Dr. Paulson breaks into my thoughts. "Your mother tells me you have a fiancé."

"Yes. William and I were supposed to be married on the first of the year, but we've postponed our wedding for now."

"That's very wise. You'll need several months to regain your strength." He packs his instruments away and closes his bag, but instead of leaving, he sits down on the bed beside me. "I'm sorry, Anna, but what I have to say next may be very difficult for you to hear." I feel my skin prickle, wondering what he is about to tell me. His voice grows soft. "After you and your husband are married, I strongly advise against having children." He pauses to give me a moment to digest his words. But I can't even swallow them, let alone digest them. I've always looked forward to being a mother. Now that Clarice's threats are gone and I can marry William, my future children are being snatched away from me.

"Never?" I ask, my throat catching. "Not even when I'm stronger?"

"In my long years of practice, I've known of two other young women who have suffered heart damage like yours, and the strain of pregnancy and childbirth proved too much for their weakened hearts. They both died in childbirth. My fellow physicians have had similar experiences, which is why the medical profession strongly advises against childbearing in cases like yours. I'm so sorry, Anna. I recommend you take precautions to avoid any chance of a pregnancy in the future."

His words devastate me. Why would God do this to me? It seems so unfair! Having children was one of the few bright spots in my future with William. I know I should stop feeling sorry for myself and be grateful to be alive, but I can't. I look up at Mother and see disappointment and pain in her expression, too.

"That doesn't preclude becoming a mother through adoption, however," Dr. Paulson adds. "You and your husband will be able to hire nannies and nursemaids to provide all the help you'll need. I understand that your parents adopted you, so I know you must be sympathetic to the idea. I can recommend a very good orphanage here in Chicago when the time is right."

I force a smile. "Yes, of course. You're right." I love my parents. And they love me every bit as much as they would their own child. My future doesn't have to be bleak. "Thank you for being honest with me, Dr. Paulson."

Mother comes to sit beside me on the bed after he leaves. Tears fill her eyes. "Oh, Anna. I'm so sorry." She holds me in her arms, and we weep together. More than anyone else, she understands the impact the doctor's words had on my heart. I feel closer to her than ever before.

"I never asked why you and Father didn't have children of your own," I say after we've dried our tears.

"There didn't seem to be a reason. The years just went by and my hopes and dreams became dashed month after month."

"Did you ever consider adopting a child from an orphanage like the doctor recommended?"

"We had just decided to look into an adoption when you came into our life. It seemed like a miracle."

I console myself with the thought that William and I will also adopt a child someday—perhaps several. There must be dozens of poor orphans in Chicago who need loving parents and a good home. Oma would tell me that everything happens for a reason, and that God can work all things together for my good. But right now, the doctor's warning not to give birth has struck me like a terrible blow.

When I am finally able to get out of bed and get dressed again, William asks to pay a visit. I go downstairs to the morning room to greet him, and he holds me briefly in his arms as if afraid I might break. "I'm glad you're feeling better, Anna."

"Thank you." I sit down on the sofa, and he sits on a chair across from me. I recall how Derk boarded the very first train to Chicago when he learned I was ill, and then burst into my bedroom, not caring if it was improper. Once again, I'm reminded of the differences between the two men. I know it isn't fair to compare them. William's formal upbringing with nannies and nursemaids was very different from Derk's. And William hasn't known loss the same way Derk has, when his mother died in the same shipwreck that killed Mama. He understands grief in a way that William probably doesn't.

"I'm still very weak," I tell William. "It took nearly all of my strength just to walk down the stairs. It's so frustrating. You can't imagine how much I long to be completely well again. I'm sorry our wedding has to be postponed."

"Yes, I am, too. But I still plan to move into our new home in January so it will be all ready for you once we're married.

I'm having some rooms on the first floor converted into our two bedroom suites, so you won't have to climb the stairs."

I smile, determined to make light of my limitations. "That's very thoughtful of you. There's no shortage of rooms to choose from in that house."

"Yes. That's true."

"I've been grateful for everyone's prayers these past few weeks," I say, hoping to steer the conversation in that direction. "God truly does hear and answer prayer."

"I'm grateful for your doctors' knowledge and skills, too."

I decide not to force the subject. I hear the mantel clock ticking loudly. We have run out of things to say. I know I need to tell William about Dr. Paulson's warning not to have children, but I can't bring myself to say the words out loud. I need more time to accept the truth in my own heart. I admit that I'm still angry with God about it. Why did He allow me to become ill in the first place?

As I search for a topic of conversation, Clarice comes to mind. I long to tell William how she tried to ruin both of our lives so he will be just as furious with her as I am, but then I would be just as guilty of spreading hurtful words as she was. I haven't forgiven her yet, but I know I need to. Even though she intended to harm me, God brought something good from it when I found my father. As the silence between William and me stretches, I decide to tell him about Judge Blackwell.

"Did your mother mention what she learned at my tea right before I got sick?"

"No. Why?"

"I know you'll recall all the gossip about my illegitimate birth and the scandal it caused."

"Yes, and I'm relieved it has all died down again." He gestures with his hands as if trying to push the topic back down.

"It died away because I learned who my real father is and

discovered that my birth wasn't shameful at all. May I tell you what I learned about him?"

"If it's important to you." I sense his wariness.

"Before I was born, my mama went to work as a maid in the home of Judge James Blackwell. Do you know him?"

"I know who he is. We may have met socially a few times."

"Judge Blackwell is my father. He and Mama fell in love and were secretly married."

William makes a face. "That sounds a little farfetched. I can't imagine a man from his social background doing something that foolish." I bristle at the word *foolish*. "Are you certain it's true?" he adds.

"Very certain. Judge Blackwell admitted it. He loved my mama. She wasn't a nameless maidservant, and he didn't make a foolish mistake. The judge showed me their marriage certificate; he is willing to make a public statement about her. The reason that the gossip halted is because he stepped forward."

"Good. Then it's over. Let's never speak of it again."

"I'm hoping to get to know him better in the future and—"

"I would prefer that your relationship to him remains a secret. For the sake of appearances. We have our future to think about."

Anger makes my heart pulse against my ribs in a dangerous way. I'm furious that William wants to dismiss my past and let it remain a secret. "The judge's parents felt the same way you do, and they conspired to have the marriage annulled. They refused to take responsibility for Mama and me, and we ended up living in poverty."

"I think you can understand why the Blackwells renounced their son's affair—"

"It wasn't an affair. It was a marriage."

"A marriage that could jeopardize his future."

"He loved Mama!"

"I assume he was very young. His parents wouldn't want this one mistake to ruin his life."

"I'm not a mistake!"

"Anna, dear, you need to calm down." He leans forward in his chair and reaches to take my hands, but I pull them away. "I didn't mean that you were a mistake. But I honestly believe that the best thing for everyone involved is to forget the fact that you're adopted. As far as society is concerned, the Nicholsons are your parents. Let's not mention your so-called 'real' parents again."

I breathe deeply, waiting for my heart to stop pounding, waiting until I can speak calmly. "I wanted to share what I discovered about my real family with you because learning who I truly am has changed me. My parents came from two different social classes, one wealthy, one poor. And I don't want to put people into categories anymore. I used to treat people differently if they weren't wealthy like me. I barely knew our servants' names. Now I see that a chambermaid has just as much value and worth as an aristocrat. Love erases all of those man-made barriers."

"I understand. You have a very compassionate heart, Anna. But don't forget that you are the Nicholsons' daughter. They raised you and gave you their wealth and prestige. You owe them everything. The best way you can honor them is to let go of your past. It must be insulting to them when you talk about your 'real' parents—as if they aren't the 'real' ones who sat by your bedside all these weeks when we didn't know if you would live or die."

I release my anger with a sigh. William is right. I would never want to hurt my parents. I'm searching for something to say when Mother sweeps into the room, and William rises to greet her. "Good afternoon, Mrs. Nicholson."

"Hello, William. I just returned home and our butler told me you were visiting. Isn't it wonderful to see Anna looking so well?" The way Mother looks at me, the love that's so apparent in her eyes, makes me feel as though I have been resurrected from the grave like Lazarus.

"We were all very worried about her," William says.

Mother looks at the empty tea table and frowns. "Why haven't you offered William some refreshments, Anna? Shall I summon one of the servants?"

"No, thank you, Mrs. Nicholson. I should be going. I don't want to tire Anna." William bends to kiss my cheek before leaving.

"I'm sorry if I interrupted the two of you," Mother says when he's gone.

"Not at all. We were done talking." In truth, we had very little to say.

"You look exhausted," Mother says. "Shall I ring for a servant to help you climb the stairs?"

"Not yet. I'm tired of the view from my bedroom. I think I'll sit here for a while longer."

I stare at the indentation on the chair where William sat and relive our conversation. He is right. I do owe Mother and Father a huge debt. And it's cruel to talk about my "real" parents in front of them, especially after Mother shared her grief with me about not bearing children. From now on, I must let go of the past and think only of my future.

CHAPTER 32

Geesje

HOLLAND, MICHIGAN

I'm sitting at my kitchen table, sipping tea and praying for all the people I love when the sun finally peeks above the eastern horizon. I haven't slept well in two days. Cornelia is still upset about her grandfather's decision to move away, but we have agreed to pray and trust God for a resolution. *How much more pain does that poor child have to endure?* I ask God as I plead for His mercy.

The house is so quiet at this hour that the gentle tapping on my back door makes me jump. Derk comes through the door a moment later. "Sorry, I didn't mean to scare you."

"What are you doing up so early?" I ask him. "Would you like some tea?"

"No, I can't stay. I got up early to study, and I saw your light on." Derk speaks softly, as if worried Cornelia will overhear him. "I wanted to tell you the latest news. Our pastor came over last night to talk to Dominie Den Herder. I went upstairs to give them privacy, but the warm air vent in my bedroom is right above the front room, and I couldn't help hearing what they said—even though it was in a mixture of Dutch and English."

"Wait. Are you sure you should be telling me this?"

"Well . . . I know Cornelia is upset about having to move again. And I know you're worried about her, too. . . ."

I hesitate before deciding to let Derk continue. "Go ahead, then."

"She'll have a temporary reprieve from leaving town with her grandfather. The pastor persuaded Dominie Den Herder to stay and help out at the church, at least through the Christmas season. He's going to preach at one of the Dutch language services, although they haven't decided when, exactly."

"I'm so glad. It will bolster Cornelia's faith to see her prayers being answered. But isn't the dominie supposed to start a new job in Kalamazoo?"

"If I understood him correctly, the job wasn't definite. And it was some sort of manual labor. He's probably better off staying here with the jobs he already has."

"So he was just running away again," I say. I'm glad I meddled.

"I told my father about what's been going on, and after the pastor left, he talked to Dominie Den Herder. Dad assured him that the rent he's been paying has been a help to us, and there was no need to move out. He said he was welcome to stay as long as he likes."

"That was very kind of him, Derk. Let's hope he convinced him. I know the dominie is carrying a huge load of grief. Was he able to confide in the pastor and share any of it?"

"Not that I could tell. They mostly talked about ways he could help at the church, and what his church back in the Netherlands did during the holidays. That sort of thing. Nothing personal as far as I could tell."

"Thanks, Derk. And while I don't condone your methods—"

He laughs. "Hey, it isn't my fault that I could hear every word they were saying."

"Well, thanks for letting me know. I'm relieved that he and Cornelia won't be leaving right away. And Cornelia will be happy, too." I hope the news will be a boost to her fragile faith.

Cornelia looks as though she hasn't slept much, either, when she shuffles into my kitchen later that morning. I tell her the good news as we eat our oatmeal. "At least you'll have time to think through what you want to do if your grandfather still decides he wants to move after Christmas."

"I'm going to be eighteen in February. Aren't I old enough to do whatever I want and live wherever I want?"

"That's probably true. We can ask someone for legal advice, if you'd like. But even if it's legal for you to stay here with me, and even if that's what you decide to do, I urge you to make peace with your grandfather before he goes away. You don't want to live with any regrets or angry words between you, do you?" She frowns and looks away. Too late, I remember that the last words between Cornelia and her mother were angry ones. We finish eating in silence.

Afterward, I open my Bible to the Gospel of Matthew, which Cornelia and I have been reading together. We read Jesus' parable about the man whose huge debt was forgiven, yet he refused to forgive a much smaller debt that was owed to him. It ends with the man being thrown into prison, and with these words: "This is how my heavenly Father will treat each of you unless you forgive your brother or sister from your heart." I close my Bible.

"Did you really mean it when you told your grandfather you hated him?" I ask Cornelia. "Hate is a very strong emotion."

"Well, I don't love him. And I don't want to live with him."

"I understand why you feel bitter toward him. But if you allow that bitterness to live in your heart, it will eventually destroy you. So many things happened that you couldn't control. You've been powerless over your life. And when your grandfather orders you around, it must make you feel even more powerless. But there is one thing that you can control, one area where you do have power. And that's the power to forgive him."

Cornelia looks up at me, eyes flashing. "Why should I?"

"Because it's what Jesus wants us to do. He forgave all of us and now we must forgive each other. In Jesus' parable, the man who wouldn't forgive was thrown into prison. The only way we can be set free is to forgive."

"But what my grandfather did was wrong! He took my baby away!"

"I know. But forgiving someone doesn't mean that what he did was right. It wasn't. Forgiving means that even though he was wrong, and even though he owes you a debt for all the pain and suffering he caused, you're choosing to forgive that debt. You're marking it *paid*, just like Jesus did when He forgave our sins. You're no longer going to hate him or desire revenge."

Cornelia shakes her head in vehement denial. "I can't do that."

"None of us can do it without God's help. For years, I was bitter toward the young man who convinced my daughter to run away with him. You heard the rest of Christina's story when we were in Chicago, and all of the things that happened to them after they left home. But God can bring joy from our sorrows, in time. And now He has brought Anneke into my life."

Cornelia looks unconvinced. I decide to let it go. We've talked enough for one day.

As Christmas approaches, Cornelia spends much of her time, when she isn't working at the store, helping me and the other ladies at church as we prepare Christmas parcels for the poor. They're packed with food and baked goods, some warm clothing for winter, and a simple toy for each child, along with bundles of firewood and sacks of coal wherever they're needed.

When the day comes to deliver the Christmas parcels, Cornelia and I borrow Arie's horse and wagon. The December afternoon is sunny but very cold, and the fresh layer of snow on the ground crunches beneath our boots and the wagon wheels. Smoke from hundreds of chimneys and factory smokestacks freezes in the air in a sparkling fog. Everyone's cheeks are rosy as we load up our wagons at the church. Dominie Den Herder has come to help, as well. I'm surprised to learn that he has been spending much of his time at the church, in between his duties at the print shop and the newspaper.

"Would you mind riding along to help your granddaughter and Mrs. de Jonge?" the pastor asks him. "They have several loads of firewood and coal to deliver along with their parcels." Dominie can hardly say no, although I can tell he would like to. He hasn't spoken to either of us since the night he told Cornelia they were moving. "And please make note of any spiritual needs these families may have so our church can help meet them," the pastor adds.

We set off to make our deliveries, the three of us pressed together on the driver's seat with Cornelia handling the reins. I have gotten to know many of the families we're helping, and I enjoy taking time to visit with them and fuss over their children. But unless he has wood or coal to carry inside, the dominie stays outside near the wagon while I chat. I feel sorry for him. He is missing a wonderful blessing.

One of our last deliveries is to a new family I haven't met before. Mrs. Miller is a tiny woman who can't be much older than Anneke. Two small boys cling to her skirts as she welcomes us inside. Everything she owns, which isn't much, is crammed into one small, drafty room. "May your boys have one of these treats?" I ask as I pull a box of homemade cookies from the basket. She nods, and Cornelia kneels beside the children to pass them out. My heart breaks when I see the joy on the little boys' faces as they bite into them.

"Say, 'thank you,'" Mrs. Miller prompts. They mumble the words through mouthfuls of shortbread.

"Is there anything else the church can do to help you, Mrs. Miller?"

"Well . . ." I see her struggling with her emotions, and I move closer to reassure her.

"Please don't be afraid to ask."

"It's just that . . . my husband is in the county jail. . . . For robbery." I hear the shame in her soft voice and see it in the way she lowers her eyes. "The boys and I haven't seen him in months. It's too far to walk in the snow."

"Do you know when he's allowed to have visitors?" I ask. "I can arrange for someone to drive you and your children to see him."

Before Mrs. Miller can reply, the dominie interrupts. He has brought two bundles of firewood inside and has heard us talking. "You should feel no duty to visit," he says in his clumsy English. "He is in jail to be punished. He is bad for your children." He looks at me. "A bad influence," he says in Dutch and waits for me to translate. I can't do it. I'm hoping Mrs. Miller hasn't understood anything he said. But she has.

"I know what John did was wrong," she says. "But he's still their father. And I want him to know that I love him."

"I will take you," Cornelia says. She has won the children's trust with the cookies, and the oldest one takes her hand as she stands. She gestures to our wagon, parked out front. "Tell me when should I come."

Marinus has already left and doesn't hear Mrs. Miller's

tearful words of thanks. We return to the wagon, and it takes every ounce of willpower I have not to lecture Marinus or tell him how wrong he was to say what he did to Mrs. Miller. Only God can change him. I certainly can't.

Our last visit is to Mrs. Hartig, an elderly widow who lives alone and struggles with melancholy. The curtains in her front room are drawn shut when we arrive, and she has allowed the fire in her stove to go out. The room is very cold. "Would you mind building a fire for her?" I ask Marinus as he brings in the coal. "Cornelia and I are going to visit with Mrs. Hartig for a bit."

The ash grates need to be emptied first, and it takes a while for the dominie to get the wood hot enough to kindle the coal and warm the room. Mrs. Hartig understands Dutch, so it's easier for Cornelia to join the conversation, but neither she nor Mrs. Hartig says much. I do most of the talking as I pass around the cookies and invite Mrs. Hartig to help us bake more of them at church next week. Once again, Cornelia offers to provide her with a ride. Mrs. Hartig shakes her head.

"We need to let the church know that she is having another spell of melancholy," I say when we return to the wagon an hour later. "We'll need to visit her more often and show her our love."

"What happened to make her so sad?" Cornelia asks.

"It's none of our business," Marinus says before I can reply. "And what makes you think she wants visitors tramping in and out, disturbing her privacy and trying to cheer her up?"

"It's not a question of cheering her up," I reply. "We simply need to walk alongside her when she has these spells. We sit with her, read to her, just to let her know she's not alone."

"And once you tell people at church that she is depressed, then all of the ladies will gossip about her."

"Some of them will. But many of them will volunteer to sit by her side, and bring her a meal, and help keep her fire going." There's so much more I want to say to him. I long to quote the

Bible verses where Jesus says, "*I was sick and you looked after me, I was in prison and you came to visit me.*" But I don't. The dominie already knows those verses. They are in his head, but they have never touched his heart.

"Thanks for your help," I say when we return to the church. The late-afternoon sky is already growing dark, and the December chill has reached my bones. I wonder if Marinus will comment on what he has seen and done today, but he merely nods and walks away.

"See why I hate him?" Cornelia says. "He's so mean."

"It's almost as if he's afraid to love, as if he's protecting his pride behind a wall of stone, and he's afraid to let anyone or anything touch his heart. I feel sorry for him, Cornelia."

"I don't."

Cornelia drives me home, then leaves again to return the horse and wagon to my son. As I stir the coals in my own stove, I can't stop thinking about the dominie. He has locked himself in a prison made of laws and rules, where grace and mercy aren't allowed. I wonder how much more pain he will have to suffer before his prison walls begin to crumble.

CHAPTER 33

Anna

CHICAGO, ILLINOIS

My health continues to improve, but as Christmas approaches, I still don't feel strong enough to face the yearly round of parties and receptions and teas that have been part of my holiday celebrations in the past. Instead, I ask Mother to plan a holiday party at our home so I can celebrate our Savior's birth without overtaxing myself. Father goes out with our driver and our butler to purchase an enormous Christmas tree that fills an entire corner of our parlor, nearly touching the ceiling. I watch from the sofa as Mrs. Dunlap and the other servants decorate it under Mother's careful supervision. Fresh evergreen boughs top every fireplace mantel and adorn the stair railings. Their aroma fills the house with the scent of Christmas. We have celebrated with these customs for as long as I can remember, but I'm seeing Jesus' incarnation and birth through different eyes this year. Maybe it's my close brush with death, or perhaps it's the fact that I have more time to reflect on those long-ago events in Bethlehem now that I'm not racing through the snowy city from one elaborate gathering to the next. Either way, I'm learning to be grateful for a simpler life.

William came to see me again, and I was careful to make no mention of my "real" parents. "I hope you'll feel free to attend all of the holiday events without me," I told him. "Please don't let my absence prevent you from enjoying the season." I was pleased when he agreed.

Now it's the night of the party at my home, and snow is falling softly outside, covering the city in a blanket of pure white. The servants have lit dozens of candles, and an abundant buffet of sliced ham and roast beef and every kind of pie and dessert is spread across our dining room table. Laughter and well-wishes fill our home as I greet our family's friends and social acquaintances for the first time since my illness. I have been marshalling my strength for this Christmas party, but I will likely have to stay in bed all day tomorrow to recover.

I've insisted that Mother invite Judge Blackwell and his family. I'm eager to get to know my half sister, Florence, who is a few years younger than me. She sits beside me near the Christmas tree, balancing a dessert plate as we chat. I search for a family resemblance between us but can't find one. She has the same mahogany-colored hair as the judge, the same dark brown eyes as her mother—so different from my fair hair and blue eyes. I think I understand why William doesn't want me to acknowledge the relationship publicly, but I can still be friends with my half sister, can't I?

"My father was very worried when he heard you might be dying," Florence says. "He told us the tragic story about him and your mother."

"I hope you won't think less of him for loving another woman before your mother."

"Not at all! It sounds so romantic. Besides, I've always wanted a sister."

"I don't have any siblings at all. It will be wonderful to finally have a sister. I hope you'll call on me some afternoon when you get a chance, Florence. I won't be able to make social calls or return to the Literary Club for a few more months, but I would love it if we could become friends."

"I would like that, too."

I watch the judge stride across the room with a glass of punch in his hand, and he halts in front of us with a wide grin. "Why, look at that! Here are the two prettiest girls at the party, talking together."

"Oh, Papa. You aren't biased at all, are you?" Florence stands and leans into him. He laughs as he wraps his free arm around her shoulder and pulls her close. He seems so warm and loving that I envy their close relationship. I don't even know what I should call him yet. "If you'll excuse me, I'm going back for another piece of this wonderful pie," Florence says.

The judge takes her place on the chair beside mine. "I see that the Wilkinsons are here tonight. Am I to understand that you're going ahead with the wedding?"

"Yes. William and I were supposed to be married on the first of January, but we had to postpone the wedding when I got sick."

He leans close, lowering his voice so only I can hear him. "You may feel free to tell me to mind my own business, Anna, but why are you going through with this marriage? It's clear that you're in love with Derk Vander Veen. And he told me that he loves you, too. If you've learned anything at all from Christina's and my story, please let it be that class distinctions and family wealth shouldn't get in the way of love. All the money in the world isn't a fair exchange for spending a lifetime with the person you love."

"I'm not marrying William because of all this," I say, gesturing to the beautiful room where we're sitting. "I don't want any of it—but my parents do. May I confide in you, Judge Blackwell?"

"Please do."

"My father has had some financial troubles recently, and he owes a lot of money to the Wilkinsons' bank. He and Mother could lose everything if I don't marry William. I heard what happened to the Kirkland family, and I don't want my parents to end up bankrupt like they did."

"That's very noble of you. But don't you deserve to be happy, too?"

"How can I be happy if my parents are ruined and disgraced? I love them."

"There must be another way out. For all of you."

"If there is, I don't know what it is." A look of sympathy fills his eyes, but then he stands abruptly as we see William approaching. "William, have you met Judge James Blackwell?" I ask.

"Only briefly. How do you do, Your Honor? I'm Anna's fiancé, William Wilkinson."

"It's a pleasure to meet you." William knows that the judge is my father, but he makes no acknowledgment of the relationship. As far as he and the rest of Chicago society are concerned, Arthur Nicholson is my father.

"If you'll excuse us, Your Honor, I would like to speak with Anna in private."

The judge gives a little bow. "Of course. Merry Christmas, my dear."

William takes my arm and helps me to my feet, leading me through the crowded room and across the foyer to the empty morning room. "I need to have you all to myself for a few minutes so I can give you your Christmas present," he says. He reaches into the pocket of his tuxedo and presents me with a small jewelry box. I open it to find a glittering ring. The huge, emerald-cut diamond is surrounded by half a dozen smaller diamonds. William takes my left hand and slips the ring onto my finger. "Merry Christmas, Anna. Do you like it?"

"It's beautiful, William!" I move into his arms, and he bends to kiss me. I feel the passion in his kiss and want so much to feel the same for him, but I don't.

When our lips part, he gazes down at me and says, "You look beautiful tonight."

"And you are the handsomest man at the party." It's true. I'm well aware of the admiring glances William draws from other women everywhere he goes. I look down at the ring he has just given me. I've lost weight during my illness and it's too big for my finger, but that can be fixed. Like the house, the ring is too large and extravagant for my taste, but I would never hurt William's feelings by mentioning it. "Thank you. It's a wonderful Christmas present."

"Our parents would like to announce the new date for our wedding," he says. "We're so grateful that you're growing stronger every day, and we thought tonight would be the perfect occasion. We've chosen the first of June, if that's all right with you."

My heart makes a nervous jitter but I smile up at him. "My social calendar is completely empty at the moment. And Dr. Paulson assures me that I'll be much stronger by June."

"We're all grateful to have you back, Anna." He pulls me close for another hug, then offers me his arm so we can join the others.

"William, wait," I say, holding back. "There's something I need to tell you before we're married. I've wanted to speak with you about it before, but I haven't known quite how to do it."

"Anna, what is it?"

I draw a breath for strength and exhale. "The doctor said

the damage to my heart will never heal. I will always be weaker than I used to be."

"Yes, so you've told me. And I promise to hire dozens of servants to pamper and spoil you. I'll wrap you in cotton batting like a delicate glass ornament." I know he means well, but his words make me feel like I'm suffocating. Even before my illness, living a pampered life of ease made me feel useless, and now I will feel even more so. How will I ever find a way to serve God if I'm wrapped up in cotton and sitting on a shelf like a fragile doll?

"I know you'll treat me well, William, but there's something more." I gather my courage, willing myself not to shed any more tears. "The doctor says it will be very dangerous for me to bear children. My heart could never withstand the strain of childbirth."

William looks stunned. I can see that he is analyzing my words, thinking them through, counting the cost, just as I had to do. I wait for him to realize what a tragic blow it must be for me to know I'll never be a mother, and then to take me in his arms and comfort me. But he doesn't. He doesn't say anything. Thankfully, Mother comes into the room and interrupts us, breaking the awkward silence.

"There you are! I've been looking all over for you. Mr. Wilkinson would like to offer a champagne toast to the two of you."

"William just gave me his Christmas present. Look, Mother." I hold out my hand to show her, and I see that my hand is trembling.

"It's beautiful, Anna. Come and show everyone. We're ready to make our announcement."

I take William's arm, and we walk into the parlor to stand together in front of the Christmas tree. The ring weighs down my hand as if it's made from lead.

CHAPTER 34

Geesje

HOLLAND, MICHIGAN

On Sunday morning, Cornelia and I are chatting with the other women after the church service when Lena Visscher approaches us, her baby bouncing and squirming in her arms. "Mrs. de Jonge? I was wondering if you and Cornelia would be able to come to my house for coffee tomorrow morning?" I look at Cornelia to see if she has understood, and she nods.

"We would be happy to come."

Lena's little house is fragrant with the aroma of coffee and cinnamon cookies when we arrive. The sketch Cornelia made of baby Willem has been framed and sits on the mantel along with fresh evergreen branches. "I want to ask you something, Cornelia," Lena says as we sip our coffee. "I would like to pay you to draw another picture of Willem. It would be a Christmas present for my mother, who doesn't get to see him very often.

She has a photograph of him, but it just isn't the same. There is so much life in your drawing."

Cornelia looks surprised but pleased. I watch as she searches for the words to reply in English. "I am happy to draw him. . . . Maybe you would like color? . . . I have now some paint." Earlier this month, I gave Cornelia a set of watercolors, brushes, and other supplies as a present for Sinterklaas Day. Her pictures now reflect the color and life that is gradually filling her soul as God heals her grief from the past.

"Even better," Lena says. "Let me know when you want to come by to sketch him—although, I don't know how we will get him to sit still." We laugh as we watch him swim across the floor using only his arms. "I think some of my friends would like to hire you, too, if you're willing. They've all admired the picture you drew." Cornelia's proud smile seems to light up the room.

Later that day, the mailman brings me an official-looking letter from the Netherlands. I'm glad Cornelia is at work as I slit it open and read it. It's from the church officials there, responding to my request for justice for Cornelia. They are willing to look into the matter, they say, but they feel that the investigation and disciplinary action should come at the request of Dominie Den Herder, Cornelia's legal guardian. At the very least, they would like him to confirm the truth and accuracy of what his teenaged granddaughter has accused this man of doing. I understand their viewpoint. But I dread another confrontation with Marinus.

I sit down by my fire and pick up my knitting as I stew over the letter, planning how to approach the dominie. I could tell Cornelia's story to our pastor and ask him to get involved. Maybe he could convince Marinus to do the right thing. My son Jakob might help me, too. But the secrets in Cornelia's past are hers alone to reveal, and I already know how furious her grandfather will be if I start sharing them with others. No, I will need to talk to Marinus myself.

I'm deep in thought when I hear my back door open and close, and in walks Derk. "Well, look at you, all rosy-cheeked from the cold! How are you, lieveling?" I stand to embrace him and feel the cold air on his clothes. "What brings you here on a Monday afternoon? Shouldn't you be in class?"

"We don't have any more classes until after Christmas— although I'll have some extra work to do to catch up. I wanted to come by and see if you've heard from Anneke lately."

I feel a prickle of uneasiness. "Yes, she's doing well and continuing to recover. She's still quite weak, so she's having a quieter Christmas this year. She says she doesn't miss all the parties and running around." Tears burn my eyes when I recall her sad news about not bearing children. I wrote back to her right away, telling her how much I wish I could console her in person. It's devastating news for any woman to hear. But it isn't something that I should share with Derk.

"Tell her I said hello when you write to her."

His expression is so eager and lovesick that it breaks my heart. I shake my head. "No. I can't do that, Derk."

"What? . . . Why not?"

"Lieveling, you have to let Anneke go." He looks devastated. "I know how hard it is, believe me. But you'll never be able to get on with your life unless you do. The wound will never heal. Anneke is going to marry William. Whether we like it or not, whether she loves him or not, that's what's going to happen. I know your heart is breaking, but you need to accept the truth and move forward. God has the perfect wife in mind for you, and it isn't Anneke." He looks away, but I can see that he's struggling with his emotions.

He gives a curt nod. "Understood."

"Listen, I thought I would never love anyone the way I loved your grandfather. But I did. I loved my husband Maarten very much, and we had a good life together. You'll love again, too." He tries to smile, but it doesn't reach his eyes.

He starts to leave, then turns back. "Did Dominie Den Herder tell you he's going to preach the sermon at the Dutch service Sunday evening?"

"No, I haven't spoken with him. But that sounds like good news." And maybe after he has that triumph, after he has returned to the pulpit and to his calling, he'll be more open to helping me talk with the Dutch officials on Cornelia's behalf.

This time I warn Cornelia ahead of time so she won't be caught off-guard on Sunday evening. "May I stay home?" she asks when I tell her that her grandfather will be preaching. "I don't want to hear him preach."

"I won't force you to go. But would you think about something for me? Your grandfather gave up his calling as a minister, and this is his chance to use that gift. If you're going to forgive him, this would be a wonderful time to tell him. So he can start all over again."

She gives her customary shrug. "I'll think about it."

"It's what God would want you to do, Cornelia. And then you'll be able to start all over again, too."

On Sunday evening I'm surprised and pleased when Cornelia comes out of her bedroom dressed for church. "I'm going to do it," she says in a shaky voice. "Will you come with me to talk to him?"

"I'll be right beside you." I offer her a hug, and the poor girl is trembling as if she's standing outside in the cold winter night without her coat. We go next door to the Vander Veens' house, but Derk tells us the dominie has already left. I pray that Cornelia doesn't change her mind as we walk to Pillar Church together.

The sanctuary is filling with parishioners arriving for the evening service, so I hurry with Cornelia to the back of the church to avoid getting entangled in conversation. We find her grandfather getting ready in the sacristy. He has already put on a clerical robe and is trying to adjust the white stole around his neck. I'm astounded when Cornelia walks forward and fixes the ends of it for him so they hang evenly. He looks surprised, too.

"Thank you," he says with a slight nod. He is an imposing figure, tall and dignified and handsome. I can see why this is the image he wants the world to see.

"I-I have something to say." Cornelia's voice is whisper soft. I silently pray for her. "I have been very angry with you for taking my baby away from me. You were wrong not to let me hold him or say good-bye. But I want you to know . . . I forgive you."

His head jerks back in surprise. "*You* forgive *me*? Isn't that the wrong way around, Cornelia? After what you did?"

She swallows and takes a breath. "I've asked God to forgive my sins, and I know He has. But I needed your love and attention after Mama and Papa died, and you didn't give them to me. You left me all alone when I needed you. You were the only person I had left in the world, but your work was always much more important than I was. You didn't even see what that man was doing to me. Instead, you ignored me and looked the other way. Then, after my baby was born, you didn't give me a chance to see him and say good-bye. It was cruel of you to take him away from me that way. . . . But now I want you to know that I forgive you . . . for everything."

For the space of a heartbeat, the dominie looks shaken, a towering oak buffeted by a strong wind. Then his imposing façade slips back into place. "Excuse me. The service is starting." He walks away.

Cornelia turns and sags in my arms like a rag doll. "I'm so proud of you," I say. "You did the right thing. It's between him and God now. Don't let his response discourage you."

She dries her eyes and straightens her shoulders. When she is ready, we go back into the sanctuary and sit in a pew. The dominie sweeps in and takes his place on the platform in front.

"I don't hate him anymore," Cornelia whispers as the service begins. "I feel sorry for him. Nobody loves him. I know how terrible it feels when nobody loves you." I squeeze her hand. It's no longer trembling.

Dominie Den Herder rises when it's time for his sermon. He looks at home in the pulpit. I have never been able to imagine him as a pastor, caring for the needs of his flock, but I see him now as a minister of God's Word for the first time. He has a commanding presence. "Let us pray," he begins. He bows his head to recite the familiar prayer: "May the words of my mouth and the meditations of my heart be acceptable in your sight, O Lord, my strength and my redeemer. Amen."

He lifts his head, taking a moment to gaze out at the sanctuary full of people, surveying the crowd as if demanding their attention before he begins. "This evening—"

He stops. His gaze comes to rest on Cornelia. Time seems to halt as he stares down at her. The air stills. The silence is immense.

There is a moment when I see him sway, and I'm reminded of how the great oak trees that we felled to build the town of Holland would teeter, as if trying to regain their balance the moment the final blow of the axe had been struck. I see his despair as he realizes, like those proud oak trees, that he has been severed from the roots that fed him, nourished him, and held him in place.

"Oh, God!" he groans as he falls to his knees. "Forgive me!"

Cornelia leaps up. She pushes past me in the pew. I watch her hurry up the aisle and mount the steps to the platform. Then she also drops to her knees and wraps her arms around her grandfather, cradling him where he has fallen.

CHAPTER 35

Anna

CHICAGO, ILLINOIS

Mr. Wilkinson has asked Mother, Father, and me to meet him for dinner downtown at the private club he and Father belong to. The January evening is bitter cold, so the servants have warmed our carriage with pans of hot coals for the ride. I have been out only a few times this past month, choosing my social events carefully so I don't overdo it. But this dinner seemed important, and I assume it has something to do with our new wedding plans.

There is a dark, gentlemanly warmth in the club's dining room, with its plush carpets, soft lighting, and hushed voices, making it feel comfortably intimate. The fragrant aroma of fine cigars fills the air. Mr. Wilkinson and another gentleman are already seated at a corner table, and they both rise as we approach. I look around for William and his mother but don't see them. Then I notice that the table has been set for only five people. I feel a prickle of unease when Mr. Wilkinson introduces the other gentleman as Mr. John Avery, his attorney.

"Where's William?" I ask.

"He won't be joining us tonight. Please, have a seat and let's order our drinks. I'll explain everything in a moment." The waiter is standing ready. I shake my head when he asks what I would like. Something is very wrong, but I can't imagine what. Father seems wary, as well. He swirls the ice around in his glass after it arrives, without drinking any of it. The others chat about the snowy weather for a few minutes.

At last Mr. Wilkinson sets down his own glass and exhales. "This is one of the most difficult decisions I've ever had to make. . . . As you know, William is our only son. You may not know, however, that I have no brothers or uncles. William is the only male in our family who can carry on the Wilkinson name. Unfortunately for all of us, Anna's illness has left her unable to bear William a son. And since our family needs an heir to carry on our business . . . I'm sorry to say we have no choice but to end the engagement."

I open my mouth to speak, but nothing comes out. I feel as if someone has just yanked the chair out from under me and I've dropped to the floor with a painful thud. My parents are speechless, too, as we try to comprehend what Mr. Wilkinson has just said. Father is the first to respond.

"You're . . . you're ending their engagement? We just announced the new wedding date to all our friends at Christmastime."

"I understand how cruel our decision must sound to you, but we have no choice. Adopting a child is not an option for our family's future." He pauses, as if to give us time to digest his words. Mother is white-faced and mute with shock as all her hopes and dreams for me are shattered. I reach for her hand, wondering if she will need her smelling salts.

"You would do this to our Anna?" Father asks. "After she has been so ill?"

Mr. Wilkinson plows forward, ignoring Father's outrage. "Since we are the ones who are breaking the engagement, our family is well aware that you have a legal right to sue us for breach of contract. And while we deeply regret any embarrassment and grief this break may cause you, it is our hope that you will spare both of our families the indignity of dragging this matter into a court of law."

"You can't do this to us!" Father says. I know he is concerned for me, but he must also be concerned that the broken engagement will result in his bankruptcy.

The lawyer, Mr. Avery, clears his throat and speaks for the first time. "Mr. Wilkinson would like to offer a very fair financial settlement for this breach of contract, with the hope that this matter can be kept out of court. I have drawn up these papers showing the amount of the proposed settlement, along with the assurance, in writing, that any outstanding loans you have with the bank, Mr. Nicholson, will not be canceled or foreclosed. In fact, we're offering to negotiate a lower rate of interest and to extend the length of the loans for as long as you feel is necessary."

I shake my head to clear it. Did I hear right? I won't have to marry William, and yet Father won't face bankruptcy? Tears fill my eyes. I must be dreaming!

Father glances at me and misinterprets my tears. "You would break my daughter's heart in such a cruel way?"

"Is there anything else we can do to compensate you, Anna?" Mr. Wilkinson asks. "William feels terrible about this."

"Why isn't he here?" Father asks. "Shouldn't William be the one to tell Anna?"

"This was my decision, not William's," Mr. Wilkinson says. "He reluctantly conceded to my wishes."

I don't believe it for a minute. I saw William's expression when I told him what Dr. Paulson said. I pull off the ring William gave me and set it on the tablecloth in front of Mr. Wilkinson. "Please give this to William for me."

He holds up both hands, as if the ring is hot and he's afraid to touch it. "No, no. That isn't necessary. The ring was a Christmas gift. William would like you to keep it."

"I would rather not." I leave it lying on the table in front of him.

Father pushes back his chair and stands. "I think we should go." We haven't ordered dinner yet, but I'm sure that no one is hungry. The other men rise, as well.

"Please, take these papers with you," the lawyer says. "Have your attorney look them over. Let me know when you're ready to talk further."

Father snatches them from his hand and stuffs them into the inside pocket of his suit coat. He pulls out Mother's chair for her and helps her to her feet, then does the same for me. I see a host of emotions in Mother's expression—anger, humiliation, shock, outrage—as the staff help us with our coats and we make our way to our carriage. I'm eager to tell Mother that I'm not at all upset by what happened here tonight. I am amazed! I feel as though I've been set free! The papers in Father's pocket are an answer to all my prayers.

"I plan to fight this," Father says when we're seated in our carriage. His voice is tight with outrage. "This is so unfair to you, Anna. Your illness and the consequences of it weren't your fault."

"William is stealing everything he promised you," Mother adds. "Your beautiful home, your future . . ." She is fighting her tears, and I can tell she doesn't want to lose control.

"But I'm not upset at all that he broke our engagement," I tell them. "I hated that house. And I don't want to marry William."

"Well, of course you don't," Father says with a huff. "Not after the way he just treated you. Imagine, not even having the courage or the decency to face you in person!"

"It isn't that. I never wanted to marry him. I was only doing it for you and Mother."

"For us?"

I hesitate to humiliate my father further by admitting the truth, but I see that I must. "Last summer I overheard you saying that your business had suffered some setbacks and that you needed the loans from the Wilkinsons' bank. I didn't want you to lose everything the way the Kirklands did. And I know how happy Mother has been to be included in Mrs. Wilkinson's social circle, joining the Literary Club and everything."

"I thought you cared for William," Mother says. "And that he cared for you."

I think about Derk's declaration of love and all the ways he showed his love for me, and for the first time, I dare to hope that I might have a future with him after all. It feels like a miracle! "I was fond of William," I finally say, "but I'm not in love with him. And he was the one who made all of the plans for our future—the huge mansion and running for political office. I didn't want any of it."

"And yet you would go ahead and marry him for our sakes?" Father asks.

"Of course. I love both of you."

"Anna! I would never ask such a sacrifice from you. I didn't even want you to know about my financial problems."

"You saved my life, Father. You and Mother gave me everything I have and made me the woman I am. I would gladly help you."

Father shakes his head. "I don't know what to say."

"Don't you see how this has all worked out in a wonderful way? I no longer have to marry William, yet your business will still be safe. Please accept Mr. Wilkinson's offer, Father. You have no idea how relieved and grateful I am that he broke the engagement." My illness and my inability to bear children seemed like such disasters, yet they are the very circumstances that have set me free from a life I would have hated. Joy born from tragedy! I feel giddy enough to laugh, but my parents don't share my happiness yet.

We arrive home, and the butler hustles us inside where a fire is blazing in the morning room. He pulls two chairs close to the hearth so Mother and I can warm up, but Father is too restless to sit. He lights a cigar and puffs clouds of smoke as he paces. Mrs. Dunlap asks if we would like something to eat, since we've returned home so soon after leaving, but none of us is hungry.

"Even if you don't want to marry William," Mother says, "what the Wilkinsons have done to you is so unfair. They've destroyed any chances you have for arranging a good marriage in the future. People are going to talk. They'll think William didn't want you because you are damaged goods, especially after all of those rumors about your past. And you're a little old at twenty-four to begin courting all over again. You'll be competing with much younger debutantes."

I know she means well, but her concerns make me want to laugh out loud. "None of that matters to me, Mother. I know you both enjoy this social life, and you've worked hard to get where you are. But even when I'm completely well again, I don't want to go back to a life of teas and luncheons and calling cards. I haven't missed it in the least while I've been ill. When I was banished from society for a week because of all the gossip and the threat of a scandal, I saw how shallow William and his family are, how concerned they are with appearances. Now that God has spared my life for a second time, I know He must have a plan for me. I want to find out what it is. Life is too short and too important to waste on things that don't interest me."

"What will you do?" Father asks.

"I don't know. But at least I'll be free now to pursue the charity work that William forbade me to do. There are so many needs among the poor here in Chicago." I see my mother wiping a tear, and I rise to wrap my arm around her shoulder. "I'm so sorry if I've disappointed you, Mother. The last thing I ever want to do is hurt you."

"You haven't disappointed me. I admire your . . . your determination. And your certainty. You've grown into such a strong woman this past year. And your faith . . . I don't know where it came from but . . . but when we nearly lost you, I realized how weak my own faith was. I wanted to turn to God, and I didn't know how."

"Maybe we can learn together."

Mother nods and blows her nose on her handkerchief. "I would like that." Another reason to thank God on this night of miracles. "My wish for you is to find a man from a fine family who is worthy of you. Someone who will support you well and care for you." She could be describing Derk. Again, I wonder if I dare to dream of a future with him. "Can you think of any worthy young gentlemen from your circle of business contacts?" she asks my father.

"My dear, you aren't listening to Anna," he says. "She has a second chance in life and she should do what makes her happy, not what pleases us. If she wants to do good deeds and help the poor, we should let her. She would have sacrificed her own happiness for ours; now let's do the same for her."

Mother looks up at me, blinking away tears. "I do want you to be happy, Anna."

"Tell us what we can do for you," Father says. "What would make you happy?"

I swallow a knot of joy. "To live a simple life with the man I'm in love with."

"The man you're . . . Does such a man exist?"

"Yes. I'm in love with Derk Vander Veen. And he loves me."

"The young man from the hotel?" Mother asks.

I laugh out loud, knowing she will probably always think of Derk that way. "Yes. But he no longer works there. He's a student at the theological seminary in Holland and will graduate in the spring. We both thought it was impossible for us to be together, but now that I no longer need to marry William—"

"He can move to Chicago and work for my firm," Father says. "I'll find a position for him."

"He won't have any social connections, at first," Mother adds, "but I'll do whatever I can to help him fit in."

I hold up my hands to stop them. "Derk wouldn't want any of that. He's going to be a minister in a few months, and he'll be called to serve a church congregation."

"We could find a church for him here. It's an unusual occupation for people of our means, but it could be arranged."

"He wouldn't want you to pull strings to serve a church in Chicago, Father. He wants to serve wherever God calls him."

"Would you have to move somewhere remote?" Mother asks. "What about your health?"

"I don't know if Derk even wants me for his wife, although I know he loves me. I won't be able to do any work, and he can't afford servants on what the church pays him. And he doesn't know I can't have children. These are all things Derk and I would need to talk about."

Father rests his hands on my shoulders as he looks at me. "And you believe that the life you're describing with this young man would make you happy?"

"I do."

"My dear little Anna!" He holds me tenderly, and I remember how strong his arms felt as he fought to keep us both afloat in the pounding waves. I love my father with all my heart. "If marrying this minister will make you truly happy, I will do whatever I can to make sure that it happens."

CHAPTER 36

Geesje

HOLLAND, MICHIGAN

"The walk will do us good," I tell Cornelia. We bundle up with scarves and hats and mittens before leaving our snug home. Cornelia offers to carry the basket with the cookies and warm bread we've just baked. The January day is crisp and cold, and the snow that sits atop the barren branches sparkles in the sunlight. We have just passed Derk's house next door when I hear someone calling my name.

"Mrs. de Jonge! Wait!" Dominie Den Herder buttons his overcoat as he hurries down the front steps and walks toward us. "I was just coming to speak with you." He has been a different man since his collapse on that Sunday evening in church. He wasn't able to preach his sermon or even return to the pulpit, but no one except Cornelia and me, and perhaps our pastor, understood that it wasn't a sudden illness that had made him unable to go on. Back in the sacristy, where no one else could hear his sobs, he begged Cornelia to forgive him.

"I wanted to tell you and Cornelia that I have mailed everything they requested to the church officials in the Netherlands," he says now.

"That's very good news. We're on our way to visit Mrs. Hartig, at the moment, but why don't you come over and have tea with us when we get back?"

He looks down at the ground as if memorizing the toes of his boots. I wait, wondering what else he wants to say. "May I join you?" he asks. "On your visit?"

I'm so surprised it takes me a moment to respond. "Yes, of course. Let's keep walking so the bread we just baked doesn't get cold."

"And so we don't freeze!" Cornelia adds. She is hopping in place as if afraid her shoes will freeze to the ground. "It never got this cold back home, did it, Grandfather?"

"Nay, not that I recall." He tucks his scarf a little tighter around his ears to keep them warm. The snow squeaks beneath our feet as we walk. When we reach Mrs. Hartig's house, the dominie slows his steps. "I hope you don't mind that I came."

"Not at all."

"I-I need to learn how . . . how to do what you do."

I smile to reassure him. "It isn't hard. We're just going to sit with her and maybe read—"

"That isn't what I mean." He stops walking as he fumbles for words. "I mean the way you give, Mrs. de Jonge. The way you . . . love."

I look up at him and see a broken man. "I think God has already been teaching you. Both of you," I add, facing Cornelia. "There was a time in my life when I said I was willing to serve God any way He chose—and I meant it. But then I began to lose the people I loved, and I became very angry with Him for making me suffer. As my resentment grew, I nearly turned away from Him altogether. Then one day I found myself praying with a friend whose baby had been stillborn, and I understood that this was how God was asking me to serve Him. Would I accept my own suffering as something He allowed in order to shape me into someone He could use? Someone who would love like Jesus? Was I willing? Over time—and it was a long time—I chose to let go of the resentment and to trust Him. Simply trust Him. I don't need to see exactly how He's going to weave together all of the broken strands—in my life or anyone else's. But I know that the finished work will be beautiful."

I expect the dominie to be uncomfortable visiting Mrs. Hartig, as he was the last time. I expect him to simply clean the ashes from her stove, stoke the fire, and add more coal while Cornelia and I talk with her. The dominie does all of those things. But then he comes into the parlor and sits down beside Mrs. Hartig and asks if he may pray with her. His words are tender and moving as he bows his head and asks God to restore her joy.

None of us says much on the way home. I repeat my offer for him to come inside with us for tea. He shakes his head. "Thank you, Mrs. de Jonge, but—"

"I wish you would call me Geesje."

"Perhaps we can have tea another day . . . Geesje." I can tell that there is something more he wants to say. I wait. "Thank you for teaching me today. I wish . . . I wish I had known to do the same things for my wife." I'm too stunned to reply as he leaves us and returns home.

Cornelia and I have finally warmed up again after our trek across town when the mailman drops a letter in my box out front. I dash outside without a coat to retrieve it and am pleased to see that it's from Anneke. I tear open the envelope and begin reading as I walk back to the house. Her words stop me dead in my tracks. I stand on the porch with my front door wide open as I read them again: *William has ended our engagement. I no longer have to marry him, and yet my father's finances will be just fine. I'm free to marry Derk! . . .*

"I don't believe it!" I cry aloud.

"Is it bad news, Tante Geesje?" Cornelia pulls me inside and shuts the door.

"No! It's wonderful news! . . . I just can't believe it! Here, let me read it to you. But first I need to sit down. . . . Oh, how I hope and pray that what Anneke writes is true, yet so rarely in life is there a 'happily ever after' ending, and she and Derk have been through so much already—"

"Read it to me!" Cornelia says, laughing. "Hurry up!"

"Dearest Oma,

William has ended our engagement. I no longer have to marry him, and yet my father's finances will be just fine. I'm free to marry Derk! I love him, Oma, and I know he loves me, but first we'll need to figure out how we can make it work. I know I'm totally unfit to serve as a minister's wife, especially after my illness. Although when Judge Blackwell heard the news that my engagement to William had ended, he promised to hire as many servants as I needed so I could marry Derk. He likes Derk, and he has given us his blessing. My father has, too. My parents said they will do everything they can to ensure my happiness with the man I love.

I haven't told Derk any of this. I wanted to write to you first, so you will stop him from racing right down here on the very first train. The winter weather is too stormy for travel, and besides, Derk needs to finish school. But if you make him promise not to race down to Chicago the moment he hears the news, we can start writing letters to each other. We will have a lot of important things to talk about during the next few months. Once we see each other again in the spring, we can decide what we want to do from there."

"Did you understand all that?" I ask Cornelia when I finish reading. She smiles and claps her hands.

"I love happy endings," she says. "I can't wait to tell Derk."

"He'll be overjoyed. He has been so lovesick for Anneke. Who would have ever guessed that such an impossible situation would be possible after all?"

"May I run next door and tell Grandfather to send Derk over here the moment he comes home?"

"Yes, why don't you do that. . . . Oh, my goodness! I still can't believe it! If I'm this happy, imagine how happy Derk and Anneke are going to be!"

Derk doesn't come over until after eight o'clock that night. I feel like an overripe melon that's about to burst with happiness by the time he gets here. "I've been studying with a group of friends," he tells us. "Dominie Den Herder says you have big news?"

"You need to sit down, Derk. I know people always say you'd better sit down when they have news, but I really think you should this time."

He's laughing as he lowers himself into a chair. "I'm guessing it must be good news by the way the two of you are grinning."

"The best news you could ever imagine. I got a letter from Anneke today—"

"She's coming to visit?"

"Even better. She isn't going to marry William. They ended their engagement. *And* . . . she is free to marry you."

Tears flood Derk's eyes. He tries to speak, but all that comes out is a sob. He leaps up and pulls me into his arms, squeezing me so tightly I can barely breathe. "I must be dreaming," he says. "Oh, I hope I'm not! Tell me this is really happening, Tante Geesje!"

"You aren't dreaming, lieveling," I say when he finally lets go. I'm weeping with joy, as well. "Best of all, Anneke's parents support her decision. And so does Judge Blackwell."

"The judge said he wanted to help me, but I never imagined . . . How did he do it? Does she say?"

"No. But she said her father won't go bankrupt after all."

"When does the next train leave? I have to go down there! Do you think there's a train leaving this late at night? How will I ever wait until tomorrow morning if there isn't?" Derk pulls his hat from his coat pocket and jams it onto his head as he stumbles toward the door.

"Whoa! Hold on, Derk. You need to read Anneke's letter first. I'm supposed to make you promise not to skip classes again and run down to Chicago." Cornelia retrieves the letter from my desk and hands it to him. He wipes his tears so he can read it. I hear him breathing deeply as he struggles not to cry. He loses the battle before reaching the second page and collapses onto the chair again, covering his face. "Thank you, God. Thank you . . ." he murmurs.

"I can't help thinking of your grandfather Hendrik. He would be so surprised and pleased to see our grandchildren falling in love and getting married. Only God could arrange something this wonderful, this miraculous."

At last Derk lifts his head. "I still can't believe it!"

"Now, you need to promise me you won't go to Chicago. Did you read what Anneke said?"

He laughs as he rises to his feet. "I read it. But do you honestly think there's anything in the world that can stop me from going?"

Stop a hopeless romantic like Derk? A man who is wildly in love? No, of course not.

CHAPTER 37

Anna

"Did any letters come for me today?" I ask our housekeeper. I've just finished dressing for this evening's party and have run into Mrs. Dunlap on the stairs. I know it's too soon to receive a reply from Oma or a letter from Derk, but I can't bear the suspense as I wait to hear from them. I think Derk wants to marry me . . . but I guess I'm still afraid to hope that we can be together.

"No, I'm sorry, Miss Anna," Mrs. Dunlap replies. "I must say you look lovely this evening. It's so good to have you well again."

"Thank you, Mrs. Dunlap." I join Mother and Father in the foyer of our home as we wait to greet our guests. My parents are hosting a formal dinner party this evening, and our house looks warm and elegant with lamps and candles sparkling in every room. The dining room table is spread with our finest

374

linens and crystal and silver tableware. I'm no longer able to make social calls every afternoon, nor am I interested in doing so even if I could. Now that the Wilkinsons aren't part of our lives, Mother has been doing less socializing with their crowd and more entertaining in our home. She seems happier and more relaxed than ever before.

The carriages begin pulling up out front, and before long, our home overflows with laughter and greetings. The servants pass trays of beverages and hors d'oeuvres, and I'm enjoying myself immensely as I chat with people I haven't seen since Christmas. It's nearly time to proceed to the dining room when our butler approaches and pulls me aside.

"Excuse me for interrupting, Miss Anna, but an uninvited gentleman is asking to speak with you." I peer around the corner but don't see anyone in the front foyer.

"Who is it? And where is he?"

"In the kitchen. He came to the servants' door."

I follow the butler to the kitchen, wondering who it could be—and there's Derk! Without thinking, I run to him. His arms surround me, holding me tightly, and I know this is where I want to be for the rest of my life! All around us, the cook and our other servants have been scrambling to get the meal ready to serve, but our little drama has distracted them. They stare, mouths agape at the sight of me embracing a man they don't know in the middle of our kitchen.

"Don't cry, Anneke," Derk says when we pull apart. His fingers are icy as he wipes my tears. "I don't ever want to make you cry."

"You're crying, too," I say, laughing through my tears.

"These are tears of joy. Ever since Tante Geesje showed me your letter, I can't seem to make them to stop." He holds me again, and we rock in place as if waltzing to our own music. For me, it's a symphony of pure joy.

"You weren't supposed to come," I murmur into his shoulder. "You have classes."

"Not on Saturday. Besides, how could I stay away?"

We part a second time and I ask, "Why did you come to the back door?"

"I saw all the lights on and the carriages parked out front, and I didn't want to interrupt anything. It looks like you have guests."

"They're my father's guests. I'm helping Mother greet everyone and make introductions."

"Look at you! You're dressed like a princess in a fairy tale!" He touches my hair, which is piled high on my head and embellished with jeweled combs. "You're so beautiful, Anna!"

"You must join us, Derk. Come on, I want everyone to meet you." I tug on his hand, but he doesn't move.

"Dressed like this? I wouldn't dare. And I didn't bring anything better to wear, either. Certainly nothing that's fit to accompany a princess."

"Would you feel better if you borrowed a tuxedo? Please, Derk. I would love to have you join me. We haven't sat down to dinner yet, and Mrs. Dunlap can easily add another place for you."

"Can I ask you something first?"

"Yes?"

He pulls a white cotton handkerchief from his coat pocket and carefully unfolds it on the palm of his hand. Tucked inside is a plain gold ring with a tiny red stone. "This was my mother's," he says as tears fill his eyes again. "Will you marry me, Anneke?"

I throw my arms around him, hugging him tightly. "Yes! I would love to marry you!" When we finally let go, he takes my left hand and slips the ring onto my finger. It fits perfectly. And it's much more to my liking than the one William gave me.

"Maybe I should have asked your father for your hand first," he says. "That's what I came here to do. You know, I don't think I've ever met your father."

"Well, you can meet him right now. I'll ask Mrs. Dunlap to find a tuxedo for you. The butler and footmen wear them for formal occasions, so there must be some extras somewhere."

I call for our housekeeper and explain what we need. "He's a tall fellow, Miss Anna," she says, looking him over. "None of the servants is as tall as he is."

"Just do the best you can. Please."

Mother's eyes go wide when Derk and I walk through the door from the kitchen a short time later. She looks him over from head to toe, assessing the trousers that are two inches too short, the ordinary brown shoes on his feet, and the tuxedo sleeves that don't reach his wrists. "Aren't you—?"

I interrupt, afraid she's about to say *the boy from the hotel*. "You remember Derk Vander Veen, Mother."

"I'm very sorry for interrupting your party, Mrs. Nicholson."

"Not at all, Derk . . . May I call you that? We're happy to have you." The smile she gives him is so warm that I want to hug her. She looks him over again and laughs. "Is that our butler's tuxedo?"

"It is. I-I'm sorry—"

"Never mind. We'll buy you one that fits a little better for next time."

"Next time . . . yes." He grins. Mother's welcome is so different from the last time Derk paid a visit that hope begins to blossom and bloom.

When it's time to proceed to the dining room, Derk seems overwhelmed by the elaborate table settings and the other guests in their finery who are taking their places around the table. The butler seats him beside me, and I quietly coach him on what to do and which fork to use. The guests seated near us engage

Derk in conversation, and they seem fascinated as he talks about becoming a minister. I know everyone is dying to know if he's my new suitor, but they're much too polite to come right out and ask. Father watches us from the far end of the table, too far away to talk to us. But he must see our joy. I can't stop gazing at Derk, nor he at me, so anyone with eyes must surely notice how we feel about each other. I don't care! I want the world to know I'm in love!

When the dinner party ends and the last guest has said goodbye, Derk and I join my parents in the morning room. "I'm glad to finally meet you, Mr. Nicholson," Derk says. "I love your daughter very much, and I've asked her to marry me. I would be honored to have your blessing."

"You have it, young man," he says, shaking Derk's hand. "Anna tells me she's also in love with you. Her happiness is very important to me."

"I don't know if Anneke told you, but we're connected by a common tragedy—the wreck of the *Ironsides*. My mother was also aboard that ship, and she drowned that day. But out of disaster, God brought Anneke into your life. And now into mine."

We talk for a while, and I can tell that Derk has won my father over with his solid, down-to-earth honesty and humility. Mother seems swayed by how much he clearly cares for me. "We'll talk more in the morning," Father says as the evening grows late.

Mrs. Dunlap has prepared a room for Derk. "You'll find your bag already in there," she tells him. "Let me know if there's anything else you need." I walk up the stairs with him, reluctant to say good night, worried that I'll wake up to find this has all been a dream.

"Derk . . . there's something else," I say when we reach the landing. The full moon illuminates the stained-glass window from outside, bathing us in colorful prisms of light. "I need to tell you that—"

"If it's about having children, I already know. Tante Geesje told me. I can't imagine how sorrowful you must feel. If you'd like, we can adopt an orphan when we're ready to start a family—a dozen orphans. My heart is open to whatever children God gives us. As I'm sure you know, the bonds of love are just as strong as the bonds of blood. And you'll make a wonderful mother, Anneke."

I sigh. How different from William's response. "But it's more than that, Derk. The doctor says I can't do work of any kind. We'll need servants to do all of the household duties like washing and cleaning and cooking. Even if I were allowed to do all those things, I wouldn't know how. I'll be a useless wife to you."

"Anyone can scrub and clean. Not everyone can be a pastor's wife."

"What does that require?"

"Things you already do wonderfully well, like taking an interest in people, and quietly listening to them, and showing them you care. You'll be praying with people and studying the Bible with them. And you'll be great at organizing charity efforts to help the poor."

"Like Oma does?"

"Exactly. You're wonderful with people, Anneke, and a gracious hostess. I watched as you made everyone feel welcome and included tonight. Especially me."

"I'll have so much to learn."

"You can do it. . . . But what concerns me most of all is that I'll be asking you to give up all of this—your home, your family, your entire way of life—to live in a drafty parsonage with none of the finer things you're used to. My monthly salary couldn't even buy the dress you're wearing. We'll rely on donations from people in my congregation. I've seen the way you live in this beautiful home, and I feel as though I'm asking too much of you."

"William offered me the opposite extreme—a life of extravagance—and it wasn't what I wanted at all. Moving to Michigan is going to be an adjustment, I'm sure. But my parents are willing to hire all the extra help I'll need."

"I wish they didn't have to. I wish I could provide for you."

"I know. But listen, Derk. I think a bigger question is, will your church accept me since I'm not one of them? And I'll be a pastor's wife with a houseful of servants. I know you feel uncomfortable in my world. Will I feel the same in yours? I'm asking this for your sake, not mine. I don't want people to think less of you because of me."

"The Bible says that man looks at the outward things, but God looks at the heart. I'll be sure to use that text for my first sermon." He breaks into a smile, but I'm still worried.

"The Bible also says that it's hard for a rich man to enter the kingdom of God."

"Anneke, you're doing exactly what the rich young ruler in that story wasn't willing to do. You're giving up all of your riches to follow Jesus and serve His church."

"And to marry the man I love."

"Yes. That too," he says, smiling. "I love you so much, Anneke." Derk bends to kiss me. I feel the touch of his lips on mine for the first time as the moon spills dazzling colors at our feet.

CHAPTER 38

Geesje

Today is the first day of June, and I've opened all of my windows to air out my house. The sky is blue, the sun is warm, and it's the kind of day that makes me feel happy to be alive. My gardens are growing again—and so are the weeds, of course. I'm poking around in my flower beds this morning, hoping I'll have enough blooms to decorate the church for Anneke's wedding next week. Next week! I've been waiting all winter and spring for this glorious day—as I'm sure she and Derk have, too.

I'm weeding along the side of my house when I hear Cornelia calling to me from inside the house. "Tante Geesje? Tante Geesje, where are you?"

I stand up and answer through the open window. "Out here. Where are you?" She's supposed to be working at the store. My screen door slams and Cornelia runs around to the side of the house, out of breath.

"Look what just came! Mrs. Van Putten said I could run home and show them to you right away." She opens a small box from our print shop while I wipe my hands on my apron. Inside are four postcards with scenes from Holland and the lakeshore. My son Arie printed them from Cornelia's hand-drawn watercolor paintings.

"Oh my! They're wonderful. Very professional."

"Mrs. Van Putten already ordered some to sell in her store. And Arie thinks the postcards will sell really well at all the big hotels. He's going to show them to the hotel managers when they come into town to give him their printing orders."

"They'll be a huge success. I'm so happy for you." I pull her into my arms for a hug.

"My new friend Janna from church also likes to draw, and we're going to walk around town tomorrow and look for more ideas for postcards." Cornelia is beaming.

"It's wonderful to see you this happy. Heaven knows, you've had enough sorrow for one lifetime."

For a moment her smile fades. "I still think about my baby, sometimes, and wonder what he looked like."

"He was a part of you, Cornelia. Of course you can't forget him."

"They told me he was given to a woman who couldn't have children—like Anneke. And so from now on, whenever I feel sad, I will imagine him with parents like Anneke and Derk."

"They will make wonderful parents, won't they? And you will, too, someday."

"Ya. I have to run back to work. I'll see you later."

"Thank you for showing me the postcards," I say as she jogs away, waving good-bye.

Cornelia is barely gone when I hear Dominie Den Herder calling my name. "Geesje? Are you home?"

"I'm out here." I walk around to meet him on my front porch.

"It's much too nice to stay inside, isn't it?" Dominie asks.

"That's for certain! The sun is coaxing all my flowers into bloom, just in time for Derk and Anneke's wedding next week. Do you have time for a cup of tea with me, Marinus?"

"I don't want to keep you from your work."

"I'm done gardening for the day. Come on in." I lead the way inside and rinse off my hands before setting out the teapot and cups. After all of my arguments with the dominie, I never could have imagined we would one day have a friendly chat over tea. He is working more hours at the Dutch newspaper now and writing a weekly devotional column for them. He has also been helping at church. *"But I don't belong in the pulpit,"* he told me privately. *"I squandered that right."*

"I have some news from my former church in the Netherlands," he begins. "The man who violated Cornelia has been confronted and punished. They have put measures in place to make sure he can never abuse another young girl."

"Thank goodness. That's wonderful news. Cornelia deserves justice."

"They have also told the man that he must make restitution for the harm he did to her. It will be in the form of monetary payments. It won't be much, but she'll be able to use it for something she wants to pursue in the future."

"She mentioned an interest in photography the other day. Maybe the money could help her get started."

"Ya. Whatever she wants."

The water has begun to boil, and I rise to pour it into the teapot. I take out the cookie tin and offer him some while we wait for the tea to steep. "May I ask your advice about something, Dominie? I'm sure Derk told you that he's been called to pastor a little country church in a community not far from here."

"Ya. Such good news for him."

"It is. But most of the men in that church are farmers, and

they tend to be very conservative and old-fashioned. I'm worried that Anneke will feel unwelcome there. I'm afraid they will judge her unfairly because she comes from a wealthy family, especially since she will have to hire help to do all of the usual household chores. Do you have any thoughts on how I can convince these men to give her a chance?"

"Listen, Geesje—"

"I know, I know . . . I'm being a meddling busybody, as usual."

"Of course you are." He offers me a rare smile. "But now that I know you better, I understand what motivates you to meddle. It's love. Something I've needed to learn."

"Thank you."

"To answer your question, you probably can't convince men like that to change their opinions. I suggest you win over their wives instead. They're the ones who will need to adjust to a pastor's wife who isn't like them. Let them convince their stubborn husbands to accept her."

"That's a very good idea. Thank you."

"I have benefitted from your . . . shall we call it 'preaching,' Geesje? I recommend that you 'preach' to the wives of that congregation about not judging people. You can be very persuasive."

"Why, thank you," I say, laughing. "I believe that's just what I'll do. In fact, Derk is coming later this afternoon with my son's carriage, and we're going to ride out to his new church together. He wants me to look over the parsonage and figure out what he and Anneke will need to set up housekeeping. Why don't you come with us?"

"Oh . . . well . . . I don't know about that. . . ."

"Please, Marinus. I think Derk could really benefit from your experience as a dominie."

"And learn from my mistakes?"

"That too."

I manage to talk Marinus into coming. We're waiting on

my porch together when Derk arrives after lunch with the carriage. The sun feels wonderfully warm as we set off through the countryside for the eight-mile journey, passing through the village of Zeeland first. Flat, fertile farmland surrounds us on all sides, and the air smells of springtime and warm, plowed earth.

"You'll soon have a lot of wonderful new beginnings," I tell Derk. "A new marriage, a new church to serve . . . I'm thrilled for you, lieveling."

"I'm still amazed that the church hired me. I'm excited and also a little terrified."

"It's good that you're afraid," Marinus says. "That way you won't be tempted to do everything on your own strength. God likes it when we lean on Him."

"I'll be doing a lot of leaning, believe me!"

"If there is any way that I can help you or advise you," Marinus says, "please don't hesitate to ask."

"Thank you. That's good to know. I think I'll be asking you often."

We spot the church in the distance, situated near the junction of two roads. It's small and plain, with white clapboard siding and a steeple on top. Four women from the congregation are waiting outside to show us around the parsonage. I can see that they're eager to meet their new pastor. Derk charms them immediately with his warmth and friendliness. He introduces Marinus and me. "Didn't your wife want to come?" one of the ladies asks Derk.

He looks flustered. "Anneke isn't . . . I mean, she's not . . . um, we're not . . ."

Marinus jumps in to help him out. "What he's trying to say is that the ceremony will take place next week." Everyone laughs, and of course the ladies want to know all about the upcoming wedding as they lead us to the parsonage behind the church. I'm amazed at how cordial and talkative the dominie is, speaking confidently in English.

The house is small and cozy inside, with a front room, a kitchen, one bedroom downstairs, and two more bedrooms upstairs. The house is furnished with the basics—a sofa and rocking chair, a dining table and chairs, iron bedframes, mattresses, and a couple of dressers in the bedrooms. I remember the mansion where Anneke grew up and wonder how she will ever get used to living in this simple house with its plain, wooden floors. "I'm happy for Anneke's sake that it has indoor plumbing," I whisper to Derk.

When we've toured all the rooms, I ask the ladies to help me look through the kitchen and make a list of what Anneke will need while Derk takes Marinus over to see the church. I'm glad to have the women all to myself for a few minutes. "May I tell you a little bit about your new pastor's wife—who is also my granddaughter?" I ask as we work. "And I would also like to ask you to help me with something." I send up a prayer as the ladies gather closer to listen. "Anneke is different from most of the women we know. You see, my family didn't know Anneke even existed until last summer. Her mother—my daughter—left home and moved to Chicago right after the Holland fire. She married, but her husband abandoned her when she was expecting Anneke. My daughter was returning home to Holland when she drowned in a shipwreck, leaving Anneke an orphan. As God would have it, she was adopted by a wealthy Chicago family, Mr. and Mrs. Arthur Nicholson. She has lived a life of wealth and privilege, in a mansion with servants to wait on all of her needs."

"It sounds like heaven," one of them says, and we all laugh.

"Anneke was also raised in a different denomination than ours. Worst of all, she's only half Dutch!" The women smile at my little joke.

"Now Anneke is giving up the only way of life she has ever known to marry your new pastor. She loves him, and she loves God and wants to serve Him more than anything else in the world. Last year, she became critically ill and nearly died. The fever damaged her heart and made it impossible for her to do any kind of housework. Of course, we all wondered why God would cause someone so young to suffer that way, leaving her weak and frail for the rest of her life. But maybe God wanted to use her trials and her brush with death to prepare her for the tasks He has planned for her—praying for the sick and the weak and the brokenhearted in your community. Don't you find that's the way God sometimes works in our lives? He'll use our difficult experiences for the good of others, if we let Him." The women nod in agreement. I see the hardships and losses they've endured written in the lines on their faces.

"Here's where I need your help," I continue. "Anneke's parents have offered to pay for the extra household help she's going to need. Maybe you know some women from your community who would like to earn a little extra money doing washing, cleaning, and so on?" They look at each other and mention a few names. "That's wonderful. But more than that, I need you to please make sure the other ladies in your church accept Anneke and give her a chance, even though she's not like you. Please try to stop the whispers and the gossip about her faults— how she is an unsuitable rich girl who can't do any work. She is giving up a life of wealth and privilege to marry Derk and to serve here because that's what she feels God is calling her to do. And once you get to know Anneke, I'm sure you will love her."

"We will be glad to help you, Mrs. de Jonge," one of them says. "Thank you for telling us about her."

"And we will ask around to find the help she's going to need," another adds. I've done my "preaching" as Marinus calls it. I can only pray that I have helped ease the way for Anneke.

Our list of needed bedding and kitchen supplies is complete by the time Derk and Marinus return. "It's a nice little church," Marinus says on the way home. "It's much like the one in the Netherlands where I first preached."

"And the parsonage will make a cozy little home for the two of you," I add.

Derk heaves an enormous sigh. "Can I be honest?" he asks. "I'm worried that Anneke is going to be shocked when she sees that house. It's so shabby and rustic compared to her mansion in Chicago. Besides, she's used to living in a city, and it's pretty lonely and desolate out here. How can I ask her to give up everything to live way out in the country with me? Maybe I should let her see the house and the church before she marries me, so she has a chance to change her mind."

"You could do that, certainly," I reply. I don't tell him that I share the same fears he does about how hard it will be for Anneke to adjust. "But you also know how much Anneke longs to serve God. Remember, she isn't moving here just for you. God is calling her to serve this church the same way He called you."

"I suppose you're right." He doesn't sound convinced.

"Anneke is a very courageous young woman. I believe she'll make the change from mansion to country parsonage with faith and joy." I pause, then add, "Her mother, on the other hand, is going to be horrified when she sees your new home!" We share a good laugh at the thought.

Derk is quiet for most of the journey, and when we return home again, he ties up the horse and follows me inside. "I want to ask you something, Tante Geesje, and you don't need to answer me right away. You can think about it and pray about it first."

"This sounds serious."

"It is." He takes a deep breath, his expression worried and somber. "Would you consider moving in with Anneke and me and helping us out for a few months or so?"

"Move in?"

"We wouldn't expect you to cook or clean or anything like that. But Anneke told me she wants to learn how to be a good minister's wife. How to be part of the church community. How to make our house a home. And you are the best teacher she could possibly have. Will you please pray about living with us for a while?" He kisses my cheek and leaves without expecting a reply.

I sink down on a kitchen chair to think, ignoring my cat who is swirling around my ankles, demanding attention. Moving in with Derk and Anneke would mean so many changes! I would have to leave all my friends, my church, my snug little house and comfortable way of life. It would mean living way out in the country instead of in town, where I can easily walk everywhere and visit with everyone. My life changed nearly a year ago when Cornelia came to live with me. I wasn't willing to make room for her at first, but look how blessed my life has been because of her. It occurs to me that she and Marinus could live here and look after my house and my cat for me if I moved in with Anneke and Derk.

I have lived a lifetime of experiences and have started all over again a number of times. In a way, I feel as though I'm too old and too settled in my ways to make another move and another new beginning. And yet . . . perhaps God doesn't want me to get too comfortable. Maybe change is His favorite tool to make sure we keep growing closer to Him. Maybe He still has work for me to do, even at my age.

CHAPTER 39

Anna

HOLLAND, MICHIGAN

I'm trembling with excitement as I climb into the hired carriage with Mother and Father for the drive from the Hotel Ottawa on Lake Michigan to Pillar Church in Holland. Today is my wedding day! I'm quite certain that it's the happiest day of my life. Father looks at me from the opposite carriage seat, and I think I must be smiling from ear to ear because I make him smile in return. "This is your big day, Anna. I hope you'll always be as happy as you are right now."

I lean across the gap to give him a hug. "Thank you, Father. And thank you for giving Derk and me your support." When I return to my seat, Mother fusses with my dress and veil, re-adjusting it. I convinced Mother that I wanted a simple white satin gown without puffed sleeves and voluminous petticoats and miles and miles of lace. Today is probably the last time I will ever have servants to help me get dressed and to arrange my hair. The thought is very liberating. "You look worried, Mother," I say when I see she isn't smiling. "Are you still picturing me living in that parsonage?"

"It's in the middle of nowhere! Our kitchen and servants' quarters are more luxurious than that house is!"

I laugh and hug her, too. "I'll be happier there with Derk than I would have been in that monstrous mansion with William. Oma will help us make the parsonage cozy, you'll see."

"Your grandmother will be good company for you. I must say I'm very relieved to know she'll be moving in with you."

"I'll miss you both. I can't remember a time when I was ever away from both of you for more than a week or so. Promise you'll visit Derk and me often?"

"Of course." Mother squeezes my hand.

I catch glimpses of Black Lake through the trees on my right as we ride, the water sparkling in the brilliant sunshine. I couldn't have ordered a more perfect day to get married.

A crowd is already gathering on the front lawn of Pillar Church when we arrive. I recognize several of my parents' friends who have traveled all the way from Chicago for the wedding. Oma is standing between the pillars with Cornelia and her grandfather. They are waiting for me but also for Uncle Arie and Uncle Jakob's family. Uncle Jakob is going to perform the ceremony for Derk and me.

"It is a very pretty church," Mother admits as we climb from the carriage.

"Wait until you see how Oma decorated it inside. She has been cutting and gathering flowers all week, from her own garden and from all of her friends' gardens." I start up the steps on Father's arm, then stop when I see Judge Blackwell and his daughter, Florence, coming to greet me.

"My dear, you look beautiful!" he says, kissing my cheek. "I wish you all of the happiness in the world." The judge knocked on Oma Geesje's door yesterday afternoon while I was visiting her, surprising both of us. We had a wonderful talk over a pot of tea and Oma's cookies, then we all walked up the hill to the cemetery to see Mama's gravesite. In so many ways, it feels like all of the loose ends of our lives are being woven back together again.

"I hope we'll have a chance to visit with you later at the wedding luncheon," Mother tells the judge. She has arranged to host a luncheon at the Hotel Ottawa after the ceremony for all of our guests. The hotel is a fitting place to celebrate our marriage, since that's where Derk and I first met and fell in love.

"Yes, we'll be there," the judge replies. "Thank you for including Florence and me today."

Oma engulfs me in her embrace when I reach the top of the steps. She already has tears in her eyes. "Don't get me started crying," I say as I dab my eyes with a handkerchief.

"You are so beautiful, lieveling! I'm so happy for you and Derk I could just burst! All of our loved ones in heaven are surely celebrating along with us today." I know she's thinking of her husband, Maarten, and of Mama. And also Derk's mother and his grandfather Hendrik.

Uncle Jakob's wife and family arrive, including his daughter, Elizabeth. Oma introduces them all to Mother and Father. "The resemblance between you and your cousin is striking," Mother says when she meets Elizabeth.

"She's the reason Derk and I first met," I explain. "Derk mistook me for Elizabeth."

"You seem very calm for your wedding day," Elizabeth says.

"That's because I'm about to marry the man I love." I never imagined I would be able to marry for love.

"Let's wait inside," Oma says. "We wouldn't want Derk to see you ahead of time, would we?" She takes us to a little room beside the sanctuary where Father and I can wait before we walk down the aisle. Mother has tears in her eyes as she makes a few last-minute adjustments to my dress and veil. Then she leaves with Oma and the rest of the family to sit together near the front.

Uncle Jakob sticks his head inside to see if we're ready. "Do you have the ring you chose for Derk?" he asks. Father fishes in his pocket and gives him the simple gold band I chose, then Uncle Jakob leaves to take his place for the ceremony. The organ has begun to play, and I hear laughter and voices in the foyer as our guests arrive and take their seats. I'm trembling with excitement again as I wait. I close my eyes and silently praise God for bringing our marriage to pass.

At last, at last, the organ begins to play the processional! It's time for Father to escort me down the aisle so I can begin the rest of my life. My heart races when I see Derk standing at the front with his father and Uncle Jakob. He looks so tall and strong and handsome in his new Sunday suit. His fair hair shines in the sunlight that's streaming through the windows. He smiles when he sees me, and my heart feels as though it might burst. I smile through tears of joy as I walk forward to marry the man I love.

Bestselling author **Lynn Austin** has sold more than one million copies of her books worldwide. She is an eight-time Christy Award winner for her historical novels, as well as a popular speaker at retreats and conventions. Lynn and her husband have raised three children and live in Michigan. Learn more at www.lynnaustin.org.

Sign Up for Lynn's Newsletter!

Keep up to date with Lynn's news on book releases and events by signing up for her email list at lynnaustin.org.

Don't Miss the Prequel!

In 1897 Michigan, Dutch immigrant Geesje de Jonge recalls the events of her past while writing a memoir, and twenty-three-year-old Anna Nicholson mourns a broken engagement. Over the course of one summer, the lives of both women will change forever.

Waves of Mercy

More from Lynn Austin

To learn more about Lynn and her books, visit lynnaustin.org.

Accompanied by their young butler and their maid, two sisters defy society's expectations as they search for a biblical manuscript. On their exotic journey to the Sinai Desert, they experience challenges and wonders, and recall the events that brought them to this time and place.

Where We Belong

This powerful series captures the incredible faith of Ezra, Nehemiah, and their families as they return to God after the Babylonian exile. These stories of faith, doubt, and love encompass the Jews' return to Jerusalem and their efforts to rebuild God's temple amid constant threat.

THE RESTORATION CHRONICLES: *Return to Me, Keepers of the Covenant, On This Foundation*

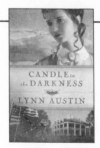

Caught between her home outside Civil War Richmond, her awakening abolitionist beliefs, and the man she loves, Caroline Fletcher sees the hard world around her for the first time. Will she choose love and the comfort of home, or sacrifice everything for the truth that burns her heart?

Candle in the Darkness

BETHANYHOUSE

You May Also Like . . .

Gentlewoman Rachel Ashford has moved into Ivy Cottage with the two Misses Groves, where she discovers mysteries hidden among her books. Together with her onetime love Sir Timothy, she searches for answers—and is forced to face her true feelings. Meanwhile, her friends Mercy and Jane face their own trials in life and love.

The Ladies of Ivy Cottage by Julie Klassen
TALES FROM IVY HILL #2
julieklassen.com

In the aftermath of tragedy, Grace hopes to reclaim her nephew from the relatives who rejected her sister because of her class. Under an alias, she becomes her nephew's nanny to observe the formidable family up close. Unexpectedly, she begins to fall for the boy's guardian, who is promised to another. Can Grace protect her nephew . . . and her heart?

The Best of Intentions by Susan Anne Mason
CANADIAN CROSSINGS #1
susanannemason.com

Vivienne Rivard fled revolutionary France and now seeks a new life for herself and a boy in her care, who some say is the Dauphin. But America is far from safe, as militiaman Liam Delaney knows. He proudly served in the American Revolution but is less sure of his role in the Whiskey Rebellion. Drawn together, will Liam and Vivienne find the peace they long for?

A Refuge Assured by Jocelyn Green
jocelyngreen.com

BETHANYHOUSE